AN ANATOMY
OF BEASTS

Also by Olivia A. Cole

A Conspiracy of Stars

AN ANATOMY OF BEASTS

OLIVIA A. COLE

KATHERINE TEGEN BOOKS
An Imprint of HarperCollins Publishers

Katherine Tegen Books is an imprint of HarperCollins Publishers.

An Anatomy of Beasts
Copyright © 2019 by Olivia A. Cole

Library of Congress Control Number: 2018941660
ISBN 978-0-06-264424-4

Typography by David Curtis
19 20 21 22 23   PC/LSCH   10 9 8 7 6 5 4 3 2 1

First Edition

For my mother, then and now.

CHAPTER 1

Three mammals whose names I don't know move slowly over my grandmother's still body. I watch for her pulse, my eyes tight and dry from lack of sleep, the desire to listen for her steady heartbeat the only thing keeping me awake. The mammals appear faceless—I'd thought they were thick blue insects at first. They travel up my grandmother's plump brown arms like furred larva, so slowly their motion is barely noticeable. It was Rasimbukar who had picked one up for me when she stopped in the infirmary to check on us: she'd curled her hand gently around one of the animals and lifted it from my grandmother's skin. Under its fuzzed body were several pairs of legs and a small rodent-like face with a mouth like a proboscis.

"It will help," Rasimbukar had told me when she first

laid the creatures upon my grandmother. "She will wake when they are finished."

Now I wait for the creatures to complete whatever task it is they must do to help my grandmother rise. It's my fault she's like this. I'd walked down the hill between Rasimbukar and her father, weaving through the dizzying city they call their home, a city whose name I still don't know. The smells and sounds of the lives around me had forced open the tunnel in my mind, pulsing louder and brighter until I felt blinded by it. When I'd arrived at the place where my grandmother lives—a low round building the color of the sky—her face in front of me had seemed more like a memory, and the man standing just behind her in the doorway had the eyes and mouth I'd seen only in old photographs—my grandfather. It was too much. The loss of my mother, the strangeness of this new place, it welled up inside me like a blue roar, and, as my grandmother opened her arms to me, I couldn't speak or move. I could only look at her familiar features and think *My mother is dead*. And there in the tunnel, my grandmother heard me; everything inside me spilling out of my mind like a hurricane, crashing into hers untethered.

Her face underwent a series of ripples. The smile, wavering, then the flickering frown, vibrating outward into shock, disbelief. Then blank. Blank open space in her features as her eyes rolled and her body careened toward the ground. Rasimbukar's sturdy arms had caught her, the tunnel in my mind flaring an orange burst of concern as she silently called for Adombukar to help. It had all been a blur, my grandfather stepping out of the photograph in my 'wam to my side, steering my shoulder with a warm, slender hand. Now we're here, my grandfather asleep in the corner, crumpled into a strange chair that resembles a leaf, me curled on the floor beside my grandmother, my tailbone numb and tingling from being still so long, searching her motionless face for remnants of my mother. I find them in every crevice, and my heart throbs like it's been crushed on a slide beneath a microscope.

The room is cool, but I've scanned it many times in the last countless hours and have found no evidence of vents like the ones that cooled our 'wams in N'Terra. N'Terra. It hardly seems like a real place now. My life there suddenly feels like fiction, a lengthy dream that my mother's death interrupted. I squeeze my eyes shut at the memory of her disappearing under the savage mass of vasana, but the darkness only makes me see her more vividly; without my grandmother's face before me, all I hear is the strangled cry from my father's throat as he realized—too late—what was happening.

Something stirs behind me and I turn abruptly, finding Rasimbukar materializing at the edge of the dim room. It's as if a blanket had been hanging in front of her and is rapidly disappearing stitch by stitch. Those imagined stitches are in fact exceptionally thin vines, plant fibers that snake aside in either direction, glistening a little like fine thread. It's only a matter of seconds until Rasimbukar stands there unobscured and then enters the room.

Octavia, she says silently. My mind mellows at the feeling of her voice coursing through it. I wonder if she intends to be comforting or if it is merely a natural effect of her presence. *We had hoped you would be sleeping.*

I glance at my grandfather, still asleep. He's turned slightly sideways in the leaflike chair and I notice that it seems to have curled around him to hold him in place.

I can't sleep, I tell her, not wanting to wake him. I've spent some time staring at him as well. But although I've spent my life knowing his face from a photo, he's a stranger to me. He'd spoken not one word when I'd arrived here, even as my grandmother was transported to this infirmary. We'd shared each other's presence like two breathing stones until he eventually slept.

Your grandmother will be all right. I regret not meeting with her first before I brought you to her. It was a mistake. Mine.

I feel the shape of her words there in my mind but there's something else there too, a deep violet color of sympathy. It's wrapped around and between her words. She is sad for me: sad for all my loss. The idea that she is apologizing to me after everything the people of N'Terra have done to her and her planet makes me feel sick. Almost without meaning to, I snap the tunnel closed, shutting her out of my head.

"It's okay," I say out loud, whispering. My grandmother's face doesn't twitch.

"Let me take you outside," Rasimbukar says in her smooth wooden voice.

I say nothing, but when she moves back toward the entrance of the room, the vines already slithering sideways to make way, I follow.

Outside, the heat makes my breath slow. In the dim healing room I'd almost forgotten where I was; even with the bright lights of the Zoo, I'd almost imagined I was back in the labs, my grandmother tranquilized on an exam table. The sun makes it easier to shake off the shudder that rises from my skin at the thought of what had happened in the labs. The heat slides into me like many golden hands, relaxing my muscles. I breathe deeply.

"Better?" Rasimbukar asks. She says it out loud. I briefly wonder if I've hurt her feelings by closing the tunnel, but when I look at her, the spots on her forehead are wide and well spaced, a look of frankness.

"Yes," I reply.

"Good. I would like for you to see someone."

I look around as we walk. When I'd first entered the city with her at dawn—had that been this morning? I've lost track of time. Maybe it was yesterday. Maybe the day before—I had been blinded by many emotions. N'Terra and all its shadows behind me, and this new place ahead. Rasimbukar and Adombukar had propelled me forward through the throngs of curious Faloii who had paused on their various paths to gaze at me. Their energy had pulsed from every direction, the lines of connection between my head and theirs illuminated and vibrating with questions just on the other end. I couldn't bear to look at any of them, the knowledge of what was happening in N'Terra weighing me down to subterranean levels. I'd closed the tunnel and followed Rasimbukar with my eyes on the ground. Now I take in the city.

It's as breathtaking now as it was when I first gazed down on it with Rasimbukar on the hill. So different from N'Terra, with its white walls and lineless ceilings. If this place reminds me of anything, it's of the communal dome in the Mammalian Compound, where our homes were decorated with flags and cloths before Dr. Albatur began to have them replaced with the hollow banners bearing the Council's seal. Bright colors are everywhere here: domed roofs of red and yellow, some with twisting peaks of complicated craftsmanship. The buildings are tall and short, small and massive. A tree that would require hundreds of arms to encircle is rooted solidly a little ways away, a circular structure built right alongside it, almost into it.

I realize, suddenly, that the circular structure, a pale purple building, appears to be pulsing. I squeeze my eyes shut and look again, thinking my exit from the dim infirmary has made me dizzy. But it's no trick of the light: the walls are billowing softly, like a field of grass all rippling and bending to the same current of wind. I reach out and catch Rasimbukar's arm.

"Do—do you see that?" I ask, still not trusting my eyes. "That building . . ."

Rasimbukar pauses on the path. Her spots gather in concentration and then loosen again as she observes.

"Its walls are moving, yes," she says neutrally. "It is growing."

I'm still touching her arm, the feeling of her skin not quite like skin, and take my hand away quickly, embarrassed that it surprises me.

"Growing?"

"We cannot expect it to remain unchanged," she says, showing her teeth in what I believe to be a smile. "It is happy, however. It will not change much."

She turns away and continues down the path, and I have to trot after her. As we pass among more structures and trees so massive I can't see the tops, I realize I should be asking more questions. But my mind feels dull, as if my curiosity has lost a wing and flaps uselessly. My mother is dead. My father is a person I don't recognize. Rondo . . . Alma . . . both far away. The last time I'd seen them, Rondo was bleeding on the ground, Alma on the roof of a 'wam holding a buzzgun. Do they think I abandoned them? Are they imprisoned? Are they dead? I picture the vasana climbing the walls of Alma's vantage point, those mad eyes rolling as the dirixi teeth slashed. . . .

I find Rasimbukar in my mind and am surprised: the tunnel

is open for her but I hadn't opened it, at least not purposely.

You must not let grief consume you. It will weaken you. You did not allow me in your thoughts, but I am here. Do you understand?

I suddenly feel as if I'm going to cry, a tide of water that has met a narrow part of the riverbed, my throat. It strains against the dam, and it's as if everything in my heart will burst out of me. My fists are clenched tightly, as if gripping the dam itself. Something soft brushes against my knuckle and my eyes snap open.

It's the gwabi, who I immediately recognize as the same one from the Zoo that had accompanied Rasimbukar and me through the jungle.

Hello, I tell her silently, and am greeted by a comforting yellow reply. Somewhere in the other colors and shapes that she sends me, I understand that she knows my mother is dead. She's sorry for me and perceives me as a baby, a motherless cub. I can't tell her that I feel like an old woman, so I just look into her eyes, comforted by her presence.

She lost her parent too, Rasimbukar says musingly, as if she isn't quite sure why the gwabi is still hanging around either.

I notice that my fingers are thrumming where the fur of the gwabi's shoulder still makes contact. I rub my fingertips together, a feeling almost like static remaining. I know, without knowing how, that the gwabi is young, but reaching the age when she will reproduce. She will not seek a mate, but will instead create the cells necessary to do so alone. I never learned this in the Greenhouse, but somehow I know. If I were in the Greenhouse, I might lean over to whisper to Alma excitedly, send Rondo a note on my slate. Their absence looms large inside me, but is still dwarfed by whatever this presence I feel is: almost like the voice of Faloiv whispers in my ear, explaining how things work.

"I feel . . . ," I say out loud, searching for the words. "How?"

Is it so hard to understand? Rasimbukar says, and gestures for me to follow her down a narrow path into the trees, deeper into the city. *You are listening. The Artery is more than communication. It is the network that connects everything on Faloiv.*

The gwabi stays with us for a while, loping at my side as we wind along the edge of a wide stream. The trees thicken, and so do the buildings, although it's sometimes hard to tell the two apart. In N'Terra, it was impossible not to differentiate between what occurred naturally on Faloiv and what we had built: everything in our compounds was smooth edges and white material, some gleaned from the wrecked *Vagantur* and some created from the plentiful clay found on the planet. Looking around now—all the structures seemingly interlaced with trees and stone—I don't see the white clay anywhere. Do the Faloii build their homes as we do, or is it another process entirely? I have many questions, but the only one that comes to my lips isn't about the city.

"Will my grandmother actually be okay?" I say. The gwabi had woven back into the trees at some point and Rasimbukar and I walk alone.

"Yes," says Rasimbukar. She turns to look at me now, her eyes unblinking. She addresses me out loud and not in the tunnel, and I'm grateful: sometimes when she's looking at me and in my mind simultaneously, it's a little too intense, like staring into the sun. "Your grandmother has experienced a trauma. The ahugwo will repair her."

"Ahugwo. The blue mammals?"

"Yes."

"We never learned about them in N'Terra."

"There are many things N'Terra does not know." She makes a slight gesture with her shoulders, an almost shrug. I wonder if she learned it from my grandparents.

Or other humans. Suddenly my brain fires: with everything that has happened, the things I, Alma, and Rondo had been investigating have been pushed to the side. They arise now in my head, all the pieces reconnecting. I stop walking.

"My grandfather is alive," I say dumbly, the truth of it still fresh and almost unpronounceable.

Rasimbukar blinks now, slowly, as if she's wondering if I need the ahugwo too.

"Yes."

"But . . . me and my friends . . . we found a list of humans who never made it to N'Terra. People we thought died. My grandfather was one of them."

A few of the spots on her forehead drift to one side, as if uncertain.

"Yes. I left this out of our conversations while you were in N'Terra. Your mother and grandmother asked that they be the ones to discuss it with you."

"So . . . so my mother knew her parents were alive."

"Yes."

"But why lie? Why pretend my grandfather was dead all these years? My whole life they told me he never even boarded the *Vagantur*. That he died on the Origin Planet. What's the point?"

"I cannot speak what your grandmother would prefer to tell you herself. And in her time."

"If my mother had just told me," I say, and I can't help it: the bitterness invades my voice like a swarm of insects, "maybe everything would be different. If she had just told me the truth—"

Rasimbukar cuts me off with a swift motion of one of her paw-like hands, brought down like an ax through the air.

"Your mother had her reasons, Octavia," she repeats. "Everything she did was to preserve peace. As I have told you, violence has grave consequences on Faloiv. It can trigger more than war between two peoples. The planet itself can become an adversary."

I say nothing to this, walking alongside her, taking in the vines and the leaves that form an almost tunnel around us. I have no real concept of war—just shadows of what Dr. Espada and other whitecoats referenced while reflecting on the past—and thinking about the planet itself as an enemy makes me shiver. I imagine the ground opening to reveal fangs and a bottomless purple throat. Having watched my mother die beneath the vasana, I can't help but think of war, of all bad things, as fangs. But when I think of all the buzzguns in N'Terra, the picture in my mind transforms: the ground opens as before, but faceless figures come swarming from its depths, a shifting army. What would the planet look like, mobilized against us? Would it turn against the Faloii too?

A sound in the brush turns my blood cold, my imaginings of war leaping out of my head and into the jungle before advancing on me with jaws flexing. The leaves rattle just beyond the path and my fear pivots, filling my head with the image of a dirixi, towering and scaled, falling upon me to finish what it started the last time I ran into it. But it's only a small group of reptiles I don't recognize, their scales so smooth and shiny they look like glass, delicate silver wings tucked along their sides. I stare at them, until I realize something larger comes from behind them, rustling through the bushes without grace. But Rasimbukar is not afraid; instead turns her attention to their arrival, as if expecting them. We're meeting someone, I remember, someone she wants me to see, and here they are emerging from the greenery that surrounds us like an airlock. I expect another of the Faloii, another face I don't recognize, something new, something strange.

I don't expect a face I recognize. I don't expect Jaquot.

CHAPTER 2

He stands there, alive, supporting himself on two thick canes made of what looks like shining green stone. His skin is his skin, tinged with the colors of the foliage around and above, but it is flesh. Not mist, the fabric of a ghost, or a dream. Flesh. His green eyes sweep over the clearing before landing finally on my face.

My mouth forms his name soundlessly.

"Hey, you're here!" he says as if our reunion is the most unsurprising thing in the world, and uses the canes to swing himself forward out of the trees. It's not until then that I look down and see that the boy in front of me is indeed Jaquot, but different. He's missing a leg. He sees my face and pauses, glancing down at himself. "Oh, this. Yeah."

The pleasure that had flashed across his face clouds. His lips twist.

"Rasimbukar and her friend rescued me from the dirixi, but not before it got a piece of me." He swallows. "Well, more than a piece."

"Everyone thinks you're dead," I finally say. I don't know whether to hug him or keep staring to prove he's actually alive. If only Rondo and Alma were here for this. "Your father thinks you're dead."

"I know," he says. "But they're taking care of me here. Your grandma too. Stars, I can't wait to see Yaya's face when she finds out the hundred are alive. And me. How is she? Does she miss me? Was she sad?"

I ignore the look of longing on his face.

"The hundred? Wait, what? You mean the missing hundred from the *Vagantur*?"

"Yeah," he says.

"They're alive?"

"I mean, yeah. You saw your grandfather by now, right?"

I whip around to face Rasimbukar, who has allowed us to speak without interjecting. Now, the spots on her forehead drift together and apart.

"I assumed you understood this as we discussed your grand-father a moment ago," she says. "He is one of the Acclimates. Your grandparents are two of many who have opted to join our city as they learn the ways of Faloiv."

"So she knew?" I say. "My mother knew about *all* this? She knew there was an entire separate population of humans living on Faloiv?"

"Yes."

"She knew . . ."

I find myself sitting on the ground without fully realizing how I got there, the jungle spinning slowly around me. Jaquot moves awkwardly over to offer help, but I wave him away. The air seems too thin, my lungs too thirsty. Of all the lies and all the secrets, the truth about my grandmother burns most hotly in my mind. I think of the photo on the wall of my 'wam, so far away in N'Terra, how my mother had stood before it, longing for her mother and father. I had believed there was nothing left of them but that photo.

"But why?" I say. "All this time . . . my grandmother just left us? I've believed she was dead since I was eleven!"

The surge of anger isn't strong enough to pull me up from the ground, so I just glare up at Rasimbukar.

"There are many things that must be explained," she says. The last time someone told me that there was much to be explained, it was my mother and Dr. Espada in the Greenhouse. Now they're both dead.

"I know it's a lot," Jaquot says softly. I stare at the green canes he leans on so I don't have to look in his eyes. "I hardly believed it myself at first. But once you talk to the others, it will make more sense."

I squeeze my eyes shut, breathing deeply to control the factory of emotions humming through me. I reach out for the smell of the ogwe, the trees that had been something of a constant companion in N'Terra. I find the scent, but it's different out here in the jungle. Wilder. More joyful.

"You smell the ogwe," Rasimbukar says, reading me. The spots on her forehead rise in curiosity.

"Yes."

"Ogwe has a smell?" Jaquot says, and for a moment I'm transported back to the day in the Beak, just moments before seeing the philax that changed everything. Even now I can't help but smile.

"Let us walk," Rasimbukar says, and I sense her relief at my smile. "We can discuss this another time."

We walk along a new path, one that winds us around the edge of a lake. From one angle, the reflection of the sky makes it look blue, but when we get closer I see the water itself is a soft pink.

"Mineral deposits?" I ask.

"Correct. This is where we will bring your grandmother when the ahugwo have finished with her. This water is very useful for healing."

As she says this, I spy someone slowly wading in from the

bank across the lake. Their careful movements tell me they are old, but from here I can't tell if they are human or Faloii. I'm suddenly eager to lay eyes on these hundred people, people like me who have lived a life I can't imagine. All this time I've been suffocated by N'Terra, imagining a life beyond the white walls, and there are people already living it.

The pink lake is bluer at its edges, and I'm admiring its purity when a voice hails us. I know the person is Faloii by the wooden timbre of their voice, and without fully meaning to I open my mind to see them before I look. She's already there, greeting me. Her name is Hamankush.

"Hello," I say when she approaches. She has just stepped out of the jungle and joins us as we make our way toward a round building that reminds me of the Greenhouse.

"Anoo," she says.

"Anoo is a species of insect," Jaquot says. "Extinct, I think. But it means *hello* in their language."

"What is it called?" I ask, looking at Rasimbukar. "Your language?"

"We speak Anooiire," she says. The spots on her forehead spread wide. "The parts that are spoken, that is. Hamankush is an archivist."

We continue toward the round building. Its brown walls are in fact mottled with a deep green, lines and ridges like veins mapping its surface, beginning at the ground.

"Come in," Rasimbukar says, and she lays her hand on the

wall, peeling up a thin opaque layer with her fingertips. It gently gives way, a sort of flap-like covering that conceals a doorway. I glance at Jaquot, but he passes through without remark. A stab of competitiveness surprises me: he's only been here for a week at most and already he is comfortable, knows more than I do.

Inside, the air is cool, and, like the Greenhouse, the light is tinged green. No windows that I can see, but the sun seems to pierce through the roof, filling the low-ceilinged hallway with a soft glow. I inhale through my nose and it hits me, with a scent as delicate as it is sturdy.

"This is a plant," I say. "Are we inside a plant?"

Rasimbukar offers me a flash of her teeth. "Yes. Good."

But she says nothing more, leaving me to trail after her beside Jaquot while she confers with Hamankush. In the tunnel I find nothing: they are having a private conversation.

"I heard your grandmother fainted," Jaquot says. "Is she going to be okay?"

I don't tell him that she hadn't merely fainted: that it was my own intensity—and inability to control it—that made my grandmother lose consciousness.

"I hope so," I say. I trail my fingers along the wall, but jerk them back when the wall trembles slightly at my touch. In the tunnel, there is a humming green presence. When I listen carefully, I get the feeling that the hum is a stream of communication that is too fast and dense for me to understand. It doesn't address me, but it is aware of me. Its hum isn't for any one audience: it's more like a heartbeat, but a heartbeat full of information. I gently close the tunnel.

"Did they tell you about my mom," I say without looking at Jaquot.

He doesn't answer right away. The dull thump of his canes is the only sound.

"Yes," he says. "I'm so sorry. Were you . . . there?"

"Yes."

Rasimbukar pauses in the hallway and lays her hand on the wall. Like in the infirmary where my grandmother is being kept, a doorway appears by way of the simultaneous separation of many tiny vines. Hamankush is gone. Rasimbukar gestures for us to enter.

At first the only thing I can focus on is the fact that I'm somehow high in the air, and seemingly outdoors. Inside the plant, it had felt as if we were walking along a level surface. We had climbed no stairs; entered no lift. And yet I look out at the Faloii city from the vantage point of what seems like a small tree. The city and the jungle sprawl out before me, the colors almost overwhelming in their vibrancy. My first impression is that we're outside, but I quickly realize a thin membrane exists between me and the outdoor air, the bright chamber I stand within still cool and smelling vaguely of soil.

It's not until my awe of the city view wears off that I notice the dozen faces tilted toward me in what turns out to be a small bright room. Both human and Faloii, they stare at me from where they sit in the sunshine, a scattering of materials between them. The humans are all my age or younger. The Faloii, I assume, are young too: they look different from Rasimbukar. Their skin is lighter, a yellower shade of the rich brown and carrying more of a greenish tinge. None of them seem to be aware of or interested in the majestic view of the city and planet.

"Your peers," Rasimbukar says. "They will help you acclimate to Mbekenkanush."

"I'm sorry, to what?"

"This is Mbekenkanush," Jaquot says. "The city."

"But my grandmother—" I start as Rasimbukar moves back toward the door.

"I will send someone for you when she wakes."

And then she's gone, leaving me staring at the place where the door had been. I almost go to the wall to try to open it again, anger sprouting in me like a sapling. My grandmother, who I thought was dead, is in a room unconscious with my grandfather, who I also thought was dead, and Rasimbukar wants me to socialize?

"Anoo," says one of the people behind me, and I turn to find a human girl a little older than me standing next to Jaquot. She studies me.

"You are the kin of Amara," she says in the same measured accent as Rasimbukar, just without the wooden timbre. "You have the same eyes. The same look."

"Yes," I say, sizing her up. Her hair is cropped very short, as short as Rondo's. She has a round face like Alma's, full cheeks, and a broad shiny forehead. I miss my friends so much I see them everywhere.

"You are a friend of Jaquot?" says another human boy, his skin as pale as the tiny roots I have seen at the base of small plants. He doesn't stand. "From the same place?"

"N'Terra," Jaquot says. With the help of the full-faced girl, he eases down to the ground. I find myself angry at how comfortable he is among them. As if he has been here all along.

A prickle in my mind grabs my attention, and I reach for the tunnel. In it, the Faloii in the room greet me with expressions of surprise and delight, a few with reservation, to find that I can hear them and they can hear me.

You are like your grandmother, one says. *You speak very well. You will learn more.*

Clumsy though, says another, but I don't think they mean any harm by it. *They,* I notice. I gather from the impressions offered by the Artery that Faloii youth decide upon both their sex and gender at a time of their choosing. In the group before me, everyone is undecided.

What are you doing in here? I ask them. I've never addressed more than one person at a time in the tunnel, and it flexes a part of my brain that I'm unaccustomed to using. It's not hard, exactly: just a matter of allowing each chain between us to remain illuminated.

Here we study, one says. They have not shown me their name. *The Faloii our business, and your people theirs.*

What is the business of my people? I ask, curious.

They enjoy learning about the past. Among other things.

Jaquot is looking at me strangely, along with the other humans. The round-cheeked girl says, "Oh, like Amara in that way too."

"Huh?" Jaquot says, not understanding at first. "Oh. *Oh.* Stars, Octavia. I guess it all makes sense now?"

"I guess. So, wait," I say, addressing the girl. "You guys don't have it? The . . . you know, the way to talk?"

"Very few," the girl says, and turns her head to look at the work she studies, as if this doesn't bother her.

Join us, someone tells me. They show me their name: Kimbullettican. *Sit.*

The humans are studying what Jaquot tells me are called books. I know this word, of course, but not like this: these are not documents on slates but thick heavy objects with many delicate leaves. We have them in N'Terra, but they are fragile and protected carefully.

"No slates?" I say, eyeing what Jaquot is reading, a thick text with many diagrams that appear to be geographical in nature.

"We have a version of them," he says. One hand goes to rub a leg that is no longer there, and he quickly snatches his hand back. "But the Elders use them mostly. Limited supply. They have us doing legwork, so they say, but these books have been read hundreds of times. They just want us to know this stuff."

Jaquot eyes the book in his hands and I can't tell if he's reading or if he's searching the page for something to say. My mind is full of noise. Not from the tunnel—the Faloii youth are quiet, absorbed in their own conversations—but a clamoring of death and questions. The shadow that looms over N'Terra feels as if it's clinging to the soles of my feet, trailing me these many miles through the jungle and hunting me here. I study the faces of the humans around me. The full-cheeked girl has turned her face down to her book and seems to be reading in earnest. How can they be studying so calmly with everything that has transpired?

"Most of these are about the Origin Planet," Jaquot says, holding up the book. "The geology of this planet isn't so different once you get underground, based on what the Faloii say. Dr. Albatur and them always made it sound like Captain Williams was an idiot for landing us here, but under the circumstances I think she did a pretty good job and got damn lucky."

"If lucky is dying in the crash," I say, trying not to sound snappish. "Why do they have you studying the Origin Planet? That seems like a waste of time."

"You think? I don't know, I guess so. But rather than starting blind, it kind of makes sense to compare things we know to find similarities in what we don't know."

"But we *don't* know," I argue. "What do you know about the Origin Planet besides what you've been told? Those books were written generations ago by people who destroyed the place they lived. I wouldn't call them the ideal models of scientific progress."

He closes the book.

"The Elders here mostly agree. Except . . . there's this nostalgia, you know? Not for the planet itself, but what they had to leave behind, kind of. Remember Dr. LaQuinta Farrow?"

"Wait . . . ," I say slowly. The name tugs a string in the back of my mind but I can't find what it's connected to. "LaQuinta Farrow . . . why do I know that name?"

"Yaya's grandmother's friend," he says with a sideways smile. "Remember, we argued about it that day in the Zoo? The woman Yaya's grandmother says died? Well, Yaya was wrong—don't tell her I said that, seriously—Dr. Farrow is still alive. Old, but alive. She's an Acclimate!"

"Starsssss," I hiss. "I wish Alma was here! She would have so much to say."

"So does Dr. Farrow." He smiles. "She's full of fire! She came in to talk to me and the other students a couple days ago. Wasn't an admirer of Dr. Albatur."

I lean forward. "What did she say?"

"In some ways she's like a lot of the Acclimates. They talk differently about the Origin Planet here. Like what they were escaping wasn't just the planet but its people."

"Hmm," I muse, making a note of this. When my grandmother wakes up, we will have a lot to discuss.

"You know how Dr. Albatur started taking down people's flags and stuff in the communes? Replacing them with the N'Terran banners?"

"Yeah."

"Well, I told Dr. Farrow about it and she lit up! *Not* in a good way. She said that's the kind of thing that happened on the Origin Planet; it's why we know so little about it. According to her, there was nothing to know. The only thing people had for themselves was their research."

"Doesn't sound so bad," I say, whitecoat logic still clinging to me.

"This is how Dr. Farrow described it: she said imagine a whole city full of Albaturs, telling you what you could and couldn't study. Deciding what was valid science and what wasn't . . . and what they decided was valid science was only ever for the benefit of the Council. And that being your whole life. No escape. Just studying what they tell you to study, and your discoveries being used to hurt people."

I chew on this. I had once dreamed of doing nothing but living in the labs, occasionally sleeping at home, the way my parents had. Those dreams had fallen away with the peeling back of N'Terra's secrets, but it leaves a void in my life, empty like lightning striking the jungle and leaving a razed patch in its wake.

"I don't know." He shrugs when I'm silent. "It's just funny how similar some things in Mbekenkanush are to N'Terra.

Different versions of the past. In N'Terra, Albatur was always trying to re-create the Origin Planet: what we ate, how we lived. But here, it's subtle things that the Acclimates are searching for. Who we were. What we were like. It's like they don't remember what the world they came from was like. Let some tell it, the ground on the Origin Planet was collapsing underneath them. Others talk about war. It's hard to ever really get one story."

The word *war* strikes a chord in me, vibrating through my ribs.

"Does everyone here know about N'Terra?" I say, dropping my voice to a whisper. All this talk about N'Terra, and we're not even discussing the truth.

"What? How N'Terra pretends everyone here died? Some people know about that, yeah."

"No, not that. I mean what's *happening* there."

He stares at me blankly, and the blankness makes me want to shake him. What does he think? That Dr. Albatur is just a regular whitecoat and that the shady practices and whispers and banners and propaganda are just . . . differences of opinion?

"I mean what's happening in the labs," I whisper. "The vasana. What they're *doing* to them."

Hamankush appears beside me. I hadn't heard her enter the room—the doors here don't give any warning like the whispers in N'Terra. She hails me in the tunnel.

Come with me, she interrupts.

Rasimbukar told me to wait, I say.

I am telling you to come.

I don't even look at Jaquot before I follow her to the wall. The eyes of the group are like lasers on my back, each of them wondering what my problem is. As I pass through the parted vines, I receive a violet shape of sympathy from the Faloii youth called Kimbullettican. They understand my grief, the way it twists everything inside me. I thank them as the vines close behind me.

Hamankush leads me back down the softly glowing hall. She peels the layer of plant and lifts it, nodding for me to pass through. Outside, the heat is thick and wet with high noon humidity, and I notice the silence of the jungle just beyond the domed plant I'd just emerged from. The animals taking shelter from the heat, at rest and conserving their energy. Except the building, I sense: it seems alert in the tunnel, its too-fast-to-comprehend language humming on and on, energized by the sun. When I look at Hamankush, her ears have unfurled, collecting solar energy. My very skeleton seems to ache at the thought of what I'd uncovered with Alma in the depths of the Zoo: the Solossius, its vile blueprint, the tower at the center of the commune, Albatur's intentions to use the bones of the Faloii in plain sight. . . .

"What is it called?" I say to distract myself, nodding at the building housing the school.

"The plant itself is called a qalandar. But when it is engaged in this task, acting as a structure, the structure is known as a qalm."

"A qalm," I repeat. "Are there many?"

"Yes. Every structure in Mbekenkanush is a qalm. *We build nothing artificially.*"

She adds this last part in the tunnel and I understand the feeling she passes with it to mean that she is referring to N'Terra, the choices of my people.

Most of us don't know, I say. *It's the people in charge. They are doing this.*

This does not change the outcome, she says.

I have nothing to say to this. I close my eyes in the sun, wishing it was giving me something. This place has always been my home, but its sun does not even love me as it could. I give nothing. I only breathe the air and eat the food. And yet my grandmother has lived here peacefully for many years. Has she found something to give?

Is my grandmother all right?

I do not know.

Then why did you bring me out here?

Because you were preparing to share information with the others that is not ready to be known.

What information? You mean about what—what my people are doing?

Yes.

29

So they don't know.

Most do not. Our Elders have determined this is for the best at this moment.

In the tunnel, the gwabi greets me from somewhere nearby. She is nesting in the shadows of the colossal trees, the trees that make everything in N'Terra look small and flimsy. Two cities. Mine, and this. Both with secrets, both deciding what to tell and what not to tell. If I had to choose where my allegiances lie . . . what would I choose?

Were you here when we got here? When we landed?

When the star people came from the sky? Yes, I was here. I did not see, but I felt the arrival. We all did. It was a very strange day.

"All this time," I say, mostly to myself. "I never knew some of us came to you."

"You refer to the Acclimates."

"Yes. They've been here this whole time."

She studies me, her eyes like galaxies shifting over my face. She studies me in the tunnel too, and I sense that even when I'm not actively communicating something, the Faloii can still get impressions, still understand things I have not made overt.

"That is correct," she says.

"Why?" I say when she doesn't continue. "We didn't even know there were others. No one ever told us. Why didn't you let them return to N'Terra?"

"Let them? Does this mean *allow* them? You are mistaken. It was your people who would not allow them to return."

I have the feeling of standing on the edge of a crack in the ground, teetering. Hamankush's face is unreadable, the spots on her forehead almost entirely still. I swallow. "Why not?"

I'm afraid of what she might tell me. Disease? Is there something infectious about the Faloii that N'Terra knows would wipe out the settlement? Is that why they've tried so hard to keep us apart? I feel guilty for harboring this thought until finally Hamankush's spots drift ever so slightly upward.

"I will show you something," she says. "Come."

She walks fast, her long legs passing over the land as if she has decided that what she wants to show me is urgent. I keep up as best as I can, jogging behind her back along the pink lake. I don't know where she's leading me, but when she ducks into the jungle I'm surprised. I was expecting her to take me somewhere where I might see records. She's an archivist, Rasimbukar had said. I imagined her leading me to an ancient building like the Council's dome, perhaps. At the very least a monument, some pillar to the past that might have answers to my questions. But she pushes deeper and deeper through the trees, our feet sometimes following a path and sometimes slipping through thick curtains of cascading leaves until we find another. I'm sweating, my palms dripping sweat onto the forest floor. My scalp pours a waterfall down the back of my neck, my skinsuit doing its best to ventilate my body heat.

I'm feeling faint by the time we stop. It can't have been longer than ten minutes since we first plunged into the jungle, but my vision seems to be expanding and contracting, like the lens of a camera trying to adjust to shifting light. Hamankush turns to me abruptly in the small clearing where she has chosen to pause, her starry eyes sweeping over me in one long blink. Her arm swipes at and removes a bell-shaped white flower from a branch. She extends it to me.

"Chew," she says, "but do not swallow."

I obey. My only other experience with food in the jungle is the rhohedron Rasimbukar gave me, and part of me had ignorantly expected this to be similar, but it couldn't be more different. The plant is crunchier than it felt in my hand, difficult to smash with my teeth.

What is it called? I ask as I chew.

It is called wahanile. Do not swallow.

I know.

It is very important that you do not swallow.

I hadn't been nervous before, but now anxiety makes my jaw slow. I chew carefully, methodically, not allowing even a drop of my own saliva to creep down my throat.

Remove it now. Into your palm.

It feels rude spitting in front of her, so I turn my head away just enough to be polite and deposit the small lump of the chewed remains of the flower into my palm. It resembles a thick white paste now, slightly sparkly, as if the flesh of the flower had contained tiny precious stones.

Your remaining saliva, she says. *Spit it there.*

She indicates the root of the tree bearing other white wa-hanile, and I obey.

Now take what is in your palm and rub it here. And here.

I mimic her motions, dipping my finger in the chewed-up paste and swiping it across my forehead and at my temples.

Then here, and here.

I use the rest of the paste to swipe a line under my chin on my throat and on the back of my neck.

"Better," she says, not as a question. She's right. I feel cooler, as if the paste has sent a wave of shade through my skin. My sweat even feels pleasant, as if rather than salty water it has been replaced with a gentle rain.

Drink, she says, and passes me a gourd-like vessel that she must have been carrying all along. When I obey she studies me again. *Rasimbukar tells me you can smell the ogwe.*

This wasn't what I expected to hear next, and I glance up at her, curious.

Yes. Sometimes. When I need to relax.

She looks at me for what seems like a long time, the spots on her forehead drifting as if deciding what to do next. When they eventually become still again, I know she has made up her mind.

I will show you now.

I expect her to immediately start showing me whatever it is her mind possesses, but instead she sits down, gesturing for me to do the same. I sink down next to her as she turns and places her long-fingered hand on the ground beside us. Her hand immediately takes on the rich black color of the soil, its depth seeping into her skin, green in places. I don't see what she sees, but I feel a pulse of her energy in the tunnel: it's as if her mind is filling up with some bright substance. She's receiving something.

What are you doing? I can't help but ask.

As you know, I am an archivist. But the archives are far from here. I am asking Faloiv to transfer the memory from there to here.

You can't access it in your own mind?

It is not my memory.

Her entire arm is now mottled black and green, an extension of the ground we sit on. It's not camouflage, I think: not the way N'Terrans have been able to reproduce it. It's another level of complexity that I can't even begin to understand: it's almost as if her arm is *becoming* soil. She seems to be focusing intensely now and the energy in her mind pulses again.

Are you prepared?

I think so. I'm nervous.

Here. See.

The memory that she passes into the tunnel surges in and brings with it the taste of dirt and plant matter. The memory smells like Faloiv; and even though it's nonphysical, its intensity causes every sensory neuron to fire as the planet itself enters my brain. No wind blows in the air, but I feel a breeze across my skin as the black soil of Faloiv fills my veins. My head snaps backward without my permission; my bones feel as if they're growing into wooden branches. It's not painful—it's almost pleasant—but it's a feeling like being buried and unearthed simultaneously.

I am a tree. Or my mind is. I sway in the breeze and I am tall and thick and content. I see more of the world than I thought possible—every inch of me is an eye: porous, both open and closed to the world. From where I'm rooted, I oversee everything. The city of Mbekenkanush, its people.

My people.

There are humans here. The tree-sense that has taken up space in my consciousness like a copilot recognizes them warily, a new species whose intentions are disconnected from the tunnel where the creatures of Faloiv converge. Their minds are small and mysterious. And yet the human in me can sense these people's joy: they are recently descended from outer space; they are on solid ground and safe; and they are happy about it. I can hear their voices, raised with laughter. They are learning about their new home. These are the Acclimates, come to Mbekenkanush.

But something is coming.

Suddenly my mind rushes with red and orange flames of pain. It blinds me—or the tree? Both of us—with its intensity. It's as if the signal connecting me to the tree's memory begins to short: I see only flares of what the tree remembers, everything else frayed and distorted. Three people come from beyond the tree line, people wearing yellow suits. I smell strangeness on them: the smell of synthetic materials. Of burning. The people that come from the jungle carry buzzguns. Maybe there are more than three. Humans from inside Mbekenkanush are running toward them, two women and a man. I recognize two of them.

Somewhere inside the tree's memory I whisper, "Nana."

And the man beside her is my grandfather. He waves his arms. He's yelling. Everyone is yelling. The buzzguns zip. People fall. Inside me, the memory of the tree is quaking and my own horror builds alongside it, so huge and terrible that I'm afraid my skin might tear. My grandmother runs beside the other woman, both of them shouting. The buzzguns fire. My grandmother screams.

The woman running with Nana has fallen. The world inside the memory is swirling as blood falls and spills, seeming to wash the whole city in its shocking redness. Then from the sky comes a buzzgun in the form of a bird: its body is all angles and edges, silver metal sharp and shining as it swoops down out of the clouds, raining violence and chaos upon the scene below.

"A drone!" my grandfather's voice thunders. "Take cover!"

Hamankush's voice is a sudden echo in my head from beyond the tree's memory:

This is war, she says.

Who were those people in the trees? I ask. I'm breathless. I've never seen people kill each other. It's staggering, almost too much to comprehend.

Your people. N'Terrans.

Why . . . why?

Periods of blackness punctuate the memories of the tree I am able to see. It feels as if a rope is tied around my waist and I'm being forcibly dragged through dark water, the sun occasionally showing me my surroundings. On the same bloodstained ground, the Faloii and my grandparents—other humans gathered around—seem to argue. In the center stands a single cloaked figure, face obscured by the green shroud that wraps them. Their presence pulses with mystery, the conflict of the humans and the Faloii seeming to swirl around them. They feel ancient and otherworldly—I sense it from the way the tree regards them: fear and awe. They stand motionless in the midst of war.

And this, Hamankush whispers from beyond the memory, *is what they do not want you to see.*

CHAPTER 3

The soil is leaking out of my veins, emptying me as the memory of the tree and my own consciousness split, becoming two again. My limbs lose their strong woodenness, the roots abandon the soles of my feet. As the last leaf shrinks from my mind, I feel small and brittle, my skin strangely exposed after the secure armor of bark.

When I open my eyes, ready to ask Hamankush the many questions that are forming in my mind, I instead find Rasimbukar, towering above me and staring at Hamankush with what can only be described as a glare. The spots on her forehead are assembled in a low rigid line. I'm almost afraid to open the tunnel, but when I do I find that I am barred from whatever conversation it is that they are having. Hamankush's fists are clenched, her own facial spots vibrating in small tight patterns.

I lower my eyes, staring at the dark soil, a sensation of being wood still leaking out of me. When Rasimbukar finally turns her eyes on me, she looks like she's about to speak when she lowers her gaze to my feet. Her spots drift higher on one side, losing some of their rigidity.

"What is this?" she says.

At my feet, a tangle of new vines has grown from the forest floor. I know for a fact that they weren't there when we arrived at this place, and as proof, they grow before my eyes. They seem to circle me, green tendrils drifting closer to my ankles as if in curiosity. From one, a single black flower—delicate and lovely—blooms.

"Interesting," Rasimbukar says.

"Yes, interesting," Hamankush says, but there is something in her tone I can't read, and Rasimbukar jerks her head to fix her with an icy stare. There is something else unspoken between them, something I don't hear.

"I have been looking for you," she says. Hamankush turns and disappears into the trees without another word. "Your grandmother has awakened."

My grandmother is sitting up in bed, the blue mammals, which had roamed her skin when I saw her last, removed. She offers me a weak smile when I enter the room. My grandfather is gone.

"Nana," I say.

"Afua," she says, and beckons me with one of her plump hands.

I approach her bedside slowly. She has been dead since I was eleven. Seeing her now, after so many years gazing out at the jungle and wondering what direction, under which tree, her body had become bones . . . it's hard.

"I owe you an apology, sweetness. Years of them," she says.

I sit on the low stool where I'd slouched earlier and study her hand to avoid her eyes. I don't remember her fingers, her nails. After five years, the edges of her have blurred in my mind. Will my memories of my mother become the same? A flower torn from the branch, fading in the sun?

"I can't believe she's dead," I whisper.

Her hand takes my chin and steers it upward so I finally look into her eyes. The grief there is bottomless—I think I should have known that my grandmother was still alive all these years because my mother's eyes did not look like this. My mother's sadness had carried the gray mist of loneliness. My nana's carries more than clouds. This grief is a mountain in her heart.

"Where is my grandfather?" I ask.

"He has gone back to his work," she says.

"You talk like them," I say softly. "Like the Faloii."

She smiles.

"Yes, I suppose I do. After so many years, it is inevitable that the tongue learns new rhythms."

Neither of us speaks after that, the silence like a third person in the room, taking up too much space. She reaches out her hand, palm up, inviting me to take it. I can't quite bring myself to do it, and the guilt is the invisible third person pinching the fat on my arm.

"Have I been gone that long, baby?" she says.

"No," I say quickly. The memory of resting between her soft knees as she braided my hair, her wordless melody floating down to my ears, her and my mother's voices darting back and forth across the 'wam in mock argument . . . it all feels close, as if I could reach out and cup it in my palm. "But, yes."

She sighs, and the sound fills the small dim qalm.

"Of course," she says. "I'm sorry. I've thought of you every day. Time passes so strangely. And now I get you here and I act like no time has passed at all. For me it doesn't feel that way sometimes, but it can't have been easy for you. N'Terra was hard enough to manage when I was there. Now . . . I can't imagine."

"So it was always this bad?" I say, grabbing what feels like neutral conversation and clinging to it. "It's like all this stuff was happening around me and I didn't even notice."

"Youth will do that." She smiles. "But, no, it wasn't always *this* bad, although it's never been good. I wandered back and forth for a while before I left: seeing Jamyle—your grandfather—but also giving my heart a rest from everything happening in that place. I missed you so much . . . but it was a relief to be away."

The possibility of neutral topics shrinks out of my grasp.

"Mom knew you were alive," I say. "And she never said anything."

At this, her fingers curl in on themselves, their tips rubbing together in thought.

"That's right," she says. "It was hard for her, sweetness, believe that."

"I need to know why everything was so secretive," I say. "I know Mom was at odds with the Council, but you weren't. . . ."

"It wasn't just your mother," she interjects. "For me to be gone and alive would mean I had to be somewhere safe. Albatur has been building toward what we're seeing right now for a long time. Me being gone but not dead wasn't going to play, baby."

"But Albatur just got elected," I say. "That's what I don't get. Everything feels so sudden."

Her lips purse a little, twisting, and this face and what it means comes swimming back up through my memory. It's the face she makes when there's a lot she wants to say but is choosing her words carefully. A face my mother inherited.

"It's never just one person," she says. "But Albatur came here with a purpose. He didn't expect the planet's effect on his biology. He spent a lot of time just trying to survive, like the rest of us, while N'Terra's roots were laid. But he never wanted to stay here. Never envisioned this as the last stop for humanity."

"I saw . . . war," I say. "Did they come here after the Acclimates left? With buzzguns?"

The weak smile transforms into a soft frown.

"You have been talking to Hamankush," she says. She prods my mind and I'm almost surprised, forgetting that she, like my mother, is able to speak in the tunnel. She seems to welcome changing the topic. "It is called the Artery," she adds, noting my surprise. "The place where you speak the quiet language. If you are looking for something to call the language itself: Arterian."

"Arterian." I nod. "What about Grandfather?"

She shakes her head. "Not all the Acclimates are able to. There needs to be what the Faloii call a willingness in the brain. You are a little different. My gift—and your mother's— was given. Yours was inherited."

Before I can ask more questions, she redirects me to the matter of what I'd seen.

"Now," she says. "Hamankush?"

"Yes, Hamankush showed me a memory. The trees' memory. People . . . died."

She nods and pushes herself a little higher in the cot, sitting up slowly.

"Yes," she says. "Including a friend of mine. Her name was Anna. We were close on the Origin Planet. When we landed here, the Faloii requested that a group of us live among them, to learn the ways of living in harmony with Faloiv. Your

43

grandfather knew right away the value of respecting the Faloii, and I think he knew as soon as he set foot on Faloiv that there was something special here. We knew that if a future here was possible, it began with peace. Anna helped us convince others aboard the *Vagantur* that living in Mbekenkanush was wise. The ones who came with us didn't see living with the Faloii as captivity but an opportunity to learn more quickly. More safely."

"But not everyone."

"No. Not everyone. Not all scientists are curious, Afua. And plenty are arrogant."

"But you went to N'Terra," I say. "You didn't come here. Not right away."

"That's right. Jamyle didn't want to bring your mother into such a circumstance if it turned out the Faloii had ulterior motives. And someone had to keep an eye on Albatur and his followers. Your mother and I stayed, and the plan was that we would join him here when the time came. But many things changed. Change happens quickly. But slow too."

"Hamankush said N'Terra wouldn't let the Acclimates come back. Is that when they . . . when they killed Anna?"

"Yes. This is what I mean when I say Albatur has been building toward this. It began far before he was elected. Far before we left the Origin Planet."

Something in the room pulses. It's not light, and it's not sound either. It's a current of some kind, which I recognize traveling through me as if I've touched an electric wire. When it fades, my toes tingle.

"The qalm," Nana says. She raises her arm from her side and rests her palm against the wall, which shudders almost imperceptibly. "It must be raining."

We pause to listen, and sure enough I can hear the distant thrum of a storm. I hadn't seen any clouds when Rasimbukar had brought me back here from the jungle.

"In N'Terra you know three days before it rains," I say, looking up as if at the sky. "The clouds start to gather far out over the trees and then slowly roll in."

"Yes," Nana says. "But Mbekenkanush is where the rain begins."

When the vines part a moment later I expect to see Rasimbukar, but it is Kimbullettican, the youth who had expressed sympathy in the school qalm. They enter and greet my grandmother silently. Then they hail me, also in Arterian.

It is raining, they say.

I know.

The qalm has agreed to grow a room for you. Rasimbukar informed me that you might like to observe.

Observe?

I hesitate, glancing at my nana. I haven't seen her in years and now we're getting interrupted—I can't help but wonder if it's on purpose. She seems to notice my indecision and shoos me off her bed.

"We will catch up," she says, her N'Terran accent creeping back in with the voice she uses for comforting. "Go on now."

I follow Kimbullettican out through the vines back into the corridor. They lead me down in the opposite direction I'd entered from, and I can't help but compare my surroundings to the Zoo. A maze of tunnels, similar in that way. But the membrane of the ceilings allows in the sun, slightly muted, and the floor isn't a hard artificial barrier between foot and ground. The soil is a comfort under my feet. The lines here are not straight either—not like the unforgiving angles of N'Terra's labs. Everything curves. All is irregular, the shape of breath, as if the qalm exhaled and the tunnels followed the whim of the air. When Kimbullettican leads me to an opening where the vines have not yet grown in, I see this imagining isn't far off.

The room before me grows with every pulse that throbs gently through the qalm. It's the rhythm of a wide green throat swallowing water: with each swallow, the space swells. The room is barely a room, existing only as the thinnest green membrane, but it thickens with each pulse. A moment ago I was looking out at the city through the thin layer, but with every passing second the details become more obscure, the rounded green bubble before me thickening and strengthening. Only the roof remains thin, but not enough to see the sky: just the faint shadowy shapes of raindrops, which land and then slide down the curved sides before dripping to the ground. Inside the membrane, a shape rises from the floor, inch by inch, growing taller and more substantial. I eventually realize it is a sleeping platform, grown from the very ground. Another structure, flat and broad, emerges, which I believe is a small desk. Compartments appear in one wall, holes like the ones I remember from our kitchen in N'Terra. I imagine my father sitting there alone and my heart sinks in my chest.

"It is finished," Kimbullettican says out loud. "There may be some adjustments over the next few days. But you may lie down and treat this space as your own."

"Thank you."

"Do you smell it?" they say, turning their eyes on me. They lack the endlessness of Rasimbukar's: there is the glimmering quality, but not quite the galactic bottomlessness of Rasimbukar's, Hamankush's, and the other adult Faloii's.

I do smell it, though I'm not sure what "it" is. A smell that seems familiar but subtle.

"I have communicated to the qalm that the room will be yours. It absorbed some of your scent while you sat with your grandmother. This is how you will identify your room in the future, as there are no other notable external differences."

"Thank you," I say. "For explaining."

"You cannot know what you do not know," they say, and flash their teeth. It reminds me of the words Alma and Rondo and I had exchanged so often in the Greenhouse: *we don't know, but we will*. Kimbullettican doesn't seem to notice my sudden sadness at the thought of my friends; they seem pleased with themselves, and I decide that this smile the Faloii perform is certainly a trait they have learned from humans, and Kimbullettican is pleased that they inserted the gesture correctly.

"How old are you?" I ask.

"Your friend Jaquot asked the same question. My age is irrelevant, as it is not comparable to your measure of time. My chronology might seem quite long to you, but we mature very differently from humans. We are similar, you and I, in terms of maturation. I believe that is what you would really like to know."

"Yes," I say. "And do you remember when the Acclimates came?"

"I do not," they say, and that's all.

"That's okay." I sigh.

"It must be." They smile again. I think this phrase, this joke, is something they have picked up from humans as well. My grandmother has their accent; they have our smiles. They stare at me for a moment and then the smile falters. "Hamankush says the plants like you."

"She did? I mean, they do?"

"I think she is right. Do you feel the curiosity of the qalm? The way it observes you?"

I had not noticed, at least not consciously, but when I stop and listen, I can feel the energy of the room I stand in focused on me, like a beam of sunlight directed by a magnifying glass.

"I do now," I say, baffled. "But what does it mean?"

"I am not sure if it means anything," Kimbullettican says. "Only that when you inherited the biology of your grandmother, it may have mutated slightly in you."

"Mutated?" I say, concerned. I know not all mutations are bad, but when my mother told me I'd been given a gift, I hadn't thought of it as a mutation.

"Do not be worried," they say. "It is merely interesting. It may make your life on Faloiv even easier than your peers'. Or even more difficult. It is hard to say with humans."

I don't know what to say to this. Between the intensity of their eyes and the focus of the qalm on my consciousness, I feel overwhelmed.

"I am sorry," Kimbullettican says, sensing my discomfort. "I realize now that this may not have been a kind thing to say."

"It's okay." I sigh. "You don't owe us any kindness."

"That may or may not be true. But I understand that this all must be very strange—discovering a side of your people that you never knew existed."

I think of what Hamankush had shown me—*this is what they do not want you to see*—and the fact that Rasimbukar has been shielding N'Terra from Mbekenkanush's consequences, but hide this thought from Kimbullettican.

"You mean the fact that the Acclimates are here, or what is happening at home in N'Terra?"

"They are the same thing," they say, looking at me with what seems to be a quizzical arrangement of their facial spots.

I will leave you now, Kimbullettican says in Arterian before I can decide how to reply. *Rasimbukar says you will need to rest.*

I almost ask them not to leave me—it's hard to feel alone with the consciousness of the qalm swirling around me. But that would be ridiculous; and after I bid them good-bye, I carefully climb onto the sleeping platform, which is higher than at home. Home. What is home now? Not just N'Terra but this whole planet: What is home?

CHAPTER 4

I wake to the sound of Jaquot's voice and startle, nearly falling out of bed. I'm curled at the edge of it, still in my skinsuit, which I've been wearing for entirely too long. I look around for Jaquot but don't see him, only a vine hanging from the ceiling, a blue cup-shaped flower at its end. I think it's a communication device of some kind, and reach for it, but the flower comes off in my hand. I jerk my hand away as the vine retracts into the ceiling. The flower quivers in my hand, then slowly opens. Then from its center, softly, drifts the sound of Jaquot's voice. I realize the only thing he's saying is my name.

When I hold the flower to my ear, Jaquot's voice continues, soft and smooth as if the sound is brought to me by the wind.

"Octavia," he says, and I realize it's some kind of recording when he continues. "Rasimbukar wants you to come with us on our assignment today. They're taking your grandmother to the pink lake, so don't worry about her. Rasim said she made sure you have clothes in one of your wall compartments. Meet us at the school when you wake up."

Then the little flower is silent, only a vague echo stirring in my ear. I take the flower away from my face and study it, trying to understand if it's organic or some kind of elegant technology. I place the flower on my cot, half expecting it to self-destruct, but it just rests there, blue and innocent. I turn to the wall compartments, wondering if Rasimbukar had come into my room as I slept, silent as a shadow.

But, no, I find; the clothing that rests inside the compartment is the work of the qalm. The material is membraneous like the first shell of the room as it had grown, and attached to a slender stem that connects to the inside of the compartment. I give it a gentle tug and withdraw what appears to be a suit much like the N'Terran one I already wear. I would like to bathe, but there's no one to ask, so I remove my white skinsuit and use the material to swipe under my arms and the back of my neck. When I pull on the new clothing, I realize right away how different it is.

There are no stitches or seams: it doesn't appear to have a beginning or end, but the neck hole seems entirely too large; my whole chest wrap will be exposed, I think, fitting my arms and legs through the appropriate holes. But as it fits to my body, I realize the opening is gradually closing, knitting itself together across my chest and back, slithering up toward my neck. My panic is involuntary. I stumble backward, half-heartedly clawing at the material and trying to get my fingers between it and my skin before it overtakes me entirely. But there is no space: it has bonded with me, more of a second skin than the N'Terran suit could ever be. And then I feel it: the sensation that soothes my panic like salve on a burn. Breath. My body breathes through the material in a way that makes me more aware than ever before of the pores of my skin, the hairs on my arms and legs and in my armpits. All of these things, these tiny human details, have a purpose, and the suit seems to understand this.

"Hello," I say, and feel stupid for saying it, but it's as if I'm greeting my body for the first time. And the hello is also for this wonderful, amazing suit. My skin drinks oxygen greedily like it's never fully enjoyed breathing on Faloiv while clothed before now. I'm running my hands over my arms and legs and chest, admiring the strangely sparkling material—like the scales of a morgantan, but plantlike—when I hear a voice from nearby. It takes a moment for me to realize the voice is speaking in Arterian, an unusual smudge of conversation that I'm somehow overhearing.

It is inevitable, the voice says. *And when the Isii is consulted, the humans must choose.*

Wearing the new suit, I slip on my shoes by the door, and rest my fingertips on the wall as I'd seen Rasimbukar do. The minuscule vines part immediately.

In the hallway, I find Hamankush, staring intently at another Faloii person, with whom she is having a silent conversation. I only hear one harsh word before the tunnel snaps shut, a reprimand of her companion.

Careless.

"Octavia," she says to me out loud. She moves toward me and the person she'd been addressing disappears through another vined door. "You will be joining your peers in the jungle today. You have heard?"

"Yes," I say, trying to look like I wasn't eavesdropping, even accidentally. "I was just on my way. If I can remember how to get there."

She shows me the path in the tunnel. The way she speaks Arterian is different from Rasimbukar: quick and rushed.

"You see?" she says, and I nod, holding the series of images and instructions in my head. "Good. Your suit fits you well. Your hands are bare?"

My hands are indeed bare.

"Uh, yeah, I guess so. I just didn't want my hands covered. I guess it understood."

She studies me. "You are an unusual human," she says.

"How?" I ask. The spots on her forehead, so still compared to Rasimbukar's constantly shifting pattern, are like a puzzle I wish to solve.

"Unusual," she says. "Where some see ocean, you see water."

She turns away, moving toward the vine door her companion had gone through.

"Hurry now," she says. "I will see you shortly."

I find my way to the school with the help of Hamankush's instructions, but I discover that she needn't have guided me. The city isn't as overwhelming as it had seemed yesterday, when the newness of it all had rained down on me like a meteor shower. And aside from the difference in appearance, the activities of the Faloii don't seem at all different from what I might have observed in the dome of any compound of N'Terra. Except rather than animals, everyone appears to be in deep concentration examining the various plants and vegetation in the city. I recognize Adombukar, standing near the trunk of a young tree, one palm on its bark, listening intently.

It's strange to see the Faloii all around me after mystery shrouded their existence for so many years. My N'Terran upbringing had prepared me for something akin to monsters, but their difference is only that: different. It's stranger, in fact, to see the humans among them—walking, talking, studying, all in the qalm-grown suits but still sticking to the shade the trees provide. The Acclimates are outnumbered, but seem unbothered by this as they go about their work. Some of them study alongside the Faloii, but many more seem to be involved in taking care of the qalms: water here, bringing different species of insects and birds. A woman my mother's age stands near one as I pass by, applying what appears to be a thick green paste to one section of the qalm's wall.

"What are you doing?" I venture to ask, pausing.

She turns, an expression of surprise on her face. "A branch fell in a recent storm, damaging the qalm. I am using a bit of phinusa to help heal it."

"It can't heal itself?" I say.

"Yes," she says. "But why should it? When we can help?"

"Is that what you study here? Healing the qalms?"

"Study?" she says, raising an eyebrow. "I do what needs to be done."

She seems eager to return to her work, and somehow I understand from the qalm that it is eager as well. Even if I can't fully comprehend its language, I understand that it feels . . . pleased.

When I finally wind my way through the city and arrive at the school, Jaquot and the same group of others stand waiting in the shade of the qalm. A habitual part of me looks for Dr. Espada, and the memory of his death is like the sting of an insect, so sharp I almost gasp.

"You have a suit!" Jaquot says, nodding at me from where he leans against the qalm. I can't help but look at his missing leg. I want to ask him how it feels, if he's lost more than just this limb, but he sees me looking and his expression closes off. This is a path I am not invited down. Not yet.

"Yes," I say, averting my eyes to my clothing. I stand in direct sunlight but only my scalp seems to notice the heat. I make a mental note to see about getting some of those bell-shaped flowers from the jungle to smear along the rows of my braids, to protect my exposed scalp. "This material is amazing."

"It is," he agrees. "N'Terra spends so much time studying animals. We should have spent more time learning from the plants."

"They would have if they had joined the Faloii," the round-cheeked girl says, stepping into the sun to join me.

"Joi is a proud Acclimate," Jaquot says, shooting me an apologetic smile.

"So are my grandparents," I say, locking my eyes on Joi's.

She smirks at this but doesn't offer a retort. The other humans in my peer group don't seem interested in talking to me. If N'Terran greencoats are focused on our studies, these kids are obsessed. Even out here surrounded by Faloiv, most of them have their faces shoved in books or notes. Not true of Kimbullettican, who watches me with the other Faloii youth.

"Your grandmother is improved?" one says. They introduce themselves as Revollettican, a sibling of Kimbullettican, in Arterian.

"I think so." I nod. "She was able to sit up."

I hesitate, then address Kimbullettican and Revollettican silently in Arterian. I don't like how Joi eyes me like a surgeon, looking for something to cut at.

I didn't see my grandfather when I was there, I tell them. *Do you know if he has a study or something?*

Your grandfather, Kimbullettican says. Their forehead spots rise in amusement. *If he is not with your grandmother, then he is by the black lake.*

His favorite place, Revollettican says.

"The black lake?" I say.

Jaquot appears not to notice that this was part of a conversation being had in private.

"Oh, I've heard about that," he says. "Apparently your grandfather's the only one who goes there. It's like his thesis."

"His Lifework," Kimbullettican corrects.

"Meaning?" I say.

"This is what Dr. Lemieux calls it," they reply. "The Acclimates study many things, but your grandfather has chosen one course above all others."

"And he studies . . . a lake?" I say.

"I must believe there is something about it he loves," Kimbullettican says. "Hamankush tells me he has been attending the black lake since the Acclimates arrived. Some scientists find comfort in their work."

"You have to love something to study it for multiple decades," Jaquot says. "Sounds like an obsession to me."

The word *obsession* lingers like a half-remembered dream, a footprint in shifting sand. *Obsession.* Dr. Albatur has an obsession. So does my father. I've seen where it got them.

I sense a familiar presence approaching in the tunnel. It's

different away from N'Terra. I almost don't notice that the tunnel is open all the time. Without the threat of fear leaking in from animals in containment, the impressions that wander in and out of the Artery are pleasant and operate just behind my consciousness. The familiar presence reveals itself a moment later when Hamankush emerges from the jungle.

"Anoo," she says to us all, then greets the Faloii and myself in Arterian. "You have your materials?"

Everyone but me nods. The Faloii youth wear the belt of pouches at their waist that Rasimbukar occasionally wears, but the human students all carry slim green cases slung across their chests. The feeling of unpreparedness seizes me, and I inexplicably think of Yaya. Always battling to stay ahead of her in the Greenhouse. Do I miss even her?

"I have a few things for you," Hamankush says, turning her eyes on me, her long arm extending a pack toward me. I accept the pack gratefully, and mutter my thanks. "Water. Wahanile paste for the parts of your skin not covered by the suit. Some dried foods that you are accustomed to. Recording materials."

I drape the pack over my chest, taking a moment to admire the fabric. Is it fabric? Or some other kind of plant adapted for this purpose? The question answers itself when I let the pack hang by my side and notice a strange sensation at my hip. I look down, and find that my suit has melded to the bag ever so gently. The two fuse loosely, keeping the case from moving around when I walk.

"Fascinating," I whisper.

Hamankush moves off toward the jungle and we follow her wordlessly. Jaquot ends up at the back of the group with his slower gait, and I hang back to walk alongside him.

"They'll make me a prosthetic eventually," he says. "Lots of Faloii have prosthetics. Well, not lots. But enough so that they know what they're doing. It's an organic material they use to make them, like everything else here. I wonder if it will look like a foot—a human foot—or like a Faloii paw. Their feet are kind of cool, you know."

"Aren't you thinking about home?" I say. "Your dad thinks you're dead, Jaquot. That doesn't bother you?"

"Of course it does. But we didn't talk much when I was in N'Terra." He averts his eyes, focusing on the path ahead. "I didn't think he'd even notice I was gone. Maybe he needs to see what life is like without me for a while."

"Petty," I say, but he shrugs.

"I like it here," he says eventually. "Things are more relaxed. Don't you feel it?"

"I do," I admit. Just the comfort of the suit I wear takes the pressure off. It feels like I'm friends with the sun for once, rather than adversaries. But the relaxation can't quite sink in. "But Jaquot . . . there's a lot going on back home. There's a lot that's happening."

Rasimbukar would not like that you are speaking of this, Hamankush tells me in Arterian. I jerk my head to look at her, chatting with Joi at the head of the group. She doesn't appear to break her conversation and I realize my understanding of the Faloii is woefully limited.

"Look, I know, okay?" Jaquot says, and in between paces he swipes irritably at a plant with one of his canes. "You're always stressed out, Octavia. Why can't you ever just loosen up?"

I bristle at this, opening my mouth to snap at him. But the sight of him glancing down at where his leg should be silences me. We continue on, quiet, and I turn my attention to the jungle around us, widening the Artery; inside, I get glimpses of animals I've never seen or heard. N'Terra knows nothing about this planet.

"We are getting close now," Hamankush calls. Then in Arterian, *Can you feel it?*

I sense the Faloii youth all expanding their consciousness, and I attempt to do the same. I have an awareness that my breadth is stunted compared to theirs, but I focus, trying to muscle it wider and wider. I'm rewarded with a sort of tingling at the edge of my mind, up ahead through the trees. I sense the Faloii youths' discomfort before it fully translates in my own mind. Something is wrong ahead, too far for my own mind to grasp, but the farther we walk, making our way through the thinning trees, the more apparent it becomes. It's familiar . . . something trembling in the tunnel . . . strange and known simultaneously. I sense Hamankush's sudden confusion, translating into unease. Whatever she had brought us to see is not here. Something else is in its place.

There's a clearing ahead, and it's just before we break through the tree line that it hits me. There's an igua ahead. But she's not herself. Something restless paces inside her. A parasite, she's saying. She's telling the air, the trees. An herbivore, she has no predators, but warns all of Faloiv. She is sick, she says. Stay away. Stay away. Stay away.

We approach. She warns us, begging. Her consciousness seems to fade in and out within the Artery, as if something is cutting her off intermittently. Joi and Jaquot and the other humans break through the trees with their minds empty and unconcerned. They don't hear her, feel her. Hamankush and the other Faloii move forward speaking to her, a more complicated tongue than anything I can conjure. They console her in her own language, a skill I know instinctively that I will never attain. I can only send green signals of comfort, so I do.

"Is something wrong?" Joi says when she finally sees the igua, lying on her side in the middle of the clearing, alone. "Is she giving birth?"

"This is not birth," Hamankush says.

We draw nearer, the igua begging us not to. Hamankush lays one of her long paw-like hands on the igua's side, assessing. Revollettican does the same, unafraid, conversing with the animal. I can't understand the conversation, but I gather from Hamankush's secondary impressions that they are having trouble ascertaining what is wrong. The igua is confused, afraid.

But there is something familiar here, something I can't quite place. The sense of it slithers around in my head, looking for a match. It slides over a particular sensory memory. A smell, flat and white . . .

"Oh, stars," I cry. "Hamankush, you have to get away, fast!"

I grab her and Revollettican, attempting to pull them away. They both regard me with a look of disbelief, Hamankush's spots quickly translating into anger.

"Child," she says harshly. "Control your Arterian. Immediately."

I realize what she means, that my sudden red panic had flowed through the tunnel, the igua sensing it and lurching with fear. I snap the tunnel closed and appeal to Hamankush with both hands.

"Please, it's dangerous!"

"It," Revollettican says out loud sternly. "*She.*"

"That's not what I meant," I plead. "Please, we need to get away from her right now!"

"Make sense," Hamankush orders. "Do not consider speaking until you do."

She turns away, Revollettican doing the same. Everyone else stands back, looking uncertain. My helplessness flails within me like a wounded bird. I cannot fly into Arterian without causing the igua to panic, and I can't calm down enough to explain in an audible language. Jaquot appears beside me, his face folded with worry.

"What's the matter?"

"I—I . . . ," I stutter. I snap my mouth shut and close my eyes, forcing myself to take deep breaths. I have to control the tunnel, and open it only to Hamankush to shield the igua. Two breaths. Three. I open my eyes and focus hard on addressing only her.

Hamankush, I say. *Danger.*

The flat white smell invades my nostrils again. The smell of the Zoo. I pass it to her, and without thinking show her the vasana from N'Terra's labs. I show her the pack of them, wild with artificial madness, frothing and flaming, their brains not their own, the rage a mechanical parasite implanted by white-coats. Here, the igua has been altered. She is not herself. The empty smell of the labs is all over her, in the very breath that snorts from her flared nostrils.

DANGER, I say again.

Hamankush stares at me hard, then takes two long strides away from the igua to stand in front of me, much too close.

Tell me this is a lie.

I'm telling you the truth.

We lock eyes, the stars of her gaze mesmerizing in their depth. I'm lost in those stars, trying to find a way to make her see, when the igua screams. A sound like a storm tearing from the clouds, rending the air with electricity. And then, as if emerging from a terrible dream, the fangs are there, flashing from that wide, bawling mouth, growing like the violent stems of strange flowers. Too white. Too long. Then those teeth are closing around the body of Revollettican, the youth's eyes opening wide in shock at the sight of their own blood, so unexpected, so unusual.

The rest is a blur. The jungle whirls around me. Something switches when the blood meets the soil. A reversal, a planetwide sigh. In a flash, Hamankush presses one long finger against the igua's neck, and in the tunnel there is a burst of painful white light, leaving glowing rings around the edges of my mind. Then everything is silent. Everything is still. The blood seeps into the ground, and above us the sun stares down.

CHAPTER 5

I am alone. I sit on my cot, my knees pulled to my chest, staring at the empty chamber of my room. I've unraveled my braids, my hands desperate for distraction, and now I sit with my back against the wall, finger-combing each zigzagging section. Every now and then I look into the Artery, but the only communication I pick up is the thrumming tongue of the qalm.

Hamankush had killed the igua, and what seemed like moments later Rasimbukar and other Faloii had appeared, all communicating soundlessly. I and the other youths were swept back to the city, and I was jostled here to my room. I had asked for my grandmother and was ignored. The Faloii man who had brought me here was as unreadable as the walls of my room, his facial spots low and solemn across his brow. All around me, the tunnels are closed, but I don't need to be told anything in

Arterian to know the scent that pulses around me. Fear. Anger.

The igua must have escaped from the labs alongside Adombukar and the rest when I left N'Terra. Why had I not sensed it? The cybertronic parasite planted in its brain by Dr. Albatur? The igua must have been partially altered and then either escaped or was let free.

I pace the small room. No one had ordered me to remain here, but venturing outside the qalm seems pointless. I don't know where to find my grandmother, or if I'm even allowed. I'm turning back to my cot when a presence makes me spin back to face the wall. Sure enough, the minuscule vines are simultaneously parting, revealing the doorway. In it stands Rasimbukar.

You are changed, she says. At first I think she's referring to my unbraided hair, but I sense a different meaning. *We all are. Come with me.*

I follow her out of my room and down the hallway. The smell of fear is stronger here. It's not the qalm that emits it, but it does seem to come from the walls.

"Where are we going?" I say when she leads me outside.

"We have questions," she says.

I follow her in silence through the city. All the pleasant motion of yesterday is gone, faded like a puddle shrunken by the sun. The odor the many trees—ogwe and others: syca, marandin, and duna—emit reminds me of the day my mother was arrested in N'Terra: a dire smell, a smell of warning.

Yes, says Rasimbukar, sensing my feelings.

She leads me to a small qalm, its green a deeper shade than the school—almost black. I lay my hand on it without thinking, sensing its complicated nature. It's very old. Perhaps older than anything else in the city.

Decisions are made here, Rasimbukar says as the vines part to admit us. Her facial spots are low and still but widespread. This look always reminds me of my mother somehow and I avert my eyes. She gazes at me a moment longer and then sweeps into the qalm.

It's one room. I'd expected a honeycomb of chambers and halls like the other buildings I've been inside, but instead I am greeted with a circular space lined with platforms that grow from the walls, jutting out at varying heights. An array of Faloii sit on these platforms, some upright and some slouched, all watching me and Rasimbukar intently. At the center of the room grows a small bent tree, giving off a soft orange light like a flame. Beside it sits Hamankush, cross-legged on a low platform that rises from the ground. Hers is the only pair of eyes not fastened on me. Hers are closed, her facial spots drifting slowly back and forth across her forehead in perpetual motion.

Your grandmother, Rasimbukar says, and indicates the back wall with one hand.

My heart leaps at the sight of her, half sitting, half lying on a platform by herself. She gives me an encouraging smile, sending me green shapes in the tunnel. I hadn't fully realized until

I saw her how afraid I am, the anxiety clawing at me as if my ribs are a cage it must escape.

You may go to her, Rasimbukar says, and I do, giving Hamankush and the center of the room a wide berth. I climb up on the platform and let my grandmother gather me against her the way she did when I was a child. She is warm and so is the room but I don't care: the feeling of her soft hands gripping me through my new suit transports me to a safe, distant place. Rasimbukar takes a seat on an empty platform.

The silence lasts a long time. The warmth from the strange tree in the center of the room fills the space with an almost smoky heat, and I find myself nodding off as the minutes turn into an hour, more. My head is just lolling sleepily against my nana's shoulder when Hamankush speaks.

"I come to tell the truth," she says. "And seek repair."

The room fills with a hum that startles me. At first I think it's the qalm, but a quick glance around shows me that the sound comes from the throats of the Faloii. Deep and resonant, it thrums from each of them and joins with the others, filling the room like an invisible cloud. They go on humming and I realize the place at the bottom of Rasimbukar's throat glows a soft green, shining gently through her skin like an incandescent jewel. I watch in awe, gazing around the room at the glowing spot on each Faloii present. My grandmother's hand squeezes my shoulder. Something tells me not to speak, even to whisper a question.

As suddenly as the humming began, it stops.

A conversation begins in Anooiire. It's the first time I've heard it spoken aloud at length, and its rapidity is almost shocking. It flows like water, nearly without pause, a rhythm of sounds and cadences foreign to my ear made familiar only by the polished wooden tones of the Faloii speaking it. The voices come from around the room, including Rasimbukar's, all their words directed at Hamankush, who sits with her head bowed by the tree. She responds occasionally, her answers short.

It's impossible to follow what is being said. I understand that Hamankush is being interrogated in some way, based on what happened in the jungle with the igua. When I look at Rasimbukar, the spots on her forehead seem unusually tight, and I wonder if she and Hamankush have some preexisting tension. Eventually the voices from around the room dwindle away, and it is only Rasimbukar and Hamankush who speak, the Anooiire getting faster and faster until I can barely make out one word from the next. Then I recognize one word.

Octavia.

There is a flutter of interest, both in the room and in the tunnel. My skin and my consciousness prickle as both eyes and minds readjust to settle on me, and suddenly, though I'm at the edge of the room, I'm at the center of it. Everyone is staring, and I don't know who to look at. My hand automatically fastens around my grandmother's wrist. I am eleven again.

"Octavia." Rasimbukar's voice carries across the silent room. I fight the chill it sends down my spine.

"They want you in the center. With Hamankush," my grandmother whispers. She gently pries my hand loose from her wrist, slipping back into a N'Terran accent. "It's okay, sweetness. I'm here. I'll be right here."

I walk to the center of the chamber, joining Hamankush by the glowing tree. Every pace feels like I'm stepping farther out into the blackness of space, the unknown yawning before me. Hamankush doesn't look up when I join her.

"You may sit," Rasimbukar says. Her voice is indecipherable but her facial spots drift gently outward, and I hold on to this small observation as I sink down on the platform beside Hamankush.

Rasimbukar says something in rapid Anooiire, and in my head there's a sensation of a flower blooming, the tunnel widening to admit the minds of the many Faloii present. It's almost dizzying, the presence of this many. I would never be able to isolate my Arterian to address only one out of so many—and perhaps this is the point—but Rasimbukar says only to me: *All is well. This is a place for truth.*

Other voices begin to ask me questions. I can't discern who they are or any identity attached to the questions. When I answer, it is as if I answer to them all.

Hamankush took a life, the Faloii say. *You saw this?*

You mean the igua? I reply. *Yes. But she had to.*

Do you understand that the killing of one who takes no prey is a violation? ask the Faloii.

I—I don't know, I say.

Do you understand what it means for one of our people to commit this violation?

I don't know.

They are angry. And somehow I am to blame. Their emotions rush into the tunnel, fear tingeing it all in deep purple hues. Suddenly the tunnel snaps shut and the Arterian is silenced. At least for me. Around the room, the looks of concentration paired with a haziness of the eyes that I have come to associate with Arterian conversations continue. I have been shut out. A lump forms in my throat. Then Rasimbukar speaks.

"This portion of this discussion will be held in your language," she says, her eyes on me. "You are overwhelmed. It is agreed that truth will be more easily discerned if you are able to fully comprehend what is being asked of you."

"It is not customary for a discussion in this chamber to be held in any language but ours," Hamankush says, raising her eyes.

"It is not customary for one of our people to take a life of Faloiv," Rasimbukar says. She adds something in Anooiire, her facial spots gathering near the center of her forehead. Hamankush bows her head even more deeply.

"It wasn't her fault," I say, my body flushing with heat at the memory of the igua's fangs. "The igua . . . it wasn't normal. It wasn't an igua anymore."

"The Faloii have a deep awareness of the life on this planet," someone says from the back of the room. "There is no parasite capable of changing the nature of a creature. We inherit the knowledge of this planet's creatures. Hamankush committed a violation."

"But she didn't have a choice," I reiterate. "It's not like she wanted to!"

I look at Hamankush, waiting for her to raise her head and tell them what happened. But her eyes remained fastened on the packed reddish dirt of the floor.

"She made a choice," another voice says.

"She had to do it," I cry. "It would have killed us all!"

"The igua do not kill," a Faloii woman says, her facial spots communicating a deep frown.

I cover my face with my hands. Too many emotions are flying inside me, a whirlwind catching all the fragments that I'm feeling and throwing them skyward. Hamankush did what she had to do, I know this. I also know that what she had to do is a direct result of what the whitecoats are doing in N'Terra. Why has Hamankush not told them what I communicated to her—the vasana? Is this a ritual of this qalm, where she is not allowed to defend herself? Or is there another, hidden reason that I can't see? I remember Rasimbukar keeping the knowledge of her father's abduction secret, knowing that the truth could start a war between her people and mine. If I tell the truth now, what could it mean?

"What are you going to do to her?" I say quietly. "To Hamankush?"

"Such a violation would mean banishment," Rasimbukar says without hesitation. "Revocation of the Arterian tongue. She would be extracted from the veins of Faloiv."

Beside me, Hamankush's body gives the smallest quake. Even with the tunnel shut, the grief seems to drift from her skin to my heart. My own chest clenches. Rasimbukar knows the truth about N'Terra. Adombukar knows. If they have knowingly kept it a secret, is it one that I can tell? What will they say?

I turn and glance over my shoulder to find the eyes of my grandmother waiting there at the back of the chamber. Round and brown. My mother's eyes. My mother's face.

"It wasn't Hamankush's fault," I say. Like her, I fasten my eyes on the soil. It offers no comfort, but I try to lose myself in it. "The igua was . . . changed. It was made into a weapon. By N'Terra. By my people."

CHAPTER 6

In another world, the silence might have been true silence. There's not a sound, not a breath. The qalm itself is soundless, as if it is repressing its heartbeat in the gravity of this moment. But around me, the patterns of facial spots ripple, constantly changing, like a storm has been contained in this small chamber and will burst forth at any moment.

"Child," a Faloii woman says, standing. Her voice does not betray any emotion but her spots are jagged, rigid across her brow. "You are telling us the star people have harmed the animals of this planet?"

"Yes," I say, my voice so small I can barely hear it.

"How is this possible? Why have the animals not told us?"

"They are cut off from the Artery," I whisper. "Their brains . . . they . . . we . . . some of the star people . . . they're changing them. They're altering them. The animals aren't . . . themselves anymore. They're gone."

Another period of silence. In the conversation they have sealed me out of, I imagine flashes of red traveling at light speed. I don't dare look at my grandmother.

Someone nearby speaks a few words in Anooiire. Though I can't understand them, something about the words feels like a blade, as if they were directed straight at my heart. Rasimbukar's eyes are on me.

"What did they say?" I ask.

"They said, 'The star people have brought a new death to Faloiv. Just as we predicted.'"

"A new death," I whisper, squeezing my eyes shut.

"We have much to discuss," Rasimbukar says.

I brace myself for more questions, but instead the room explodes into Anooiire. After the prolonged silence it makes me jump, and I think even Hamankush does too. Her eyes are still fixated on the soil. Her future depends on what is being said. I wish I could speak to her. Touch her. I can't decipher the flurry of words being spoken around me, but her terror is a language I understand. The storm of conversation goes on for some time, until Rasimbukar says a few words that send quiet rippling out through the chamber. She looks at me and I quail under her eyes.

"Hamankush took the life of an igua," she says. "And your truth is that this igua would have meant her harm?"

Rasimbukar knows this already.

"Her. All of us. Did you not see the teeth? How do you think Revollettican got . . . hurt?"

Hurt. I don't want to ask if the youth is dead.

"We noticed nothing unusual about the corpse of the igua," a Faloii man says from near Rasimbukar.

I hadn't seen the body after Hamankush had killed her. The scene had erupted into chaos, Hamankush trying to staunch the blood of Revollettican, the other Faloii youth scrambling, Jaquot and the other humans all but hyperventilating. Then Rasimbukar and the others had appeared and swept us all away.

"The teeth can be hidden," I say. "I don't understand how it works. Maybe when the igua died the teeth retracted."

"You did not see these teeth when you approached the igua, Hamankush?" Rasimbukar says.

I hear the smallest intake of breath, Hamankush raising her eyes to speak.

"I did not."

"But you saw them when the igua attacked, as this child says?"

"I did."

Another flurry of Anooiire ripples through the room, which Rasimbukar silences in Arterian.

"Hamankush, leave the qalm. We are finished with you for now."

Hamankush rises immediately and passes through the

parting vines. I'm alone on the platform—the many Faloii eyes upon me feel almost too intense to bear.

My grandmother appears at my side and it's all I can do to keep from reaching for her like an infant. Instead I bite my lip and hope my eyes tell her how grateful I am that she is now sitting there on the platform beside me. I half expect one of the Faloii to object, but Rasimbukar merely nods.

"Your truth is that Hamankush is not responsible for the death of the igua," she says.

Rasimbukar knows she's not. She knows we are.

"Yes," I manage to get out.

"Your truth is that the igua died another kind of death. Before coming to the trees."

"Yes."

"And your truth is that the responsibility for that death lies with your people."

The "yes" catches in my throat. It gags me. All the fears that drove me to get Adombukar out of the labs, to avoid the light of truth shining on what N'Terra had done . . . why did I think this could be avoided?

"Yes," I finally say.

I can't tell if the silence in the room is true silence or if within a private tunnel my fate is being decided in the colorful, wordless language of Arterian. Or maybe I only think it's silent. The world around me seems to have faded as my mind creates different outcomes for this scenario without my bidding. I imagine N'Terra crumbling, my people cast back out into the stars. Or maybe just buried in the soil of Faloiv.

"We have reached an agreement," Rasimbukar says. Beside me, my grandmother doesn't move a muscle. I wish I could tell if her heart is beating as hard as mine, or if her cool demeanor is the extension of some inner certainty. I squeeze my hands into fists, my nails digging into my palms, waiting for Rasimbukar to speak to me again, to tell me what's happening.

But she doesn't. She speaks in Anooiire, and the words sound slower this time. As if she is enunciating carefully, delivering something solemn to the ears of the listening Faloii. Then she looks at me, and I think her facial spots look like the leaves of an ogwe after heavy rain, low and heavy, bearing the gray storm.

"You are finished here," she says. Then turns her eyes away.

CHAPTER 7

My grandfather is waiting in my nana's qalm when we return. No Faloii had accompanied us, no one steering me back to my room as a prisoner. We had left the single-chambered qalm and walked in silence through Mbekenkanush. Even if we had wanted to speak, it was as if the city forbade it. The trees were still, the hush that I felt creeping on me like insects since Hamankush killed the igua ever present.

When the vines weave back together at our backs, my nana goes to my grandfather, who sits motionless in the leaflike chair as before.

"They have decided?" he says. It's the first time I've heard his voice. Deep, rumbling.

"They have decided . . . something," Nana says. "I don't know what."

"Isn't it obvious?" I blurt. All my fears have nipped at my heels as we passed through the city. Now, in this dim room, they burst from the corners with teeth bared. "They're going to make us leave Faloiv. All of us."

"That may be," my nana says, sinking onto her bed.

I recoil from her words as if burned. "How can you sound so calm?" I demand. "Where would we go? And how? The *Vagantur* is dead. Your home planet is dead."

"These are not questions the Faloii will be concerned with if their decision is to expel us."

"Us," I snap. "It's not *us*! It's them! Dr. Albatur and those other idiots!"

"We are responsible for them," she says. "Your mother and I worked very hard to change the path N'Terra was walking upon. Your grandfather too, in his way. But it wasn't enough."

My grandfather nods silently.

"There has to be something we can do," I plead, as if my grandmother is the one I must convince.

"What is done is done," she says. "Events have been set into motion. What Albatur and the others have done has violated the nature of Faloiv. There is a very delicate balance here. The planet has already begun to change."

"I feel it," I say.

"You feel it?" she says, raising an eyebrow. She exchanges a look with my grandfather.

"Yes." I sigh. "When the igua died . . . I felt something.

Something in the ground. Something in Faloiv. I can't explain it. Like the whole planet froze."

"If you can feel it, then the Faloii certainly can," my grandmother says, standing from her bed. She moves toward my grandfather and perches on his knee. "You hypothesize about expulsion. War may in fact be the outcome."

"War," I breathe, squeezing my eyes shut. "Rasimbukar always said she wanted to avoid war."

"Whatever decision the Faloii make will be in the best interest of the planet. This is not our home. We will do what they ask."

"But it is my home," I cry. "It's *my* home!"

My grandparents stare at me, sad and still.

"There has to be something we can do," I say again.

"What was needed should have happened a long time ago," she says, the irritation leaking into the river of her voice. I don't know if it's for me or for N'Terra. "You are young, and this all feels new, but Albatur and the Council were warned. Your father was warned."

She pauses, her eyes shooting to my face, assessing for damage her words might have caused. I get the feeling that my father is a wound in her life as well as my own. I glance at my grandfather and his face has hardened, his eyes fastened on the floor.

"I don't like it either, baby," my grandmother says, her N'Terran accent peeking through again. She bites her lip. I'd forgotten she does this. She does it when she's worried and doesn't want you to know. Would the Faloii spare her? Or would they turn against all humans, even those who have lived among them for so many years? The idea of my grandmother, who only just joined me again in the world of the living . . .

I shake off the thought before it can fully form, and turn to leave the qalm.

"Octavia," she says, her voice grabbing me as the vines begin to part. "We have to do what we have to do."

"There has to be something that can be done besides just . . . *waiting*," I say forcefully. "Otherwise it's a countdown to the inevitable."

When she doesn't reply, I leave.

I wander aimlessly through Mbekenkanush, winding my way around the trees and the qalms, the silence crushing me. I wonder how long I would have to live here to become used to the animals that roam freely. They hunt one another. They feed their young. They cross the path and the sky. I go back to the day I had seen the philax in the main dome of the Beak: how the transparent ceiling far above had seemed like plenty of room for the birds to wing and cry. I see now how wrong I was: how some of them climb so high in the sky they become specks against the blue before plummeting toward the ground, pulling up before they reach the dirt. They relish their freedom. Mbekenkanush pulses with their liberty. The memory of N'Terra's walls fills me with guilt: its boundaries had seemed suffocating to me, but I had never questioned whether keeping the animals of Faloiv in the labs was just. Here, feeling how deeply the planet breathes when free, I know how cruel our prison was.

I walk for what feels like hours, and I keep expecting someone to stop me, to drag me off and interrogate me further about the happenings inside N'Terra. But they don't need to. Adombukar knows plenty, and so does his daughter. Were they just waiting for confirmation? For something to happen? Was this all a test, seeing if I would tell the truth about my people when the time came, testing where my loyalties lie, seeing if we really are all the same?

"We're not," I whisper.

"Talking to yourself?" says a voice, and I gasp, turning to find Joi standing by the qalm I had just passed by. I realize now it's the school, that my feet have been carrying me along the city's well-worn paths, my mind on another trail. The school appears to be deserted now except for her.

"What are you doing?" I snap, embarrassed. "Where is everyone else?"

"I came to return a book," she says. "I have been told we are all supposed to be reporting to our own qalms right now. What are *you* doing?"

"Just . . . walking," I say. "Clearing my mind."

She moves off toward the pink lake, which will lead us back toward the part of Mbekenkanush where my qalm is. She pauses and gives me a pointed look, as if she doesn't quite trust me to be unsupervised, and I'm too weary to be annoyed so I follow.

"I heard about the hearing," she says. "But everyone is being secretive. Do you know if Hamankush will be . . . exiled?"

"I don't think so." I sigh. "They're trying to figure out what to do with us."

"You mean the N'Terrans?" she says.

Beside us, the pink lake is motionless within its gentle black banks. Had there been ripples before? A sign of the planet's breath? If there had, the pink water, powdery looking with its dense minerals, is motionless now, its surface eerily placid.

"I guess so," I reply. How can I tell her that what the N'Terrans have done might affect her as well? "My grandmother says there might be war."

"There was not war last time," she says. "But perhaps this is one leaf too many on the pile."

"You know about that?" I say, referring to the memory Hamankush had shown me. "You weren't even born yet."

She shoots me a sideways look. "What do you speak of? The last time your people"—she pauses, deciding whether to be kind—"I was certainly born. The last time the N'Terrans sent a weapon to Mbekenkanush, its target was Dr. Lemieux. I don't know if that was the goal this time as well, but in any case perhaps our hosts grow tired of human skirmishes."

I stop walking, and when Joi continues I reach out and

grab her bicep, dragging her backward more forcefully than I intended.

"Excuse me? Dr. Lemieux?" I snap. "You mean my grandmother?"

She wrenches her arm from my grasp, with the assistance of her suit. It's a strange feeling under my bare fingers, the material growing slippery to loosen my grip.

"No," she says. "Your grandfather. The last time this happened, the thing they sent was not an animal. I do not have much memory of it. I was very young."

I think of the thing that had come from the sky that I had seen in the memory, the thing my grandfather called a drone.

"Why him?" I wonder out loud.

"As I said, I was very young. But my mother says N'Terrans only ever think about one thing, so whatever that one thing is, it must be that. But in that way, your grandfather is very N'Terran."

"What do you mean?" I say.

"His one thing is the black lake," she says. "For the N'Terrans it's something else, but good science isn't single-minded."

I shoot her an ugly look, lacking the energy to debate what good science is. But she's right about N'Terran whitecoats: all their discoveries, all their studies, and it's all done while looking backward at the Origin Planet.

"The N'Terrans sent an envoy to Mbekenkanush a few months back," she said. "Did you know?"

"What? Why would they do that?"

"They wanted to search the city. We said no, of course."

"Search it for what?"

"I do not know," she says. "You did not know they came? I am surprised your grandmother did not tell you. Though she has a lot on her mind. Grief is a heavy thing."

The disdain on her features softens into regret then, and it's as if my mother has risen from the ground and floats between us before settling onto my shoulders, the weight of which Joi can't imagine.

"What was it like?" she says. "Growing up there? With them?"

"With who? The N'Terrans?"

"Yes," she says.

"It was . . . I don't know. Normal. I don't have anything to compare it to."

"You do now," she prods as we round the last edge of the pink lake.

"Barely," I say, glancing at her sideways. "I just got here."

"True. I think I am trying to understand if you are more aware of your people than Jaquot is."

"They're your people too," I say.

"Yes and no."

"What are you asking me, Joi?"

"Where do you want to be?" she says abruptly, turning away from the city and settling her eyes on mine. "You have come here, away from your place of birth. But you do not seem to think this is a place for you. Why is that?"

Anger and grief converge in my throat, ready to become a stream of sharp words. But the rush of them settles almost as quickly as it rises, Joi's frankness like a splash of water over a young flame. She doesn't understand. How could she?

"It's complicated," I tell her. "I just got here. I lost my mother. My father is back there."

"So you are not like Jaquot in that way," she says, looking curious. "You are close with your family. Or at least your mother?"

"I mean, yes," I reply, confused. "We didn't see each other much. They were in the labs. Studying. A lot."

Something about the way she nods in response to this makes me feel that while I'm having a conversation, Joi is taking notes.

"What?" I say sharply.

"Like the Origin Planet," she says. "In that way. This is why humans have so little knowledge of who we were before we came here. Forcing people to work rather than create."

"No one forced my mother."

"Maybe not," she says. "Not exactly."

A tongue of wind makes the nearby trees tremble and I glance over, my heart jumping unconsciously, afraid of what else might emerge from the leaves. When I look back at Joi, her expression is an annoying mix of amusement and condescension.

"You are afraid," she says. "Like Jaquot."

"I didn't grow up in the trees," I snap. "Not like you. It's still weird to me."

"How can where you live . . . be weird?" she says, almost laughing. "How can you be afraid of the place where you are?"

"Because where I was is different from where I am," I say. "I don't know what you think N'Terra is like, but whatever you think, it's different. We weren't meant to stay here. We weren't prepared."

"My grandparents wanted to be prepared," she says, shrugging. "That's why we came here."

She gestures at the qalms around us now that we've edged closer to the center of the city. Far down what becomes a wide path there are several Faloii on their way to various places, the trees far over their heads like guardians, the vines looping from trunk to trunk. Joi's gesture seems to encompass all this, and something larger too: a history connecting the humans that live here and the ones I left behind, the line that connects them smudging somewhere in the middle. I'm about to ask her what her grandparents hoped to find on this planet, if their journey's ending here was a thing they were satisfied with, but she's turning away, leaving me.

"Where are you going?" I call.

"To my qalm," she says. "I suggest you do the same."

The qalm admits me readily, everything in my chamber exactly as I left it: my rumpled white N'Terran skinsuit discarded on the floor from this morning. I pick it up, squeezing its familiar fabric in both hands, remembering my last day in the Mammalian Compound, everything that had transpired. I thought discovering the truth about the Albaturean process and the plans for the Solossius would unravel the truth, all of it, but those bits of yarn had only led me to more knots. Two attacks on Mbekenkanush: once before I was born, and once with my grandfather as a target? How long had N'Terrans been chipping away at the Faloii's fragile trust—who is the enemy of who, and where does that leave me?

I cast the skinsuit aside angrily and turn back toward the qalm wall. Joi said the instructions were to return to my chamber, but this new information drives me to disobey. I need to go back to my nana and this time demand answers.

I press my fingertips lightly against the wall and wait for the creepy stirring feeling that tells me the vines recognize what I want. But nothing happens.

I ignore the sinking feeling in my gut and try another spot on the wall, fanning my fingers out wide this time.

Nothing.

"Stars," I whisper.

I rub my fingers together and try one more time, pressing each fingertip firmly against the cool greenish material.

Nothing. It's exactly as I had feared. I am a prisoner. Rasimbukar and the Faloii have made their decision. I am not to be trusted, and even the qalm knows it. I back away from the wall and sink down to the ground. I can sense the never-ending stream of communication from the qalm, fast and fluid and green, but it ignores me. The words aren't for me. Nothing is.

CHAPTER 8

In the dream, my mother is alive. I'm in my room back in N'Terra, swallowed by the darkness of our 'wam, when my door folds open. She enters the room carrying a light in her palm, a glow that illuminates the smile on the lips that look like mine.

She speaks, and her lips move, but they don't match the words. I hear them in my head as if in Arterian but different somehow.

We used to sing, she says in her dream language. *I don't remember the words, but we used to sing.*

"I've never heard you sing," I tell her.

I don't remember the words.

Whatever glowing thing she carries, she places on the desk in my N'Terran bedroom. She's not wearing a white coat but a tunic made of yellow material. It reminds me of the yellow cloth that used to hang on our 'wam's door in the commune. My grandmother's cloth. Carried from far across the universe, my mother wears it in whatever universe is now her home.

We didn't have much to bring, she says. *Scraps. But songs don't have any weight. We carried what we could.*

"Sing me one," I plead. She's fading. I need her to stay. "Sing me one of the songs."

I don't remember the words.

It's not a sound that wakes me, or light. It's still deeply night—I can feel that in the still thickness of the air and see it from the moonlight that fades in softly through the ceiling of my qalm. But when my eyes flutter open, it's as if someone shook me awake, a fingerless hand reaching out from nothing and plucking a string in my mind. The reverberation still travels through me as I raise my head from the floor.

I don't remember lying down. I'd fallen asleep right here on the ground by the wall, my hip pressed slightly against it. Though the miraculous pulse of the organic wall is ever present, I must have gone on half conscious of it in my sleep, because the flowing rhythm is barely noticeable now, steady and constantly changing, a stream of unintelligible thought and knowledge, forever a mystery to the simple wood of my brain.

Until it's not.

I bolt upright, the sudden change almost incomprehensible

at first. But there it is: a shape of something emerging from the impossibly complicated stream of its consciousness. I can't make it out: it's like the music of Rondo's izinusa but sped up by a machine more powerful than anything I can fathom. And yet . . . one or two notes reach me where they hadn't before, finding me in the Artery and resonating there like spinning planets.

"What is it?" I whisper in the dark. My mind streaks back to the moment in my mother's office, so far away in my 'wam, when she'd spoken to me in Arterian for the first time. A jolt of longing rips through me: this language of the qalm feels as unreachable as my mother.

The qalm is changing. The room is so dim I barely notice at first, but between shadows I can make out the solid green and brown and dark. A smell of soil and sky reaches my nostrils, as a shape grows from the wall, twisting and stretching like a tentacle, forming itself, reaching for me. . . .

Not a tentacle. A hand. A hand almost like mine and almost like the Faloii's but not quite like either. One moment it has too few digits, one moment too many, but it's trying very hard to maintain the shape, bits of soil sprinkling from it every second or two. It beckons to me, and in my head the notes of the qalm's strange complex music are still surging, but with the hand before me, I think the one or two notes that find my inner ear mean a certain thing. I reach out for the hand and it recoils, shrinking and disappearing as I continue to extend. By the time it has gone, swallowed back up by the qalm, my palm is against the smooth dark wall and the vines are parting with their usual rapid snakiness.

The qalm is allowing me to leave.

I understand this with a certainty as solid as the ground beneath my feet. In the language I only comprehend but a breath of, this building—the very stuff of Faloiv—is making way for me to depart. Beyond my parted vine door, the corridor is dark and silent. I could be the only person on this planet, just me and the world itself.

I almost leave right then. But I pause, turning back to the small space that the qalm had arranged just for me, my scent like a wafting fingerprint I leave behind. In the pale moonlight, my eye falls upon my old skinsuit, discarded at the foot of my sleeping platform. It looks limp, lifeless, a shell of a former life that seems more and more ancient with every second. I turn away and pass through the vines.

The moon lights my way to the jungle's edge. The silence is almost suffocating. My mind wanders back to the night out in the main dome with Rondo; the night I saw my father tranquilize Adombukar. The same moon. The same ground beneath my feet. But in N'Terra, the hum of the compound's energy stores and the distant voices of whitecoats, the sound of Rondo's breath in the shadows beside me . . . I didn't feel alone. Here, I am the only one who knows where I am. What I plan to do. What *do* I plan to do? I tilt my head back and look up at the stars, like the eyes of the Faloii but infinitely more vast. I try to envision a path through those stars, a black map that my veins can follow like a familiar scent. But nothing up there looks like home. My ancestors had looked to the stars and seen a future . . . all I see is the end. Ahead, the stalks of a plant whose name I don't know but whose red petals are like the faces of kin sway stiffly in a night breeze.

Behind me, the shapes of Mbekenkanush rising against the sky remind me of Dr. Albatur's towers inside N'Terra. The feeling of my room inside the qalm being aware of me and watching me returns, and I shudder with the thought that the city itself watches me go, and I can't quite shake the idea that Mbekenkanush will keep me from leaving. I move slowly and softly, thinking of what Joi had said earlier and cringing away from my own fear: *How can you be afraid of the place where you are?*

When the hand grabs me in the dark, I have every intention of screaming. But it catches at my mouth before any sound escapes.

"Shh," comes a soft voice through the dark. "Afua, quiet."

"Nana," I whisper as her hand comes away. "I was just . . ."

"I already know what you were doing," she says. "I would expect nothing less of my daughter's child."

"I have to do something," I whisper, giving voice to my intentions for the first time. "We can't just . . ."

"If you're going to do something, you must hurry," she says, her face shifting in and out of sight as clouds pass over the moon. "The Faloii have made a decision. We don't have much time."

"What decision," I whisper. "About us? About humans?"

"They are going to the Isii," she says, speaking quickly. "It is the brain of Faloiv. It was where Adombukar was headed when N'Terra abducted him. The Faloii are going to deploy a small group of their people there, where the greater decision may be made."

The urgency in her voice is like a prod of electricity delivered straight to my neurons.

"What does that mean? What does the Isii do?"

"Many things," she says. "Listen."

My mind is widening before I'm even consciously asking it to, and my grandmother sweeps into my head. I sense that she has never seen the Isii herself—and perhaps would not be permitted to—but that it carries great power. The impressions rush over me: the essence of Faloiv swirling inside what feels like the core of the planet. My grandmother said this is where the greater decision will be made, but *decision* is a pale word: our human expressions lack the ability to illustrate what really happens at the Isii, so she tries her best to show me. At the Isii, planets are made. Species are born . . . and eradicated.

"Stars," I whisper.

"Yes," she says. "The Faloii have decided that N'Terrans have gone too far."

Somewhere behind us in Mbekenkanush, something stirs. We both feel it: a pulse in the Artery. Someone is awake and is aware of our presence. My grandmother turns back to me in a hurry, snapping her mind shut. I follow suit, feeling suddenly guilty and panicky.

"You know where my heart lies," she whispers. "I have no love for N'Terra. But the Faloii Elders would not take kindly to me sending you off to interrupt their plans. That is why you must be quick. It will take a few days for the Faloii to choose their group and to prepare for the trip—there are rituals involved. By then maybe you can have changed this course. It is not dangerous for us yet, but depending on what the Isii feels from the human presence, that could change very quickly. That's why if there will be action, it must be from you."

"Me?" I say as loudly as I dare.

"Flowers don't just grow at other humans' feet," she says, her face lost in shadow.

"So?"

My mind is closed, so it is with my physical senses that I hear the approach of Faloii.

"You need to go now," she says. "Find the one who keeps the eyenu. Her memory is deeper than ours could ever be, and the past will answer for the present."

"The who?"

"Quickly! There is a mineral I have found. When it encounters water, it erupts with crimson smoke. If the Faloii decide there will be war with the humans, I will release the smoke. If you look to the sky and see it, you will know what is to come. Now go!"

She's pushing me, trying to bury me in the darkness. She moves quickly, hoping to head off whoever comes our way. I step into the jungle.

It's as if a curtain has been pulled back, the silence of Mbekenkanush's clearing disintegrating like sand meeting water. The chorus of night surrounds me. The sound of trees swaying against each other, blurred like many deep breaths. The close and faraway calls of animals N'Terra doesn't yet know exist, animals with skins made of shadows and stars. I open the tunnel reluctantly, afraid of what it might show me. I think of the myn in the stream of the Mammalian Compound, how Alma had said that being able to hear in the tunnel was an advantage as well as a handicap: I can hear the animals, but they can hear me too. I wonder if they hear how angry I am at my grandmother.

Even as I am surrounded by life—in the jungle and the Artery—all I can feel is my anger. This feels too familiar: everyone around me knowing something I don't, while I blunder through the mess trying to solve the puzzle. A stream of moonlight breaks through the foliage, illuminating what appears to be a reptile with deep blue skin. It hovers with the assistance of a double set of wings, using its long prehensile tongue to grip the buds of glowing white flowers. The flowers are opening one at a time, as nocturnal as the animals around them. The reptile picks them off one by one, the wings thrumming like a chorus of insects. I wish I could ask them what the eyenu are. A plant? An animal? An object of the Faloii? The mystery of it only feeds my anger.

I am going to N'Terra. Damn the secrets. Damn the eyenu, whatever they are. Instead of adding more pieces to the puzzle, I will go back to where this puzzle began.

I step slowly and carefully over branches, sometimes climbing over trees that fell long before I was born. The suit I wear, grown by the qalm, doesn't tear or snag. When I slide on my stomach over the rough surface of a massive trunk, the suit seems to grow smooth, helping me along. I catch glimpses of the moon as I move north—but the glimpses are farther apart, the moments in shadow longer and deeper. There is the occasional iridescent flower, but the soft glow is enough to show me my hands, and never the nonexistent path. I tell myself my feet will know it when they find it. That some unknown force will draw me to N'Terra. *That is not science*, a voice like Alma whispers from the back of my mind.

And neither is my decision to go back home, I think. But the similarities between my mother's approach and my grandmother's are too glaring to ignore: mystery. Puzzles. Secrecy. Secrecy got my mother killed, I think, and swipe a tear from my face.

I'm just starting to get angry about the irrationality of crying when a sound stops me cold. It's different from the gentle rhythms of the trees, the ubiquitous movements of a hundred unseen animals. It is purposeful. Every step has a goal. A crackle of twigs, the hush of leaves pushed aside with urgency. I stand rooted to the spot, one hand clutching a branch in the dark. The sounds are louder, come closer, the steps quick and heavy.

It can't be a dirixi. I would have felt the quake of its arrival. Am I bleeding? Had the smallest thorn pricked my skin through the suit, the smell of blood drawing the beast from its faraway cave? A small one, perhaps. A young one, sent out to hunt for the first time. No one would ever find my body, consumed by its fledgling jaws.

I force myself to widen the tunnel. Too late to arm myself: the branch I clutch is attached to a tree, and it's too thick to break off. In the dark I can't even discern a climbable perch. I inhale hurriedly, wondering if a field of rhohedron will rescue me this time, but my nostrils are empty, and the sound of the creature rushing toward me is closer than ever. When the tunnel spirals fully open, its consciousness is almost upon me.

I recognize the presence just as the dense plants part to reveal the creature. A surge of energy, purple with worry. The gwabi bursts from the greenery and closes the space between the bushes and me with a single leap.

"Oh," I whisper.

She butts me with her massive head, intending to be gentle

but sending me stumbling backward with her strength. She growls low in her throat, but I know from the signals she passes me in the Artery that she means me no harm.

"I'm okay," I say. I run a hand along her back, still in awe of the rock-hard muscles her sable fur conceals, the sticky electric buzz it seems to leave on my fingertips.

She regards me with luminous eyes, sizing me up, searching for wounds. I assure her in the tunnel that I am unharmed, but she continues to express her worry. I don't know how she found me. She makes it clear that I shouldn't be alone. Not out here.

"I have to go back," I say to her, the best way I can in Arterian. Arterian is never words, but it's different with animals than with the Faloii. She gazes at me, understanding—I think—where I'm going but worried about why. She knows what is in N'Terra. She had been a prisoner there.

"I have to do something," I whisper, passing her colors and shapes: my fear for my people and the Faloii, my dread for what will happen to the planet if N'Terra's actions bring war. She gazes at me impassively, her eyes like two glowing orbs. She is angry, her disgust for N'Terra smoldering inside her. She doesn't wonder what it is I plan to do—she merely assesses me in that motherly way, and I feel from her the same sentiment my mother would have provided. Something that strengthens my resolve.

My hand is still on her back, and she turns away, guiding me around the reaching tentacles of a skinny tree that may not be a tree at all. She warns me to stay close—I'm her blind furless cub in a jungle of thorns. I walk along beside her, comforted by the rumble in her throat. Together we walk south.

The night has thinned in the hours before dawn. Sunrise is a miracle that I have never experienced within the isolated security of the Mammalian Compound: the way the sun, still hidden below the horizon, manages to dilute night's opacity. The jungle is no longer one jagged shadow after another: I can differentiate between ogwe and marandin trunks.

And I smell water. I have no idea how many miles I have traveled in the secure company of the gwabi, but even with the help of the qalm suit, my body is telling me hydration is necessary. When I communicate this to the gwabi, she is reluctant to deviate from the invisible path she follows, but her concern for my well-being outweighs her desire to press on. She leads me to the right, cutting through the walls of green that surround us on all sides. She moves quickly and I trot to keep up, vines whipping across my cheeks. I use my arms to shield my face as we continue on, but a few moments later I am able to lower them as we break through into what seems to be a clearing. True dawn is still an hour or so away, but its approach shows me that I was correct about the scent of water. There is a lake, shadowy in what's left of the moonlight, but smelling perfectly drinkable.

Still, I wait until the gwabi lowers her head to drink before I dare scoop up a palmful of it. My father would have a seizure if he could see me these past few days: rubbing the fluids of strange flowers on my skin, attempting to drink water that hasn't been properly tested. But if it's good enough for the gwabi, it's good enough for me. I'm just bending my neck to sip from my hands when the sound of the water stirring far out in the lake causes me to jerk my eyes up.

It's still too dark to see well, and the forgotten water flows down my wrists as I scan the surface desperately, seeking the source of the sound. I back away from the water's edge and find the gwabi doing the same thing, a nervous growl rumbling in her throat. I squint, the clouds over the moon playing tricks on my sight: Is that a shadowy figure there in the center of the lake? Something sinking down under the water? A massive something, slipping below the surface just as my eyes fasten on the bulk of it.

I don't know if it's me or the gwabi that screeches when the figure appears on the bank, not far from where we stand. We both leap back, the gwabi bristling, ready to lunge. The figure grows larger, standing from where it had been crouched at the water's edge. I can't move, too terrified to open the Artery and ascertain whether the creature is harmless or means to attack. The gwabi hasn't moved, so surely this means the shadowy figure before me is an herbivore? She would know if it was a predator. Any logic that is solid and strong inside me crumbles into powder as the figure moves toward me.

And then the clouds shift. The moonlight is my friend.

The shadow is my grandfather.

"You," I gasp, my lungs finally deciding to work again. I have a name for him—Jamyle Lemieux—but not a name of the heart, like *Nana*. This man whose face I know is part of my blood but is a stranger to me.

"Octavia," he says. The first time hearing my name from his mouth and it's accompanied by a frown. "What are you doing here? Does your nana know you're here?"

"Y-yes," I stammer. "She's the one who told me I should go."

"Go where?" he says. "In the middle of the night?"

I hesitate.

"To N'Terra," I lie. "The Faloii are going to the . . . the Isii? They might turn the planet against the humans. If I can get back to N'Terra and make everyone see the truth, then maybe we can stop this."

"Back to N'Terra." He frowns. "I would have thought your nana wanted you far from that place. I don't think logic and reason are tools that work on those people."

"Logic and reason are what I was raised on," I say, and when I hear it out loud, I feel stronger. The idea of going back and facing Albatur and his lies takes the shiver out of my skin. My grandfather says nothing.

"Someone said that N'Terra sent a weapon for you," I say before he can challenge me. "Why? Why you?"

His eyes had been wandering out over the black water, but now he peers at me through the dark.

"Not just me," he said. "Your grandmother too. Albatur blames us for the delay of his life's work. And he's right. About this I have no regrets."

The words *life's work* catch my ear and now I'm gazing out over the lake as well.

"Why do you come here?" I say. "Why is this what you study?"

"Study," he repeats with a smile. "I don't study the black lake. I protect it."

"Protect it? Protect it from what?"

"From who," he says. "I protect it from myself: N'Terra. There is nothing on this planet that our people would not seek to exploit. Your grandmother now protects Mbekenkanush; I protect the black lake. Like everything else on this planet, it carries something."

I cast my eyes back out to the black waters. "What does it carry?"

"Trees carry memory. Water carries words. Kawa carry everything."

I eye my grandfather in the pale light, his skin taking on a bluish tint beneath it. I wonder silently if he's not a little bit . . . off. He's older than my grandmother, and after everything he's been through, maybe something in his mind has loosened.

"I thought I saw something sinking out there," I say.

"Something huge. Is it a specimen? An animal, I mean?"

He turns away from the lake, his eyes on me again and the smile faded from his mouth. It's strange finding pieces of my mother in the creases of this man's face. Her worry is a gene, passed on from this jaw.

"This entire planet is an animal," he says. "Which is why we must be very cautious about what happens next."

"You mean with what the Faloii are planning?"

"Yes and no. The Faloii may pass along the fact that humans have become parasitic and Faloiv remains hospitable. But the planet and its creatures will always have their own ideas. The very plants we eat could turn against us."

Beside me, the gwabi gives a low grumble in her throat. My grandfather isn't able to speak Arterian, but I wonder if she understands his meaning nonetheless. As I'd walked through the jungle with her, the shadows had lost their sinister quality, but now they seem ominous again as I imagine the trees growing fangs and swallowing us whole. My grandfather moves toward me, and he seems to see the fear growing in my eyes.

"Courage isn't the only thing that will help us survive," he says. "But it is one thing. Going back to N'Terra will take courage. Especially if you fail."

"I won't," I say, setting my jaw, against my fear and against his words. "People just need to know what's going on. Albatur is running the show and keeping everyone in the dark. If people knew . . . this wouldn't be happening."

He studies me for a long moment, his expression so like my mother's I almost wince. But when he speaks, it's his voice, not hers, and the loneliness in what lies ahead of me swoops down from the sky like a night bird.

"I hope you're right."

CHAPTER 9

It's well past dawn when I glimpse the red road through the trees. We've been walking all night and my limbs had begun to feel as if they've been replaced by pillars of stone, each countless step through the dense jungle more painful than the last. But when my eyes find the swirls of rosy dust rising in the wind, all the fatigue that had been building in my bones crumbles away. I find myself gripping the fur of the gwabi's shoulder, energy pulsing through me. She growls gently to make me relax, but instead I pull her to a stop.

"You have to stay here," I whisper, as if the ears of N'Terra reach this far. Maybe they do. "It's not safe for you."

She understands the shapes I pass her in the Artery, and her fear reflects back to me in a pulse of orange, the memory of the containment room still fresh. Still, she is worried for my well-being and butts me powerfully on the shoulder. I brace myself and cradle her massive head in my arms.

"I'll be okay," I say, squeezing my eyes shut. "Just stay far away. Don't let anyone see you."

I think of Manx and her group of finders, and the idea of them combing the jungle for the gwabi and any other escaped specimens sends a blaze of fury through me. I pass the gwabi a series of comforting messages and then step out onto the road.

I know immediately where I am. The branch arcing over the road curves the way it always has, marking the way to the Beak. I'm about halfway there from the Mammalian Compound. Somehow the branch looks too familiar. I've been gone less than a week, I tell myself. It shouldn't look any different. But even if every leaf is the same, I know the world has changed.

I point my feet east down the road, trying not to think about the times I had traveled this very route with my father in one of N'Terra's chariots. *Slow down, Octavia,* I hear him say in my head, the wind whipping past us carrying the colors and smells of Faloiv, things he was oblivious to. My previous fatigue returns to me, weighing down each step. The suit from the qalm keeps me miraculously cool, but suddenly sweat is pouring from my scalp and beading up on the bridge of my nose. My father. Will the news of war be exactly what he wants to hear? I make my way down the road, staying close to the tree line in case I need to dive in for cover. I've spent the last hours of walking with the gwabi mentally going over my plan, but even after all that, it's not much of one.

I'm going to the Greenhouse first. More than anything I want to reunite with Alma and Rondo, but strolling in through the gates of one of the compounds doesn't seem like an option. I need help, and with Dr. Espada gone, I think my best chance is with Dr. Yang. She taught me when I was a child, and had been kind to me the last time I'd seen her—the day my mother was arrested. I don't know whether she'll listen to me, but at least I'll have access to the greencoats. Maybe Yaya and the others are back in the Greenhouse after the disaster in the Zoo. Maybe I can convince them too. I don't know who else I can trust.

Every step on the road stirs up the powdery red dust, and I imagine this is what my blood must look like churning through my heart—so frenetic it disintegrates. By the time the school appears through the trees ahead, I'm panting, not from the heat but from my own anxiety. I swallow hard as I approach the front door, trying to remember the resolve I'd felt by the black lake and grip it like a weapon. I am here for a reason.

But as soon as I duck inside the Greenhouse I know that something is off. Dr. Yang's classroom is closest to the door, and for as long as I can remember, the first thing one hears when entering the school is the sound of the kids chanting whatever song she had made up that week to help them remember their species classification charts.

Today there is silence.

Not thick silence—the kind where people are present but wordless, hushed with study. This is empty silence that encases the ear in solitude—the kind that lets you know you're alone.

Dr. Yang's door is open, as always, but when I peek my head around the corner to peer in, everything has changed. The colorful charts that had once covered the walls as learning aids have been stripped away, the illustrations of animals that I know Dr. Yang had lovingly sketched with her own hand are gone. And so are the children.

"Octavia?"

I jump hard. Dr. Yang emerges from the back of the room, the green glow from the windows, which had once been so calming, now creepy and damp.

"Dr. Yang," I say. "Where is everyone? The kids?"

"They've been moved into the labs," she says. She seems to float across the classroom, her face drawn. "What are you doing here? You shouldn't be here. Not alone."

At first I think her worried expression is for my face: that the fear rising in her eyes is a reflection of what she thinks I have done, figments of whatever story the Council has woven about me. But as she gets closer, I find that her eyes look past me: they hover over my shoulder, eyeing the hall.

"The little kids are in the Zoo?" I say, entering the classroom. The green glow sweeps over my skin. "Why? For what?"

"Things are changing quickly," she says. "The Council has decided to rethink the path of N'Terran education. Theory is out, they say. Hands-on is in."

"They're only, like, eight years old," I say, incredulous. "They have them working in the labs?"

"Yes. A lot of it is watching and listening. Children do what they're told." She bites her lip. "Do you remember the drums?"

"The drums?"

"In the communes. When people would leave the labs, they would return to the communes and pick up drums?"

"Yes," I say, baffled. "Of course."

"Albatur has banned them. They are not what we should remember, he says. The Origin Planet he wants us to re-create has no music. Not that kind."

"What does that even mean?"

"You shouldn't have come back," she says, shaking her head. "You may have been safer in the jungle."

"It's not about what's safe," I say. "It's about what's true. I need to get into the compounds. I need to talk to people!"

"That's not a good idea," Dr. Yang says. She steps past me toward the door, motioning for me to follow. "Come with me quickly. It's better if we leave from the rear exit. I can escort you to the tree line but after that you must continue alone, I'm afraid."

"No," I say, remaining where I am. "I need to get inside before things get even worse."

"Worse?" Dr. Yang says. There is a shade of angry amusement somewhere in her voice: as if someone my age can't possibly imagine worse, but she can.

The sound of voices makes us both jerk our heads toward the doorway.

"Stars," she whispers. "You need to hide. Quickly, Octavia."

But I recognize these voices: this isn't the sound of a stern group of whitecoats. I hear banter and laughter. Greencoats. One voice rises above the others: "You're not fooling me, Yaya. I saw your eyes bug out. You don't have to admit it, but next time you ask me to dissect a morgantan for you I'll know why."

Yaya. And the voice: Julian. Other voices laugh, at least two. I move quickly away from Dr. Yang and step into the hall.

The group of greencoats stops abruptly at the sight of me.

"Yaya," I say, surprised by the relief in my own voice. "It's you!"

I don't know what I expected from her, but it wasn't a look of almost revulsion. She looks nauseated at the sight of me, as if my appearance were the equivalent of a troubling specimen of fungus showing up in her path.

"Octavia," she says eventually. "What—?"

Julian cuts her off. "What are you doing here?" he says. "They said you defected."

"Defected?" I say. It's a strange word to have chosen to describe my disappearance. "Do you even know what happened?"

"You helped one of them break in," a girl named Janelle says. She had sat near me in the Greenhouse, but now her eyes are cold and hard as if she's never seen me before. "You got multiple N'Terrans killed."

"We know exactly what happened," Julian says.

"Why are you here?" Yaya says before anyone else can continue.

"That's not what happened," I snap. "It's Albatur who's getting people killed. We have to stop him. *That's* why I'm here."

"Did your mother tell you that?" Janelle sneers.

"Octavia, don't!" Yaya shouts when I lunge forward, my fist raised. I've never hit anyone in my life, but I'm prepared to take off Janelle's head.

Yaya and I scuffle, me still swinging and her holding me back while trying to avoid my flying hands. Julian yells something. Dr. Yang is gone.

"Octavia, *don't*!" Yaya shouts again, but over her words I hear Janelle repeating something about my mother. I stop fighting Yaya, and I hang back, panting.

"I called them," Julian says.

"Who?"

"This is exactly what the Council said would happen," Janelle says, her face a combination of anger and ruffled fear. "They're drawing people into their lies and turning them against us."

"*They*," I say, my chest heaving. "Are you really this dense? It's Albatur and the Council that are lying! Stars, he killed my mother!"

My eyes are filling with tears even as I grit my teeth against them. The tremble in my chin feels like a betrayal, but I stare at the greencoats in front of me with as much steely cool as I can muster. Yaya's eyes waver, but Janelle and Julian return my steel.

"There are two sides here," Julian says, and I remember that his father is on the Council, that he's been advocating for N'Terran control over the Faloii for years now, echoing his parents' venom. "If you're not for N'Terran progress, then you're against it. Dr. English—your mom, not your dad—was against it."

I can't believe what I'm hearing. It's as if they have swallowed every lie that Albatur ever dreamed and now regurgitate them in a stream of blood and poison. I had come here with such resolve, but the look in Julian's eyes is impenetrable to reason. I think of all the people in N'Terra with this same look in their eyes. The day the graysuits had searched people's 'wams . . . some had resisted, but even more had gulped down the fear and let it roost in them, building nests.

Behind Julian, the door of the Greenhouse slams open, and against the sudden glare of sunlight from outside, two figures appear. They pause there in silhouette only for a moment, and then the two figures move swiftly toward us, fast becoming the bodies of two guards.

"She's here," Janelle calls unnecessarily. "We kept her here."

"Good," says one of the graysuits.

"I need to talk to Dr. Albatur," I say. "Or my father. He—"

One of them grabs me before I can continue, their grip around my bicep like metal shackles.

"Zap her," the voice says. It's then that I realize they have on the same masks I'd seen the night we broke Adombukar out of the Zoo: the strange armor that conceals their faces, leaving only a smooth featureless countenance, a reflective visor across the eyes.

"Why are you wearing those masks?" I demand, hoping my voice sounds stronger than the fear betraying me.

"Zap her," the voice says again, and my left arm is freed for the second it takes for the hand to reappear with a tranq gun. My mouth has just started to form the word *no* when my body convulses, a burst of yellow light exploding behind my eyes before it all goes dark.

The air isn't right. Before my eyes even open, my lungs, my skin, tell me that wherever I am is not . . . normal. The sky is gone. The smell of the jungle is gone. I am in a tomb. I feel empty and alone, as if drifting deep into outer space, where the world is so dark it's blindingly white. . . .

"The monitor reads that the subject is regaining consciousness," says a familiar voice. My brain is still swimming. I'm not quite awake, not quite alive.

Nearby, something beeps. A machine. It has no smell.

"Yes, I see. Fluids have been administered?"

"Yes, doctor. Though she didn't really need much."

My head swims toward one of these voices. I know it. In the white darkness, my mind tries to put things in order. How did I get to this place? The only part of my body I can feel is a piece of my arm, the vague pain there the only thing defining it as real.

"English," the voice I don't know says. "Can you hear my voice?"

I try, but I can't. I'm still rising from the bottom of a deep pool. The white darkness is beginning to fall away, and I struggle against it, trying to swim higher.

"The subject's heart rate is climbing," the voice I know says.

"Good. She's with us."

When I open my eyes, I'm blinded by the whiteness again, and I shrink back, thinking I left it behind. But the bleariness is clearing away with every blink. I feel as if I'm emerging from a cocoon. My skin feels exposed and thirsty, like whatever had protected it inside the cocoon has been stripped from me in this dry, scentless place. I can move my hands. The fingers of one brush the bare skin of my thigh.

"My suit," I can hear myself whisper. "Where is my suit?"

"We have confiscated your clothing for further analysis," says the familiar voice. I had thought it was familiar but it sounds different to me now: like the thing that had made it familiar has been clipped, shorn somehow.

"I need my suit," I whisper. My eyes are less blurred, and I find that I'm wearing a thin white garment. It ties around my neck. The back of me is bare against the stiff white cot I lie on.

"English," comes the other voice from farther across the room. "Quiet now. You'll want to save your energy for what is to come."

"What is to come?"

"Yes," says the familiar but clipped voice. Right next to me, fiddling with the painful spot on my arm. I use all my strength to turn my eyes toward that voice, force my vision to focus.

"Alma," I whisper.

Her round brown eyes hold mine for only a moment before they dart back down to the task at hand, injecting more fluids into my intravenous. Her mouth is pulled down ever so slightly in a practiced frown. When she looks back up, the eyes I've always known to sparkle with curiosity, with mirth, are expressionless.

"Alma," I say again, afraid she hadn't heard me, that my voice is not working.

The once-familiar eyes squint slightly.

"It's Intern Entra," she says.

CHAPTER 10

Whatever Alma injected me with makes me sleep again. But not the deep sleep of a tranquilization: a half sleep, where my body is aware of itself and my ears pick up nearby sounds, but my eyes are not controlled by my brain, and time has no definition. I have no idea how long I lie in this state of halfness. As the immeasurable time passes, I find the panic growing from tremor to earthquake inside me. Will I lie like this forever? Is this my punishment for betraying first one world and then the other? Eternal unsleep?

But then there is a spark in the darkness. A tiny thing at first, so faint it's like an indistinct spot you see after glancing at the sun. It persists there on the periphery of my consciousness like a distant star. My mind is numbed by whatever Alma introduced into my veins, but gradually the clouds that come and go clear, and the familiarity of the faint blaze grows stronger.

A child of Faloiv. They're too far for me to grasp who or what they are, but the realization that, even in this prison of pale darkness, the Artery still exists fills me with a new energy. It's not enough to give me the power to move, or even speak, but my mind sharpens, strengthens as it clings to consciousness. I struggle against the noxious invasion in my veins, trying to focus on the tiny burning star of consciousness in the Artery. But it's fading away, either because my mind is weak or because the actual presence has disappeared.

Just beyond the small universe of my mind comes a sound. A hum that I recognize from some part of myself that feels ancient. Then I hear the hum again . . . the closing of a door. I'm in the Zoo. Beyond my closed eyes that I have no control of, I remember the white walls I had seen so briefly before Alma had put me under again, into this half sleep. Now I know I haven't been moved. I am in the same bed, in the same white room, but I have no idea who I now share the room with. Terror creeps from every corner. I imagine Dr. Albatur slithering in, caped in his sinister red hood, clutching a cylinder of one final injection—the lethal one that will send me into a permanent sleep. My mind grows antennae, tentacles, as I try to reach out with every one of my senses to feel the danger before it comes any nearer. . . .

Something touches my hand. If I could jerk away, I would,

but I am trapped in the soft paralysis. I brace myself for the feeling of a needle pricking at one of the vulnerable veins on the back of my hand, but instead my skin experiences . . . a caress.

A thumb brushed across my flesh. Almost nonexistent pressure, as if the hand touching mine isn't there at all. Maybe it's not.

"I'm here, O," comes a deep voice, so soft it could be made of smoke. My mind experiences the voice as a code: I know it but the drugs keep me from recognizing it, and I struggle to unscramble the cypher, fighting against the injection's clouds. It's all too much. Fear, hope, and the almost imaginary feeling of someone stroking my hand . . . I slip back into the emptiness, spinning in space.

Times passes. I don't know how much. I open my eyes. The world I perceive now is real, and my brain crawls over every detail, first the white-paneled ceiling, artificial lights glaring down on me. I cringe from them, my head lolling to the side, and my eyes find the tower of blinking lights and tubes, some of which lead down to my intravenous. My brain tells my hand to reach out and grasp these tubes, tug them from my skin. But my fingers only wiggle. I am waking up, but in pieces. My body hasn't realized that we belong to each other yet.

"I know what you're thinking," says a voice. "Better to leave those alone."

My eyes slowly search the area before me for a face, but find only more white walls, more blinking lights. With considerable effort, I loll my head in the other direction, and come face-to-face with a dark-haired man in a white coat. His features swim, arranging and rearranging. Eyebrows, thick but neat. A white surgical mask obscures his chin, but only his chin: he's pulled it down from where it is supposed to cover his nose and mouth. I recognize that mouth, a blur of a memory.

"Doctor . . . ," I croak.

The eyes before me, just a mere foot away, crease at the corners with a smile. It's not pleasant.

"Yes, I am a doctor. Your memory is returning. Good."

I squint, trying to focus, jerk the memory to the surface of my brain. His voice. More than the mouth, I know the voice. The hidden sneer within it, the slanted enjoyment of the specimen on the table before him . . .

"Dr. Jain," I say. The words sound like shards of glass, jagged and irregular.

Those eyebrows rise in surprise. "Oh?" I can't tell if it's a pleased sound or not. "He will find this very interesting."

He. He's talking about Dr. Albatur. This is Dr. Jain, Dr. Albatur's assistant: the whitecoat I'd seen first experimenting on the helpless vasana. When the feeling first begins to buzz inside me, I almost don't recognize it: a red invasion, like a virus lancing through my biology. It flows through me, clenching my fists and tightening my jaw. Rage. There it is. Rage, hot and red and flaming through every vein.

Dr. Jain notices. "Good." He smiles, and pulls up his mask.

As it turns out, Dr. Jain is there to remove me from this room. But I know better than to be grateful. He hums under his breath as he wheels me down the hallway. There is nothing to see here. This is a hopeless déjà vu. The endless white hallways. The windows full of nothing. At least this time most of the illusions of emptiness are true: the Zoo is almost empty. I close my eyes tightly as my wheeled cot passes infinite doors, trying to remember what it had felt like as the animals rushed past me in a river of fangs and claws, eager for their freedom, the smell of it filling their noses and mine. There are still specimens here, but nothing like before. We had all but depleted them in our battle in the containment room. I hold this thought in my mind as the hum of a door once opening, and then again closing, fills my ears. I know before cracking my eyes that I am being watched.

At first I see only him. Indoors, he doesn't need his red cloak, but the pale sickliness of him is indicator enough of who stands before me. He looks even sicker than before, the creases around his mouth purplish. He looks like he needs more blood, like some essential element has been drained from him, pooled somewhere he can't reach. His eyes are as cold as the metal table alongside my cot.

"We meet again," Dr. Albatur says.

I don't trust my voice to sound brave, because I'm gradually realizing where I am. This is the man who killed my mother. Rage leaves me wordless, and fearful. The metal table. Its attached lariat used to trap specimens in place. The nearby tray bearing its collection of glittering tools. The recording device. The window.

The faces in the window.

Rows of faces. All clad in white coats.

I'm in an observation room. I am a specimen.

"We are curious about your suit," Dr. Albatur says. "And it is under analysis. But we are curious about you as well. I don't think you can be too surprised that we have many questions. After your . . . departure."

Again he pauses, his metal eyes dissecting my face. I stare back as calmly as I can manage, remembering that while he may have the tools to cut my skin, he doesn't possess the ability to read my mind. He doesn't have that gift. In a lurch, I'm remembering where I'd found my mother the night she died. Alone in a room. Strapped bleeding to a table. Had she endured what I'm about to experience?

"As you can see, we're all riveted by where you went and where you came back from. And wearing such a wondrous suit! How did you describe her vitals, Dr. Jain?"

"Remarkable," Dr. Jain says.

"Remarkable," Dr. Albatur repeats in a low voice. "*Remarkable*. One might assume it might have something to do with the suit. But of course the curious mind wonders if it's something more."

I glare at him until he moves away, adjusting some dials on the recording device and rearranging a few instruments. He slips on a pair of exam gloves before turning to the window filled with faces.

"I'm not the only inquiring mind, as you can see," he says, gesturing broadly. "Much of the N'Terran scientific community is as thirsty for answers as I. Based on the events that took place here in these labs, N'Terran priorities have shifted. We can only assume that your biology was compromised in some way. Perhaps a mere toxin. Perhaps some implantation of the bones. Perhaps something hidden more deeply. Something in your brain."

He turns back to me as he says these last few words. My horror has surpassed fear. I am frozen by the meaning of his words, their roots sinking through my skin and down to my skeleton. I can only stare at him, my teeth clenching and unclenching.

"Yes, compromised," he says softly. "I have been a patient man, slowly rebuilding the world we were cut off from, moving toward a bridge back to that world. There has been entirely too much tolerance for variance of opinion on the matter. I don't know what it is that makes a person stand in the way of their own species, but we will find the answer. Layer by layer, we will dig until we find it. And along the way perhaps we will find something advantageous, like your special suit. I can see many uses for that back home."

He moves closer, his gloved hands shining like wax. This

can't be real. Dr. Jain has moved around to the foot of my cot, tightening the strap that binds my feet. I hadn't even noticed them until now, I'm so out of touch with my body. But the pressure around my ankles wakes my skin. I wriggle, weakly at first. Then more strongly, desperately as Dr. Albatur comes nearer. His hands are empty of any tool, but the idea of his fingers on me is torture enough.

"Don't," I finally wheeze. "If you touch me . . ."

He waves away my words.

"We are past the place where threats have meaning," he says. "And, in any case, I have yet to encounter a threat I couldn't neutralize. How do you think I got here? Why do you think I was sent?"

I don't know what this means and I don't care. I look frantically around the room, searching for some means of escape. It's in vain. I cast my eyes toward the glass of the observation room, taking in the faces in a frenzy, hoping to find just one pair of eyes that carry empathy. Nothing. The reflection of white light in spectacles. Alma's words from the Greenhouse come echoing through my mind: *Knowledge is power.* I had come here thinking that if they just knew what Albatur was doing, they would do the right thing. But they do know. I stare into the face of their knowledge, the blank stare of a cold sort of science. They are two dozen strangers: I am not real.

And then the side of a face I know, moving toward the back of the room. Tall. Taller than the rest. Broad through the shoulders. Hair gray at the temples. He is not looking at me, instead seems intent on getting out of the room, away from the window.

It is my father.

He looks back one more time as the door opens silently before him. I can't read his face. It's as empty as my lungs. And then he's gone.

CHAPTER 11

I lose track of the days. I haven't seen my father since the first day, when Dr. Albatur attempted to lift knowledge from my skin. It had started as a tingling sensation on my bicep, a tool shaped like a hammer but electronic, emitting tiny red sparks. Gradually the tingle had kindled to a burn, then an all-out inferno on my arm, the skin lasered off layer by layer as he gathered the samples of my epidermis needed to examine in his many tests. The next day, my other arm. The next day, my back. The patches are treated with narruf gel when I am returned to my white-walled cell, and every time the attending whitecoat applies the thin layer of goo to my burned skin, I think of Dr. Adibuah, the day he'd applied it to my neck. The day I'd seen the philax. The day this all began. I wonder if he knows I'm here, if he knows what they're doing. Maybe he's dead too. Or maybe he's one of the faces watching coolly from the window.

But my father knows. And I know he's not coming. And the pain of every cell of my skin they steal is even worse with the knowledge that he knows. My father knows. And still I am alone.

Dr. Jain will be in for me soon. The days blur together, but I was given sustenance through my intravenous some time ago, and they usually come to retrieve me a few hours later. That allows enough time for the morning drugs to wear off, helped by the tube food midday. They want me alert for their evening experiments. My reactions must be clear and observable, not artificially enhanced or stunted in any way. This is the worst part of the day, my body weak, but my mind awake. I sit like a stone in the lonely white room, wondering if the Faloii have left for the Isii, if they've already convinced the planet to swallow us up. If I could see Alma again, maybe I could try to get through to her, break whatever chain has tethered her to the Council.

I think the same thoughts over and over again. Escape. My father. My mother. The Faloii. War. Dr. Albatur. Escape. My father. They give me only enough liquefied food to keep me going. They want me weak.

The door hums open.

"Awake," Dr. Jain says, his smirk ever present. "Good. Today will be a little different."

"Different," I repeat. My fists are already clenched. They

keep my limbs tethered to the cot. I might choke him if I had half the chance.

"Yes. We've finished with your dermis and epidermis." He studies his slate. "Today we'll be moving on to your bones."

"I'm not Faloii," I spit. "Nothing in my bones is going to help you. And theirs won't either. I won't let you."

He doesn't have to say what his eyes express: that I'm not in any position to make threats.

"You don't have to let me go," I say. "But I need to talk to the Council. They need to know what they're doing has consequences. If we start a war, it's not something we can win."

"War," he says. "You don't know the meaning of that word."

"I don't," I say. "Neither do you! You're younger than my parents. You were probably a baby when they left the Origin Planet."

He squints. "I don't need to remember it to know where I belong."

"Maybe not," I say, desperate. "But that's not the point. The point is, what you think you know about war isn't what's going to happen here. I've seen the drones. This isn't that. The whole planet will turn against us."

"It's always been against us," he says, and returns his eyes to the screen of his slate.

"That's such a stupid thing to believe!" I cry. "Do you not even think about what he tells you before imagining yourself as a victim? Stars!"

I hang my head when he doesn't respond. "Just let me talk to the Council," I say. "They need to know more than just what he tells them. Does he not have to prove his theories? Isn't that *science*?"

He stares at me, his lips pursed, his dark eyes clouded. He's hearing me, I think, and my pulse quickens. He understands.

"This isn't about science," he says, putting his slate away. He's reaching for the cot. "It's about power."

I jerk away, the clang of my bonds echoing in the small stark room. I hear the snarl rise out of my throat and can't recognize the sound of it as myself. The beast in the white coat takes me out into the hall, away to where they will prod at my anatomy as if it is I who is the monster. I keep snarling. I can't stop.

When I'm returned to the white room, the snarls have been drained from me by a series of syringes. I lie limp and sweaty on the cot, near unconsciousness. I hadn't even bothered looking for my father as Dr. Albatur prodded my bones. I had expected the Head of the Council to continue pontificating about the future of N'Terra, but when the needles came out, his mouth was sealed into a thin line, the weak blue of his irises turning shiny and hard. I don't see a future. When my eyes are open all I see is the vicious white of the room; when they're closed, nothing but faint patterns of stars on the backs of my eyelids.

Dr. Jain is there in the room, staring down at his slate, swiping through what must be data gathered from my anatomy.

The light of the screen glows in his square spectacles, and he takes on the beast-like quality again. Glowing eyes. A smirk. He barely looks up when the door hums open.

It's Alma. The sight of her expressionless face floating above her white coat is like another needle plunging through my skin and into my breastbone. I can't take it, her round eyes empty when they pass over my face. Has she been coming in and out of my room as I slept these days away? The idea that she has seen me held prisoner day after day and done nothing makes me want to die.

"The tranquilizer?" Dr. Jain says, still not looking up but addressing his words to Alma.

"Yes, doctor."

"Good, right on time. You may administer it now. Her vitals are stable enough."

"Yes, doctor."

She approaches my cot, the syringe gleaming on a small silver tray. I don't even try to twist away, as I had the last two nights when drugs were administered. What's the point now?

The hands of the girl who had been my best friend are cool on my clammy skin. I remember when she'd removed my intravenous after I'd been lost in the jungle, so long ago, when my reappearance meant relief for her. Her fingers had been deft and expert in their movements, as always. She seems to be having some trouble now, fiddling with the port where the syringe goes in. Then a pinch. Not inside my vein. On my wrist.

OLIVIA A. COLE

I crack open one eye. I don't have the energy for both. The syringe is there in her fingers, but the liquid inside it is clear— not the blue substance I know to be the tranquilization drug. Is this new? I force open both eyes, afraid that they have invented some new superserum that will immobilize me even further. But then I see Alma's eyes.

They're hers again. The flat, lifeless stare of the last few days falls away, the disguise put aside. Her two fingers are still at my wrist where she'd pinched me to get my attention.

I'm wide awake now.

She flashes her eyes down to the syringe in her other hand and, darting her eyes in the direction of Dr. Jain, gives one quick nod. Then she lifts the syringe to the intravenous port, fits the needle in, and injects me with whatever is in the syringe.

I feel it immediately. Not the deadening effect of drugs but the sweep of energy and vitality usually associated with a vitamin compound. She's given me the opposite of a tranquilizer: she's given me some kind of liquid energy.

"She shouldn't give you too much trouble," Dr. Jain says, but his voice is distracted, his eyes still on the slate's screen.

"None at all, doctor," Alma says in that dead voice. But her gaze holds mine, as bright as before. Now she closes her eyes and tilts her head ever so slightly. I know her meaning: *Be asleep.*

I close my eyes, my heart pounding. I know I need to get it under control in case Dr. Jain checks my pulse. I focus on

134

breathing deeply, slowly, even as the burst of energy from the vitamin compound rushes through my circulatory system. *Alma*, I think, hope taking off in my stomach like a flock of oscree.

"All done, doctor," she says. With my eyes closed, I feel her move away from my bedside and make her way toward the door. "She is unconscious."

"Good work," Dr. Jain says, and his slate case snaps shut. The door hums open. I pray that he will go, that he won't bother to come touch my wrist, my chest. His voice is eager: there must be some results from my data that he wants to go chatter with Dr. Albatur about. Or some other specimen that they have imprisoned nearby that he can't wait to go prod with another set of needles. Either way, I am forgotten as they leave together.

I remain still. I have no idea what is to come, but Alma has a plan. Her eyes were on fire with it. Now all I have to do is wait.

CHAPTER 12

Even if I wanted to sleep to pass the time, I couldn't. The vitamin compound Alma had injected me with buzzes through my veins like beetles: I am a swarm in my cot. The room seems to get darker and darker, even with my eyes wide open. As the hours ooze into one another, a terrifying thought occurs to me: Had I imagined the whole thing? Had I hallucinated the light in Alma's eyes?

There's a sound beyond the door. Not the hum of it opening, but tapping, shuffling. Like someone has pressed themselves against the other side and inches sideways down the hall. *I'm here*, I want to call. Had Alma forgotten which room I am in? Or is this all a hallucination too?

My ears pick up a low, muffled beep. A long, heavy silence. Then the whisper of the door sliding open. It's too dark for me to make out who stands there in the hall until they step into the room, and then the motion sensors bathe the room in harsh white light. I blink rapidly, and when the spots clear from my vision, I am rewarded with the two familiar shapes of Alma and Rondo.

Rondo immediately goes to the wall, his body blocking my line of vision. He does something to the lights: there's a click, and two sharp clips, as if he's cutting wires. They are abruptly extinguished, and the tower of blinking lights attached to my intravenous goes dark and quiet.

"I needed the light," comes Alma's voice through the pitch black, an irritated whisper.

"Use the slate," he says.

"Are you . . . are you real?" I croak. Tears are gathering in my eyes.

Rondo is at my side a heartbeat later. I can't see him, but his thumb caresses the back of my hand. A soft, gentle pressure that I had felt my first night in N'Terra . . .

"You were here," I whisper. "I thought . . . I thought it was a dream."

"I was here, O," he says. He seems to know I'm crying, because his other hand finds my face in the dark, searching gently upward until his fingers find my tears. He carries them away, and for a moment all that is heavy in me is made light. I know those hands. I know this heart.

"Oh please." Alma sighs. "No time."

She appears beside us and a rectangular light glows from her hands. The slate illuminates one side of the bed, the crook of my elbow centered in the glare.

"First things first," she says.

She passes the slate to Rondo, who reluctantly unhands my face, and with him holding the slate steady, Alma removes the bonds and my intravenous. The feeling of the needle pulling free of my body is as uncomfortable and bizarre as ever, but it's as if light and life rushes into the tiny hole it left in my skin and fills me up. Free. I sit up from the cot and start to swing my legs over the edge.

"Whoa, whoa," Alma whispers. "I know the injection I gave you makes you think you're invincible right now, but if you go too fast you're going to regret it later. Take it slow—"

"*No time*," Rondo mocks.

"But not too slow," she finishes. She shoots him a poisonous look, and the smile that stretches my dry lips is almost painful.

"What's the plan?" I say. I've got both my legs over the edge now, and my toes stretch for the cold white floor. It's strange feeling the artificial ground of the Zoo again, especially with bare feet. I hate it: just one more cold, dead thing in this place.

"The plan is stay with me," she says. "I'm going to have to help you walk because Rondo needs to navigate with the slate. We've got a route laid out."

Rondo gives my knee a comforting squeeze and moves toward the door. He raises the slate and bends his neck the way I'm used to him doing: hacking.

"This door is locked from the inside?" I say.

"Yes," Alma says. "They all are now, thanks to you. They changed all the access points from handprints to ocular scans since the night we busted Adombukar out."

"Speaking of which," I whisper, leaning on Alma as she walks me closer to the door. "How are you working in the labs? You tranquilized Dr. Albatur, if I remember correctly."

She chuckles under her breath.

"Yes, but I must have stunned the stars out of him because he didn't remember a thing. I don't know how it wasn't on camera. All he remembers is you. He's fixated on you as the cause of all of this. Now that . . . now that your mom is gone."

The sound of Rondo's fingers tapping away on the slate pauses for the briefest moment as the mention of my mother's death blooms in the air around us. *Gone*, she said. Like my mother lives, just elsewhere. I don't even know what they did with her body. A fiery lump forms in my throat.

The door hums open, light spilling in.

"Time to go," Rondo whispers.

The hallway is empty. It must be very late. Even the most dedicated whitecoats have gone home to their communes.

"No guards?" I whisper.

"Sometimes."

I lean on Alma only slightly: the injection she had administered thrums through my veins. I shiver in the flimsy gown the whitecoats had dressed me in.

"I need clothes eventually," I say as we slowly round a corner, Rondo squinting at whatever system on his slate guides us.

Alma nods.

"I have a package hidden outside," she says. "Water and a skinsuit and shoes and stuff. We just have to get there."

"Shh," Rondo hisses, and throws an arm backward, pressing us against the wall. I hold my breath. Some distance away I hear one pair of steady footsteps. Rondo peers around the corner. "They're going the other way. Just wait."

We remain frozen, the blood pulsing in my ears.

"It was a guard," he whispers when I can't hear the footsteps anymore. "They must not have had a comm or they would have shown up on my screen."

"New program he made," Alma whispers. "He had a lot of time on his hands when they had him on house arrest."

"House arrest?" I breathe.

"For knocking out that guard. Aiding and abetting or something," he says, motioning with his head for us to continue. I want to touch him, inspect him for harm. The task at hand stands between us. We creep down the hall as before.

"Speaking of which," I whisper to Alma, "Dr. Albatur doesn't remember you tranqing him, but they must know you helped get Adombukar out, right?"

"Not really," she says. "Honestly, they were incredibly disorganized about the whole thing. That's definitely changed, by the way. But they knew I was your friend—I just convinced them I was jealous of you and never really liked you."

"Who is *they*?" I hiss.

"In here. Now." Rondo jerks sideways in the hall and we immediately follow suit. After a few lightning-fast taps on the slate, a section of the wall hisses open, revealing what seems to be a linen closet. Racks of antimicrobial cloth. Shelves of gowns like the one I'm wearing right now. Rondo shoves me and Alma into the small space. *"In."*

The door hisses closed behind us, and the only light inside is Rondo's slate. I smell everyone's breath, the worst of which is, of course, my own. I try to breathe shallowly and away from Rondo, straining my ears for any sound in the hallway. I detect the faint murmur of two or more voices, and peer over Rondo's shoulder at his screen.

"Two guards," he whispers. "Both have comms."

On his screen is what appears to be a map of the labyrinthine Zoo, an orange line winding its way through the corridors. The route, I assume, that Rondo has laid out for us. Very close to one section of the orange line are two red glowing dots, moving slowly along.

"Is that them?" Alma whispers, nodding at his screen.

"Yes. The program picks up the comms and registers them as red dots. I don't have any way of tracking the whitecoats unless they have a slate, which registers as a blue dot."

"Where are we?" I ask.

"We're invisible," he says, and I can see his smile from behind by the rise of his cheekbone. "I'm encrypted."

The voices beyond our linen closet sound clearer: they are very close to passing just outside the door. I fasten my eyes on the two red dots, praying they won't pause in this little section of orange line. *Keep going,* I think. *Keep going. Let me out of here.*

"They have them on a stricter patrol now," Alma whispers. "Since Adombukar escaped."

"Who is *they?*" I repeat.

"The Council," Alma says, her voice sounding jagged in the dark. "It was honestly Dr. Albatur's dream: a reason to crack down. A couple of the animals we released killed some of the guards in the stampede. Dr. Albatur blamed Adombukar. Called it an act of war."

"He was already sowing the seeds before. All his fear tactics," Rondo mutters, his eyes glued to the screen. "This gave him all the justification he needed. He's running the Council like his private army."

"And my father?" I hear myself say. I hadn't wanted to say it.

"He—he still sits on the Council," Alma says softly.

I watch the two red dots continue down the corridor, going deeper into the maze. My father could be with them for all I know. Walking like a ghost beside them and Rondo's program wouldn't know the difference. I shudder.

"They're gone," I whisper.

"Yes. Let's go."

We don't meet anyone else as we make our way along Rondo's orange path. Occasionally I widen the Artery to see if there are any animals here that I might be able to take with me. But the tunnel is dark, lifeless. What if they are here, imprisoned as before, but Albatur and his Council have discovered how to keep us from hearing each other?

"Should be right around here," Rondo says, finally raising his eyes from the screen and scanning the empty hall before us.

I pause, leaning on Alma's shoulder, sweeping my eyes over the motionless corridor.

"What should be?"

"Our route."

"You don't know where it is?"

"I've only seen it digitally. We didn't have time to come check it out first since we didn't exactly know you were coming."

"What is *it*?" I demand in a whisper.

Alma shushes me. "Let him concentrate!"

Rondo passes me the slate, whispering, "Hold this. Look out for red dots."

"What about blue ones?"

"Those too."

He moves slowly down the hallway, running his hands along the walls inch by inch.

"Here somewhere . . . ." he mutters.

"What are we looking for?" I whisper.

"It's a ventilation shaft," he says, pausing to inspect a seam in the wall. "The early blueprints of N'Terra show it as being in this corridor. They closed it off twenty years ago when they learned a better way to cycle the air. It was one big shaft before that served as a kind of vacuum to force the air to move. . . ."

He pauses again, inspecting some tiny spot I can't see from where I stand.

"So hot here, you know . . . ," he murmurs. "They dealt with the noise just to get some airflow."

"Rondo, focus," Alma hisses.

"I am."

He continues to inspect each inch of the wall. I'm starting to sweat, even wearing this stupid skimpy gown. It's fear that sends my pores into overdrive, not heat. I hold the back of the gown closed with one hand and hold the slate with the other, anxiously glancing down at it every few seconds before looking back at Rondo to see if he's found anything. Alma has moved to the opposite wall now, mirroring his inspection of every seam and irregularity in the smooth white clay walls. I stand alone in the middle of the hall, helpless except to keep watch and try to tame my pulse.

"What are we going to do when we find it?" I say. "Break through the wall?"

Alma taps her hip pocket but doesn't look up. "I have pavi extract. I steal a little whenever I can. Just like it dissolved Adombukar's cage, it should dissolve the wall."

"Not exactly subtle," I mutter. "All it takes is someone walking by and seeing a huge hole in the wall and we're busted."

"Yeah, well . . ." Alma trails off.

"Stars," I groan.

"I think I found something," Rondo says, and Alma and I rush over before he can go on.

A ridge in the clay, raised ever so slightly above the surface of the rest of the wall. I sweep my eyes anxiously over the surrounding area, looking for more. Sure enough, there is another ridge farther along to the right, running parallel to the first.

"Up there," Alma whispers, pointing. We all take a step back and tilt our heads, taking in the ridge near the ceiling.

"A square," Rondo murmurs, gazing at a faint line near the floor. "This is it. They just patched it up. It *is* huge."

Alma is already reaching for her pocket, withdrawing a long vial of pavi extract.

"I hope I have enough." She frowns, and crouches. She uncorks the vial and extends her hand to pass me the stopper.

But my hands aren't free. I'm gripping the slate with all ten fingers, staring at the maze of the Zoo, trying to map where we are. Trying to decide if the blue dot coming in our direction is actually our direction or somewhere else in the lab.

"Rondo," I whisper, scarcely daring to breathe. "Is this . . . is this where we are?"

I want to be wrong. I shove the slate in his face, and he has to wrench it from my shaking hands.

I watch each muscle in his face go slack.

"What? What is it?" Alma demands, standing, craning her neck to see the screen.

I'm not looking at the screen anymore. I'm looking at the corner just six feet away, hearing the sound of footsteps over the pounding of my own heart. They're coming right toward us. Not a harmless blue dot. But a person. Blue means whitecoat. Blue means . . . it's over.

There's nowhere to hide. I stare at the corridor before me, at the shadow bearing our capture.

He comes around the corner. White coat. A slate clutched in tan fingers. I only see pieces at first, the horror of being caught causing my brain to fire in intermittent bursts. Then in a rush of adrenaline it all comes together as the whitecoat takes one step toward us and stops.

It's not just a whitecoat. It's my father.

CHAPTER 13

"Don't try to run," he says. His voice is a skeletal version of itself, all bone and no blood. I'm not close enough to see his eyes, but I know the ghosts that lurk there. They've always been there, but now have more company with the addition of my mother.

The three of us stand motionless before him, three kunike waiting to decide on fight or flight. But I know neither is an option. Where to run? Fight with what? The only weapon I have is my eyes, and I use every bit of viciousness they can muster as I stare him down.

"Octavia," he says, but his mouth can't quite form whatever words his mind had planned. His lips are empty like his eyes. "I think you three had better come with me."

Alma takes one tiny step backward, as if at least one muscle had decided on flight.

"Don't," my father says quickly. "You wouldn't get far."

Another long moment of silence, of staring. "This way," he says. He stands to the side in the corridor, swinging one arm out to show us the way. He doesn't appear to be armed. In one hand is his slate, the one that had registered the blue dot on Rondo's device. The other hand is empty, but who knows what his white coat conceals.

"How did you find us?" Rondo says, searching for the flaw in his plan even now that it doesn't matter.

"Because I was looking," my father says. "Now move."

I move first. Forcing my feet forward is like walking through a treacherous swamp, and I give him a wide berth, nearly pressing myself against the wall in order to be as far from him as possible. For a brief moment I consider lunging at him, wrapping my arm around his neck and squeezing, giving my friends time to escape. But even with Alma's vitamin in my veins, I know I'm too weak. Alma and Rondo follow, my father bringing up the rear.

We continue down the hall in silence. I keep my eyes straight ahead, waiting for my father's voice to tell me where to go.

"What do we do?" Rondo whispers. I know my father can hear him. My eyes are open for an opportunity, but I know better than to hope there will actually be one. The Zoo had once been a place for hope. Not now.

"Just here," my father says. I stop moving, casting my eyes left and right. Doors surround us like any other place in the labs. I have a vague feeling of recognition. I think if we were to continue down the hall we would run into the Atrium.

My father comes from behind us and chooses a door. He rubs his eyes, then leans close to the lineless white surface, opening them wide. A thin blue line that I hadn't noticed before illuminates, emitting a subtle flash as the hidden device performs the ocular scan. A muted beep of recognition, and the door slides open.

I recognize it right away: the sorting room where the other interns and I had spent our very first day inside the Zoo. The bins are not nearly as full as they were the week we were on duty, but there are still dozens of eggs of various sizes and colors shining all around us. Something has changed though: the relaxing atmosphere that the eggs had once provided seems faded and dull. I can't put my finger on it exactly . . . something in them has shifted.

"What are we doing here?" Alma says as the door hums shut behind us. I know her well enough to know that she's terrified, but she does her best to put on a brave face, daring to look my father square in the eyes.

"Octavia," my father says, ignoring her. "There are so many things I wish you would have done differently."

I look away from Alma and go back to staring at the eggs. The rage that's building inside me could shatter every shell in this room. In this moment I wish my father could speak Arterian, so that I could fully communicate the violence of my anger, shove the shapes of my fury into his mind. Our language seems so rudimentary. It lacks the power of what I feel.

"You don't see the whole picture," he says, his voice harder than it had been a moment before. "And why should you? We said our children wouldn't know the pain of our world. . . ."

"Who's we?" I snap, unable to stop myself. "You and my mother? She's dead. Because of *you*."

He stops short and moves so quickly that I almost don't have time to dodge. I spring sideways, avoiding whatever blow he's intending to land on me. But he merely brushes past, almost shoving me out of the way as he lunges toward the back of the sorting room. He kicks a bin of eggs out of the way, and I leap forward to catch a lavender egg before it crashes to the ground. My anger spikes again, filling the tunnel in my head. But there is no one there to receive it as my father shoves the examination tables out of the way. A metered scale is next: he nearly sends it toppling in his effort to clear a path. I cradle the lavender egg, staring at him in furious bafflement.

"What is he doing?" Alma says under her breath.

"I've worked my whole life so that you wouldn't have to know," my father goes on. He sends a shelf bearing a projector and slides careening to the floor, the crash filling the room with an orchestra of echoes. I cringe, cupping the egg to my chest as if to protect it. "Just to create a world for you that's safe."

"You sound just like Albatur," I spit. "Always going on about how no one understands what you're trying to create, no matter who you *kill* in the process!"

"If Albatur doesn't get what he wants, the death has not even begun," he says, not looking at me, forcibly moving another shelf.

"And you think that's a good thing?" I cry. "We killed our home planet, and now we're going to kill this one? You don't even know what you've done—"

He whirls on me, cutting me off. "The death followed us here, Octavia," he says. But the fire is fading from his voice, sputtering out. "It was a stowaway. There's so much you don't understand. And that's why I need you to do what I cannot do."

His eyes are damp coals. All the wind that had swept my angry ship forward dies, and I stare at him, at a loss. "I need you to do what I cannot do," he repeats, pleading. "I need you to understand."

He turns away, back to the wall he has cleared of shelves and tables and charts. He places two hands against the smooth white clay and slides them slowly in a gentle circular pattern, the motion of someone feeling their way through a dark room. They seem to find something after a moment of seeking and stop abruptly. His hands flex against the wall, and something shifts.

"Stars," Rondo says, impressed.

The wall is sinking in. Not all of it, just a section. Twice as wide as my father and almost as tall. It's as if a mouth is open-ing in the clay, swallowing itself. It retreats from my father's hands, then folds sideways in a loose way, like fabric. Had it ever been a wall at all, or was it a mirage, like so many other pieces of the Zoo?

"What . . . ?" I trail off, amazed. I return the lavender egg to its bin and against my better judgment move toward what has revealed itself to be a passage at the back of the sorting room.

"It's time for you to leave," my father says. He doesn't even look at me. He stares ahead into the mouth of the tunnel, and then disappears into its shadows.

I stand frozen for what feels like an eternity, hope and logic battling in my mind. If my father is helping us escape—and he seems to be—then surely there must be a motive greater than fatherly love. Love hadn't made him put a stop to Albatur's experiments, after all. But through the tunnel comes the drift-ing scent of Faloiv, and it's too much to resist.

Somehow Alma is already ahead of me, eager to explore whatever secrets this strange turn of events contains. Rondo is at my side a half second later, taking my arm and letting me lean on him as we take our first step into the dark. My father's slate is a lantern ahead of us, and his steps are brisk and pur-poseful. He knows where he's going, obviously. I should know by now that anything shocking to me is old hat to him.

There's not much to see. I had expected dampness, the dis-tant sound of dripping water. But this is not a cave, hollowed out by the powers of the planet itself. This is man-made, a human tunnel. The ground doesn't have the comforting give of soil—it is the same artificial substance as the Zoo, firm and cold against the soles of my feet. But warmer than the labs, I observe: the temperature is changing. We're leaving the cool filtered air of N'Terra and inching closer to the hot natural breath of Faloiv. And something else. Heat and stench are ahead, something that crawls into my very skin as well as my nostrils.

"Do you smell that?" Alma says, but I don't reply. I might be sick if I do.

"This will be unpleasant," my father says.

There's a blur of light ahead, and he puts his slate to sleep, its glow no longer needed. The moon is guiding us now. The moon and the stench.

"They're dead," I whisper, so quiet that only I can hear.

In a few steps I know that I'm right. At the end of the tunnel is the edge of the jungle, but even the smell of the ogwe and syca cannot mask what lies on the ground before us. Dead animals. A half dozen. Two vasana. One lonely gwabi. The other bodies are unidentifiable. I falter against Rondo, my hands over my nose and mouth, horrified. The empty eyes of the dead stare up at the black sky of Faloiv, the stars too far to reflect in them.

"Killed the night Adombukar escaped. The night your mother . . ."

"What are they doing here?" I say. I fasten my eyes on the jungle instead of the bodies. I'm afraid if I stare too long that I will find the bloody hands of my mother emerging from the pile of hooves and paws.

"This is the tunnel Manx and the finders use to smuggle in specimens," he says. "Hidden."

"That doesn't answer my question," I say. "Why are the bodies here? Just . . . here?"

"I have no answer," he says, his voice a husk. I want to strike him.

Rondo and Alma have moved close to me, sensing my anguish. But their nearness does nothing to ease the stench. Not just of death but the smell of anger that seeps from the trees down upon me and my people. I dare not widen the Artery, afraid of what other witnesses to this horror I will find. The ogwe see. The syca know. Their anger burrows into my head, becoming my own; and in that instant I think of the Faloii, the small group my nana said is heading to the Isii. Had they already arrived? Is this why the trees' anger feels so much more intense? Or is it because the part of me that is connected to Faloiv is naturally siding against the damage my people seem to insist on doing?

My father turns to me, and the pain in his eyes isn't enough—it will never be enough. "We don't have much time," he says. "There is more at work than you realize. The Solossius was always a backup plan. For the years we have been studying its construction, we believed it to be our only option. But then you reignited Albatur's original desire. You and your friend."

"Me?" Alma says.

"No, not you. Him. The Faloii man."

"His name is Adombukar," I snap, bristling. "But what do you mean? We reignited what?"

"He brought Albatur's desire right into the labs. Not just his bones. Something infinitely more powerful. The thing that brought Albatur to this planet to begin with."

"The kawa," Rondo says softly. "You're talking about the kawa."

I turn to my father, trying to see him with the eyes necessary to understand everything that's happening.

"The kawa? Albatur wants that? But why . . ." I pause, the pieces floating together. "Power. Adombukar was able to extract energy from it. Albatur thinks he can do the same thing."

"More than thinks," he says, his mouth a hard line. "Knows."

"How? How does he know?"

"The kawa powered the *Vagantur*," he says.

"What?" Alma says. "Come again?"

"A kawa powered the *Vagantur*," he says again. "But it was lost when we landed. Albatur and the first N'Terrans spent many years looking for it as they attempted to repair the ship. The Faloii told us there were no more. But when you helped Adombukar leave the labs, we learned that they lied—we saw

Adombukar use the egg. There *is* another kawa. Maybe many more."

"How did a kawa power the *Vagantur*?" I say. "It's an object of Faloiv!"

"We only have time to discuss the present just now," he says. I again fight the urge to strike him. "And what you must do."

"What I must do?" I cry. "Must? What I thought I *must* do was come here and expose Albatur. But . . ."

"You can't expose that which you don't see the whole of," he says roughly. "This can't be your aim now, Octavia. The only course of action now is to give him what he wants. What we're owed. Before this gets worse."

"Give him what he wants?" I spit. "What we're *owed*? You must be out of your—"

"There will be violence," he says, raising his voice. "War. You don't know what war is, but—"

"I saw a bit of it," I say, remembering the vibration of the drone through the memory's air. "And I know it was N'Terrans who brought war to Faloiv."

His eyes find mine and hold them, and the expression I find there seems muddy, conflicted.

"We only have time to discuss the present just now," he repeats. "And what you must do."

"Which is what?" I demand. "Everyone has this idea of what I need to do. . . ."

I almost repeat the instructions my grandmother sent me

into the jungle with—"find the keeper of the eyenu"—but despite the fact that my father had helped me escape the labs, I still don't trust his eyes. They shine with desperation, and I'm not sure about what they're desperate for.

But now he's not looking at me, he's casting his eyes back over his shoulder, down the tunnel.

"You must find us the kawa," he says when he turns back. "We can still save a lot of bloodshed if we can just give him a means to leave. The rest can be negotiated. There is so much that he wants, Octavia, but above all, he wants to return to the Origin Planet. Give us the kawa, so we can go."

"Us," I say, glaring at him. "*Us.*"

"You are us too," he snaps, reaching out for me, but under the flare of anger there's a plea in his tone. I pull away from it and him.

"The Origin Planet is dead though," Alma says, and maybe it's my father's voice still echoing in my ears, but there's a trace of a plea in hers as well, the Origin Planet like a string tethered to her heart, pulling her always. "Why do you want to go back?"

"To rebuild!" he cries, and then flinches, glancing back into the tunnel again. "What he wanted when we first came. He never wanted to stay."

"Because we crashed," I say.

"It's more complicated than that," he says, his voice still low but grating. He glances over his shoulder again, becoming more and more agitated. "It's time for you to go. You have come from their city: go back. Get the kawa. If you have to . . ."

He pauses, assessing me, and I get the feeling that the same way I had bitten back my grandmother's words, there is something he holds back from me now.

"Just one will be enough. Get a kawa. Just one, Octavia. Bring it to me. You may hate me, but I am your kind. Think of your people, your flesh. This is about our survival."

I feel as if I'm choking on everything he has told me, but he continues on past my silence.

"You'll need this," he says. He reaches into the deep pocket of his white coat and withdraws the strange mottled material of my qalm-grown suit. My heart leaps at the sight of it.

"My suit!" I cry, and snatch it from his hand. I clutch it to my chest. It's only been mine for a few days, but it feels as much a part of me as my hands.

"And this," he says. He takes a few quick steps away, moving just outside the mouth of the tunnel. He leans down and when he straightens again he's holding a gray bundle.

"What's that?" I say, peering at it.

"Our packs!" It's Alma's turn to snatch something from his hand. She immediately opens one of the packs and withdraws the items within: a skinsuit, shoes, water canteens, and other odds and ends.

"How did you find this?" she says, shooting a look at my father.

"The rest of the Council may not be wise to your loyalties," he says, turning back toward the tunnel. "But I am. I have to go. We're out of time."

"Wait," I cry, snatching at him. "You're telling me I need to go find the kawa, as if it's that simple! I don't know where they come from: they don't just have them lying around in Mbe-kenkanush!"

"If you have questions about the kawa," he says over his shoulder, a hint of a sneer in his voice, "then Captain Williams can answer them."

"Captain Williams? The captain of the *Vagantur*? But she died in the crash," Alma pipes up, still clutching her pack.

"You don't even know what's happening," I interject. "The Faloii are on the verge of turning the planet against humans. You know what that means, right? If they convince the planet to see us as parasites? Do you know what that *means*?"

"Yes," he says, already turning away, moving back into the dark. "It means we have to leave. And it means you have to hurry."

CHAPTER 14

When the sun had risen, the first thing I did was scan the sky for red smoke. The dread which has taken up residence in my body had fully expected to find it hovering somewhere on the distant horizon, a symbol of the bloodshed to come. But there are only clouds and the usual red eye of the sun. I still have time.

We've walked all night, the soles of our rubbery N'Terran shoes carrying us miles through the jungle. Alma still doesn't believe that Jaquot is alive.

"How?" she says for the hundredth time, following as I lead us through the jungle. "I was there. I saw his blood. I saw a piece of his skinsuit. I think I would have noticed if the Faloii had a battle with the dirixi to save Jaquot."

"Well, they didn't save all of him," I say, ducking under a low-hanging branch. "I told you it got his leg."

"Stars," Rondo says, behind Alma. "How did they heal it? Can he walk?"

"The Faloii seem to have effective medicine," I say. "He has tools that help him walk. Physically I think he's okay. But I think he's depressed."

They nod, both sipping from the canteens Alma had stowed in the packs. Resourceful Alma. Between the water and the dried hava strips, I feel restored, if sore and stiff.

"I'd kiss that idiot if I ever saw him again," Alma says, her voice rising happily. The silence that had clung to us in the first hours of our journey has fallen away with the coming of the sun. The more distance between us and N'Terra, the more freely we talk. "I wish I could see Yaya's face when she learns he is alive. She still hasn't been the same since that day."

"She has in some ways," Rondo says, sounding annoyed. "More devoted to the Council than ever. Her theory that the Faloii actually killed Jaquot? She believes that for sure since Adombukar broke out. Albatur spun it so that everyone believes Adombukar broke *in*. Half N'Terra probably thinks a whole army of Faloii came charging through the Paw's gates."

"She definitely does," I say, and tell them about how she'd kept me from attacking Janelle in the Greenhouse. "She's under whatever spell he's cast over the whole settlement. I can't believe this. I really thought I'd be able to talk some sense into the greencoats at least. . . ."

My grandfather hadn't liked the idea of me going back

to N'Terra and now I see why. I'm embarrassed by my own naïveté, my insistence that showing people the truth would be enough.

"It's not your fault," Rondo says, and his tone makes me look at him. Everything in me that's rigid softens whenever I meet his eyes. Is love supposed to make you weak or strong?

"It's like Yaya and Julian were learning a whole different curriculum," I say to take my mind off love.

"In a way they were," he says.

"Fools," I mutter, swiping at a shiny purple insect that seems interested in my hair.

"There's another one on the back of your head," Alma says.

"What?" I snap, freezing, afraid to reach behind my head. "Why didn't you say something? Get it off!"

"It's just a melinoovo." She laughs, passing me on the trail. "Harmless. They're curious."

"How do you know?" I say, following her, hating the idea of a bug using me as a chariot.

She looks over her shoulder with an arched eyebrow. "What *don't* I know?"

"You're so annoying."

"You're annoyed because now you're second in line," she says. "Just like in class."

She laughs her long musical laugh and I smile. It had taken me several hours to fully realize that this is reality: walking through the jungle with Rondo and Alma. No Manx. No guides. No protections. After traveling from Mbekenkanush with the gwabi overnight, I'm less fearful than I might have been, but I can still sense the anxiety that clings to my friends. The sunlight helps melt it away, but I can tell by Alma's jokes that she's trying to force herself to relax.

"So your grandmother said find the keeper of the eyenu," she says. I'd filled them in as we made our way through the jungle and now her brain is cranking again. "Yay for cryptic, I guess, but what does that mean?"

"You know I don't know," I say. "Maybe it has to do with the Isii."

"I guess we'll find out if we're headed back to Mbeken-kanush," she says, slapping at a leaf. "We'll just ask her."

I frown to myself. The idea of going back to the city appeals to me because I want to be back with my grandparents, back with Rasimbukar. But it feels like hiding. Retreating to what feels like safety, letting everyone else handle the problems that seem bigger and more dangerous every second.

"So what's it like?" Rondo says from behind me. "Mbeken-kanush. Is it big? How many people are there? Do they eat the same stuff we eat? How long until we get there?"

Alma casts a glance back at him before I can answer.

"You'd perform better on exams if you asked this many questions in the Greenhouse," she says.

"Well, luckily I don't have to worry about that anymore," he says.

"What do you mean?"

"I don't really see classes resuming as normal anytime soon."

"I mean, maybe not now," Alma says, sounding distressed, "but eventually!"

"You're ridiculous," I say, laughing. I wonder if it sounds as forced as it feels. It's hard to imagine a resolution to all this, particularly one in which things go back to normal. I don't think normal ever existed: one more N'Terran mirage.

"Things may be different once we figure everything out," she says airily. "But research is always going to be part of what we do."

"I wonder if Dr. Albatur even cares about science," Rondo says. We pause as Alma scurries over a fallen tree in our path, and he takes the opportunity to pluck the melinoovo off the back of my head, tossing it into the bushes. I shoot him a look of gratitude. "It seems like of everything he loves, discovery is toward the bottom of the list."

"Not all scientists are curious, and plenty are arrogant," I say, echoing my grandmother's words.

"For sure," Alma agrees, finally on the other side of the hill of the fallen tree. The path we've been following opens up now, expanding from a thread of a trail into a path wide enough for all three of us to walk side by side. "But arrogant or not, Albatur has a plan. These past few days working in the Zoo with Dr. Jain? Those guys are focused."

"How so?" I say, sliding down on her side of the tree.

"They're still cautious about what they say in front of who, so I didn't hear a whole lot. But at least twice I overheard Jain saying to Albatur that 'if they found them,' N'Terra wouldn't need the Solossius at all."

"Referring to the kawa, I'm guessing," Rondo says.

"Based on what Dr. English said, I'd say so," she says. "But he said they only need one."

"Even if they only need one," I say, bitterness creeping into my tone, "who's to say they won't take more than they need? I don't really imagine Dr. Albatur as the guy who only takes the bare minimum."

"So what are you going to do when we get back to the city?" Alma says over her shoulder. She's leading like she knows where we're going, when I barely do. "Say, *Hey, let me get one of those kawa, please and thanks*? Do we have to . . . you know . . . steal one?"

"I'm not stealing anything from the Faloii," I snap, and surprise myself with the suddenness of my temper. "If my dad thinks I'm going to be his little spy, he can forget it."

"So . . . plan?" Alma says, and I can tell by the look on Rondo's face that he's wondering the same thing.

Nearby, another voice joins our dialogue, although it seems to be engaged in a conversation of its own.

"I just want a sip," the voice complains, loudly. "Just a sip."

My blood runs cold, both hands shooting out to grab my friends.

"Then you shouldn't have left your canteen at the ship," another voice says, cutting through the trees from up ahead. "You could've had a sip from your own."

"We only left five minutes ago! We can still go back!"

"Stars," Alma whispers.

"Hide!" I hiss, and I dive into the bushes that hug the path, dragging Alma and Rondo with me. Thick green leaves like tongues slap me in my face, still wet from dawn's dew, but I only lurch through them more quickly, determined to get off and away from the trail. Due to the jungle's density, distance isn't required: the greenery swallows us, and being plunged deeper into the leaves immediately makes it cooler, out of the direct stare of the sun. Even with the qalm-grown suit, being in the shade is a relief: I almost sigh within the cool, but I swallow it as the sound of several pairs of feet approach on the trail, only a few paces away.

"I might die," the first voice protests. "How are you going to feel if I die because you wouldn't share your water?"

"Better than I would feel if *I* died because I gave you too much of my water."

"Manx! I need water!"

A third voice cuts in now, the presence of the three people almost even with us on the path. Alma catches my eye.

"Finders," she mouths.

"How old are you two?" the voice of Manx snaps. I almost recognize her by her footsteps alone: quick and snappy. "I knew

I should have brought Ivy and Alicia instead of you dolts."

"Aw, don't be like that, boss," the first voice says, the whine leaking out of it. "We're just messing around."

"Well, save it. We only have five hours between us and N'Terra and you need to be sharp with a reason for why we haven't found anything yet."

"But we've found a bunch of stuff!" one of the other voices says. They're passing us now, so close I can hear the water sloshing in their canteens. "He may see everything we've salvaged and decide to just build a smaller ship instead of repairing the *Vagantur.*"

Manx pauses on the path, and between the dense foliage I can make out a flash of her curly white hair. I try to sink lower in the plants without actually moving, and I realize I'm still holding Rondo's hand. I relax my grip to let it go, but he tightens his, so I squeeze back.

"Let's get one thing clear," Manx says, her tone as sharp as I know her face to be. "I thought we'd been over this but I guess I need to reiterate. There will be no mention of *any* alternate plan. No suggestion of anything besides the repair of the *Vagantur.* Do you understand? If he ends up thinking something else up, then that's on him. But we do not suggest that. Our job is to salvage parts, find the pods, and if we come across any Faloii for the machine in the meantime, great."

"What about Dr. English?" one of them says. My heart spasms.

"What about him?"

"He might like the idea of building another ship instead."

"You treat English and Albatur as a single entity, is that clear?" Manx snaps. "They want the same thing. Again, our *job* is to get them what they want. Focus on the *Vagantur* and the pods."

I let go of Rondo's fingers. My hands need to be fists.

"What's the big deal?" the second voice says. "If we can't find the pods, there's no reason to fix the ship at all, right? We'd just stay here."

Manx lets out an exasperated sigh, and between the leaves I see her turn away, back toward the direction of N'Terra.

"Yep, I should have brought Ivy and Alicia." She groans. "Come on. Watch out for the syca seeds that have fallen right there. If you step on one, it will burst and I don't want to have to carry you back to N'Terra because you're temporarily blinded by your own stupidity."

The sound of the two men grumbling makes its way to my ears through the trees, and the three finders move off down the path, back down the direction we'd come.

"Too close," Rondo whispers.

"Should we wait until they've been gone awhile?" Alma whispers back.

"No," I say, and push through the branches back toward the path. A plan is forming in my mind, parts of its blueprint drawn from the conversation we'd just overheard. A magnet in my head draws the metallic dust of my various clues together, and the urgency of it flows through me, sending me speed walking down the path in the opposite direction of the finders.

"Um, Octavia . . . ?" Alma says, drawing even with me. "Something you'd like to share?"

"Didn't you hear them?" I toss over my shoulder. "They just came from the *Vagantur*. We're close to the ship."

"And?" Rondo says. If I am eagerness personified, he is caution.

"So don't you want to see it?" I say, not slowing. "All these years of people talking about it crashing, and now with Albatur wanting to fix it again . . . There's something significant about the ship. The finders are usually combing the jungle for specimens, but today they're out here by the *Vagantur* looking for something?"

"For pods," Alma says, quoting Manx.

"Yes, pods. Maybe that's what they call the kawa. Energy pods or something. If they're out here looking already, maybe that means they know a kawa is close? Then we could just get it and . . . and . . ."

"And what?" Alma says.

"I don't know! Fix things! Let Albatur drag his deformed hide out into space. Get this over with!"

Surprisingly, it's Rondo's hand that wraps itself around my bicep and tugs me to a stop.

"This isn't much of a plan," he says, his brown eyes serious.

"You're making a lot of assumptions about the finders and what they're doing. If they were even close to finding the kawa they need, your dad wouldn't have broken you out of the labs and sent you looking for it."

"What else would they be looking for?"

"The ship's power cell," he offers. "They always said it had been damaged in the crash, but your dad said it was lost."

"Well, to be fair, based on what her dad said, the power cell *is* a kawa. But that makes no sense, so . . ."

"We need to go to Mbekenkanush," Rondo says, pulling me again when I try to continue down the path.

"He's right, O," Alma says. "We can see what your grandmother meant about the eyenu, and then think of a strategy from there."

"No," I say, pulling away. The half plan solidifies in my mind, and it doesn't include going back to the city. "No. Don't you see? I was in the Zoo for days. My nana said it may take a few days for the Faloii to gather the group that's going to the Isii. That means they could already be on their way! Or worse. If we go back to Mbekenkanush, we may not be allowed to leave."

I turn to move again, but Rondo catches at me once more.

"So we're doing what? Going to the *Vagantur*? A shipwreck?"

I jerk away one more time, fixing him with an angry glare. Something inside me feels like it's being drawn into two halves: the half that is attached to N'Terra and the half that is part of

Faloiv. Something about being immersed in the jungle again makes the latter half grow and pulse. This isn't the time for N'Terran indecision and inaction. The jungle is making moves and we need to do the same thing. Rondo seems to feel my resolution and takes a step back, letting his hand drop. It makes my heart squeeze but I look away.

"My dad said that if we had questions about the kawa, to ask Captain Williams," I say.

"Octavia," Alma says, exasperated. "No offense, but your father was being a sarcastic ass. How are we supposed to ask a dead woman anything?"

"I don't know," I say, finally moving back down the path without being stopped. "Maybe she's not even dead? We thought the hundred were dead, and they're all living in Mbekenkanush. Either way, there are too many things pointing me toward the ship right now, so that's where I'm going."

"At least get off the path." Rondo sighs. "If Manx and her goons were on this trail, then anybody else could be too."

His logic is a needle through the thick skin of my insistence, but I pause briefly before diving into the jungle once more, ducking under limbs and mossy branches, leaving Alma and Rondo to scramble after me. The only sound I hear is our own breathing and the noises of the jungle, birds calling far above in the trees that seem to have no tops. And, of course, beneath it all, the pulse of Faloiv in the Artery. Has it always been this loud? Has it always been this . . . on edge?

"It gets thinner up ahead," Alma says from just behind me. Despite her protestations, I can sense the eagerness in her voice. Alma, who had always been the one obsessing over the past, cataloging old words from the Origin Planet, will finally get to see the ship that had brought our parents and grandparents here. Her curiosity, contained only by the insistent ignorance of the whitecoats she was asking, is blooming into hope. I feel it too, but it's a different hope, the hope of the syca and the ogwe: I hope to find the answer that will take the plague out of the parasite.

She and I reach the edge of the clearing at the same time, the sound of Rondo's feet in the leaves drawing up behind.

"Stars," Alma whispers, her voice quivering. "Wow."

Why do I feel so nervous? As if laying eyes on the ship will confirm something, or contradict it. As if my brain doesn't quite trust that what I'm about to see is a ship; as if what might be revealed is in fact one of Albatur's beasts, the thing that carried us here just one more organism capable of murder.

But it is a ship.

"It's . . . ," I say.

"It's real," Rondo says. Maybe we've been carrying the doubt all our lives; the inability to fathom a time before Faloiv, a past that actually existed somewhere else. But this is proof.

The *Vagantur* is long, easily longer than the span of the Mammalian Compound, excluding the commune. It rears up high from the ground, white-gray but nearly buried under the embrace of many green and brown vines and mosses, struggling to remain separate from the planet that it had made its final landing upon. It tapers closer to the hull, a rounded nose that saw most of the damage from the crash, scorch marks still apparent even under the wear of four decades. Toward the tail of the ship it widens, wedge shaped, its massive body streaked brown from the rains of Faloiv, perhaps trying to wash this stubborn lump of space matter away. But here it sits. I stare at it, openmouthed, wondering where in its shell the power cell existed: Is its cell as enormous as the ship itself, or would it be a small thing to behold, a surprise for the person sent in to repair it? And where had it gone? Where is the part of this machine that makes the whole organism tick, the thing that is causing bloodshed on the planet that's my home?

Then I see the guards.

"See, this is what I'm talking about," Rondo hisses, seeing them at the same time. "There's two dozen people out there, Octavia! This is such a bad place to be right now."

I can't disagree.

The people that roam around the clearing aren't exactly guards, or even finders like Manx and her cronies. They wear the gray suits I'm used to seeing in N'Terra, but they're not patrolling, despite the buzzguns slung down each of their backs. There are white tents set up all over the area, long like the Worms of N'Terra with transparent flaps on all sides. The people in gray suits comb the clearing, baskets and tools in hand, peering down at the ground, which is still mostly rock and soil since the *Vagantur* plowed through. The place where humans landed on Faloiv is a scar on the planet's face.

"What are they looking for?" I whisper.

"The pods?" Alma says. We're all crouching. "Surely in the years since the crash people have already searched this area for them."

"Maybe," Rondo says quietly, and even though he doesn't offer any other words, I can tell his brain is ticking away, weighing new theories. "Manx said salvaging. To repair the ship. They must need more than power: the shell itself needs to be fixed. I mean, look at it."

He's right: the nose of the vessel gapes with various holes. Daylight shines through several from the other side.

"There are so many people out here," Alma says. "I wonder if this is what most of the finders do. Come out here and fiddle with the ship instead of looking for new specimens."

"I wouldn't be surprised." I nod. "Especially now that it seems Albatur isn't pretending to care about anything except his goal of leaving Faloiv. They probably don't even care about discovering new species now. They have what they need to exploit the ones they do know about."

Rondo makes a sound of disgust. No words necessary. But then he points.

"That's the guy that put me on house arrest," he says, gesturing at a tall graysuit with a square jaw and reddish hair. He stands near what looks like an entrance to the ship, talking on his comm and looking at his slate.

"I know him," I whisper. "He was the one who arrested my mother and Dr. Espada. I think he's in charge. He seemed like it that day."

"He looks so young," Alma says.

"Impressionable," Rondo mutters.

The young man is oblivious to our presence, eyeing his slate, shielding its screen from the glare of sun. Then he's slipping it into his belt and speaking into the comm, squinting.

"We should try to get his slate," I whisper.

"His slate?"

"Yeah," I say, staring at the graysuit so hard my eyes burn. "What we need is information. If we know more about the kawa, or the power cell or whatever, then maybe we can go back to Mbekenkanush with something worth offering them. So if they *are* about to turn Faloiv against humans, we can give them a reason to protect . . . you know . . . some of us."

"Bold," Alma says, pursing her lips. "Very bold."

I expect Rondo to argue, but when I glance at him, he's staring at the graysuit with his jaw set, saying nothing. He agrees but he doesn't want to admit it. It gives me a rush of brassy courage.

"Okay," I say. "Alma, let's do it. I'll create a diversion, and you snatch it from his belt. Rondo, you stay here."

I'm punishing him and I don't know why. Maybe I'm

punishing N'Terra, that place I had once loved so fiercely. Rondo is the last person to blame for my loss of it, but my grief is so cold it feels hot. I don't give myself any more time to think about it. I grab Alma's wrist and tow her out into the clearing.

Our path is laid out clearly ahead. Between the *Vagantur* and us is a boulder—or maybe a piece of wreckage from the ship—that will be large enough to hide us until we make our next move. Dragging Alma with me, I dash toward it and as soon as its shadow touches my toes, dive down behind it. Alma collapses next to me, panting.

"Not your best plan," she says. From the trees at our back, I can make out the sound of Rondo's curses, under his breath and barely reaching our ears.

By the ship, the graysuit has put his comm away. The slate remains on his belt, but for how long? No time to come up with a better plan. The time is now.

"Go," I whisper.

All my muscles are clenched as if synced with Alma's, so when she sprints, my whole body jerks. I realize too late that I've already messed it up. I'm supposed to be the diversion.

I step out from behind the boulder, ready to let the graysuit see me, to allow Alma some time to either get the slate or get away. But he's turned away, facing the tail of the ship, eyeing the progress of the many graysuits working in the clearing. Alma approaches him from behind, miraculously unnoticed.

I throw myself back behind the boulder before I draw the

attention of anyone else I hadn't included in our plan. I peep my head around the edge of my hiding place, watching as Alma creeps up behind our target, her hand outstretched for his waistband.

My heart has either stopped or it's beating so fast that its rhythm is undetectable. The graysuit stands, hands on hips, unaware of Alma at his back. Her hand pauses midair, unsure if she should take the slate or not. I know she's thinking the same thing as I am: Could our luck possibly be this good?

She slides the slate from its holster on his hip, an inch at a time. I taste the tiniest tinge of blood—I'm gnawing the side of my tongue, my jaws a vise.

And then she has it. It's in her hand, black and sleek in the bright sun, the graysuit oblivious. She flashes her teeth in a self-congratulatory smile, and she's moving to slide the slate inside her skinsuit's inner pocket when the graysuit moves to turn around.

Alma's reflexes are superhuman. She doesn't pause or falter. His muscles have barely twitched when she's diving into the open space of the *Vagantur*, which from my vantage point behind the boulder I can now see is a door. When the graysuit has turned around, Alma is gone, a phantom.

But two more graysuits are approaching. They are ducking under the half-repaired body of the ship, hailing the graysuit we'd made our target. They hadn't seen Alma, but if they go inside the *Vagantur* right now, they will.

Don't go in, I chant silently. *Don't go in.*

"Nothing to see on the other side," one of them says, his voice carrying over to where I hide. "If I didn't know better, I'd say we have too many buzzguns."

"Never too many buzzguns," the graysuit with the square jaw says with a smile. He still hasn't noticed he's missing his slate.

"Still," the first one says, "I'm going to grab an MX instead of an MZ. The MZs are so damn heavy to be hauling around for no reason."

And then he's angling his body toward the door. His partner moves to follow, and a breath later they're disappearing inside the ship. The slateless captain shouts something obscene at their backs that makes them laugh and then he strides away, down toward the tail.

And then I'm running. I can't be as fast as I feel right now—it must be adrenaline lying to me, assuring me of escape. But maybe I am this fast, urgency adding wings to my feet as I sprint toward the ship, the artifact that brought my family to this place so many years ago. My mother had huddled inside this ship as a child, trying to decide if she was excited or afraid. And now she's dead, her wonder snuffed out by Dr. Albatur's dreams of dominance. No time to think about the past. I reach the door and throw myself inside.

CHAPTER 15

It's familiar and I'm surprised. Inside the mossy husk of the *Vagantur*, a seemingly ancient bone, I'd expected something rudimentary: a wooden version of the facilities we have in N'Terra. But I realize some of it seems to be the same material; much of what I know back home was built with parts of the ship we've salvaged to accomplish what we need to survive.

I stand in what appears to be a sanitation room; the doors, to what might have been an airlock at one point, open on either side to allow traffic in and out of the ship. The walls are smooth, and here the light is good; but beyond, deeper in the ship, there are dim tunnels, shadows where the sunlight can't reach. I imagine the interior filled with holes, broken gaps that we've emptied to excavate the past and drag it up to where we stand in the present. Inside, protected from the eyes of the scavengers in the clearing, I take a moment to gently lay my fingertips on the wall, knowing this material was made on the Origin Planet; and something in my skin calls to it, like my atoms and its atoms recognize each other.

"I saw the bushes moving, but there was nothing there. Hell. There could be an army of them for all we know."

More graysuits. The voices snap me back to reality and I look frantically around me, searching for a place to hide. I don't see Alma, but there's another short hallway connecting to this sanitation room and I dive through its entryway, shoving myself into the first crevice I find, a sort of open closet housing the gray suits the guards wear. I sink backward into the flexible material, willing myself to be invisible.

"Their camouflage gives me the chills," another voice says, closer now, coming from outside. "You don't know if it's animal or one of the people. When you can't see them, it could be anything."

"That's why we needed more time to study the one Dr. Albatur captured. If we could have had more time, we could have figured out how to get through his skin."

They're talking about Adombukar. The knowledge sends heat rushing up to my head, filling me like liquid flame. I feel my qalm suit perceive me, and it does something in its biology, cooling me, trying to keep me alive. It doesn't understand that the heat is rage, that the thing endangering me isn't my heat but the two guards whose footsteps draw nearer and nearer. Or does it? The suit is tickling my throat, a creeping sensation like the legs of many insects making their way across my skin. Higher. Up to my ears, enveloping them. I freeze, not daring to claw at the expanding suit lest I attract the guards.

"We don't need their camouflage. We just need them to ante up with the power cells. We should have known they stole it from us."

My lips are covered.

"I don't know why they want anything we have: they have everything."

"Greedy," his companion says.

My nose. The space around my eyes. I can still breathe, but the air smells like soil, the warm earthy scent of the qalm. I feel every coil of my hair being flattened by the creep of the suit. I am utterly encased. My hands, which I had left bare, are hidden from me. Their shape is all that defines them: my skin has become gray, bluish white—the colors of the guard suits that hang around me, the shadows of the slim closet.

Then the guards are there before me, removing their masks, placing them inside one of the compartments in the closet wall. They stare right at me, continuing their conversation like I am one of the suits.

"We have to be close, with or without it, right?" one says. I can almost count his eyelashes.

"We wouldn't be out here working on the ship if we weren't."

His hand nearly brushes my face as he reaches in, withdrawing another suit. I close my eyes, breathing shallowly. I search for the smell of ogwe trees and it's obscured by metal and sweat, but I find fragments of it, try to inhale the comfort of the pieces as softly as I can.

"Wait, who the hell is that?" one says suddenly, and I can't help it: my eyes snap open, ready to find one of those gloved hands reaching for my throat. But he's squinting down the hall.

"Who?" says the other.

"That girl. Did you see her? She just . . . she was just there."

Stars. They've seen Alma. They're turning away, there's nothing to be done. The sound of them moving down the hall.

"Hey," says one. *"Hey!"*

I rush out of the closet, clawing past the suits. Back out in the short hallway, I catch the last snatch of gray as the two of them disappear around the corner, deeper into the ship. Just two, I think, giving chase, but what I plan to do to subdue them isn't a calculation that exists in my head yet. I just know Alma's getting captured is not an option.

I see her as soon as I turn the corner, her Afro bobbing back and forth as she dashes down the hall. The corridors are wider than I expected but dim. Solar panels have been affixed to the walls—the *Vagantur* still has no power. The guards stampede after her, yelling curses, tripping on the occasional vine that has found its way through the cracks in the hull. She trips too: the slate she'd had clutched in her hand falls and shatters on the floor. My heart sinks, but Alma keeps running, and I dash after them, all of us moving closer to the nose of the ship where crash damage lets in sporadic beams of light.

"There she goes," one of the guards shouts. I put on a last burst of speed, desperate to catch them as they round another corner, veering still closer to the nose of the ship. I can read Alma's logic like a map: she is hoping she can clamber out one of the many gaping holes here toward the front of the *Vagantur*.

They have her cornered. Alma stands at the end of the hall, close to what must be the very front of the ship, her chest heaving. There are three doors around her, but I can't read their signs, obscured by dust.

"You did our work for us," one of the guards is saying, buzzgun aimed squarely at her chest. I stand there frozen behind them, desperately looking for a way to intercede.

"Back up," the other says. The sight of Alma's eyes, wider than I've ever seen them, fills my heart with ice.

"Back . . . *up*," the guard says again when Alma doesn't move. Finally, one shaky step after another, she retreats three paces. The guard aiming the buzzgun uses the weapon to gesture at one of the three doors. "Open it up," he says to his partner.

The door is opened with a wheel, as if it's a cryo chamber. They have them in the Zoo—when opened, a burst of frozen mist escapes with a wheeze. Not so here. The only thing that exits the chamber now is a vague rotten scent, decaying leaves and stale air.

"In," the guard with the buzzgun says. "Until we comm back to N'Terra and figure out what to do with you."

I wish Alma could see me. Every time her eyes flicker over the shoulders of the guards, I pray that she'll catch sight of me, the blur of my camouflage waking before her, but if she notices anything unusual about the sight of the hall, her face doesn't betray it. Both guards outweigh me by one hundred pounds and they're armed. I just have to pray they don't lock the door.

Alma steps hesitantly toward the vault, every pace heavy with dread. The guard who stands waiting makes a sound of impatience and grabs her hard by the arm.

"In," the man says, and drags her the last few feet into the room. As soon as she clears the door, he swings it shut behind her, the clang echoing through the close halls and reverberating in my teeth for the brief moment of silence after the door has closed behind her. And then I hear her screaming.

The guards laugh on cue, and one spins the wheel to latch the door. I have to press myself against the wall, grinding my knuckles into the hard surface, shutting my eyes tight to keep from throwing myself at them in rage. The dry dead smell from my best friend's cell lingers in my nostrils as they go on chuckling.

"It won't hurt her," one says. They're moving back toward me now, and I keep my eyes shut, praying my suit continues to

protect me, that the dim light and the colors of the crisscrossing vines remain my friends.

"Think she's one of them?" the other says. They're close
enough for me to smell their sweat. "One of the traitors who
lives with the aliens?"

"Must be. I don't know how the hell she would've gotten
way out here otherwise."

"Did that look like a N'Terran suit to you?"

"Unlikely."

"It looked like it to me."

"If it was, she stole it. Albatur said there was a break-in from
outside, right? All those specimens that escaped. They probably took more than just animals."

They pass by, and I have to hold the sigh of relief that builds
in my lungs. I have to wait. I have to be patient. The suit knows
it and cools me, gives me extra air, feeding my skin with oxygen. I sense that it has to work harder to do so here inside
the *Vagantur*, where the sweet air of Faloiv is less free. Alma's
screams have quieted. I hear the buzz of her voice but can't
make out the words. Whatever she's saying, she's repeating it
over and over. I focus on the receding sound of the guards'
shoes, and when I can't hear them anymore, I sprint the ten
yards to where Alma has been trapped.

"Alma," I whisper, my mouth nearly kissing the door. "Alma."

She can't hear me. Her voice floats through the door. "Oh,
stars. Oh, stars. Oh, stars . . ."

"*Alma*," I say, as loud as I dare.

A pause.

"Oc-Octavia?"

"Yes, I'm here."

"Oh, stars, O, you have to get me out!" she cries, almost hysterical. "There's a dead body in here."

My hands fly to the wheel latch. It's much heavier and stiffer than I anticipated, and I have to use my strength and weight to turn it. It creaks an inch, the sound like a crack of lightning, rending the still air. I freeze, but all I hear is the shuffle of Alma against the inside of the door, struggling to stay as far away from whatever she saw as possible. I heave on the wheel once more, and it creaks again, though not as loud this time. Another full-body jerk gets it going and then I just have to maintain the momentum, turning the wheel as if steering a massive ship. I turn faster and faster until the bones in my arms are jolted with a sudden stop. The door cracks open.

Alma topples out, gasping for breath.

"It's in the air." She heaves. "I can't breathe it. It's like the air is dead too."

She knows it's me, but when she actually looks up at me, she startles anyway.

"Octavia, oh my . . . how? What is this? Camouflage?"

"It's the suit," I say, reaching down with my blurry arms and trying to yank her to a stand. "It's . . . special."

Alma's mouth opens and closes, and in her eyes I see the

mechanics of her brain whirring. But the logic of it all is too heavy for the moment, and she can only look back into the dark room I've sprung her from.

"Look," she says. "I mean . . . look."

Bones. They gleam out from the folds of old cloth like jewels buried in sand. A hand. A skull. Everything else is obscured. Alma's breath seems to come from the skull itself: I'm fixated on it, the caverns of its eyes seeming to be the source of the chamber's darkness.

I take a step toward it.

"Octavia, we need to get out of here." Alma pants. She rubs her arms, as if the skull's breath had filled the room and sunk in through her skinsuit.

"Hold on." I move into the chamber, and the smell of old death slides over my nostrils like a clammy hand.

The suit on my body isn't alarmed though; no extra burst of oxygen or prickle of warning. It gives me courage and I edge farther into the room.

"Stay just outside," I whisper. "So no one closes us in."

"Obviously," Alma says, but her voice is still thick with dread.

The skeleton is crumpled in a corner of the chamber, and the closer I get the more of its teeth I can count. I realize now that the doorway isn't the only source of light: there are no windows, but the vines outside have begun to force their way in through what looks like a valve of some kind, as delicate as eyelashes but with the force of Faloiv allowing them to muscle in and make cracks where there had been none. How does Albatur think he can make the *Vagantur* space-worthy again? This ship wouldn't get them to the moon, let alone a brand-new galaxy.

There's something glittering there among the bones, a shiny edge that I glimpse through the skeletal fingers of the shrouded hand. I squint, reluctant to move any closer, but the glitter sticks in my eye, holding my gaze.

"Open the door a little wider," I whisper.

"Octavia, we need—"

"Come on, Alma! Quick!"

A creak of metal, and the angle of dim solar panel light from the corridor falls over my back, shining on what had once been a human's body.

"They have something in their hand," I say.

"So what? Let's *go.*"

But it is calling to me. I inch closer, reaching out to gingerly swipe at the dust and grime that have formed a glove of age around the hand. I try to reach the object without touching the bones but even when using two fingers as pincers, it's impossible. I try to ignore the brittle feeling of the skeleton as I reach between the dead thumb and forefinger to withdraw the shining object.

It's a pin, smaller than the space of my palm. Stupidly, I expect the gold pin of the Council: the *Vagantur* surrounded by the round representations of the compounds. But this is something else. The remnants of four letters, caked in grime, worn by age. A circle behind them, a flowing forked design arching across the face of it. Wings on either side, and beneath, one word, which I extend a single finger to clear the dust from. Some letters are missing, too faint to make out after so many years of darkness and dirt. But I can read the word.

"Williams," I breathe.

CHAPTER 16

Alma is at my side in a flash, her dread of the room and its dead smell fallen away like an old skin.

"Captain Williams?" she whispers. "This is her?"

"It has to be." I point. "Look at the wings. She flew the *Vagantur*. I mean, there were others. But she was *the* captain."

"So she *is* dead," Alma says, recalling my father's words. "Shouldn't she have been, you know, cremated?"

I stare at the bones, a sudden anger seizing my tongue. My father had sneered about Captain Williams—mocking a dead woman, and a woman who had saved hundreds of lives no less. At one point I might have cared that he would think me emotional for defending a pile of bones, but that point is long past. Now I can only think about him with the same disdain: a crooked finger on the hand of N'Terra.

"What else is in here?" I cast my eyes around the small dark room, looking for I don't know what. A reason. A clue. Some explanation for why the woman who delivered us safely from the ruin of the Origin Planet would be cast aside in a dark cell.

"Nothing," Alma says. "Just her. Four walls. No windows. Not even a bed."

"This wasn't sleeping quarters," I say, taking a step away. "It's not like this could have been her room and she died in her sleep or something. This makes no sense."

"She was just holding her pin," Alma says, her voice sinking. I've only seen Alma cry a few times, and it's more something you hear than you see: no tears, just a tremble in her voice and her lip. The trembling is here in this room with us now. She echoes me: "This makes no sense."

"How long do you think she's been here?" I whisper. I can't take my eyes off the empty caverns of the skull—the skull of Captain Williams. "Or . . . you know . . . how long was she here, before . . ."

"Before she died," Alma finishes, her jaw shaking. Before I can find words of comfort, her gaze has sharpened, the shine of unfallen tears evaporating to make way for a laser.

"What's that," she demands, and she's elbowing past me, crouching by the wall opposite the body of Captain Williams. There's just enough light let in by the vines and the vault door to make out the presence of a disturbance on the graying *Vagantur* walls. Alma quickly runs a palm over it, then uses her fingertips to search more closely.

"Something scratched in the wall," she says under her breath. "Something . . . words."

She snaps her head around at me. "Octavia, get out of the light!"

I stand there for a moment, confused. Her eyes widen with impatience and one hand shoots out, swiping at the air.

"Move!"

I step sideways, back toward the skeleton. Light falls across the wall, illuminating the back of Alma's head, her face close to whatever she has found.

"She left a message," Alma whispers. "The captain left a message."

"What does it say?" I demand, stepping closer.

"Get out of the light!" she snaps, not looking back. Her fingers move slowly over the shapes. Then she spits.

I move backward, giving her as much light as I can. She's rubbing vigorously, desperately, using her saliva to clear away the grime.

"The dirt has sunk into the letters," she says in wonder. "And . . . blood maybe. Stars."

I keep staring at the skull, transfixed. I'm waiting for Alma to tell me what the wall says. I'm waiting for Captain Williams's empty jagged mouth to tell me what she knew, why she's here. I gaze down at her captain's pin in my open palm like a key to a lock that may not even exist. The floor seems to be made of something softer than real ground: the sensation of sinking into this ship and its many secrets is so vivid I have to look down at my feet to ensure they're not being lost in melted metal. Alma whispers under her breath, the words unintelligible and blurring into a hum. When she reads what's on the wall so that I can hear it, the words might as well be rattling from the silent mouth of Captain Williams.

"'Only one will make it run. Three pieces to return.'"

There is a long moment of silence.

"Three pieces of what?" Alma says.

"Read it again," I whisper.

She repeats herself, but the words still don't make sense. I imagine Captain Williams alone for weeks in this small dank room, before the vines had pried the wall apart and let in the ribbons of light. Darkness. She can't have come here to die on her own. Someone would have found her, cremated her, let her ashes rise to the stars and become part of the galaxy. She was forgotten, purposefully. This square shadow of a room was not the place she chose to rest but the place that had been chosen for her.

"We need to go," Alma says. I hear the disappointment in her voice, that her hero Captain Williams had not had more wisdom to impart.

"She may have lost her mind," I say quietly. I squeeze the pin and let it dig into my palm. "Who knows how long she was here."

"We need to go," Alma repeats.

I crouch, planning to return the pin to the skeletal hand, when Alma stops me.

"Bring the pin."

"Why?"

"We might need it," she says, but I know *we* means her.

I pause, staring down at the empty bone hand. The idea of leaving those fingers void, without the one thing they've clung to for so many years, makes my lip tremble. I tell myself that when everything is figured out, I will come back and get her, and cremate her the way she ought to have been.

"Come on," Alma whispers. She's already out in the corridor, her plan unfolding as I slip the pin into one of the hidden pockets of my suit.

Together we close the vault door, sealing in Captain Williams and the shadowy smell of her tomb.

"Don't tell Rondo that we almost got caught," she says. "He's already going to be super mad that we up and left him in the forest."

"I was going to say the same thing. But we were so close. We almost had the slate."

"Sorry I dropped it," she mumbles, glum.

"Don't apologize," I say quickly so that she doesn't hear my disappointment.

Alma leads us toward what had been the nose of the ship; and as anticipated, there are more holes the closer we get.

Neither of us speaks: the hauntedness of the cell is here in the rest of the ship as well, the breaths of passengers from the Origin Planet lingering like an invisible smoke in the hallways. They had been here. All my life, in N'Terra, the place my people had been born seemed far away, unnecessary to acquaint myself with: a dead place to which I had no connection. It wasn't real. But it is real—or was.

"There has to be a way out," she says, but I hear the dragging of feet in her voice, regretting that she can't stay longer, soaking in everything, looking for clues about the past. She's slowed down, her eyes sweeping the ship around us not for an escape route but for anything, everything. The dust that coats it all is only a thin disguise that she thinks she can wipe away.

I step ahead, quickening my pace. Her longing is contagious and we don't have time for this.

"There," I say, pointing. "Up ahead. There's light."

She says nothing, following me. I sharpen my ears for the sound of the guards, any minute expecting them to appear before us, or for the sound of an alarm wailing through the labyrinth of the ship. This all feels too much like the night we helped Adombukar escape, the night my mother died, and I have to swallow the dread that expands like a wormhole in my throat. Alma wants to stay here inside these dim-lit walls, but I need to be outside as soon as possible and let the sun and the ogwe clear my lungs. They call to me.

The hole in the side of the ship is large enough for us to

escape through—that's not the problem. The problem is the crew of three gray-suited guards on the ground below, milling around with their tools and their covered tents, combing the ground for either parts and pieces they can use to make repairs or for the mysterious pods that Manx calls their mission. They're not directly below, but the sight of two people dropping to the ground from inside the ship is guaranteed to draw their attention. I wonder if they've seen Rondo, if they're on the alert for more of us. I dismiss the possibility that he's been taken captive. Not an option.

"Now what?" Alma mutters.

"I—I don't know," I say.

"This was your plan," she says, and I can tell she's biting back attitude, that she's being gentle with me. It's like a scalpel prodding just under my skin.

"You can be mad," I snap. "You can be mad if you damn well please."

"I know I can," she snaps back. "But what good is it going to do?"

"What good will *any* of this do? You might as well be honest about how you feel!"

"Honest? I think *you* need to be honest, O. Because I don't think you are. Not with yourself. I mean, I want to help Rasimbukar and them too, but your dad has a point. Shouldn't you be thinking about N'Terra? Our families? Why don't we just go back to Mbekenkanush and ask for a kawa? They know you!

Maybe they'll just give it to you and all this will be over!"

"Is that what you think?" I say, feeling breathless. Through the ship's holes, the ground suddenly seems dizzyingly far below. "That we should just go get a kawa because Albatur and those other fools demand it? I don't understand exactly what the kawa are, but I do know they're important. To the Faloii. To Faloiv."

Alma averts her eyes, and I know she's ashamed of what she's said, of what she's about to say.

"I know, but—but if you have to choose a side, you know? Shouldn't it be . . . I don't know . . . ours?"

The fury rises up in me in the form of the smell of syca. I barely recognize my own anger, cloaked as it is in the Artery's different languages. Is it me that's angry or the trees? I open my mouth to rage at her.

"If you think—"

"Octavia, shh!"

"*No*, you started this, so—"

"Octavia, shut up! Look!"

She grabs my shoulder and jerks me toward the hole in the ship wall, pointing at the scene on the ground below. The three gray-suited people who had been combing the dirt are all still, fingers to one ear. They stand frozen, slightly hunched, listening to their comms. Then, as if called by a single whistle, they drop what they're doing and run toward the rear of the *Vagantur*. I lean out of the hole, trying to watch their progress, but they either disappear inside the ship or go around under the tail to the other side.

"This is our chance," Alma says, and throws one leg through the hole, out into the sun.

"Wait." I hold her by the arm. "What if they come back?"

"And what if they come inside? The guards who caught me probably already commed back to N'Terra and told them they found me!"

She's right, but I feel the way the myn feel in the stream, every shadow a lurking predator. Either way carries a threat: ahead and behind.

"Fine," I say. "Let's go."

The side of the *Vagantur* is steeper than I thought. I had imagined us merely climbing out the hole the crash landing had made in the hull and sliding down the body to the ground below. In practice, this is difficult. There are other holes to be wary of, the ship jagged in places where it had met the planet so suddenly.

"No one died in the landing? Captain Williams must have been quite a pilot," Alma mutters.

"I was thinking the same thing."

We're both stalling. I lay my hand on the pocket housing the captain's pin, and once more make a silent promise that I'll put her to rest one day.

"It's the only way," I say, trying to sound more confident than I feel. We might have gone on sitting there indecisively if the sound of shouting from inside the ship hadn't reached our ears.

"Did you hear that?"

"What did they say?"

"It doesn't matter," she says.

She grabs my hand, squeezes it, and pushes off, yanking me with her.

The wind in my ears feels as if we're dropping from a cliff. The momentum immediately tears our hands apart, and I clamp my lips inside my teeth to keep from screaming. Just in front of me, the side of the ship opens in a row of fangs, the exoskeleton torn, and I'm sliding straight toward it. I slam my palms against the ship beneath me, trying to stop, but feel only the blazing heat of the metal, fired by the sun. Still, I manage to shove myself to the right, and I go spinning on the slick surface, careening sideways, continuing my chaotic journey to the ground hip first: the distance feels a mile long. It might be. One of the soles of my N'Terran shoes, rubbery, catches on the *Vagantur*, and spins me again. I tumble downward, the ground getting closer and greener and my own breath thunder in my ears, everything happening quickly and in a series of blurs.

Alma lands before me: I hear her cry out nearby before a breath later tumbling down myself. I land in a heap by a crumpled pile of wreckage, and thank the stars I hadn't landed directly on it, surely impaled. I lie there for a moment, my lungs heaving for air, the sky a rude shade of merry blue in the face of my terror. I try to make myself sit up, but my limbs won't respond. Every part of me seems to be catching its breath. Only my eyes obey, and when they strain upward at the *Vagantur*, they take in first the hole from which we'd leaped, then, beyond, the few observation deck windows from which the passengers of this ship, when airborne, had watched the galaxy passing by. And then, inside those windows, the faces of a dozen guards. If I wasn't already motionless I would have gone still, but I realize quickly that the faces aren't interested in me. Some look at me, but only in passing, their gazes vacating quickly to aim beyond, sweeping the clearing that had become the *Vagantur*'s home. They're looking for something else, and even from here I can read their expressions like slides in Dr. Espada's projector. Fear. Bald, blinding fear.

My limbs come alive.

"Alma," I croak, clambering up from where I'm sprawled. "Alma, something is wrong. They . . . they went inside because there's something out here."

Alma doesn't reply. She lies where she had fallen, about five feet away. I stand fully, swaying slightly, and then move to her side. She's out cold. I don't see any blood, but she must have hit her head in the fall.

"Alma," I cry, shaking her shoulder. "I really, really, really need you to wake up!"

Her eyelids flutter but she doesn't stir. I sweep my eyes over the now-empty clearing. None of the graysuits in sight, and no creature making its way out of the jungle either. But I've learned there are other ways of seeing. Reluctantly, as if opening a door that may suck me out into space, I slowly allow the Artery to spiral open.

It's the silence that terrifies me. As if the invisible mouth of every animal has sealed itself, faded itself away. There is not a sound in the Artery, even when I widen it, curious: not a whisper, not a shade of color. Everyone has gone mute. It can only mean one thing.

I've just lifted Alma's wrists to pull her when the roar shakes the ground beneath my feet. I squeeze my eyes shut but don't let go, trying to fight the tremor that starts in the soles of my feet and forces its way up through my bones. I heave on Alma's hands and begin pulling her toward the jungle. There is no plan, there is no outline: I just know we can't get back into the ship, and we can't stay out here in the open. For all I know I'm moving toward the dirixi, but I have to move. Alma's head is raised from the ground as I pull her along, and all I can do is hope that a jagged rock or a piece of the ship doesn't cut her as I drag her toward the trees. I know very well that we're near death with a dirixi in the vicinity. But if one of us bleeds, death is certain.

I've just reached the tree line when the massive predator emerges from the jungle across the clearing. I glimpse its bulk in my peripheral vision, as tall as a few of the syca. I can't look. I can't let myself. I use every bit of strength to haul my best friend into the cover of the trees and collapse there among the duna, my muscles trembling. Alma makes a groaning sound but still does not wake. I turn my eyes to the dirixi.

It's more terrifying than any Greenhouse projection could have prepared me for. Much of its body blends into the surrounding trees, but it doesn't change like my suit or the Faloii's skin. This is not camouflage. It is pure jungle: deep green with overlapping patches of brown and gray, like shadows woven between foliage, as if the beast had hatched from the forest itself, the vines becoming veins in its tough skin. I can see its teeth from here, the vicious mouth held slightly open as if laughing, as if ready to chuckle while it devours whatever's in its path. It moves smoothly forward on all fours—too smoothly for something that large—but as it passes through the clearing, it rises occasionally to its barbed back legs, pausing and raising its powerful jaws to the sky, scenting whatever in the air has drawn it to this place. There are protrusions around the end of its snout: I can't tell, but from here they resemble tentacles, extending out into the air and swaying every time the dirixi pauses to inhale the smell of blood. Had one of the workers cut themselves? Is that what had drawn it here? I look down again at Alma, anxiously searching for any sign of a wound. Her skinsuit is filthy from our travels from N'Terra, but while she's covered in streaks of brown and green, no blaze of red draws my eye. I rack my brains for whatever other hunting adaptations the dirixi possesses besides that incredible talent for blood, but the sight of the beast in the clearing devours everything in my mind: knowledge, action. The only thing left is fear. I stare numbly out at the dirixi. Perhaps this is another of its skills. A psychic predator as well as a flesh eater.

"Why is the ground shaking," Alma says, her voice groggy. I whirl around to face her and find her pushing up on one elbow, her face screwed up with pain.

"Don't get up too fast," I say, moving to her side. "You hit your head."

She looks past me into the clearing, and, just like that, the foggy barrier between her eyes and full consciousness melts away. Behind me, the dirixi has all four legs on the ground and is snuffling at the base of the *Vagantur*. Even this monster isn't large enough to shift the ship, but I get the feeling that if it decided there was something inside the ship worth eating, even the metal exoskeleton wouldn't keep the teeth out.

Alma makes a sound. She chokes on it.

"I know," I say quickly. "But if we just stay hidden . . . maybe . . ."

The frailty of this small hope crumbles as the leaves directly behind us rattle and crash. Turning my back on the dirixi is like . . . turning your back on a dirixi. But the creature in the clearing is cloned in my mind: suddenly I imagine them all around us, and I find myself clinging to Alma's arm, both of us frozen, our eyes fastened on the place in the trees where the sounds of snapping twigs and crashing undergrowth grow louder.

But it's not a roar that comes next. It's the sound of a voice, addressing someone we can't see.

"Thought you could just ambush me, did you? I don't know how you got out here, kid, but when I get you back to the ship we'll figure out just what's what!"

I see the buzzgun first, emerging from the bushes behind us, and then the person holding it: a gray-suited guard with a facemask, only his angry eyes visible above its top edge. His voice sounds muffled and almost electronic through the mask, but I make out his words clearly as he breaks through the thickest of the undergrowth into the sparser area where Alma and I crouch.

"I know your face," the guard goes on, and he steps clear from the tangle of foliage. "I don't know where I know it from, but I know it. I look forward to getting you in front of Albatur."

He's dragging someone with him, someone with their hands bound in front of them, someone tall and stocky with skin the color of an izinusa.

"Rondo," I cry.

Rondo stumbles out from the undergrowth behind the guard, and they both look as surprised to see Alma and me as we do them. We all stand there staring for a moment, the buzzgun wavering from being pointed at Rondo's ribs, as if the guard can't decide who he needs to threaten to shoot. And then he sees the dirixi beyond us. His face goes through the opposite transition as Alma's had: where there had been sharp clarity a moment before is a fading expression of slackness, disbelief like a concussion that momentarily deadens his mind.

And then Rondo hits him.

With his hands bound together, the blow ends up being a double-fisted strike that connects directly with the guard's nose, the crack of the bone as audible as a breaking branch.

"Oooh," Alma cries, flinching.

The guard crumples, his buzzgun tumbling to the ground. The blast it emits is a combination of a bang and a slash of electricity, the projectile invisible except for the blur of energy that lances up into the trees.

No one moves. Rondo and I lock eyes and then, as if connected to one brain, we slowly turn and look toward the *Vagantur.*

The dirixi has paused, its monstrous head tilted away from the ship; and I glimpse one gargantuan eye, streaked with red and yellow like a vicious, shrunken sun, dart across the clearing, scanning for movement.

"You broke my nose," the guard growls from the ground. He removes one hand from his face, swiping blindly for his buzzgun. With his face only half-covered, the fountain of blood streaming from his nostrils catches my eye like a magnet.

"Oh no," Alma says, then repeats herself. "Oh no . . ."

I hear it before I see it. The shift in the ground as the dirixi rises slowly from all fours to its back two legs, the mammoth snout lifted into the clear blue sky, two cavernous nostrils flexing, the tip of a neon-yellow tongue appearing from between its deep-green lips, scenting the trickle of blood that the breeze carries to it . . .

I'm running before the beast returns its front claws to the ground, Alma on my tail. I shove Rondo back into the trees he had just emerged from, and we're all shouting, but no one's words actually sound like words. Everything is noise. Behind us, the sound of the buzzgun firing again, and just ahead of me a gash appears in a tree trunk from the blast. He's shooting at *us*, the fool! We duck and run, crashing through the trees with our arms guarding our faces against the many thorny vines, Rondo with his hands still bound together. At one point he trips, and unable to catch himself, falls down with a thud, his cry of pain like a stab in my ribs. Alma and I haul him up on either side, and I think I'm babbling about *keep going, keep running*, and *stay with me*, but I have no idea where I'm leading them. There is no blaze of rhohedron, no Dr. Espada telling me where to go. There's not even any Rasimbukar here to rescue me. It's me and Faloiv, the planet a green haze of violence around me, and I can't tell if the ground shaking is the dirixi close behind, jaws open, or if it's just my heartbeat that shakes the whole world.

I suddenly smell water. It invades my brain like a dream, like the scent of ogwe that beckons me when I need to calm down. The water doesn't calm me, but it does tell me something.

"Water," I cry. "Do you smell it?"

"Of *course* not!" Alma shouts.

"Come on, come on," I yell, making sure Rondo is with me. His face is bruised from his fall, but he's not bleeding.

Far behind, I think I hear the guard shout. The dirixi doesn't roar, but maybe it doesn't need to when its prey is so easily conquered. I push the thought out of my mind and focus on the smell of water. The Artery is still empty with the exception of a few small carnivores from above eyeing my consciousness with caution, ensuring I'm not another threat. I sense that they are moving toward the water too—I don't know why, but there's no time for hypotheses.

"There." I point at the dip in the land ahead, my breath ragged. My quadriceps are locking up. We've been running too long, and we're all dehydrated. Closer now, the water doesn't smell like the water we drink in N'Terra, but I forge ahead, the presence of the carnivores in the trees encouraging me. They are hurrying for the same destination, they must be.

I shove through a row of plants with thin fronds as long as I am tall: they droop forward, their tips coming to rest on the surface of the river ahead. They appear to be drinking. I watch, breathless, as one or two seem to have drunk their fill and slowly straighten until they are pointing at the sky. Several then release bubbles, floating upward, transparent with a lavender iridescence.

"I smell it now," Alma says, panting. She looks over her shoulder at the jungle, terror making her eyes huge. "That's . . . that's not water."

"It is," I say, even though I'm not convinced either. But some combination of my nose and the Artery tells me I'm right: it is water, but strange water.

All three of us lurch when three animals drop from the trees nearby. Rondo was busy trying to wriggle out of the rope the guard had bound his wrists with, but now he stands frozen, staring at the creatures who stand beside us on the bank.

"I—I don't know what they are," Alma says quietly, as much to herself as to us. The animals, the same pale purple as the water, are four legged, and the toes on their front feet appear to be webbed. Their fur stands out straight from their bodies in a rugged kind of puff, every bit of them cluttered by various pollen and other tree matter. Their faces, almost flat, bear luminous eyes, perfectly round. We're deeper in the jungle than any finder has gone: the life that surrounds us is as unknown as the lavender water.

The animals don't know what we are either. I sense their curiosity about us as they approach the river's edge, but their urgency overcomes any wonderment. They wade in without caution, violet splashes soaking the bank as the roar of the dirixi reverberates through the trees. It's impossible to tell how close it is, but it's close enough.

"What do we do?" Rondo says. He's succeeded in removing

the bonds from his wrists, and I feel like an idiot for not having helped him.

"I don't know." The carnivores that dropped from the trees haven't waded across as I expected; instead they pause there in the water, the current rocking them gently. But they stay put. They watch the shore with vigilant eyes.

"They're using the water to hide," Alma says quickly. "The dirixi must not be able to swim."

"But . . ."

"They know their predators better than we do!" she cries. "We should do the same thing."

She moves toward the water and I'm biting my lip, unsure about whether or not to follow, when Rondo grabs her arm.

"Wait!" he cries. "Look!"

Something is swarming out of the water, slithering up over the bodies of the three carnivores. Whatever it is, it's a mass of many small creatures: too tiny to make out from where we stand openmouthed on the bank, perceived only as what looks to be a violet slime, stirring the surface of the water where the animals stand otherwise motionless.

Alma stumbles backward away from the river's edge, falling against me and Rondo.

"What is happening?" she cries. "Are they getting eaten?"

The dirixi's roar shatters the air again, and we stand stupidly as all prey must do at some point—there's nowhere to hide. The dirixi is at our back. The river and its infestation of microscopic predators at our front. If the three animals in the water are being eaten alive, then perhaps they are simultaneously rotting too—that must account for the sudden smell that fills the air: a pungent aroma shoves its way into my nose like a fist. It's so powerfully nauseating that I almost forget about the threat of the dirixi. . . . All I can think about is vomiting.

Alma actually does. It hits her suddenly, as if her organs are grabbed by an invisible claw. She doubles over, the force of her nausea choking a groan from her throat. Rondo is leaning against a tree, not yet throwing up but with a twisted face like he could at any moment. And then I see the other animals on the bank.

All of them sick.

There are at least a dozen: carnivores and herbivores alike streaming from the forest, all of them either retching or stumbling to the ground, where they lie heaving. My knees feel weak. I sink down next to Rondo where he slumps, sweating, at the base of the tree. The smell rises in waves . . . from the river. Through watering eyes, I realize I can almost see the smell: a purplish haze surrounds the three carnivores where they still continue to be swarmed by the microscopic creatures in the water. They are the only creatures present who look unbothered by the stench. Underneath us, the ground shakes as the dirixi approaches. I can't bring myself to care: the nausea has robbed me of all ability to plan escape.

"Look at the plants." Alma pants. She has crawled away

from the water's edge and sits shivering next to me. Animals continue to limp out of the jungle, collapsing at the river's edge. Despite the nausea they all seem to be experiencing . . . they move *toward* the water. Not away.

I shift my eyes to the plants Alma indicates, the tall straw-like growths that had blown the lavender bubbles when we first arrived at the river's edge. They appear to be drinking again, their tubular blades drawing purple water up from the river. Then, one by one, they straighten, pointing at the sky before releasing a series of shimmering, noxious bubbles that drift toward the jungle.

The roar of the dirixi fills my ears, and through the haze of sickness, I find myself still staring at all the animals on the bank. They don't run, they don't plunge into the water. They lie there in plain view, the terrifying cracking of trees announcing the arrival of Faloiv's apex predator not enough to scare them into retreat. And even now, when I peek into the Artery, it is empty: every creature present has sealed themselves off. They all stare silently at the jungle with wide eyes and I turn my head to do the same.

The colossal head clears the tree line first, and I'm only twenty feet away. The one eye I can see is an inferno two feet across, with no eyelid to speak of. The teeth are more terrible up close than I could ever have imagined, red at the gums and yellow at the point, still carrying the last shred of a gray uniform. Its shoulders emerge next from the trees, and I take in the beginning of what looks like a crest of spikes down its back but on second glance I find to be trees: not big ones but solid-looking plant life that took up residence along the path of its spine. The dirixi is a planet all its own, a whole ecosystem of terror, and I swear that giant fiery eye lights up when it spots the collection of helpless animals there along the bank of the lavender river. It takes a lurching step forward, the ground shaking.

And then it stops.

The eye narrows, the black nostrils quivering. All along the edge of the water, the straw-like plants release the harmless-looking bubbles from their slender stems, and it might all be beautiful if the dirixi wasn't standing there with its mouth partially open, its monstrous fangs on display. Out from between those teeth slithers the impossibly bright tongue, separated, I see, into three forks, which taste the air hesitantly.

The dirixi makes a sound like a grunt, erupting from the cavern of its long, scaled throat. It shifts the weight from one front leg to the other, giving it an appearance of indecision. The smell is as thick and horrid as ever; I breathe through my mouth but it's almost worse—the stench seems to make the air thicker, and my lungs reject it. Some of the animals on the bank seem to have the same reaction, a variety of furred and scaled chests rising and falling quickly, panting. I feel light-headed, but I can't take my eyes off the dirixi, who hulks there, half in and half out of the forest like an angry landform.

The stalks along the edge of the river release a fresh wave of lavender bubbles, and the only sound I can hear is the ragged grunt of the dirixi, erupting like thunder from its throat. It shambles backward a step or two, a movement that doesn't appear to come naturally to it. The ground trembles, and several smaller trees are cracked in half by its bulk. Out of one of the damaged trees falls a blue-furred mammal I can't identify, and the dirixi snaps it up eagerly, the blue fur gone as quickly as it had appeared. The reptile continues shuffling backward, its nostrils snorting heavily, trying to expel the stench. The rest of us lie there, weak and sick, but the reptile we're all terrified of can't seem to tolerate it: froth gathers at the corners of its hideous mouth, its scaled throat convulsing, fighting to keep down the animal it just devoured.

None of us moves, human or animal. The bubbles rise silently around us, shiny and innocuous. When the ground has ceased to shake and the rumble of the monster's throat has faded from our ears, I finally lean sideways into the jungle and vomit.

CHAPTER 17

"Mutualism," Alma says when we've recovered. The three nameless carnivores that had waded into the river have climbed out, unharmed. Their coats, still rugged and puffy, are now absent of all the pollen and debris from the jungle that had coated them prior to entering the river. "Their coats must collect stuff from the foliage, and when they go in the water, the microorganisms feed on it. That must produce the smell—a chemical reaction maybe? Whatever it is, the dirixi hates it. *Fascinating.*"

I'm pretending to examine the tall plants that still dip in and out of the river, blowing bubbles. I had thrown up partially on Rondo's shoe, and he said he doesn't care, but how could he not, and it feels so stupid to be embarrassed about something like that after we'd nearly been eaten alive, but

I can't help it. The plants go on releasing their transparent floating orbs, but they, like the rest of the air, seem to have lost their horrendous odor. One by one the animals that had sprawled, heaving, on the bank had righted themselves and returned to the jungle. The three web-footed carnivores return to the trees, and when the last of the creatures have gone, it's just the three of us.

"So what happened to *you* two?" Rondo says, his sarcasm dulled by the fading nausea but still apparent. "Enjoy your little adventure?"

"We found a prison cell," Alma says. "With Captain Williams's skeleton in it."

He raises his eyebrows. "Come again?"

"'Only one will make it run. Three pieces to return,'" she recites. "That's what we found scratched into the wall of her cell. Show him the pin, O."

I withdraw the pin from my pocket and pass it to Rondo, who regards it with his eyes wide. "This is . . . a lot."

"I know," Alma says excitedly. I'm still reeling from our near escape from both the *Vagantur* and the dirixi, but she's already moved on in spite of the bump that has grown on her forehead. She rubs it absentmindedly, her eyes bright.

"We've been on Faloiv for forty years," I say. "Now Albatur gets elected and there's all this stuff about bones and kawa. It makes no sense."

"Whatever this is, it's not sudden," Alma says, taking the

pin from Rondo and examining it more closely. "Look at this situation with Captain Williams. I mean, no one has ever told us how she died. I'm pretty sure I've heard whitecoats say it was old age. That was obviously a lie, so what else have they lied about?"

She's right, of course. I feel distracted. All this about the kawa . . . the looming shadow of war . . . it seems too large. As if I've been handed a single screw and have been asked to build a space shuttle.

"I lost my pack when the guard caught me," Rondo says. He's rubbing his wrists, and I know they'll be bruised from the restraints. I reach out and take one of his hands in mine, rubbing my thumbs gently over the tender skin. "Including my canteen."

He might have been about to say more, but he pauses, eyeing me as I rub his wrist. I almost drop his hand, embarrassed that twenty minutes ago I'd been angry at him for no reason. But his skin is a comfort. I don't know what home is anymore, but maybe it's here in his palm.

"Yeah," I say. "And you guys need water."

"So do you," he says, frowning.

"Yeah, but not like you two. My suit helps me a lot. I wish I could have brought two more."

Alma casts her eye enviously over my body.

"It is amazing," she says. "Rondo, you should have seen her camouflage inside the *Vagantur*. Absolutely incredible."

"I saw it when the dirixi was here," he says. "She was almost invisible."

"Really?" I look down, but my suit has returned to its usual grayish green color of the qalm. "I don't even notice when it does stuff anymore."

Alma withdraws two canteens from her pack and moves to hand one to me, but I pass it to Rondo. The sun on his face reminds me of the first morning I'd walked outside the Paw and found him standing there waiting for the Worm. Warm. Gold illuminating the rich brown of him. I almost can't look.

"Drink."

He hesitates, studying me, but eventually he takes it and drinks deeply. We'd been careful to drink as we walked through the night from N'Terra, but since we'd found the *Vagantur* it had been nothing but running and sweating. They're out here because of me, and I refuse to allow anything to happen to either of them. I let my eyes wander into the jungle, still half expecting the dirixi to emerge. But I find only endless trees. Near the middle of one I spot a collection of twigs and moss, camouflaged in the crook of two branches. A nest.

"So I hate to ask," Alma says, munching on a thin strip of zarum from her pack. "But . . ."

"But what are we going to do about the kawa," I say, turning to her. "I know."

She looks wary, as if prepared for a resurgence of my anger, but I ignore it.

"So I was thinking," I say. "There is definitely more than one kawa on Faloiv. I thought maybe the one Adombukar had in the Zoo was the only one. But then I thought about the sorting room. Remember? On the first day of our internships? The egg Jaquot couldn't touch but I could for some reason?"

"That makes sense." Alma nods. "But it doesn't help us think about where to find them. The finders roam all over; they could have found them anywhere. Although I don't think they've ever been this far out."

"And I don't think they knew what they had," Rondo says. "Otherwise they wouldn't have even put them in the same holding area as actual eggs. It wasn't until after your mom was arrested that your dad had the guards looking for the kawa inside N'Terra. So they must have learned something and have been looking since then."

I still feel distracted. It's like the Artery is full of voices, but none of them are decipherable. Noise from the jungle, quick and impossible to read like the qalm's language.

"What's wrong?" Alma says, pausing her nibbling.

"I don't—nothing. I think throwing up just made me feel weird," I say, avoiding Rondo's eyes. "But we should start moving. Who knows if the guards at the *Vagantur* are going to sweep the jungle looking for us."

"Not likely," Rondo says. "They probably won't leave the ship for hours after seeing the dirixi. But you're right. Which way?"

This was the question I was hoping I would have an answer to before someone asked. I look beyond Rondo to avoid having to speak right away, and my eyes land on the river once more. The movement of the water holds my gaze, and something about it calls to me. Is this the sound that had filled my inner ear? Something about it is familiar. I find myself wandering to its edge.

"The dirixi is gone," Alma calls, but without being able to explain why, I find myself kneeling by the water's edge, and then dipping one hand down into it.

At first I think the buzzing sensation is just shock from how cold the water is—because it *is* shockingly cold. It seems hard to believe that on a planet as hot as Faloiv, anything could be this cold. But when the initial shock wears off, the buzz remains and I find myself smiling: it's pleasant, like reuniting with a friend I haven't seen in a long time.

"What's so funny?" Alma says, moving toward me. She does it hesitantly, as if she can sense that something about what's happening is odd.

"Shh," I say, because just as she's spoken, I hear another kind of voice. It's low and soft, and half hidden by the language of the water. But the river seems to carry it along, bearing it up to my ears. I listen hard, harder than I've ever listened before.

And then I hear it.

Afua.

I shoot my eyes over at Alma and Rondo, but I can tell by

the mystified looks on their faces that they cannot hear what I hear. Somehow, in the river, I hear my grandmother's voice.

Nana, where are you?

I am at the black lake with your grandfather, she says. *Are you all right? We cannot speak long this way.*

I'm okay, I . . .

You went to N'Terra?

I swallow. I wonder if she feels my guilt through this strange connection we have made.

Yes.

The fact that you have found me here tells me you did not find what you hoped to find there.

Her voice seems to travel up my arm. She's too far to connect with in the Artery, but the water seems to act as a conductor. My grandfather's words drift back to me: "Water carries words."

No, I didn't. I thought that if they just knew the truth . . .

But they were not interested in truth.

No. No, they weren't.

"Octavia?" Rondo says, looking puzzled.

"Shh," I say again.

Did you see your father?

Yes. He—he told me a lot of stuff. Stuff about Albatur and what they want. They're trying to repair the Vagantur. *They figured out what the kawa do, and my dad wants me to find one for Albatur. He says they only need one and then they can leave.*

I didn't think it was possible for the water to feel colder, but suddenly it does: it jolts up my arm, and it's as if it has transformed into the icy hand of my grandmother herself, gripping me.

There is only one kawa they are allowed and it is the one they came with, Afua. Do not under any circumstances give them that which they did not earn.

For a moment, in her sudden anger, I can almost feel her next to me. But then just as quickly, she's fading. The water seems to be carrying her presence downstream, away from me.

They have left for the Isii, she says, and the rest of the planet's noise seems to strengthen, drowning her out. *You must hurry.*

She says something else, but I can't make it out.

Nana, I say. And then out loud, just in case, "Nana."

The sound of breath and water is all I hear for a moment and then one last word before the river returns to being only a river, my nana's voice carried away: *North.*

I withdraw my hand from the water, shaking off its icy droplets, and turn back to Alma and Rondo, who stand watching me openmouthed.

"Were you . . . were you talking to your grandmother?" Alma says, her strip of zarum forgotten.

"Yes. She . . ." It's too much to explain. "Yes."

Alma stares at me for a moment, then seems to decide to let it go. "And did she . . . have any advice?"

"North," I say. "She says we should go north."

"North?" Rondo repeats. I can only nod.

Alma doesn't look convinced, but she doesn't have an alternative plan—yet—so she merely shrugs. I don't tell her the rest of what my grandmother had said, about not giving N'Terra the kawa. I need to think about it myself for a while. This problem of the kawa—what Albatur wants and what Mbekenkanush might think—feels large and cloudy in my mind, like a fin just breaking the water, beneath which lurks a much larger beast, its anatomy a mystery.

"It would help if we knew the animal that laid the kawa," Alma says. We walk along the river, headed north. We stay in the shade as much as we can. The sun is nearly at the top of the sky, and even in the qalm suit I can feel its intensity.

"I'm not even sure an animal lays them," I say, ducking a branch with scary-looking yellow thorns. "They don't feel like the other eggs. For all I know they come right out of the ground. Maybe there's a cave or something where they can be mined."

"Now there's a hypothesis," Alma says, taking a swig of water from her canteen. Rondo's usually quiet, but he doesn't even seem to be listening to our conversation.

"Drink, Rondo," I say, and when he eventually looks ahead at me, it's as if it takes him a moment to understand what I've said. He nods vaguely and takes a drink from the canteen that had originally been mine, not meeting my eyes again. I turn my head quickly in case the hurt registers on my face—is he still mad about my attitude at the ship? Maybe he's regretting coming with me at all now. He's done so much to help me— getting house arrest in N'Terra and risking his life out here in the jungle. I imagine reality sinking into him like the hush that falls over the trees at the approach of the dirixi, and without meaning to, I imagine myself as the beast. Am I the monster for dragging the two people closest to me out into this mess?

"If only we had a shell of the kawa to use as we go," Alma continues, oblivious to the storm swirling in my head. "We could, at the very least, identify some properties of the shell and see if that helps us track down what kind of ecosystem might have supported it."

"But we don't," I say under my breath. Alma's leading our small group now, sweat making the back of her neck shine. She has no idea where she's going and still she leads. Ordinarily I would smile: typical Alma. But the doubt born in my brain gnaws a path through everything ordinary and a worm of irritability crawls through. Does she think that if we find the kawa, I'm going to give it over to my father? To Albatur? The possibility of having to choose a side emerges again and it makes me sick.

The lavender of the river alongside us eventually fades, the purplish tint of the water getting paler every few minutes. Eventually it runs clear, and I wonder where it leads, what color it turns in two miles, in ten. The pink lake in Mbeken-kanush comes to mind, the black lake where my grandfather spends his time . . . so much on this planet to love and cherish. I'd grown up wanting to see and know every part of it, only to find that Albatur has been plotting—maybe for years—to exploit it. Can a planet hold a grudge? I imagine the water making itself undrinkable, the plants we eat shrinking from our fingers.

"We should stop and refill the canteens," Alma says.

I peer at the water. "It looks clear now," I say. "Just because the color doesn't show any microorganisms doesn't mean they're not there."

"Let's see if the canteen detects anything," she says, swigging the last of her own water.

Scooting down the bank on her butt, she stretches an arm to reach the fast-flowing water. She holds the mouth of the canteen against the current, allowing the water to flow in, and waits for the sensor on the side to indicate whether the liquid inside is drinkable. Rondo and I stand watching from the bank as Alma squints at the vessel. I glance at him, but he's staring off across the river, not making eye contact. The worm of irritation in my brain wriggles.

"Looks mostly safe," Alma says from the bank. "Pale green sensor light. So could be some microbes but nothing that should be too dangerous. Octavia, if they're microscopic organisms, shouldn't you technically be able to communicate with them?"

The question takes me aback. She's right, I guess, but when I listen in the Artery, I sense only the blur of noise that I've come to associate with Faloiv, with specific consciousnesses registering when a nearby animal makes itself known. But in my sudden attention to the Artery, a vague flare catches my attention. A spark of blue from nearby, there and then not there. I'm only starting to sharpen my focus on it when Rondo collapses.

"Stars!" cries Alma, leaping up from the embankment alongside the river. She spills most of what she's gathered in her canteen as she moves toward him, but I'm already at his side.

"Rondo!" I'm just inches above his face, practically screaming at him, and his eyelids flutter but do not open.

"Green wings," he says softly, in a voice I don't recognize as his. "Red stars. I love their eyes."

"What?" Alma says, kneeling at his other side. "What is he talking about?"

"I don't know! Rondo? What's wrong?"

"They disappear when you point," he says. "But I'm invisible. How do they see?"

"He's delirious," Alma says. "He's speaking nonsense!"

I grab his hand and pinch a bit of his skin, watching for how quickly it flattens, searching for signs of dehydration. He needs water, but his skin doesn't respond the way it would if he was severely dehydrated. I grasp his chin and open his mouth slightly, touching the inside of his cheek. It is wet and warm.

"I don't think it's just dehydration," I cry. "Did something bite him?"

I scan his suit with my eyes, searching for any splashes of red.

"The dirixi would be hanging around if he was bleeding," Alma says. "Maybe an adverse reaction to the odor released by the microbes?"

"I don't know!" My heart pounds and my hands shake. "His breath seems shallow. I don't know what to do!"

Without bidding, the vague blue flare appears on the edge of my consciousness again, stronger this time. I ignore it as it fades in and out, as if deciding if it wants to be seen. I grasp Rondo's face in both hands.

"Rondo!" I cry. "Tell me something! What's going on?"

"Like fins," he says.

I hold him tighter, forcing back the tears that burn in the corners of my eyes. His skin under my hands is slick with sweat, perspiration that increases with every second, his breaths almost hollow. *I'm about to watch him die,* I think. Another person I can't bear to lose. I knit my fingers behind his neck to elevate his head, and my finger brushes something stiff.

"What is that?" I murmur.

"What?" Alma snaps. "What is it?"

"Help me turn him over!"

I let his head back down onto the ground as gently as I can and with Alma's help we tilt him onto his side. I yank the neck of his skinsuit down, searching for the thing I had felt. I see the holes in the suit before I find what caused them. Three pinpoints, almost undetectable, through the material. I tear the skinsuit, my heart running away into the jungle, exposing more of his neck.

Spines. Three spines. My lungs constrict with panic at the sight of them. Each of them a quarter of an inch long, reddish where they enter Rondo's skin but a soft blue color out to their tip. They stick out from his neck stiffly like the beginning of tiny trees growing from his body. As if to confirm this, one of them sprouts the smallest, thinnest branch right before my eyes.

"Something . . . something is in him," I whisper. "His neck."

Alma shoulders me aside so she can see. "Stars," she says. "What is that, O? What *is* that?"

"I don't know! What is it?"

"You're the one who wanted to study plants!"

"Ones you *eat*, Alma! Not vicious ones!"

"Your grandma studied plants! She never said anything about this?"

"There are a million plants on this planet, Alma!" I scream.

"Like stars," Rondo murmurs.

"Rondo, hang on," I cry, cupping his face. "I'm going . . . I'm going to figure this out."

"They never taught us this stuff!" Alma says.

"Just wait," I say. "Let me think."

But there's nothing to think of. There is no lesson that correlates with this problem. This is not an animal specimen we can identify from the database of our memories—N'Terra has spent forty years teaching us the wrong things. My head is empty right now because of them, and I suddenly want to burn down every white dome in the settlement. . . .

The blue flash appears in my mind again, this time fully visible. It is a presence that demands my attention.

"What," I cry, lacking the focus to say so internally. "What is this?"

You require antivenin, someone tells me. *The plant from which the quills come provides it at the root.*

I give the blue presence all my attention.

Antivenin, I say. *What plant?*

You will not find it by its name, so I will show you.

Like a phantom, a smell wafts through the Artery, a sharp reminder of my first day in the jungle, when Dr. Espada showed me the image of the rhohedron field. But this is different, the sensation of the plant I'm being shown sharper and more vibrant, its smell as real and present as if it were blossoming right under my nose.

In the hallway of my mind emerges a plant with bluish leaves that taper into points. It grows in a cluster of its kin, the stems thin but sturdy, with a covering of fuzz along the length. The leaves jut out every six inches or so, and at the joint where the leaves connect with the stem grows a beautiful flower: purplish and downy looking, fluffed like the breast of a baby bird. I gather from its smell that it needs shade to live, and my eyes immediately dart to the tree line along which we've been walking.

You see it, then? the presence says. *So unusual.*

"What is it?" Alma cries. "What do you hear?"

"Stay here," I bark, and force myself to leave Rondo's side. I dash back the way we'd come, scanning the edge of the jungle for the bluish leaves.

"Octavia," Alma cries, panic tingeing her voice. "Where are you going? You can't be out here by yourself!"

She's still afraid of the jungle, but I'm not: there's no point. The dirixi is somewhere out there among the trees, but so is the plant that will help Rondo. The presence in the Artery has faded away again, but I don't have time to wonder about who they are. I take in the tangle of flora, searching for the one I'd been shown. It doesn't have an odor the way the rhohedron does, at least nothing that I can pick up in the tunnel, so I have to rely on my eyes. There are so many red plants here! Splashes of yellow, the overwhelming green of everything. I search for the violet blossom. I need violet. Rondo needs violet.

I would have missed it if it hadn't called to me. Not in the tunnel the way an animal would but with its blossom. I've just passed a cluster of plants, the thick green leaves of a rounded bush obscuring the trees behind it. But a small movement catches the corner of my eye, and when I look back I find the violet head of a flower extending up above the layer of the bushes. It's almost as if it's greeting me: it grows before my eyes, stretching up toward the sun periscope-like, the downy fluff of its blossom expanding in the light as if preening.

"There you are," I whisper, and move toward it. The bluish leaves have reached above the bushes that obscure the rest of the plant now as well: it's definitely the plant I had seen in the Artery.

Something snatches at me, sharp and sudden like the snap of teeth. Its origin is obscure, like a bruise I'd awoken to find, unsure of when I got it. I pull up short.

The friendly-looking violet blossom sways atop its bluish stalk in a breeze I don't feel, beckoning me. I don't move, regarding it carefully. Some kind of warning travels from my brain down through the rest of my body, but I can't identify where it's coming from.

Until the quills come out.

The violet flower unsheathes them faster than even my eyes can react—the petals whip back, exposing the quills like a row of fangs. Before I realize what's happened, the quills are buried in the soil mere inches from my feet. The violet blossom looks pleasant and inviting once more, as if it hadn't just shot at me like a tranq gun. I'm so busy watching the flower I almost fail to notice the slow approach of two vines, creeping out of the thick guard of bushes like green spies.

I stumble backward, my mouth dry. The vines reach only the place where the quills had penetrated the ground, and like the hands of an eyeless monster, grope blindly about in the dirt, surprisingly tactile and with a slithering, reptilian quality.

At the root, the voice tells me, but even before I've fully registered what's been said, I find myself leaping forward. I crush the quills under one of my shoes and grasp one vine in each hand.

The plant's reaction is immediate. The vines, initially pliable when I'd first grasped them, stiffen at my touch; the slightly hollow feeling of their insides solidifies into something like muscle, the parent plant realizing its minions require defense. It's as if the vines are the tails of a creature whose body I can't see: they writhe, using considerable strength to drag me toward the bush where the parent plant hides. I'm afraid of more vines, but I'm more afraid of the violet flower, which seems to rear even higher now, as if gazing down at me imperiously. Can it see me? Sense me? The neck of the stem beneath it appears to be rippling upward, and I know somehow that it is drawing up more quills from someplace in its blue body, ready for a second attack.

I yank on the vines with all my strength, even as they seem to thicken in my hands. Not seem to: they *have* thickened. When I first grabbed them, I could close my fingers around each side. Now I feel the strain in my palm as I attempt to keep my grip. But I don't let go. Gritting my teeth, I dig my heels into the ground, the muscles in my back stretching and flexing. I lean all my weight backward, keeping my eye on the violet blossom, which fluffs itself daintily as the throat of its stem ripples upward, preparing more ammunition.

But worse than the fear of being attacked is the odd sensation of understanding that sprouts somewhere inside me—a buzzing language whose words I can't decipher but whose meaning is clear: *you are not prey.* Its confusion is almost amusement: it regards me not as a plant, exactly, but as an ally. It reaches for me, almost apologetic about its assault. It sees me as a child of Faloiv, and it is uncertain about why I'm traveling with what it considers a dangerous species.

Humans.

I choke. Have the Faloii already reached the Isii? In the rush of colors and sensations I am connected to inside the plant, I don't sense any great shift has occurred in its biology. But there's something else . . . something that makes my blood seem to run backward in my veins. A message. A message that the planet itself has begun to pass on its own. *Humans. Danger.* And behind it, a message for me: *Don't you agree?*

It's a silent, green invitation and it yawns over me like the mouth of the jungle itself. A smell, sweet and sharp like torn leaves, invades my nostrils. *Don't you agree?*

Something snaps. I experience a floating sensation in the brief moment that inertia and gravity battle for my body, and then I fly backward, still clutching the vines with both hands, a shower of black soil raining down on me. I land hard on my butt, but the pain I notice isn't a dull ache—it's a sharp stab on my shin. I can't see my own legs: the entire plant lies on top of me, blue stems tangled, leaves overlapping, and, just beyond my reach, the purple blossom, no longer fluffing itself but lying slack against its parent plant.

I've pulled the entire plant out of the ground. I realize there are many purple blossoms just like the one that had watched me like a carnivorous eye. And I realize carnivorous is exactly what it is: below each harmless-looking violet flower is what looks like a slit in the stem. One of them is slightly open as the plant wilts and I can make out two rows of many sharp spines, thicker than the quills the purple blossom had aimed in my direction.

My foot throbs. I slowly allow my hands to let go of the vines and they slip limply through my fingers, falling onto the bluish leaves with a rustle. They've shrunk back down to their original thinness, the muscle died away. I almost feel like vomiting again—the sudden de-escalation of the plant's attack and my rising adrenaline clash somewhere in my guts. And the pain in my foot . . .

I kick weakly at the jumble of stems and blossoms, trying to avoid the areas below the flowers where the mouthlike places are and scrabbling backward away from any remaining danger the plant may mean. When the leaves are cleared away, I can see my feet. The left one has a quill sticking straight out of the shoe. The little spine is so harmless looking by itself; only an inch long, it could be a thorn or a splinter. But it's not. The nausea I noted swirling through my stomach isn't just fear and adrenaline: it's this.

Quickly, the blue presence says. *The root.*

I snatch the quill out of my shoe, expecting a welling of blood to rise. But no red appears, no sign that the quill had even touched my skin. Whatever poison the hostile blue plants offer is subtle and slow: Rondo could have been walking for many minutes before feeling the effects.

Quickly, the voice says again, and I haul myself to my feet. The place where the plant had been nestled amidst the bushes is an empty hole now that I've yanked it from the soil. I stare down at the hole in the soil, some of the smaller adjacent stems still holding on by strings to the dirt—I scan them quickly for purple blossoms, but either they'd all been yanked out or these plants were too young to bloom. I bury my hands in soil.

There's a layer of heat that rises from the dirt, as if a mouth of Faloiv is open and breathes upward. But beneath the top most layer, the soil is cool—I almost sigh in relief as my hands dig. There are many small roots of the plant that give way easily, thin and stiff. It's beneath them that my fingers come in contact with a thicker root, and it feels so much like the vines from before that I flinch from it at first. But it's still and doesn't writhe in my grasp, so I get a tight grip and brace myself to yank once more.

I topple backward again, but this time stagger, catching myself before I fall.

"Octavia," I hear Alma cry from down the path where I'd left her. My heart lurches, imagining Rondo's condition deteriorating while I'm here digging around in the dirt. Meanwhile I feel the poison stirring in my own body: my tongue feels thick and my throat dry. And still in the back of my mind, the green words that hang there, tinged with my guilt: an invitation. A fading thing that sees my friends as prey and wants me to see them as prey too.

"I'm coming," I whisper, pushing the remnants of the feeling away, and eye the root. It's long and thick, lumpy like waji before it's cooked down and mashed, but bright orange. I can't tell which part should be the antivenin, so I take another look at the hole I'd dug in the soil to ensure I'm not missing anything and then just pick up the whole thing. It's heavier than it looks, and I hoist it over my shoulder, turning back down the path to Alma and Rondo.

I try jogging, but after three steps the world around me feels unstable, as if the ground has shifted invisibly under my feet. I slow, noticing the edges of my vision looking shiny. I blink hard and swallow, willing the effects of the toxin to remain still in my blood. Alma is ahead of me on the path, standing when I approach, but the distance between us first stretches and then shrinks before expanding again like elastic. I put a hand out in front of me to steady myself, the root like an anchor on my shoulder.

"What happened?" comes Alma's voice, and I know this must be how Rondo had felt, his tongue heavy in his mouth and the air thick around him.

"I've got the root," I say, but maybe I don't say it, because my ears feel dense, filled with ringing.

Inside, the blue presence tells me in the Artery, but by now it feels like a hallucination. I move toward Alma as if through water, her voice like a blur around my head, not fully entering my brain. Rondo is on the ground at her feet, his eyes cracked, his lips parted. He doesn't move. I stumble onto my knees next to him.

"Inside," I repeat, fumbling with the thick orange root. The half-moons of my fingernails are black with soil, and I use them to tear clumsily at the skin of the root. It peels off but reveals nothing but a paler orange meat. I want to bite it. The desire to use my teeth and gnaw open this strange thing that supposedly holds the key to our survival is strong—I feel like an animal, like fangs could sprout from my mouth. But instead of biting the root, I punch it, frustration and panic making my fists unfeeling. I punch it again, then raise it over my head and slam it against the ground. It has no sound. Nothing in the world does.

I don't hear it, but I feel it: the slackening of the root, the softening of its outer skin. Something shining inside, a version of thirst hatching in me as the sight of it catches my eye like a glimmer of water. Red, glinting like precious stones but soft and wet: a nest of many round seeds, clinging together within a jelly of brilliant crimson.

Eat.

I don't hesitate. I dig my fingers into the core of the root and snatch at the seeds, surprised by their coldness. They stay together in one moist string, and I drop the whole thing into my mouth without taking another breath. The cold somehow intensifies once in my throat, and my body seizes in surprise.

"Octavia, what are you doing?" Alma screams. All our lives we've been told not to taste anything, touch anything, or get too close to anything without having identified it first. Right now the only identification I can rely on is the blue voice.

I fight the cold that expands outward from my throat and grab another handful of the seeds, the red of them like a jewel in my eye. Rondo's lips are already open but I have to squeeze his jaw to make room for the root's guarded prize, and then drop them into his open mouth.

"Sit him up," I wheeze around the cold in my chest. "Sit him up."

Alma obeys, jaw hanging, helping me pull his supine form into a sitting position. I try not to notice how stiff his body feels, refusing to acknowledge the possibility that I'm too late and he's already dead. Refusing to acknowledge that this plant wanted me to be part of that death. I massage his throat to help the seeds go down, but if they behave anything like they did in my body, they don't need help: they slide and dissolve like balls of cold space.

The seeds reach my stomach and my body stiffens like metal. My fingers go rigid and Rondo's shoulder slips out of my grasp, held only by Alma. I stare at my hands, expecting them to transform into something else, into something hard and stony, as if I am about to watch myself become part of the ground I kneel upon. But a moment later I can't see my hands at all: my vision goes orange, like the sun has exploded behind my eyelids. The cold that had been almost overwhelming a moment before seems to swallow itself, leaving behind a burst of heat that sends sweat fleeing from my skin. I sense my qalm suit working diligently to release the extra moisture, and it's as if my very body is evaporating. Sweat flows freely down my face, my nose running, my eyes filling with tears I can't see. The seeds, whatever they are, have done their work and now my body takes its turn in banishing the toxin from my skin.

When the orange glare behind my eyes clears, I see two things. Rondo, his body dripping as if he had just emerged from the river running quietly alongside us. He stares up at the sky, blinking rapidly as what must be the same burst of internal sun clears itself from his vision. And beyond, stepping from the edge of the trees, is Kimbullettican, sitting astride a gwabi.

CHAPTER 18

"You," I say when I find my voice. I'm still kneeling on the ground and don't yet feel stable enough to stand. The gwabi greets me in the Artery—the gwabi I've come to think of as a friend—a smudge of concern for my condition that passes when she realizes the venom has been purged.

Kimbullettican dismounts from the gwabi's back. "You are all right now?" they say. They wear a woven sack on either shoulder, the straps crisscrossing over their narrow chest.

"Y-yes," I stammer, the last of the orange burst clearing from my eyes. "But what are you doing here?"

"I have been following you since the wreckage of your people's vessel," they say, removing first one of the sacks and then the other. "I was forced to hide after the dirixi appeared. I am surprised you knew to approach the water."

"I smelled it," I say. "Something told me I needed to get to it."

Kimbullettican pauses, leveling the endless blackness of their eyes at me. "Hamankush is correct—you are unusual."

Rondo coughs and I turn to where he's attempting to rise. I want to help him up—my arm even jerks as if it's going to do so on its own—but I'm afraid to touch him. I'm afraid that if I touch him again, the vile green voice will beckon to me once more, that something in me will start to see him as prey.

"That was fun," he says when he's standing. He's still blinking the invisible sun from his eyes. They land on Kimbullettican. "Oh. Hello."

"Anoo," Kimbullettican says. "You are all right? Surviving vusabo venom is good but unpleasant."

"He's all right now," Alma interjects. "But is that all they need to do? Swallow those weird berries?"

"Not berries," Kimbullettican corrects. "The antivenin you both consumed is actually a collection of insect eggs that cluster in the root of the plant."

"Insect eggs," Rondo repeats. He looks queasy. I stare down at the red stain the eggs had left on my fingers, which I had scooped so eagerly, thinking them seeds.

"Nonviable, of course," Kimbullettican goes on. "The shell of the root can only be cracked when the insects capable of survival have already left the nest."

"Wait," I say. "So what if the eggs were viable? I wouldn't have been able to open the nest?"

"That is correct."

I stare at them, torn between numbness and anger. "So I dragged out the vusabo plant or whatever and got stabbed by its quills . . . and the antivenin may not even have been accessible?"

"That is correct. The vusabo will reroot itself: do not worry."

"So we might have died. Both of us."

Kimbullettican blinks. "That is correct."

"Well, that's lovely." Alma sighs, exasperated. "Octavia, are you going to introduce us?"

In the Artery, Kimbullettican assesses me, and I know right away that they sense whatever it was that had transpired between me and the vusabo. I feel their internal gaze pass over me with concerned interest, but they give away nothing about whether the subtle shifting I sensed within the plant was the result of Faloii intervention. Still, I close myself off abruptly.

"This is Kimbullettican. They live in Mbekenkanush with Rasimbukar and my grandparents." I pause, looking the Faloii youth up and down. "But what they're doing here I couldn't tell you."

Kimbullettican nods at Alma and Rondo in a friendly way, and then seems to catch the meaning of my words a beat later.

"Doing here? You mean why am I here? I was sent by Rasimbukar."

My heart doesn't know whether it wants to lift or sink. Rasimbukar has become a source of comfort, but I had left

Mbekenkanush under the cover of night because I assumed Rasimbukar and her father—all the Faloii—had decided I was the enemy. If she sent Kimbullettican in pursuit of me, it seems I was correct.

"So she . . . what? Sent you to take me back to Mbekenkanush?" I draw away from them toward Rondo and Alma, ready to flee, even if I don't know how far we would get in this jungle that Kimbullettican knows so well.

Kimbullettican tilts their head, the spots on their forehead clustering with puzzlement.

"Back to Mbekenkanush?"

"Yeah."

"No," they say. "Rasimbukar knew you would return to your people's settlement but could not be sure what you hoped to accomplish there. You were inside longer than she believed you would be, but I waited beyond the walls. When you emerged, I tracked you until you required assistance."

"So you've been spying on us?" Alma says, hands on hips.

Kimbullettican's forehead spots rise and disperse. "Spy? I have been spying you, correct. Is this what you mean?"

"No, it's *not* what I *mean*," Alma says. Her voice is higher than is natural, and I recognize this veneer. Alma doesn't do conflict. This is the tone that emerges when forced to debate in the Greenhouse. She'd rather disprove everyone through twenty pages of meticulous research.

"Alma," I say, and lay a hand on her shoulder. Rondo stands

back, squinting at us all. He has retrieved a canteen from the ground and I'm relieved. I didn't want to have to tell him to keep drinking and risk sounding like Manx, or worse, my father. "Take it easy. Kimbullettican, why did Rasimbukar send you after me?"

"To help you," they say simply.

"To help me do what?"

"She did not specify. But knowing my parent, I can hypothesize."

"Wait," I say. "Rasimbukar is your mother?"

"Yes. She parented both Revollettican and myself."

"I . . . oh. I didn't know that." I pause, afraid to ask. "Is . . . Revollettican okay?"

"You are asking if they are alive?"

"Yes."

"Revollettican lives. I would not be away from Mbekenkanush or my parent otherwise."

Relief opens like a flower in my chest.

"Okay. Good. Well, if you could hypothesize, then, why did Rasimbukar send you after me?"

"Rasimbukar loved your mother," they say. "They were good friends. There are many in Mbekenkanush who do not see the good of your people, but my parent does."

"So she . . . sent you to help me do what?"

"You are a person who does things, she said. I am here to ensure you do not do wrong things."

Alma makes a wide gesture. "Can we get some specifics? Is that an option? Or is there another secret involved?"

"The Faloii have no secrets," Kimbullettican says without emotion, and I realize for the first time that I may know some things they do not. "At least not from each other."

"This is all about power," Alma says. "The people in N'Terra who are responsible for all this madness just want an energy source that will enable the *Vagantur* to leave Faloiv."

"The Elders of Mbekenkanush have told us that this energy source you seek is within our bones."

"Not us," Alma corrects before I can interject about the Solossius. "Dr. Albatur."

"The Elders are having difficulty distinguishing one N'Terran from all of N'Terra," Kimbullettican says. "As there has been no measurable response against this person you speak of."

"We helped an entire laboratory of animals escape!" Alma says, indignant. "And Adombukar!"

"But he and the animals should not have been there at all," Kimbullettican says, as if puzzled by this argument.

"Look," I say, my hands spread out between them. "Kimbullettican. What about the people living in Mbekenkanush? People like my grandparents?"

Kimbullettican turns their eyes on me, their darkness almost soothing under the bright light of the sun.

"Humans," they say. "A different kind from N'Terrans, the Elders believe. It is understood that humans like your grandparents have not contributed to the current state of things. But Faloiv is in a delicate state. Their safety is not guaranteed if the planet should shift and require rebalancing."

"Rebalancing," Rondo says. "What does that mean exactly?"

"I do not know," Kimbullettican says. "I am not an Elder."

"Helpful," Alma mutters, but I say nothing. I'm not an Elder either, but my grandparents both had warned me about the Faloii's journey to the Isii. Does Kimbullettican really not know?

In response to Alma's sarcasm, Kimbullettican's forehead spots drift in puzzlement once more, and I realize that our body language and ways of speaking are probably baffling to them. The humans they have become accustomed to sharing space with in Mbekenkanush have, for the most part, been raised among the Faloii. Their mannerisms have been molded by the people of Mbekenkanush.

"So what's in the bags?" I say.

Kimbullettican's spots rise, and they bare their teeth as they had in Mbekenkanush, the smile at least one thing they have inherited from humans. They turn to the bags they had placed at their feet, opening one, its material releasing a rich planty smell that prickles my nostrils.

"Suits," Kimbullettican says, and withdraws a gathering of gray-green material, slightly iridescent in the sun. "Qalm grown."

Alma brightens instantaneously. "For us?" she says quickly, peering.

"Yes," Kimbullettican says, their spots communicating that they are pleased. "And a third for you, Octavia. Rasimbukar wasn't sure if you would be allowed to keep it upon your exit from N'Terra."

"I almost wasn't," I say, stroking the sleeve of my suit.

"Thank you," Alma says. She's already accepted one of the suits from Kimbullettican's paw-like hands and holds it up to the sun, admiring it. "This is amazing. What all is it capable of?"

"It will hydrate you more efficiently than your home versions can. It will cool you. It will provide a measure of camouflage. These suits were harvested from a relatively old qalm, so they cannot do some of the things one harvested from a younger qalm might offer. But they will do."

Alma has stepped behind a tree trunk to change, her eagerness irrepressible. She calls from behind it: "What's the difference?"

"Many of the older qalms did not encounter human genes until they had reached maturity, some well after. Young qalms were introduced to people like Octavia's grandmother early on in their life cycle, and therefore had absorbed the information necessary to bond with your biology."

"So my suit works for me because the qalm I was sleeping in was comfortable with human biology?" I ask. I extend another of the suits to Rondo, who has mostly been staring at Kimbullettican in awe. When he accepts it, he's still so busy watching them that he begins to change out of his N'Terran suit without caring that he stands in plain sight. Just as his chest emerges from under his suit, the shape of the muscles there surprisingly square, I jerk my eyes away to hear Kimbullettican's response.

"That is correct. There are parts of Faloiv that have become accustomed to human presence and incorporated it into their being. There are other parts that have not."

It's such a simple statement, but it contains shadows.

Alma emerges from behind the syca wearing her new suit, her arms extended to either side. "What do you think? Octavia, this thing is amazing. It's like it's talking to my actual cells. I feel so much cooler. Does everyone in Mbekenkanush wear these?"

"All the humans," Kimbullettican says, then turns their eyes back on me. "I have also brought something from your grandfather."

They reach into the other bag and a second later withdraw what looks like a book: one of the bound books that Jaquot and the other human youth in Mbekenkanush were studying the day I entered their classroom. This one, however, doesn't look as worn as the ones they had pored over, and its spine is much thinner. It, like the bag it had been withdrawn from, gives off a somewhat planty smell.

I take it from Kimbullettican's outstretched hand. I'm a little disappointed at the sight of it: A book? When Kimbullettican said they had a gift from my grandfather, my heart had swelled irrationally with a burst of sudden hope. For the briefest moment I had envisioned him sending me something that might explain it all, a disk filled with the information I need to overthrow Albatur, or even a weapon of some kind he'd been working painstakingly on at the black lake, capable of shutting down the Solossius for good—perhaps that's what I had seen sinking beneath the water. Instead, the object in my hand is barely a book: it's hardly the width of my smallest finger, and rather than being bound at the spine, I find that it's merely a thick piece of material that has been folded and creased to stack like a book.

"What is it?" I say. The outside bears no markings or words.

"I do not know," Kimbullettican says. "I merely agreed to bring it to you."

"Does Rasimbukar know he sent it with you?"

"My parent was present when it was given to me. She agreed that you need it."

Rondo and Alma, both suited and appearing to be enjoying the benefits of their new suits, crowd in on either side of me.

"What's it made of?" Alma says, squinting. "Some type of pressed fiber."

"It smells like a plant," I say, turning it over in my hands. "Some kind of weird paper."

Rondo reaches out to touch it and his fingers brush mine. I withdraw my hand immediately. The thought that had attempted to invade my head—the thought that saw Rondo as prey—still feels too present. It's like some kind of venom has invaded my blood and some irrational part of my brain thinks that touching him will spread the poison.

"It's soft," Rondo says. I can tell by the way he avoids my eyes that he noticed me pulling away. "The paper, I mean. I didn't expect it to be soft."

I unfold it, gently at first until I start to get it uncreased and realize the material is tougher than it appears. It has an oily quality to it, as if it's been treated with a substance to make it more durable. Fully unfolded, it's more than a foot wide, and blank, I think, until the sun comes out from behind a cloud and reveals the ghosts of lettering on the other side.

I flip it over to find a panorama of intricate shapes and lettering, illustrations extending from one edge of the material to the other.

"What is it?" Alma says, leaning in to get a better look. We're quiet for a moment, taking it in. It's like nothing I've ever seen. Images that look like trees almost cover the entire surface of the paper, uniform at first glance but imperfect: some taller, some shorter, the black lines that render them thicker in some places than others. In many places the trees are interrupted by other shapes. Here, an angular shape with hard-lined wings; nearby, many rounded shapes like a nest full of scattered eggs viewed from the sky. I rest a finger against one of these round shapes.

"I think it's a map," I say. "I think . . . this is N'Terra."

"You're right," Rondo says. He's pointing now too, at the angular shape with wings. "That's the *Vagantur*. This is a map of Faloiv."

"All of it?" Alma breathes. She's pulling the map toward her, her eyes darting back and forth across its surface, absorbing it all. "It's . . . it's huge."

Kimbullettican leans in now to look too, and I angle the map toward them.

"We are a small planet, but you have only seen a corner of it. Like this, though, it looks massive."

In the Artery I feel Kimbullettican's pleasure glowing like an open flame. The map in my hands is a vast stretch of unfamiliarity, overwhelming in its scope: mountains here to the north, what looks like an immense waterfall farther east. The trees go on and on, the black lines that make them smudged with age in some places, before they give way to other landmarks: what looks like a long stretch of bones north of Mbekenkanush, one huge tree taking up a clearing the size of the *Vagantur*'s farther north still. But to Kimbullettican, these illustrations must look very different: a map of adoration, representations of places they have lived among and loved for longer than I've been breathing. Every stone is a bone in their body, every tree rooted in their history. I look at the map in my hands. Kimbullettican feels comforted in the tunnel, as if the very sight of their planet laid out in any form is a great gift. I let my eye rest on the shape of the *Vagantur* and wonder if the sight of it is a pain in their heart: this foreign wreck immovable and ugly, a marker for all that has happened at the hands of N'Terrans.

"Is this Mbekenkanush?" Alma says, pointing. Her finger hovers over a cluster of rounded buildings almost like N'Terra, but smaller and north.

"No," I say, holding the map closer to my face. I've found the black lake on the map, a shaded irregular shape, somewhat elliptical. There is a range of mountains to the west. One massive, lonely mountain to the east. Disks indicating lakes and lagoons, one stretch of shadow so large it must be a sea. But the cluster of shapes Alma indicates is north of where the *Vagantur* rests, farther east from the Faloii city. "I don't know what that is. Kimbullettican?"

"You are indicating the archives," they say. "It is where the Faloii keep much of the physical history of our people and this planet."

"The archives," I repeat. "Is that where Hamankush usually is? She's an archivist, right?"

"That is correct," Kimbullettican says, and I note the sinking of their forehead spots, their expression hardening into seriousness. "That is where she will remain until the Elders solve the business of her culpability in the death of the igua."

"I thought that was decided?" I protest, lowering the map. "It wasn't her fault."

"Responsibility is a more complicated matter than fault," Kimbullettican says.

"Wait, what happened?" Rondo says.

"The igua I told you guys about," I say. "The one that the N'Terrans tampered with. When Hamankush left the qalm that night, I thought the Elders had decided she wasn't to blame. But now Kimbullettican is saying she's banished to the archives."

"*Banished* is not an accurate word," Kimbullettican says. "She is being asked to stay there and continue her work until the Elders decide what is next. It is good work. It is her work."

"What does she do there?" Alma says, lifting the map again to stare at the place where the archives are drawn.

"She minds the past," Kimbullettican says.

Alma points at a long winding line, which she has traced from near the site of the *Vagantur*.

"Is this the river we're next to right now?" she asks.

"Yes," Kimbullettican says.

"That means if we go this way," Alma says, still tracing, "then we will end up back at Mbekenkanush."

"Yes."

Alma lifts her eyes to mine. "Well, there we have it then. No need to wander around now. We can get back easily by following this. And with your friend's help," she says, nodding at Kimbullettican.

"No, we're going to the archives," I say, lowering my eyes to the map.

"Come again?"

I'm gazing at the map, the bones of my plan growing flesh. From where we stand by the winding river, the archives lie north.

"Everyone has this idea of what I should do," I say, mostly to myself. "But we're not going to know what to do for the future if we don't know what happened in the past."

"The past?" Alma says. "Remember what your dad said, Octavia. We only have time for the present right now."

A flash of anger stabs through my tongue. Alma used to love learning about the past. But now the N'Terrans' agenda has infected even her: the only part of the past she cares about is getting the *Vagantur* up and running. To give Albatur what he wants, regardless of context. I shake my head, telling myself that if I find what I need to find, I can interrupt the Faloii's journey to the Isii.

"No," I said. "The only way we are going to figure this out is if we figure out the truth. The truth about the *Vagantur*'s power cell. The truth about Captain Williams. All of that."

"The archives hold Faloiv's history," Rondo says carefully. "Not ours."

I bristle. "Ever since the ship landed here, our history and their history have been running parallel. If Hamankush minds the past in the archives, then some of our past will be there too."

I don't tell them that it was Hamankush who had shown me the memory of war. That she had shown me a mysterious cloaked figure. *This is what they do not want you to see.* I don't even know who "they" is at this point, but I'm ready to know.

I stare down at the map, at what must be miles upon miles of Faloiv jungle between where I estimate we stand and where the archives are noted in the thick black ink.

"Are you coming or what?" I say, not daring to meet their eyes. I'm so afraid they'll say no—and just as afraid that they'll say yes. Somehow a distance has sprung up between us: like a long stretch of dry ground, absent of trees and grass. Neither of them says a word, which I know to mean agreement. I sigh.

"This is going to take a long time," I whisper, eyeing the miles and miles of illustrated jungle between us and the archives.

"Not necessarily," Kimbullettican says, reaching one of their large hands toward the map and indicating another elliptical shape surrounded by trees. It is larger than the one I know to be the black lake and surrounded by jagged shapes that I can't identify. "If you wish to go to the archives, there is a more efficient way. But it will require you to trust me."

CHAPTER 19

I had hoped the gwabi would accompany us on our new route, but Kimbullettican had other ideas. Noting that Alma's and Rondo's discarded N'Terran skinsuits were not biodegradable, Kimbullettican had opted to put them in one of the sacks they had brought with them from Mbekenkanush and asked the gwabi to return to the city with the items.

"We could carry them in our packs," Alma had said. "We might need them."

Kimbullettican shook their head. "They will only get in the way. You will need to be agile for what we plan to do."

And so the gwabi had disappeared into the trees, the sack strapped to her sturdy shoulders, flashing me a green splash of farewell in the Artery.

"You are fond of her," Kimbullettican says as they lead us on the route they have planned. "The gwabi."

We walk side by side on a path—a grazing trail, Kimbullet-tican said, of ground-dwelling herbivores.

"Yes. I'm not sure why, but we have . . . an understanding? Maybe because she knew my mother."

Kimbullettican nods, continuing on through the greenery. I'd been half hoping they would offer some wisdom that would explain the bond the gwabi and I seem to share—merely chalk-ing it up to happenstance seems unscientific. Is there always a reason for the way things are, or can some things just *be*?

"This suit is incredible," Alma says from behind me. "Every time I start to sweat it's like the suit drinks it."

"The suit benefits from your biological necessities," Kim-bullettican says. "Your sweat provides it with nutrients."

"More mutualism," Alma says. "Amazing."

"Do you ever wear a skinsuit?" Rondo says, appearing next to me and aiming the question at Kimbullettican.

"No. There is no need."

I glance at Rondo, who looks like he wants to ask more questions but isn't sure how. I think about how different his life would be if he had grown up as an Acclimate and not a greencoat of N'Terra. It's all just chance. I hadn't gotten the opportunity to ask my grandmother about the events that led her to Mbekenkanush and back to my grandfather. I wonder if the archives will have answers to that.

"What's the deal with that tree?" Alma says. She'd continued past Kimbullettican and me, confident in our route, but now she's paused on the path, examining a tree that is unlike any of its neighbors. I don't recognize it at first, its bark slick and shiny, but as we draw nearer I realize it's a syca.

"Strange," I say, joining her.

Kimbullettican stands behind me, the rigidity of their forehead spots a nearly solid line across their brow.

"This tree has sensed a shift in the material of Faloiv," they say. "It is not the first. It will not be the last. This is one of the events I have been tasked with monitoring with the other Faloii youth in Mbekenkanush."

"Faloii youth? How old are you?" Rondo says.

"Irrelevant," I interject. "They age differently than us. But we're similar in terms of maturation."

Kimbullettican's forehead spots spike in amusement before returning to their rigid pattern.

"This is accurate. Look." They point. "Do you see the secretions emerging from the knot?"

We all crane our necks to look, and the light filtering through the canopy above makes the syca's bark dance and sparkle. It's a fluid, oozing from a tree knot so gradually that the movement is almost undetectable. As it surfaces from the inner tree, it moves slowly down the trunk. But the secretions don't wholly obey gravity: I can make out upward movement too as whatever the tree excretes travels along its body to coat the bark.

"What exactly have you been monitoring?" Alma says.

She reaches out to touch the bark of the tree but Kimbullet-tican's hand-paw flashes out in an instant, halting her.

"Do not," they say. "You would find it very uncomfortable."

Alma quickly backs up from the tree and Kimbullettican reaches down to the ground to retrieve a stray stick. It has a few small leaves sprouting from its end, which Kimbullettican extends toward the shiny coating of the syca. Upon contact, the secretion seems to swallow the leaves, sticky-looking fingers oozing out from the coating to draw the stick into and under the layer.

"Would I have gotten stuck?" Alma says nervously.

"Yes. I would have been able to remove you, but it would be painful."

"Stars, Alma, don't touch anything," I mutter, my heart hammering. Something about the slow creep of the secretions feels like stumbling upon bones in open ground.

"So what is causing this? What are you monitoring?" Alma says again.

"Changes in several species' defensive strategies. The behavior of the vusabo plant toward you is another example. It usually preys solely on birds. It feels . . . confused to me."

I don't look at them, instead staring at the secretions oozing from the knot of the syca, the fluid coating the once pale-barked tree, sealing it off from the rest of the planet. Is this what awaits Faloiv if Albatur continues down the path he has chosen? A sealed world? A frightened world? All that is wonderful about this planet seems suddenly to be trembling. I widen the Artery, seeking more of the changes that Kimbullettican speaks of, but while I sense the presence of many consciousnesses around me, the rest of the planet doesn't seem drastically different. I tell myself that this means the Faloii have not yet reached the Isii. That there's still time.

You know about the Isii, Kimbullettican says.

Yes, is all I say. I don't think I'm skilled enough in my Arterian to lie.

This is another reason Rasimbukar sent me to you, they say.

What reason?

If the planet should shift, you will need one of the Faloii with you.

Will it matter?

We are not sure.

"We should keep moving," Alma says, ahead again on the path. Her fear has returned. She has realized what I realized in Mbekenkanush: that wearing the suit does not change the fact that we are human. Before, I had imagined war with the Faloii as the endpoint for humans on Faloiv. . . . Perhaps it will be the planet itself that evicts us.

Kimbullettican moves down the path toward Alma, leaving me and Rondo to follow them. It feels strange to be alone with him now. So much has happened between the moon that watched Rondo kiss me and this sun that watches us now . . .

I wonder if I would even recognize his lips against mine. Every part of me feels new and old at the same time. I think of the way the syca has sealed itself off and wonder if humans do the same thing.

We walk in silence for a moment, our hands swinging near one another's but not touching.

"Back in N'Terra," he says after a moment, "I was afraid you were dead. After I saw you leave the Zoo, my dad showed up. The guards had reported me earlier in the night and he finally came: he was freaking out. Then we saw Dr. Albatur's vasana go toward the entrance to the dome. When I heard your mother was dead . . . I thought you were too."

I don't know if it's the mention of my mother's death or the sadness in Rondo's voice at the thought of mine, but a hole in my chest I've been trying to ignore widens, its edges falling in. And like the syca, I feel myself sealing off. N'Terra. Death. My family: my parents' decisions a swirling black hole that my entire life disappears into, Rondo somewhere on the outside. I clasp my hands so my fingers don't brush his.

"Is that what they told people?" I say.

"No. They pretended Adombukar killed your mom. They said you were missing—made it sound like you were taken. I knew that wasn't true, but I didn't know if you were alive either. . . ."

"Who actually reported you? That ended with you under house arrest?"

"The guard I hit," he says, and when I glance at him I see that his lips are curled sideways. "What a snitch."

"A snitch? What is that?"

He laughs in his low, quiet way. "I don't know, really. My dad said it."

"Don't let Alma hear you. She'll want the etymology of it and a list of related terms."

We let this rest between us, the silence less thorny than it had been before. Still, I keep my distance. When I sneak looks at him, I get the feeling he has just done the same.

"Do you think your parents are worried about you?" I say eventually, just to fill the air.

"Yes," he says. "But I'm pretty sure they're not really buying all of Albatur's propaganda. They heard you were found outside the compound. When they hear that the three of us disappeared, they'll know what's up."

"What about everyone else?" I say. "Do *they* buy the propaganda?"

"Yes."

"Everybody?"

"A lot of people. It all seems so ridiculous. Who would believe that the Faloii invaded our compound out of nowhere, after all this time?"

"Fear makes people stupid," I say, echoing Dr. Espada's words, which feel so long ago they look fuzzy in my mind.

"Alma is always investigating what we brought from the

Origin Planet," he says. "And what we left behind. It seems like the only thing we brought with us is . . . I don't know."

"A penchant for destruction?" I mutter.

He laughs, but I can't make myself look at him, even to enjoy his smile. A few bits of pollen catch on the coils of his hair. His hair is longer since the last time I saw him—he looks taller. Older. Is this how time passes? Years blended into the span of days? A brief absence stretched into a lifetime? Without thinking, I pause, catching him by the elbow, and reach to pluck the pollen from his hair.

He catches my fingers before I can reach him, holding me by the wrist. He looks down to inspect my hand, as if there is something there he might need to remove. Instead, he plants a kiss there in my palm, where the lines of my life meet. And I can't make myself smile.

"I wish there was space in this world for you to be funny," he says. "Maybe one day there will be."

I stare back at him. In the Greenhouse I learned so many words. I know so many facts. My head is filled with knowledge and lately none of it has mattered. How can I tell him I wish there was space in this world for me to feel what he wants me to feel? What I had once felt? When I look in his eyes I see starlight, but how can I tell him that starlight—that otherworldly glow—is beginning to feel like a threat? That the only light I want to feel is the warmth from Faloiv's sun?

"Octavia," he says, that starlight emanating out of him.

He wants me to feel something. He wants me to say it. I look in his eyes, my lips opening, words shimmering there.

"I can't," I say. A meteor. It crashes down between us.

"You . . . can't," he repeats, his lips trying to make sense of it. The shadow that crosses behind his eyes grips my heart in a vise.

"I can't, Rondo," I say, and I'm transported back to my 'wam in the Mammalian Compound, when my mother had said these same words, staring at the portrait of her parents I thought dead. Had she felt like this? The tearing of her skin between two worlds? The anguish when she realized one side was winning?

"It would help if you could tell me exactly what it is you can't do," he says softly. His hands twitch and I remember how they had played the izinusa in the sunshine. I squeeze my eyes shut, against this memory, against the feeling of his lips on my palm.

"There's too much going on," I say. "I feel . . ."

But there's no way to explain. Why do I suddenly feel that, between the language of Faloiv and the language of my people, I speak neither one fluently?

"What is it? You can tell me."

The softness of his words almost bends me. But when I raise my eyes from the ground and let them settle on his face, all I can see is N'Terra.

Alma hails us from farther up the path. She stands looking

back with Kimbullettican, the pair of them far ahead. They hadn't been walking *that* quickly, I think: more evidence that when it comes to Rondo, time shapes itself in unusual ways.

"Guys," Alma calls. Her voice has a note of something I can't identify. Not quite panic. The sound of something shrinking.

"What is it?" I say, quickening my step. After a moment, Rondo follows.

She turns away, gazing ahead at something I can't see. My heartbeat starts to rush.

"You need to see this."

CHAPTER 20

An eye gazes up at us, massive and bluer than anything I've ever seen, green at its edges, peering out from ground far below, at least two hundred feet down. It's as if the flesh of Faloiv has parted to reveal this unblinking iris that stares at the sky, and it's not until fish splash from its surface that I fully realize it's not an actual eye but water.

"Whoa," Rondo mutters. "It's like it just . . . appeared."

"It did," Kimbullettican says. "In a way. This is a result of the work of multukwu. They spent many years tunneling through the bedrock in the groundwater beneath. This is one mouth to their tunnels."

"Multukwu," Alma says. "What class of animal is that?"

"Class?" Kimbullettican says, a number of their forehead spots arching.

"I mean, what kind of animal is a multukwu? What . . . is it?"

"Multukwu are water-dwelling life-forms. They briefly come ashore from time to time, but the groundwater is where they prefer to be."

"What do they look like?" Alma presses.

"You will see very shortly," Kimbullettican says, and turns to me. "It is good that Rasimbukar sent suits for your friends. This will be useful. Are you ready?"

I hesitate. "Ready? For what exactly?"

"For the water."

"We're—we're going in?"

"Of course. I told you I knew a way to the archives that is more efficient. This is it."

"The . . ." I pause. "The water?"

Kimbullettican blinks. "The tunnels, Octavia."

I look down at the water, which seems farther by the second, and then back at them.

"The tunnels . . . under the water?"

"Yes."

"Um . . . Kimbullettican. So, I'm not really sure how to say this. But, you know. We're human. I'm not positive what your biological capabilities are when it comes to oxygen and stuff but . . ."

Kimbullettican's forehead spots lower in confusion, and then rise quickly after, almost vibrating. "You are concerned about breathing underwater," they say, their spots still vibrating, amused.

"I mean, yeah."

"Do not be concerned. You will breathe. With the help of your suit. Now come."

They turn away then, to the edge of the cliff. They don't pause or look back to ensure we will follow. They step out into space as if the ground goes on invisibly before them, so confidently that I almost expect them to float. But they don't, of course. They plunge down, and even though they had stepped out purposefully, I can't contain the gasp that seizes my throat.

"*Stars!*" Alma curses. "Are they serious?"

I crane my neck over the side, down at the perfect blue water, the clear green at the edges like a crystal mined from a forest's heart. I don't hear the splash when Kimbullettican hits the water, but the last of a few rings spread out from where they must have entered.

"Can they breathe underwater?" Rondo says.

"Apparently."

"And we're—we're going too?" Alma says.

"Apparently."

We're quiet for a moment. Alma clutches the straps of her pack, her fingers fiddling up and down their length.

"I mean, we slid down the *Vagantur*," she says, persuading herself. "And it's just water. Animals can swim. We can swim too. It's just a matter of buoyancy, right?"

"Kimbullettican said the suit would help?" I offer.

"And they said it's safe, right?" Rondo says, and he might have been talking to himself too, but he looks at me for confirmation. I don't see any remnants of our conversation. He has buried it in himself, and I feel a mix of guilt and gratitude.

"They wouldn't tell us to go in if it wasn't," I said. "I don't think."

"Stars," Alma mutters. "Are we really about to do this?"

"We are if we want to get to the archives," I say.

"Do we really *need* to go to the archives?" Alma says.

I give her a flat look.

"Okay, okay," she says. "But I am not jumping first."

I take another look down at the water. My blood has caught up to the realization of what I'm about to do, and it begins to thump in my ears.

"On three," I say.

"One," Rondo says. I can feel him reach for my hand and then change his mind.

"Two," I say. Alma moves between us, grabs both our hands, linking us. She squeezes me so hard I wince.

"Three."

I think I hear him say it but don't wait for the word to fully form before I leap out into the nothing. I have no idea if I'm falling or floating. I'm weightless. The thrum of the wind in my ears could be my heartbeat. In that moment of blurring nothingness, I could be bodiless. Just a breath surrounded by many breaths.

Until I hit the water.

It's so cold I scream. I feel the sound rising from somewhere deep beneath my ribs, as if a hook has caught hold of its root and reeled it out into the sunlight. But the sun is gone as I sink beneath the water, deep blue crushing in on my ears and nose. I realize I'd been holding my breath the whole way down, shock freezing my lungs, but the jolt of the frigid water wakes them, and they're burning for air. I claw for the surface, the haze of sun somewhere above like a star signaling my path. When my head breaks through, the remnants of the scream cracks out of my mouth, muffled by water and the ragged intake of breath that my body demands.

"Are you all right?" Kimbullettican says. They're next to me in the water, looking exactly as they do on land except for the fact that their skin has taken on a blue shade. Not camouflage exactly; just a tinge of indigo as if their skin had swallowed a bit of the water and is enjoying holding it there.

"I'm . . . fine," I gasp. My legs and arms thrash somewhat, clawing and kicking at the cold water, every motion spurred by stale instinct.

My only experience with water has been the narrow shower cell in my family's 'wam, brief interactions in which I rinse, getting as clean as I can, before using a disinfecting solution afterward, applied directly to the skin. Never submerged. Never . . . floating. The weightlessness I had felt while falling is nothing compared to this phenomenon. Is this how oscree feel? Unfettered by the ground, the laws of physics somehow defied? I know the science behind swimming. There are many animals that swim. But to feel it for the first time . . . My arms and legs measure their thrashing as I slowly realize that it's not as difficult to stay afloat as my fear would have me believe.

"You will find that it does not require much effort to stay afloat," Kimbullettican says. They bob effortlessly alongside me, the only motion an occasional stroke of their hand-paws through the water. I shoot a glance into the water beneath us but can't see their feet—the water is too deeply blue. "This water is dense with minerals. It makes us buoyant. Your suit contributes as well."

Nearby, Alma is still thrashing. She doesn't realize that she is floating, and as a consequence is sprawled almost facedown across the surface, her chin angled backward to stay out of the water, arms and legs spread wide like an insect.

"Alma," I call. "Relax! You can float."

Rondo, on the other hand, has taken to the water as naturally as Kimbullettican. He floats several feet away from me, turning himself in a slow circle. Like Kimbullettican, he strokes the water every now and then, the look on his face supremely pleased, as if he has discovered a secret in the dense blue water.

"This is . . . unbelievable," he says.

"You get used to the cold," I say. The heat of the day has not faded despite the fact that the sun moved lower in the sky, and after the frigid shock, the water is soothing.

"Speak for yourself," Alma cries. She has managed to move closer to us, but I don't think on purpose. Her thrashing propels her.

"Alma, *relax*!" I repeat.

"This isn't normal," she sputters, spitting out water.

"How could it be abnormal?" Kimbullettican says.

"We don't have fins," Alma says. She has slowed her thrashing, allowing the water's minerals and her suit to let her float. "We don't belong in water."

Kimbullettican says nothing to this, but in the Artery I detect a flash of resentment, red and green. *Without the suit, we don't belong on Faloiv*, I think, and I don't mean for it to reach Kimbullettican, but it does, and their eyes shoot in my direction over the top of the water with an expression I can't read.

"I will call the multukwu now," they say.

At this Alma stops moving entirely except for the occasional kick of her obscured feet. She has remembered that the water is not empty. We had seen the glimmer of fish splashing from the cliff; we are not alone, as one never is on this planet, and the realization sinks into each of us.

I retain my attention in the Artery to observe the way Kimbullettican reaches out to the creatures who made this water formation. As usual I am awed by the fluency of the Faloii's language: they speak to the unseen multukwu in their own tongue, a unique succession of shapes and silent intonations that my brain can't decipher. It's like music, but complicated and played by many instruments at once. At first I think the multukwu have decided to remain silent, but then I sense them appearing at the edge of my consciousness, the radius my mind can reach much smaller than Kimbullettican's.

They're coming from below. I should have guessed this, knowing they are water-dwelling organisms. But the water beneath us is like the galaxy beyond the sky—opaque and unknowable.

"Do you feel them?" Alma says, her voice shivering too.

"Yes. But I don't see them."

We bob there in the water, helpless, and I try to avoid kicking my feet too much. The idea of feeling something where a moment before had been nothing is a sensation I don't want to imagine. I try to mirror Kimbullettican, their lack of concern and the way they seem to enjoy the sun and the water. But my eyes can't help but sweep the still surface, searching for ripples, trying to see a sign of the multukwu before they see us.

"They've got to be pretty big to have created something this large," Rondo says softly.

"They will not harm you," Kimbullettican says, swimming farther away, interested in a floating bit of aquatic plant. But this doesn't feel as reassuring as if Rasimbukar had said it for some reason. Kimbullettican is our age, kind of. What if they're wrong?

"How far away are they?" Alma says. She has floated nearer to me still, and now bobs directly in front of me, her eyes large and serious. "Can you tell? Did they . . ."

She stops, unblinking. I stare back at her, waiting for her to continue, until I realize her eyes aren't exactly on me. She's gazing over my shoulder, rapt.

"Octavia," she says. "Turn around very slowly."

Every muscle in my body wants to start thrashing. But shore is a hundred yards away, and anything born to the water on Faloiv could outswim me in two. I don't even know how to swim—I've only just learned to float. I fight every natural impulse in my body and slowly, slowly maneuver my hands through the water to rotate.

I hadn't even felt the water stir. Nothing to announce the arrival of this new addition to our party. Two large brown eyes stare back at me from a substantial head the size of the gwabi's. They might have been mistaken for having skin and not fur from a distance, but I could reach out and touch the multukwu if I wanted to, and its nearness reveals the fine covering of green-black velvet coating its body. Around its eyes and mouth the hair is a little longer, as if the creature has eyelashes and a mustache. It blinks its round, wet eyes.

"It's . . . it's . . . ," I whisper.

"Adorable," Alma says.

She's right. It is quite possibly the cutest animal I have ever seen in our years of study in the Greenhouse. The globular eyes shine, reflecting my face back to me, and I've never felt the urge to pet a specimen until this moment. A paw-like flipper breaks the surface of the still blue water as the multukwu feeds itself a clump of leafy green algae, and it goes on staring at me with innocent curiosity.

"Aww," Alma says.

"I mean, wow," Rondo says. "That's . . . so cute."

Now I do feel the water around me stir, but only barely. More must be coming up from the depths, I tell myself, but I'm disarmed by how harmless this one seems, and now look around eagerly for more.

"Something is on your back, O," Rondo says, moving closer. "I think it's algae?"

"Get it off," I say, distracted still by the multukwu.

I feel Rondo's hand on my suit, a quick brushing of his fingers, but then he splashes, suddenly frantic to get closer.

"Octavia, something is on your back!"

"What is it?" I say quickly.

"It's a tentacle," Alma cries. "Kimbullettican, do something!"

Kimbullettican has swum farther away in the last several minutes, eating algae like the multukwu. Now they turn their eyes on us from several yards away, their forehead spots clustered with confusion.

"Stars, it's wrapped all the way around you," Alma says, her voice rising into a near scream.

I feel it now. It had been like a whisper at first—a gentle undercurrent of the water, a thicket of algae flowing past. But now there is pressure, not just against my back but around my ribs as well. I'm encircled. Some instinct in me tells me not to panic—that whatever has me in its grasp may tighten if I struggle. But my heartbeat races against the pressure, and my hands rush to my body before I can stop them.

We are in water, so everything already feels wet—but whatever this is somehow feels wetter. The slickness of whatever holds me is pure muscle, like the vines of the violet-bloomed plant in the jungle, but stripped of the fuzz and soil. This is slimy but strong, so strong I can feel that although it has me in its grasp, it could squeeze me much more tightly if it chose to. The fact that I can't see through the dense blue water only makes my blood rush faster through my veins.

The water before me ripples, a hushed sound like a single finger dipping in. I slowly raise my eyes and take in the sight of the multukwu rising farther out of the water, its muscular shoulders all brawny power, the same green-black coating of fur shining wetly outside the water. I have a flash of a fantasy that it will do something about the tentacle that is wrapped around my body: bite it, eat it, save me. But I slowly realize the tentacles are growing from the multukwu's body.

I hear Rondo yell and I know without looking that he has

been wrapped up as well. Alma is thrashing again, but it's no good. The other multukwu appeared like ghosts from the blue deep, as silent as the first one, rising from nowhere. We are outnumbered and certainly no match for their strength. My heartbeat seems to have faded away. Maybe this means I'm dead already, but my fear is gone. I am calm in the face of these two adorable eyes, and I shouldn't be, but what's the point in fighting what is unfightable? We came into the water. This is what we earned.

Why do you not speak? Kimbullettican is there in the Artery but is swimming leisurely back from where they had been enjoying some of the surface algae. *They will be gentler if you ask.*

Ask. My mind is suddenly like the water, their words lightly breaking the surface like a fallen leaf. And just like that I am communicating with the multukwu.

Gently, I think, and the tentacle loosens, the large brown eyes blinking and the powerful jaws continuing to munch their algae unconcernedly.

They are here to take us through, Kimbullettican says. *Why are you afraid?*

Because . . . because . . . I didn't know.

The multukwu are herbivores. You would know this if you were listening.

In the Artery I can sense the subtle tones of Kimbullettican's disapproval.

I don't know why I do that, I tell them. *It's like I forget I can hear them and they can hear me.*

You are too busy being afraid, they say, and turn to the multukwu.

"It's okay," I say to Rondo and Alma. Alma's thrashing has lessened, so I'm assuming the tentacles have loosened around her too. "They—they don't mean any harm."

"It's still holding me," Rondo says, his voice carrying over to me from nearby. "Why is it still holding me?"

"They're going to take us through," I say, echoing Kimbullettican. "Down there."

"I will help you with your suits," Kimbullettican says, and moves toward Alma in the water.

The tentacle around my waist shifts, turning me gently and carefully as if I am merely another strand of algae. The multukwu rotates me so that we are facing one another again and takes this moment to study me with his shiny eyes. They are expressive, I find, almost in the way that Kimbullettican's forehead spots are: between the eyes and the flashes of pink in the Artery, I gather that he is amused by my initial fear.

You surprised me, I try to tell him. *So quiet.*

I don't speak his language, so it's useless, but I try to communicate an apology of sorts. They dismiss it with a wisp of green energy. All forgiven. I sense that he is pleased by the weather he found when he surfaced: the sun has warmed the algae and he continues snacking as Kimbullettican floats near

Alma and the multukwu who she is partnered with, fiddling with the neck of Alma's suit.

"Do not be frightened by what happens next," Kimbullettican says. "It may feel strange."

As if on cue, the upper neck of Alma's suit begins to change: a slight shift at first as the qalm-grown material receives some kind of instruction from Kimbullettican, and then slowly creeps upward.

"Um . . . ," Alma says.

"Relax," I say.

Nothing moves on Alma except her eyes, which dart between Kimbullettican and me and occasionally down to the tentacle of the silent staring multukwu that holds her around the waist. The suit, oblivious to her concern, slowly expands, crawling up her throat, making its way over her chin, and then upward over her nose and eyes. Watching it raises the hairs on the back of my neck, as if I'm watching her being suffocated. But despite her eyes, widening farther still, she doesn't betray any sign of being unable to breathe. Eventually the suit is covering her entire face like a vaguely green transparent mask.

"Can you breathe?" I call.

"Yes," she says, her voice muffled but understandable. "Is this for the water?"

"Correct," Kimbullettican says, moving toward Rondo. "The suit will filter the water as we dive. You will need to breathe shallowly, but you will have no trouble getting oxygen.

Octavia, you can manage your own?"

I hear a shade of my father in their words, a subtle test, and although I don't have any idea how to manage my own, I hear myself saying,"Yes."

My suit is already on my body, so I figure I don't need to do anything special as far as creating a physical connection. Instead, I try to tap into it, the way I have almost without meaning to in the past when it has cooled me, camouflaged me, hydrated me. When I focus, I can feel the thrum of its presence, but like the qalm back in Mbekenkanush, its language is far too complex for me to comprehend. I think back to when I first put it on in the room the qalm had grown for me—how I had preferred that my hands not be covered and the suit had seemed to understand this, leaving my fingers bare. Floating in the water, I try to communicate my need to the suit: the water around me and the breath in my lungs. It doesn't feel ridiculous to be addressing my thoughts to a suit, because I can feel the material's awareness of me. It's like whispering to someone in the dark.

And then the suit begins to creep. It feels like the water lapping my chin at first, but then it rises, up my throat and over my jaw. It covers my ears, and I force myself not to hold my breath when it covers my nose and mouth. By the time it reaches my hairline, I'm breathing through the membrane the suit has created and looking at the world through the transparency of it.

You are ready? Kimbullettican says, finishing with Rondo and turning to me in the water. I nod in response.

"We will go down now," they say out loud for the benefit of Rondo and Alma. Rondo's face has relaxed again, enjoying the water, his chest rising and falling easily under the mask and in the grasp of the multukwu. "I will be with you the entire way."

The multukwu, which has me wrapped in its tentacle, swallows the rest of the algae he had been grazing on and readjusts me in his grip. Another one of his tentacles snakes through the water, and a moment later I have been rotated so that my back is against the animal's belly, both tentacles securing me there as if the multukwu's body is a huge backpack. If anything, he carries me like a front pack. Once he has settled his tentacles, he shoots me a signal or comfort. *Don't worry*, he seems to say. *I'm good at this.*

We sink so fast it's as if we'd been pulled by an invisible chain. I reflexively take a gulp of air, but I don't need it. My suit protects my lungs from the water. But my eyes are useless. The darkness of the water is impenetrable, and as we sink down, down, down, I feel Captain Williams's pin jutting into my leg inside my suit. It's like an echo, a reminder: this must have been what my ancestors might have felt as they disappeared into space for the first time.

CHAPTER 21

I don't know how deep we've gone until the multukwu begin to glow. The light radiates softly at first, like a barely kindled fire, and I blink hard, thinking I might be imagining it after so many minutes of solid, swirling blackness. But the glow emerges from other parts of the deep as well: three or four other bits of light in the dark that get brighter every second. Soon enough I can see my own hands, the many strange plants and formations growing from the floor beneath us, their fronds swaying with the breath of deep water: that's when I realize the glow is coming from the multukwu. And that's when I realize there are many more than the three who carry me, Alma, and Rondo.

Dozens of them, the soft yellowish light emanating from them like floating torches. The deeper we dive, closer to the population of multukwu, the brighter the light is, illuminating the entire area in a dusk-like glow, revealing the bedrock, the bottom of this immense body of water.

Bioluminescence, I think.

Yes, Kimbullettican says. *They make many things. Including light.*

Some of the multukwu are grazing on the swaying plants; others are busying themselves with what I can only assume is tunneling. Their tentacles are prehensile: many of them clutch some kind of tool that they use for the chipping away of bedrock, the dust swelling in slow clouds before gradually sinking to the floor. I want to be sure Alma and Rondo are seeing this, but they're too far on either side of me, and they probably wouldn't be able to hear me anyway.

The Artery feels different down here as we move effortlessly through the water. Harder to grip, somehow, like the connections with other organisms' consciousness are as slippery as the algae-covered stones must be.

Are you there? I say, looking for Kimbullettican.

A moment passes, the bizarre sensation of cold water rushing over my suit-covered face. Then an answer: *Yes, I am nearby. I am using this opportunity to speak with the multukwu. They are digging a new tunnel I was not aware of.*

There's a flash of movement to my right, and when I turn my head I catch sight of Alma waving an arm in my direction. It's hard to tell because of the blur of the transparent mask over her features, but I think she's smiling. Rondo is closer to me and I can definitely make out his teeth through the transparent blur of his suit. Remembering the easy way he had adapted to the water makes me smile too, but it fades almost as soon as it appears on my lips—there is so much more to this world than what we had been exposed to in N'Terra. But this may be the last time anyone human ever witnesses what we are witnessing right now.

The multukwu are sensing a shift as well, comes Kimbulletti-can's presence in the Artery. *Perhaps due to the violence on land. Many small plants at the bottom of the water are retreating into the bedrock. Sealing themselves the way the syca we encountered has done.*

This is what Rasimbukar meant when she said war has grave consequences on Faloiv, I reply.

Yes. They pause, and I finally catch sight of them ahead, moving easily through the water with long powerful strokes of their paw-like hands. *There is a delicate balance on our planet. My people have been responsible for maintaining much of it, but we can't control everything.*

So they're making a new tunnel . . . for what exactly?

I am not entirely sure. I believe they are seeking to make a secure cavern in the event of catastrophe.

Alma and the multukwu who carries her seem to be getting along well, despite their inability to communicate. The multukwu swims in spirals, dipping between tall towers rising from the bedrock that could be either some kind of stationary underwater life or the fossilized remains of them. I get a flash of Alma's smile as they rise again, swimming faster and faster. The powerful back flipper of the multukwu pumps hard, sending waves of bubbles in all directions as they continue their game.

The multukwu carrying Rondo decides to join in the amusement. It whizzes forward, more bubbles exploding. They dip and dart together, weaving in and out of plant clusters as massive as some of the trees on land, moving ever forward on the route that they know intimately. We are making our way through a tunnel, I realize: the endless dense blue above has transitioned into stone, a ceiling that I can make out from the glow provided by the multukwu's bodies. There are many fewer of them here than in the open area we have just left, but the light remains, emanating from various plants and, it seems, massive shells set into the walls of the tunnel.

Do those occur naturally? I ask, pointing at the shells. A piece of algae whizzing by wraps around my finger. I keep it, exploring its texture as we continue swimming.

No. Those were implanted by the multukwu for the benefit of the Faloii. We have acquired many traits that enable us to be comfortable for periods of time under the water, but we still need our eyes in ways they do not.

Fascinating, I say.

I suppose it is.

Another wave of bubbles erupts just ahead as the multukwu carrying Rondo and Alma zoom through a structure appearing to be made of shell but which I quickly realize is the skeleton of a very large organism. They weave in between the bones, zigzagging like children. I catch sight of one of the multukwu's faces and the delight is as apparent in their bright brown eyes as in my friends'. I smile as the group of them disappears through a thick cluster of swaying plants, lost to my eyes as they play tag deeper in the underwater jungle.

When they come racing out, I'm still smiling, assuming the game is still under way. But the glimpse I catch of the multukwu's faces sobers me immediately. Something is wrong. Behind them, among the wave of bubbles in their wake, is an inky black cloud, creeping through the water like a stain.

Kimbullettican doesn't speak—they don't need to. The lance of fear that surges through the Artery is sharp and unmistakable, like a strike of lightning through the dense blue water. I sense the same from the multukwu, confusion and fear braided together and cracking through the tunnel.

Something is wrong, Kimbullettican says, and then I sense them communicating with the three multukwu, the two carrying Rondo and Alma clustered close to us now. Rondo and Alma have already seen whatever there was to be seen: the smiles are robbed from their faces, Rondo gripping the tentacles holding him with both hands. He's trying to say something to me, and Alma is saying something to him. Their voices are too small beneath the mass of the water—I can only read their fear and translate it into my own terror.

More than theirs, it's Kimbullettican's fear that infects me. And then there's the presence that lurks in the tunnel, fading in and out of my mind's reach. It's not a matter of distance. Whatever the presence is, it is testing the Artery, weaving in and out of obscurity, peering in at those in the tunnel before sealing itself off, and then peering in again. It feels restless, unsure. But above all else, it is hungry.

Into the bones, Kimbullettican says, but the multukwu have already decided this is their plan of action and dart forward, still bearing Rondo and Alma, toward the skull of the massive skeleton that had been their recreation area only moments before. They squeeze through what had once been the eye caverns, and the multukwu carrying me is close on their flippers. I cross my arms over my chest as we go through, but the tips of my shoes still brush against the bone, leaving a small cloud of dust that Kimbullettican swims straight through when they enter the skull behind us. We all float in this small dark space, and I try not to think about how this animal died, how we hide where its brain was once housed. I focus on the water beyond our shelter, still glowing beautifully with the light from the shells on the tunnel wall, the floating shadows of algae and other plant matter occasionally stirring my heart into a frenzy. Like Rondo I clutch the tentacles securing me against the body of the multukwu, and the strong muscle feels even stiffer than before. I don't care to widen the Artery to peer inside: if whatever is lurking outside the skull within the cover of the thicket of plants is using the tunnel to track us, I need to be silent in every possible way.

All three multukwu move backward at the same moment the swaying plants part. It's an instinctual synchronization, their bodies becoming muscle as whatever they see fills them with dread. I see nothing. Only the continuous motion of the water through the tunnel, a gently tugging current I had not felt until unmoving within the skull, alerts me to any motion, plants and debris floating along in the same direction as if of their own volition. It's not until a small school of unidentifiable fish pass by our hiding place that I see what they see.

A long, bulky shape darts from the cover of the plants faster than something so large should be able to move. It's dark blue, almost invisible in the water, its flesh dappled all over with a powdering of white-gray speckles. It blends in almost perfectly with the fragments of floating sand and minerals, as if a bit of the ocean had decided to grow muscle and come together to hunt.

Because it is certainly hunting.

It's upon the school of pale red fish before they can scatter, and although many of them escape, many more are locked within the trap of its jaws. I have no idea if it even chews, if it needs to. The teeth are the only thing that don't blend, white as hot stars and serrated. I watch wide-eyed as the teeth are obscured by the deep blue mouth, rendering it invisible once more. But it doesn't appear satisfied; it skulks back and forth, its shape not fully visible due to its camouflage. I can make out four legs and perhaps three fins—it doesn't appear to have eyes.

Until the eyes are on us.

The eyes are almost transparent, milky white with a tinge of pink. Sightless, one might think, if they were not so clearly trained on you. They look right at us. Maybe one of the multukwu had chanced a look in the Artery, perhaps it was Kimbullettican. Perhaps it was me, unschooled and sloppy in the ways of sealing myself off from the network of Faloiv. Whoever had done it, the creature had heard, and it moves toward the skull we hide within with alarming speed. The water does not lend grace to all animals: it scrabbles through the water toward us in a terrifying way, as if its plan is to attack the whole skull. I grip the tentacles holding me even tighter, and I notice them squeeze me back.

The creature gives one last powerful propulsion through the water to reach the skull, extending all four of its legs to grip it. It ends up slightly upside down, its body on the top of the skull and its face and neck peering down, crooked, into the eye we hide within. It won't fit, I tell myself. It's too big. Much bigger than the multukwu, and we had to squeeze into the eye cavern. *Too big*, I tell myself. *We are safe. We are safe.* The madness of it makes my own skull hurt. Based on those teeth, this animal is a carnivore. The multukwu are herbivores. Predators only hunt other predators on Faloiv. It makes no sense that the multukwu should be prey in this moment.

The creature's eyes roll wildly around in its sockets, taking in each of us. The jaws part slightly, revealing the teeth, stark white against the dark flesh, only the tips visible and not fully bared. It seems undecided, one moment shoving its snout toward the skull's opening and the next withdrawing, changing its position on the bone above, rocking the whole thing with its bulk. My feet, I find, can reach the floor of the skull, and I brace them there.

A sound travels through the water. Not a true sound, as I would hear it on land, but the distorted echo of noise, a clicking accompanying it. It's coming from the creature, I'm sure of it. The three multukwu withdraw even farther, nearly pressing against the back of the skull. What is the sound the creature is making? I imagine it hailing an entire group of its kin, calling them to help crack the skull open and consume us. The idea of waiting for the pack of the near-invisible predators to come prowling out of the algae is too much, and I slowly widen the Artery to see if I can learn what its plan is. Perhaps there is a chance of escape. . . .

Kimbullettican is already in the Artery, communicating with the creature. As usual, I can't decipher the language being spoken, but Kimbullettican's calm is legendary. The rows of teeth are mere feet away, and Kimbullettican floats between the creature and the multukwu, having a conversation. They are still afraid—the orange flares of it linger in the Artery like fumes—but they set this aside. I feel the creature too. It is hungry, yes. But there is something more than hunger there. There is confusion, wildness. The scrabbling of the claws on the top of the skull is a reflection of the animal's mind: something is out of order, a puzzle piece out of place.

Has it gone mad? I find myself asking.

Kimbullettican addresses me simultaneously in the tunnel, not breaking their conversation with the creature.

Be silent.

I obey, but I remain in the Artery, still vigilant for the approach of other predators. All around us, the many other consciousnesses I expect to find have gone silent. It is like the effect of the dirixi in the jungle, all surrounding life understanding that those teeth are the great disturbance of order. Is this animal the underwater version of the dirixi? Does such a thing exist? If it did, I don't think Kimbullettican would be as confused as they feel. Meanwhile the panic of the multukwu rattles around in the tunnel like a rain of stones. Herbivores on Faloiv, they have never experienced being hunted.

The creature above us on the skull shifts again, its bulk rocking our hideout even more roughly. It clambers sideways, readjusting its position. It is no longer on top of the skull but on the side of it, looking straight into the eye cavern. It is certainly too large to fit, but I think if it wanted to, it could force its jaws into the opening. Kimbullettican said we would need to breathe shallowly with the suit's mask over our faces—it's almost impossible. My lungs heave against the tentacles that hold me, and behind me the multukwu's heart races against my spine.

And then the beast is leaving. The wild white eyes peer into the shadows of our refuge one more time, rolling in their sockets, its hungry confusion roiling within the Artery, and then turn in a flurry of bubbles, the skull rocking in the wake of its departure. A ripple in the forest of aquatic plants betrays its exit, but only when the plants have returned to the regular gentle sway of the current does Kimbullettican turn to us.

One among you has eaten flesh, they say.

What?

The qararac sensed a predator in this group. He knew the multukwu were not game, and yet his prey drive drove him to pursue them. You are within the Artery, and I believe he would have been able to sense you directly if you had consumed meat. Your friends, however. Not connected to the Artery, but if they have consumed flesh, it will have altered their biology, however slightly. What do you have to say about this?

The zunile. The memory of the odor of what they had served in the Zoo's Atrium emerges from a sealed passage in my mind and fills me with a memory of nausea. Meat, my parents called it. The idea of it twists my stomach, the remembrance of its shape and color, and what it had meant . . .

Kimbullettican's anger builds in the tunnel, making the multukwu shift and sway in the confined space of the skull. They are communicating something I don't understand and Kimbullettican turns their attention to the animals. Through the slight blur of the suit's mask I watch the changing position of Kimbullettican's forehead spots, how they sink and separate, then cluster before separating again. Alma and Rondo look on, their relief at the departure of the qararac mixing with their confusion about what's happening now, the looks of gravity on the faces of both Kimbullettican and me. Had they both eaten zunile? Just one of them?

Your people are a risk, Kimbullettican says finally, turning back to me. *The multukwu do not wish to carry you any farther. They are afraid.*

Are they going to leave us here? I say, panicked. We've already swum so far with their assistance. . . . I can't imagine having to do it alone.

I have convinced them to guide us to the next cavern. They will allow us to surface there and then make their departure.

We didn't know, I say. I try to communicate this to the multukwu as well as Kimbullettican, but the animals are reluctant to accept my intonations. They are confused, afraid. I get the feeling that we have been transformed into parasites in their eyes; they want to be rid of us, and fast.

What if the qararac comes back? I ask Kimbullettican.

I have explained the situation as best as I am able. The sooner we return to land, the better.

I want them to know I'm sorry, I say. *Do they understand that? That we're sorry? We didn't know.*

The outcome is the same, they say, and push off from the skull wall, returning to the vast deep blue of the underwater tunnel. The animals bearing me and my friends follow, the playfulness of before left behind in the bones. Their round bright eyes seem sunken now, and they avoid looking at us. They seal themselves off from me and carry us forward, more quickly than before. We continue on the route, Kimbullettican swimming steadily at the rear of the group, their anger still smoldering in the Artery.

CHAPTER 22

Land feels strange under my feet when we are returned to the surface. My body feels heavier and lighter at the same time, my limbs wobbly. When the mask of the suit withdraws from my face, allowing me to breathe air unassisted again, I have to be careful not to take in too much. Rondo makes himself dizzy breathing too deeply and he sits on a large stone, regaining his bearings as Kimbullettican pauses in the shallows, discussing with the multukwu. I stand nearby, my attention torn between their conversation and the sensation of the sun and my suit simultaneously drying me. It's pleasant, and somehow reminds me of my mother—warm, comforting strokes drawing the chill of the water out of my skin. My shoes, on the other hand, are N'Terran material and feel clammy against my feet.

"What did they say?" I pry when Kimbullettican turns back

to land. Behind them, the multukwu sink quickly into the deep, the dense blue water obscuring their path. A single ring of ripples spreads and then it's as if they were never there at all.

"They are confused about what your people are. They are having trouble differentiating between you and your friends, as you are connected to the Artery and they are not."

"So what happened?" Alma says, appearing next to me. "Was that thing down there after them or us?"

"One of you," I say, turning on her. "Because one of you ate the zunile in N'Terra."

Her mouth falls open and snaps shut in almost one motion. Behind her, from the stone he rests on, Rondo says nothing, staring intensely.

"It was me," she says slowly. "I only had a couple pieces. Before I knew what it was. It was weird. Jaquot was the one who liked it. . . ."

"Jaquot," I say with a groan. "Kimbullettican, do they know he's eaten it in Mbekenkanush?"

"I do not know," they say, and I sense their anger rising again in the tunnel. "If the qararac is sensing the carnivore in you, then it is entirely possible other predators will do the same."

"But we're not carnivores," Alma protests. "We had no idea it was flesh! We grew up eating plants."

"The outcome is the same," Kimbullettican snaps, the same words I have heard multiple times from the Faloii.

I turn away, a flood of tears building in my eyes. There's

no way around this. We do need to leave Faloiv, I think, and the idea of it feels like massive jaws closing around my chest. The multukwu were so beautiful, so wondrous . . . now they will likely never allow humans near their world again. It's like Rondo said, about what our people brought with us from the Origin Planet. Had they brought nothing good? Had they carried only destruction across the galaxy?

"What are we supposed to do?" Alma says. Her jaw is trembling, so I know she wants to cry too. Rondo sits with his hand covering his face.

I'm suddenly so angry at them I can't speak. I clench my fists and inside the tightness of my hand, the feeling of my mother's fingers slipping away rises up. And I'm angry at her too. For her lies. For her silence. At the fact that she's not here. I stare down at the qalm-grown suit, and at the bottom of it, my once-white N'Terran shoes. I glare at them, the only thing on my body still wet besides my hair, which, unbraided, has puffed in the humidity. These shoes. These stupid white shoes. N'Terra had stolen the animals' secrets to make clothing like this: clothing that pales in comparison to that which it was stolen from.

I find myself leaning against one of the many boulders at the edge of the water, tearing at my shoe with my still-pruny fingertips, my anger climbing and climbing.

"Octavia," I hear Alma say, but I ignore her, snatching at the fastenings that keep the shoe on my foot. When it's off, I fling it away from me before starting on the other, my hands shaking with rage.

I throw the other shoe after the first one, and stand there barefoot in the loamy soil, panting. I don't look at Rondo, Alma, and Kimbullettican—I don't know what their faces will say, and I don't want to know. Everything in me feels sodden and inflamed all at once. I try to focus on the feeling of the soil finding its way between my toes, and this momentarily displaces my rage. Under the warm top layer, the dirt is cool and damp, the true form of my grief when it's not stirred by helpless anger. I breathe deeply, sinking into this feeling, and my tears have just begun to prickle again when something else draws my attention, something almost inside me but not quite.

It seems to have crept up into me through my feet, a tingling sensation that is half sharp and half soft. I'd be panicking about the possibility of parasites if my suit didn't suddenly seem to wriggle with energy. I can only stare down at my feet, silently searching for a sign of what this means, while my skin seems to vibrate under the sudden joy of the suit. There's no explanation I can discern: just my bare feet, half submerged in the deep green and black soil, my suit nearly throbbing.

You feel it, Kimbullettican says. They've moved closer from the edge of the water, their spots floating in small circles as they study me with their serious, sparkling eyes.

"What is that?" I whisper, looking back down at my suit. I still see nothing, but the vibrating sensation continues, and my skin feels bright underneath it.

"Interesting," Kimbullettican says. "I do not believe this is a common occurrence with humans."

"What is it?" Alma says, appearing beside them, Rondo a step behind her looking sad.

"You are aware your suits are organic living material," Kimbullettican says. "They gather energy and sustenance from our bodies as well as the sun. But also from the ground, when there is a proper conduit."

"Me," I say. "I am the conduit?"

"Yes. With your foot coverings, there has not been a connection. Or if there has, perhaps you were not paying suitable attention. The suit is grateful for it now."

"Why is it unusual for a human?" Rondo says.

"Not unusual to be a conduit," Kimbullettican says. "We are all channels of energy. But unusual for a human to detect the energy at all. One must be . . . highly sensitive."

I think back to the day my mother was arrested. She had just told me to remove my shoes when the graysuits had arrived. She had known, and that means my nana must too. Does she ever lose track of the lies she's had to tell? Maybe when it had become too much was when she decided to fade into the jungle. After years of mourning her disappearance, I think I understand now. I feel the call of the green breath of Faloiv. I think it might be a relief to answer it.

And then, like a storm that exists only in my bones, the

calling of Faloiv abruptly gets louder. The creeping feeling that I had felt in the soles of my feet intensifies. I hear another voice that's not a voice. I recognize it only vaguely at first: thrumming green energy, a rushing current of language and understanding that feels old and new at the same time. . . .

It is the language of the qalm. Like the rest of the communi-cation I experience in the Artery, it's not words that I hear but a combination of instinct and emotion and understanding that swirls together in a rush of color and silent sound. It calls me. It feels me as a part of the Artery and tells me the same way it tells the rest of Faloiv:

Danger. Humans are nearby.

I'm running before I fully know why. The warning is not for me—it's for the planet, for the animals and the people. But my feet fly down a path, the sound of Kimbullettican and my friends shrinking behind me. The green language guides me, a yellow glow of warning like a beacon ahead. Branches whip my cheeks, and my suit feeds me bursts of more oxygen as it senses my sudden panic. The fear is only dwarfed by the strangeness: I move toward other humans based only on the guides of Faloiv. I can sense the planet, but I can't even sense my own people. Has the Isii decided something? Are humans in danger?

I hear them before I see them. The buzz of many voices, the sound of many feet. Finders? Graysuits from N'Terra scanning the jungle for kawa? I burst through the tree line, my chest heaving, taking in the scene before me without caution, and the first person I see is Jaquot.

"Octavia?" he calls. He stands at the edge of what seems to be a campsite, the numbers of which are hidden by the coming of night. At his side is Joi, and one or two other human youths from the school in Mbekenkanush.

"Jaquot?" I haven't caught my breath and his name comes out like a wheeze. A heartbeat later I hear it shouted from behind me in Alma's voice.

"Jaquot!"

She bursts from the tree line with Rondo and Kimbulletti-can carrying my shoes. We're attracting stares now from other people in the campsite, but Alma ignores them all.

"You're alive," she says to Jaquot, and then looks at me, her eyebrow raised. "But I am not kissing him."

Shortly after, we sit around a glowing orange flower with Jaquot, Joi, and the others. The flower is a mobile plant that generally grows in a drier part of Faloiv, I learn. Kimbullettican tells us it had been watered and thereby gives off heat, which it would ordinarily use to subdue prey. We use it to cook strips of zarum and chunks of hava.

"So every human in Mbekenkanush is here?" I say. I can't eat: I'm focused on the story Jaquot is telling.

"Almost all," he says, chewing. Nothing ever keeps him from enjoying his food. "Your grandparents and a few others stayed behind. Sorry. I know you were probably hoping to see them."

"I was when I saw you," I admit. "But if they're still in the city, that at least means the Faloii haven't turned against humans entirely."

"Turned against?" Joi says. "Why would that be your assumption? They are taking us somewhere where we can be safe. From whatever conflict is to come between Mbeken-kanush and N'Terra."

Her tone irks me, and I almost start to say what I know about the Isii, but Kimbullettican catches me in the Artery.

Do not, they say. *If they do not know, they do not need to know. Not now.*

I bite my tongue. I hate the secrets. Who keeps what from who is too complicated a maze to walk through and I'd rather us speak plainly.

"Look," I snap. "All I'm saying is with everything going on between the N'Terrans and the Faloii, it's only a matter of time until the Faloii end up looking at humans as a problem that needs to be solved."

"N'Terrans," Joi says. "Not humans."

I catch the look of agreement on Alma's face as she roasts a strip of zarum, but she avoids my eyes. Embarrassment floods through me, but it takes me a moment to realize it's not my own. I feel shame, but it's for these people. My people. They don't get it. I don't know if they ever will.

"So where are they taking you?" Rondo says. He, like me, hasn't eaten a bite.

"I'm not sure," Jaquot says. "Somewhere far north. There are mountains there, I hear. They must be hiding us away."

I stare at the orange flower instead of speaking. Through the material of my suit, Captain Williams's pin jabs my leg. The idea that the Faloii are hiding humans from a war their own people instigated make the shame burn even hotter in my stomach.

"Is that why there are Faloii standing guard?" Alma says, and her tone makes me look up. There's a question behind the question, but Jaquot doesn't hear it. He glances around the encampment, around which Faloii stand here and there. They carry no weapons but there's no mistaking their posture: vigilance. Caution.

"It must be," Joi says. "My mother said that the soulless animals the N'Terrans send are for us. To eradicate the humans that betrayed the ship."

"The soulless animals," Alma repeats, but Joi misinterprets it as a question.

"Yes, animals your people have cut off from the heart of Faloiv." There's judgment in her voice. "N'Terra sends them as weapons, first for Octavia's grandparents and now for the rest of us."

Night has fallen. The flower is an orange smudge at the center of our small circle. I silently widen the Artery, trying to see what I can gather, if anything, from the Faloii standing guard. But the only person I find in the tunnel is Kimbullettican.

You do not follow this theory, they say.

Which one?

That my people are protecting yours.

I do. I think you've been protecting us for a long time. I just don't think N'Terra is what you're protecting us from.

They don't ask, but I say it anyway:

The planet is shifting, I say. *I can feel it.*

Perhaps, Kimbullettican says. *But perhaps you too are shifting. What you hear has always been.*

Above, a sudden cacophony of birdcalls makes us all jump—everyone but Kimbullettican. They gaze, spots wide with pleasure, up into the trees, seeing something the rest of us can't. I widen the Artery, and while I can see the crowds of birds clearly—a species I'm not familiar with who greet me excitedly—I can't sense anything that should have caused the sudden screeching.

"Are they afraid?" I ask Kimbullettican. "They don't seem afraid."

"No, not afraid. They are arguing with the trees."

"Sorry?" Alma says.

"It is a friendly argument," Kimbullettican says. "A nightly one. They are asking the syca for light."

"For light?"

"It is their ritual. During the day, the male ikya birds draw the syca's prey to the treetops. In exchange, the syca provide light that they have gathered from the energy of their prey.

The female ikya then use the light to hunt for their own prey at night."

"Symbiotic," Joi says.

"So, the birds and the trees are . . . both carnivores?" Alma says.

"Yes. But they have very specific prey. You have nothing to be afraid of. Not here."

"We always thought it was a free-for-all," Rondo says, looking up into the trees in awe. "That carnivores ate carnivores no matter what."

"An oversimplification," Kimbullettican says. "Most predators, if pressed, will feed outside their small web. The only thing that is guaranteed is that herbivores are never prey."

"Except by the dirixi," I say.

"Yes. The great exception."

"Why don't you kill it?" Jaquot says, still looking up into the trees.

Kimbullettican snaps their head sideways to fix him with a sharp stare. Their forehead spots harden into a stiff line that I recognize from Rasimbukar. In the Artery, their anger and disgust is a sudden green blaze that sweeps down the tunnel. They're not alone: even Joi and Jaquot's friends within Mbe-kenkanush regard him with stony expressions.

"You lack education," Kimbullettican says, and I brace myself for what flame falls out of their mouth next when the air is suddenly illuminated with pale pink light. Kimbullettican turns away, looking back up into the trees, many of which now glow.

It's the syca. The ikya have won their nightly argument and the trees have agreed to open the petals of their formerly slumbering blossoms, which now bathe the forest in light. It's gentle, the same pale color as the last of sunset, and with this new glow we barely notice the rest of the darkening evening.

"It's so beautiful," I say. So beautiful I almost forget to scan the remaining light for the red smoke my grandmother had warned me to watch for. There is nothing.

Kimbullettican doesn't look at me, continuing to stare up into the treetops. "Yes, it is. This is my most cherished thing."

Beyond the pink of the syca's glow, I can make out the sound of many pairs of wings, the ikya taking flight, off into the rose-tinged night to find their own prey.

"I wonder why they haven't adapted better night vision," Alma ponders, peering up into the trees.

"The arrangement works for them," Kimbullettican says. "Both plant and animal benefit."

"What if something happened to the syca?" Alma says, frowning. "What would the ikya do?"

"This is why the Faloii are here," Kimbullettican says.

Another sound now joins the ikya's calling, low at first and then stronger, a thrumming like rhythmic wind, but with a melody buried between measures. Rondo's head snaps up.

"Hey," he says, and that's all before he's standing up and

moving, walking quickly away from our huddle and weaving through the other small groups of Mbekenkanush's humans. Alma and I exchange glances, hesitating only a moment before we're on our feet and following him.

He's already found the source of the sound by the time we catch up: two Faloii women stand near one of the orange flowers, both swaying and humming, their voices indistinguishable from one another. Their humming is many layered and is emitted from their throats, glowing as they had the day I had sat before the council of Mbekenkanush. But then I see what had drawn Rondo to this place, around which both humans and Faloii cluster.

Both the women bear an izinusa in their arms, and play its long elegant strings effortlessly, the music rising and falling like both wind and water, sunshine as much a part of the music as the strings themselves.

"How?" I breathe, the harmony sinking into my muscles like a balm.

"You have seen an izinusa before today?" Kimbullettican says, appearing behind me.

"Did one of the humans from the *Vagantur* bring these to Mbekenkanush?" I ask. "Rondo knows how to play one."

"Sort of," Rondo adds shyly, and the memory of his music slithers pleasantly through me.

"Humans bring one?" Kimbullettican says, confused. "If you have one among your people, it was brought *from*

Mbekenkanush. It is an instrument of the Faloii."

"What? How?" Rondo says. "It was given to me by someone in N'Terra when she died."

"I am not sure of this. Its wood is formed from an ogwe's inner core. There are but a few izinusa on the planet," Kimbullettican says, looking thoughtful. "The wood is given upon the death of the tree. This happens only once every many hundred years."

One of the Faloii women looks up at us and her eyes find Rondo's face. She must see something there—a portrait of his longing—because she pauses her humming, allowing her partner to continue the melody alone. She moves toward where we stand and extends the instrument to him. Rondo doesn't speak. He accepts the izinusa readily, the instrument in one hand and its slender bow in the other, and begins to play.

The music should be too soft to hear, but somehow it rises above all the chatter of the campsite, over the calling of the ikya, who seem to quiet at the sound of it. The two Faloii women continue their humming, exchanging smiles, their forehead spots rippling in time to the music, enjoying the tune he lifts from the strings. They find its rhythm with their voices, match it with the other izinusa.

The music seems to surround us all like the very air of Faloiv. The entire planet may have paused to listen. I can't take my eyes off Rondo, and when I finally blink I'm surprised by the tears that escape onto my cheeks. The melody that he releases into the sky is both N'Terra and Faloiv, his humanness meld-ing with the agelessness of the izinusa's wood. It's so beautiful but it fills me only with sadness, so deeply blue it could be the multukwu's domain. Here is everything that I love, human and not, and none of it feels within reach.

CHAPTER 23

The light that wakes me is not morning. Eyes roused open, it takes me a moment to remember where I am, that the warmth to my left is Rondo and the soft snores to my right are Alma. We had all fallen asleep around the orange flower, which had cooled as night fell, eventually going dark. The light I sense now comes from the trees, but it's not the soft pink released from the syca, which had faded hours ago.

Now the trees glow red.

My grandmother's smoke? No, this isn't smoke; it's something else, something of Faloiv. I bite down on the rising alarm that floats up from my bones. The campsite is silent: no one else seems to be awake, let alone aware of the strange glow that bathes my skin and the grass.

I rise, glancing down at Rondo's face, illuminated in the

reddish light. I almost wake him, not because I don't want to be alone, but because I want to be alone with him. Still, I know I would have nothing to say. How can I tell him that at one time the music he plays drew him closer to my heart, and now it makes me want to push him away? The day he played in the compound, it had filled my body with light. Now the shadows of uncertainty seem to loom only lower. The music calls to me, but something else calls louder.

I hear it now.

The green language. It seems to rustle through the Artery, sighing, carrying words that are just beyond the reach of my comprehension. The reddish glow seems to pulse downward from the trees. No sign of the moon: the sky is blotted out by canopy and clouds. No sign of the ikya.

No sign of Kimbullettican.

Their absence draws my alarm back to the surface of my skin, the hairs on the back of my neck prickling in sudden caution.

"Kimbullettican," I whisper, taking a few silent steps. My feet, bare, connect with the jungle soil and my suit comes alive. Any sleep that had clung to me sheds now as the suit's infectious vigor flows into my skin, dew that must have accumulated in the night hours soaking into me as if I'd drunk it myself. The suit is grateful that I am acting as a conduit, and it almost seems to reward me for doing so. When I first feel the prickle of information in the Artery, I barely notice it among the activity of the suit—it's hard to keep everything in my head sorted with so much input. But the information beckons me, as if with imperceptible fingers, a steady stream of communication that I eventually notice and isolate. Where I had once stood in my qalm in Mbekenkanush and found the language unintelligible, I can now pull out the meaning, even if the words themselves are a blur.

There is something nearby, something strange. The planet is aware of it—has always been aware of it—but its presence draws a new kind of caution that I pick up on like a scab scratched open.

Kimbullettican, I call in my mind, reaching out for their presence with the hope that they might be able to explain what I am experiencing, but they are either sealed off in the Artery or too far for me to contact. Or perhaps the messages from the soil are too dense to break through, clogging my ability to hear anything else. Around me, the jungle seems to pulse with life, the red glow of the syca adding a dreamlike layer between me and the sounds of night.

That's when the suit passes me something I can understand.

It's not in the language that I use to communicate with the Faloii and the planet's animals, the shapes and impressions that I had seemed born to fluency with. It's rudimentary—even more so than my usual attempts. It's as if whatever consciousness that passes me these fragments of meanings understands my mind's clumsiness and has broken it down into some primary form of itself. An impression, an understanding that emerges from the tunnel almost as a scent.

It is a scent. It fills my nose while still occupying a section of my mind, an odor as real as the smell of the ogwe but with a different meaning. In a flash I remember the day of my mother's arrest, when I'd returned to the Mammalian Compound and inhaled the smell of warning that the trees radiated into the main dome, a stark transition from the usual aroma of comfort. This is like that: not a message, exactly, but a command; the smell orders my biology to do something. . . .

Follow.

It's a trail. It's as if my sensory receptors have crunched through the data of an unseen formula and finally translated it into meaning I can comprehend: follow.

I glance backward, where Alma and Rondo sleep peacefully alongside the other human youth. Do the Faloii still stand guard? Will they stop me? I pick up my pack from where I'd been using it as a pillow and slip away toward the jungle's edge.

My feet find their own path. The light of the syca is bright enough that I make my way over tree limbs and stones without much trouble, wincing only when thinner branches scratch my face. I could turn back—I'm not without agency. But my curiosity is a mighty force that keeps me placing one bare foot after another, barely noticing the occasional stone and twig.

The light pales ahead, the syca's red fading into white: pure moonlight breaking in from the canopy. This means the trees are thinning, I think, and wonder if this means I will soon be reaching a body of water. But I would hear the water by now if a lake, the gentle lap of waves; or if a river, the muted current carrying on without sleep. It can't be water. A clearing, then, I tell myself, slowing. But I can't stop now: my curiosity is a magnet swimming darkly in my blood, drawing me toward whatever lies ahead.

It's a meadow: bright with moonlight and ringed with trees that reach up toward the stars, unveiling themselves without secret now that I have emerged from the thick kingdom of jungle. The meadow feels familiar: open and sweet smelling, an odor that rises from the expanse of short green plants bearing many round buds. I look down at them, examining them in moonlight—so familiar. My bare feet are buried in them, the softness of their blossoms a strange comfort. A delicate breeze causes a few of them to brush against my ankles. I can't have been here before, but its familiarity is a scratch at the back of my skull that I can't reach. A dream? A memory? I sweep my eyes over the rest of the meadow, wide and flat except for the bulk of a white boulder rising out of the ground one hundred yards ahead. Round, almost impossibly so; nothing in nature is so smooth unless found underwater. Perhaps this meadow had once been the multukwu's domain.

I move toward the boulder, the short plants and their spherical blossoms a carpet beneath my feet. Had this place been in a photograph kept on my mother's slate in N'Terra? A record of my grandmother's adventures before she disappeared? The familiarity clings to me, the moonlight the only thing that tells me I'm imagining it. If I know this place, I know it in sunlight. With everything made silver and white, it's hard to be sure of anything. Hard to be sure that the boulder ahead is a boulder at all.

A cloud passes over the moon as I arrive next to it, and it's not until I place my hand on its surface that I realize the scent that had led me to this clearing has faded away. Whatever trail I was following has gone cold. Or perhaps this is the end of the trail, and I have followed it to its farthest point. Under my fingers, the boulder—several feet taller than me, and almost as wide as a 'wam—is, again, impossible. Too smooth. Too round.

Somewhere in the jungle that rings the meadow I hear the triumphant orchestra of ikya, their hunt successful. I wonder if this means dawn is near, and gaze up to gauge the position of the moon. It's too high, I think. Not dawn for a while yet: more night between me and whatever comes next. While I watch, the remaining clouds masking the moon continue on their journey across the sky, and I allow my eyes to fall back to the surface of the lonely boulder.

Letters. I stare dumbly at them for a moment, shocked by their presence here. I must be imagining them—how else is it possible? But there it is. The letter *N*. The letter *T*. The rest hidden by moss. Faded by age but here nonetheless. Inside me, the green language whispers, *This. This thing. Another of their things. Caution.*

It takes only another breath for me to become frantic. A moment later my fingers are fast at work, tearing at the spongy layers of plant life that have made the boulder—the what?—their home. It all collects under my fingernails, blunting my hands, but I keep at it, swiping with my palms here, scratching there. The moon comes and goes, but when it shows its face, it shows me that the letters I'm uncovering are red—something more vibrant, once upon a time, than ink: at one point this word had been stark and immovable against the white of this lump of mystery.

The moon is hidden again and I stand there panting, unaware until now of how hard I'd been working, sweat gathering along my scalp before my suit quickly offers hydration and oxygen. I stand there, waiting for the light to return. But some part of me doesn't need it. I know what I've found. When the moon is generous again, I read the words silently.

Vagantur Capsule 3.

"Here you are," I whisper to the meadow and its strangely familiar blossoms. "Here you are."

"Here you are," rasps a voice, and I'm jerking away from the hand on my arm before I'm fully aware of its presence. I stumble backward, my voice empty with shock, falling first against the pod and then away from it, my feet instinctually seeking empty ground to run on.

It's Kimbullettican.

"You could have said something!" I snap.

I did. You were preoccupied.

"I . . ." I'm still catching my breath, both from uncovering the text and from my sudden terror. "Still. Stars, Kimbullettican."

"My apologies," they say. "I was nearby and found your presence in the Artery. Needless to say, I was surprised."

"I woke up. I heard"—I pause, trying to decide how to describe it. "Something? Something in the Artery. It reminds me of the qalm."

Kimbullettican's forehead spots cluster and disperse like a trail of bubbles flicked by a fin. "This too woke me," they say. "Your listening has improved."

"How?"

"It is a question for yourself."

I stare at the capsule in the moonlight. The moss that coats its surface seems to obscure so much more than just the pod itself.

"I think . . . I think Faloiv knows something about me," I say, almost to myself.

"Something."

I meet their eyes. In the Artery, I know they see the flurry of events and emotions that swirls there. The vusabo and its attack on Rondo, how it had beckoned for me to join it. The breath that blows the green language of Faloiv into my inner ear, the way it seems to feel my anger for N'Terra and whisper to it. I try to conceal these things from Kimbullettican—I try to conceal them from myself. I fail.

Do you still wish to go to the archives? Kimbullettican asks silently. *Or have you made another decision?*

The archives. The red letters before me on this cast-off piece of the *Vagantur* have removed everything else of significance from my mind. This thing here in the middle of the meadow feels related to the archives somehow. The armed graysuits at the ship yesterday had been combing the jungle for pieces of the *Vagantur*, and they were looking for what Manx called the pods. My father and Albatur want the kawa, but they want these pods too.

"I wonder where the first two are," I murmur.

"I do not understand."

"It says Capsule three," I say, still staring at the structure. "That means there has to be a Capsule one and two some-where."

Something about it itches my brain, remembering Captain Williams's message: three pieces to return. Is the three a coin-cidence?

"What is this?" Kimbullettican says. They are stand-ing nearer to the capsule now too, their sparkling black eyes studying its surface. At first I think they are asking me what the capsule itself is, but I notice one of their hands is pressed against it, one long thumb caressing the shell.

"What did you find?"

"A doorway, I believe. A seam in the shell."

"Let me see."

Faloii vision must be superior to human, because I don't see anything—but when I press my fingertips where their hand indicates, there's a seam. A slight indentation, running vertical along the capsule. I allow my fingers to follow it like a map, and find that it extends about a foot above my head before curving sideways and then down again. Yes, a doorway of some kind, sealed by moss and age.

"I wonder how it opens," I say, my fingers still tracing the outline of its doorway. "It's so old. It probably doesn't open anymore."

"All doors open," Kimbullettican says. "It is only a matter of finding the key."

I say nothing, running my hand over the words *Vagantur Capsule 3*. Part of me doesn't even want it to open. I imagine finding another skeleton like Captain Williams's, the remnants of someone who had died alone, perhaps while trying to flee what they believed would be the fate of the ship. I have seen enough death over the last few days: old and new, and in some cases death that has not yet occurred but is inevitable. I think if I opened this pod, whatever I would find would only make me wilt.

But then my hand wanders onto another indentation. It could have been merely a dent in the capsule, a nick taken out of its shell in what might have been a tumultuous journey to the ground from the sky. But it's too even, too uniform.

Symmetrical. A circular shape, my fingers hunting it out more frantically with each second, with an edge that extends on either side. Like wings.

"Oh . . . ," I whisper, a half-formed thought.

"You have found something," Kimbullettican says, not a question.

My fingers remain on the indentation, refusing to break contact in case what I have found is then lost in shadow, adrift again in moss and mystery. My other hand goes to the hidden pocket of my suit, from which I withdraw the pin I had taken from Captain Williams. I know before I press it into the shape on the capsule that it will fit.

It makes a soft, satisfying sound that could have been a single beat of a heart, almost immediately followed by the rusty sigh of the door juddering open. At one time it might have been a smooth process. But here, so many years since the last time the doors had parted, weighed down by grit and moss and the air of a new planet, its grace is antiquated. The door can only open partway, but it reveals a tiny circular space that I can see straight through. Like the ceilings of the domes in N'Terra, what appears to be white from the outside is transparent from the inside, and I imagine that whoever had stepped into this capsule must have felt surrounded by glass as they hurtled from the ship to this lonely place.

"Interesting," Kimbullettican says, peering in over my shoulder.

I withdraw Captain Williams's pin from what I can only think of as a keyhole, clutching it in my palm. It feels warm, although nothing on the inside of the capsule glows to indicate a source of power. I stare at the silent space, lost for words.

"Are you not curious?" Kimbullettican says, and I think I hear humor in their voice, an amused puzzlement at my hesitancy.

"I am," I say. "But . . ."

"But you are afraid."

"That's not the right word."

"I think I understand," they say, but they can't. Faloiv is unequivocally their planet—their history is rooted here. There's no part of their past that is shrouded in mystery. Not like this. I've always teased Alma for her vivid interest in our history, but now, the feeling of my own fear like a tense web being spun in my shoulders, I think I may have been more like Jaquot than I ever believed: using jokes to put distance between myself and uncomfortable truths. The past is no longer hidden behind the deliberate silences of N'Terra's whitecoats—it's right here in front of me.

"Strange that it is empty," Kimbullettican says, still peering in over my shoulder.

Yes, it is. I had fully anticipated the light of the moon sliding in through the half-open door and illuminating what was left of the capsule's lone escapee. All I see from where I stand is an array of simple controls, presumably all one would need to

jettison the pod from the *Vagantur*. I take a step forward, leaning my head into the doorway. The air is stale, even as Faloiv's
oxygen seeps in and makes it new. There's a single seat, empty,
the restraint belts dangling, purposeless.

I can't help it . . . all the fear is no match for my curiosity.
I step through the doorway into *Vagantur* Capsule 3, ducking to avoid the few drooping vines that opening the door had
disturbed. Kimbullettican leans in after me. It would be too
crowded if we both stood inside, so they get as close as they
can, head and shoulders inside the door, eyes sweeping this
place of unknown. I can feel their excitement in the Artery,
the first time they've actually felt my age: their fascination is
bare and bright, eager to discover some bit of truth.

"It does not feel as old as it looks," they observe.

They're right. The dust and growths on the outside of the
capsule give an impression of the ancient, but inside, apart
from dust, the pod feels like it could be any unused room
of the Zoo. The round transparent space is so similar to the
domes of the commune . . . it's like being in a shrunken version of N'Terra.

"I wonder if it was ejected from the *Vagantur* by mistake," I
ponder. "Since there's no one inside, I don't see the point."

"A consequence of the crash, perhaps," Kimbullettican says.
"A malfunction. What is that? A compartment?"

There's the faint rectangular outline of a compartment, a
drawer of some kind.

Suddenly Kimbullettican's shoulder is crushed up against mine. I cry out in surprise, moved roughly sideways by their presence in the pod. My backpack crunches against my spine.

"Close the capsule," they say. "Quickly!"

I fumble with Captain Williams's pin, still clutched in my left hand.

"Close it? I don't know how!"

"Here," Kimbullettican says, snatching the pin from my grasp. Their skin has taken on a mottled color, trying to blend with the silvers and whites of the capsule's interior. They sweep a hand-paw over the slim bit of wall near the doorway.

"What's going on?" I demand, moving farther away from the door, as far as I can before running into the dashboard.

"Listen," they say, still searching for a place to press the pin.

I turn my eyes to the simple dashboard of the capsule, nothing labeled with instructions or clues of what the few buttons and levers might do. In my head, the Artery fills with something like static—a presence that isn't fully a presence, choppy and unstable, a feeling like sickness permeating its aura. When I finally recognize the presence of one of Albatur's creations, I turn to the dashboard, urgency pumping through me.

There are ten buttons. Two levers. I decide to press them all. None of the buttons do anything at all—whatever power source they rely upon is long dead. One lever makes a grating sound when I yank it, but nothing happens.

"Hurry," Kimbullettican says, and I'm not sure if they're

talking to me or themselves, crouching now, looking for an indentation for the pin.

I pull the other lever downward, and the door that had opened only partially before now opens entirely. Kimbulletti-can jumps back, slamming into me.

"Again," they order, and I shove the lever upward this time, a metallic clang echoing within the small space of the capsule.

The door stiffly, reluctantly, slides shut. There's a hiss as whatever air between it and the world beyond is squeezed out.

"Be still," Kimbullettican says, but I already am, frozen against the dashboard, my eyes prying at the moonlight beyond the transparent hull of the capsule.

"It's from N'Terra," I whisper.

"Yes. A similar creature to what harmed my sibling."

The clouds drift over the moon once more, blanketing the meadow in shadow. The crush of jungle that borders the clearing isn't visible as anything but a dense black barrier and I glimpse only snatches of the round blossoms that line the ground. Whatever the thing is that I sense in the Artery—its consciousness butchered by the work of Albatur—it is not visible from where we hide in the capsule.

There, Kimbullettican says, and I feel their energy pricked toward a place near the trees where I had first emerged, a dark shape that might have been the trunk of a long-fallen tree. I stare at it so hard my eyes water, hoping it doesn't move, praying it remains a dead stump.

It doesn't.

When it moves, every muscle in my body jerks; if it weren't for my hands gripping the dashboard of the capsule, my body would have fled. But fled where? Kimbullettican and I are pressed shoulder to shoulder in the small space of the *Vagantur* pod, with no escape possible without going out into the meadow where whatever it is skulks. The transparency of the capsule is terrifying until I remind myself that from the outside, it is a smooth white shell.

It won't be able to see us, I say in the Artery.

No, not see, Kimbullettican replies, and I shiver. I imagine my scent drifting through the meadow, a trail that the N'Terran beast follows with its nose to the ground. How much air is inside this capsule? How long will we be able to hide here if it discovers where we are and decides to wait us out?

It's a gwabi. I sense Kimbullettican's dread immediately, a gray cloud that enters the tunnel and swells like a bruise. A single vasana we might have been able to overpower if forced. A gwabi weighs five hundred pounds, and the teeth wouldn't require implantation of dirixi fangs—they are born predators, but its biological laws have always prohibited it from hunting herbivores as prey. Until now.

It smells us, Kimbullettican says, but they didn't need to: I know. The creature weaves a wandering path across the meadow, following exactly the trail I had walked when I had entered the meadow and seen what I thought was a boulder.

It is not here by coincidence, Kimbullettican says. *It has fol-lowed you here from N'Terra.*

How?

I do not know. How did you escape? Were you seen?

No, we weren't seen, I say, racking my brains. *It was dark: the middle of the night. My father helped us. . . .*

My father had helped us escape. Every muscle in my body goes rigid, the pack on my back suddenly a thousand pounds weighing me down.

What is it? Kimbullettican says.

"My father . . ."

Crushing against them even more, I turn and rip the back-pack off my shoulders, jerking open its top and shoving my arm inside. A canteen. The extra suit from Mbekenkanush. Loose strips of zarum. I slide my hands along every inch of the inside of the pack, searching for anything strange. My fingers freeze when they find it.

A tiny knot. So small it could be a stray stone stuck inside the fabric. But it's not. I can feel it; round and perfect. Ignoring Kimbullettican's discomfort, I turn the bag inside out, dump-ing everything onto the floor. The moonlight provides just enough light for me to find the tiny metallic bug, adhered to the very bottom of the inside of the pack.

"A tracker," I whisper. "My father has been tracking us."

"To what end?" Kimbullettican says, their eyes darting from the bug in my hand to the gwabi that prowls ever closer outside the pod.

"I don't know," I say. "He wanted me to go find kawa to bring back to N'Terra. He must have known I wouldn't do it. He wanted to be able to track me so that he could come get it himself!"

Kimbullettican stares at me hard, their forehead spots congested in a knot near the center.

"Crush it," they say.

I drop it onto the dashboard and with one slam of my fist send its delicate inner mechanisms scattering around the pod.

"I do not know how much good this will do us," Kimbullettican says, their spots still clustered. "We have already been followed to this place."

The gwabi is fully visible now, slinking closer to the pod. Its blank eyes sweep over us, confirming that even if my scent is in its nostrils, the capsule is indeed still opaque from the outside. The creature's mouth is slightly open, moonlight catching on the blaze of saliva coating its mouth. I think of the gwabi that had accompanied me from N'Terra after my mother's death, my occasional companion. She never salivates this way. Another aspect of this animal's nature that Albatur has made ugly and vicious.

The pod shudders as the gwabi's shoulder butts up against it, and I grip the dashboard even more tightly. This capsule had fallen from the sky and landed here without so much as a crack; there is no way that this creature alone can smash it open like an egg. But that doesn't mean it won't try.

Being in the capsule, transparent from the inside, is like being in a bubble: I would almost rather the gwabi's movements be invisible to me. Instead, my eyes are glued to it as it stalks slowly, jerkily, around the pod, circling. Even its languid grace has been stolen from its nature. It doesn't move like what it is but as what N'Terra has made it.

Everything is changing, Kimbullettican says, but they don't mean it for me. I feel rude for having heard them, as if I'd eavesdropped on some private prayer.

Time passes. My muscles cramp, crammed in the capsule and trying not to bump Kimbullettican with my movements. The dashboard digs painfully into my hip. And around the capsule, the gwabi circles. Around and around. Tirelessly, ceaselessly.

"Why does it not leave," Kimbullettican mutters, and I almost jump at the sound of their voice, despite its quiet.

"The signal died when I broke the tracker," I say. "It's probably stuck here until it does what it's programmed to do."

"What is it programmed to do?"

I don't answer.

"It is strange to fear a creature besides the dirixi," Kimbullettican says quietly. "It is strange to not be able to reach her."

The gwabi passes by the part of the shell closest to me and I flinch, as I do every time its slow, mechanical gait brings it past me. I avert my eyes, as if looking at it will pass some signal to the creature holding us hostage.

"I'm sorry" is all I can say to Kimbullettican. There are much bigger things they need than an apology.

I flinch as the gwabi passes by my shoulder, close enough to touch if the transparent barrier of the capsule were not between us. I shrink away as I had before, but this time it doesn't continue on its endless circular path. It pauses.

Silence, Kimbullettican says.

I look into the Artery to see what the gwabi might be experiencing, but of course the connection is broken. I can only stare at its frozen form with wide eyes, waiting for those blank, fanged features to turn on the capsule and attempt to get inside.

But its eyes are on the tree line, its ears pricked forward, its nostrils quivering. It crouches almost imperceptibly. Despite its prime directive of tracking me, the creature does seem to maintain its instincts. Its lips pull back in a silent snarl.

"Rondo," I whisper.

I see him first, and then Alma. They are two shadows, but I know him by the set of his shoulders and her by the shape of her hair, high and proud even in the near dark.

"Oh no," I cry. "No! They can't be here!"

I reach for the Artery reflexively before I remember they can't be reached within it. Panic floods through me. Whatever barrier I have built between myself and them since we've been on this journey, it disappears in this moment. I can't let my friends be killed. I reach for the lever, but Kimbullettican's hand encircles my wrist.

"You cannot," they say.

"I have to!" I say. "It sees them!"

It does. It has altered its course, the tracker leaving it listless. I imagine its prime directive glowing red in its mechanical brain: *destroy*. Alma and Rondo have stepped into the meadow, oblivious to what awaits them.

"Kimbullettican, move!" I say, trying to jerk free, but their strength is breathtaking, their grip unbroken.

"I will not," they say. "It would mean my death, and yours, and possibly the death of the gwabi."

"It's not a gwabi anymore! Kimbullettican, *move*!"

Alma and Rondo have begun to make their way across the meadow. I don't know how they found me: my footsteps, perhaps, or maybe they had seen me leave and trailed me like two shadows. I can tell by the way they move that they are afraid, but their fear doesn't stop them from searching for me, and guilt and love throb inside me in tandem.

"They shouldn't have come," I cry. "They shouldn't be here!"

Alma spots the gwabi. In the moonlight, the silhouette of her shoots out and grabs Rondo's arm. It's too late to run. The gwabi is faster than they could ever be. But there is another presence joining us in the meadow. Close and fast, glowing blue in the Artery. It appears suddenly, a blaze emerging from the jungle, heading straight toward my friends. My heart seizes: another predator. A faster death. But then the moonlight shifts.

Hamankush, Kimbullettican says at the same time that I see her.

She's tall and straight-backed, carrying something in her hand as she crosses the meadow. Kimbullettican and I both sense her intention.

Do not, Kimbullettican says to her. *The gwabi is ill.*
I know this.

I can't make out what she's carrying in her hands, but it's long and slim, like a cane or a walking stick. She grasps it in her right hand, holding it slightly out to the side of her body as she moves directly across the meadow toward Rondo and Alma. The gwabi sees her now and has turned fully toward her, its muscles twitching. The capsule shell is too thick to hear anything through, but I can almost feel the rumble of the beast's growls in my own rib cage.

Caution, Kimbullettican warns.

Not feasible, Hamankush says.

When she's close enough for me to make out her face, the gwabi leaps. An instant of fear pulses through the Artery from Hamankush, orange and almost dizzying, but it's a mere flash that fades as she sidesteps the gwabi's attack. I hold my breath, and Kimbullettican moves quickly forward inside the pod, both palms pressed against the shell that protects us.

You must not kill her, Kimbullettican says, their desperation a web of blue tendrils exploding from their words inside the Artery.

I will not.

When the gwabi leaps again, Hamankush sidesteps again, and then swings the long walking stick in a swooping arc. It connects with the beast's skull, sending it stumbling sideways, discombobulated. It's strange watching this in silence, the capsule deadening all noise. It feels like a dream. Kimbullettican's fists are balled against the capsule, their breaths shallow.

The gwabi leaps a third time, and Hamankush's walking stick cracks against its skull again. It's enough. The animal stumbles sideways, then falls. It has only just slumped to the ground when Hamankush is upon it, withdrawing what looks like thin rope from the pack she carries over her shoulder and using it to bind the gwabi's feet. Rondo and Alma stand frozen, as if unsure of what has just transpired.

Out, she says to us, and I merely stare for a moment until Kimbullettican nudges me, nodding at the lever. I pull it, and the air from the meadow whooshes in, a breeze that feels like love after the hour in the small cramped capsule. My friends come running the remaining distance of the meadow, their breath loud and shaking.

"Octavia," Alma says, almost a shout. "What in the stars are you doing out here? What happened? You *left* us!"

"I know," I say, and I try to follow up with *I'm sorry*, but I can't. "I—I know."

Kimbullettican rushes to the side of the gwabi.

"Unconscious," Hamankush reassures them.

"These bonds will not hold her," they say.

"No. Which is why we must continue on our way before it wakes."

"Which is where?" I say, turning to her so I can avoid the eyes of my friends, who are staring at me like I have grown a new face, like they don't recognize who I am. "What are you doing here? I thought you were supposed to stay at the archives?"

"I will escort you back to the encampment," she says, nodding toward the part of the jungle I had come from. "I was summoned here to assist with human relocation. The Elders of Mbekenkanush have decided I am not responsible for the death of the igua. The igua that had been altered by the N'Terrans."

I freeze, staring at her.

"So that means . . . they hold N'Terra responsible."

"N'Terra *is* responsible," she says, and I think again of the memory she had shown me in the jungle outside Mbekenkanush: war, brought by N'Terrans all those years ago. Drones. Death. And now here we are again.

"Yes," I say. "I know. They . . . have made their decision."

"Yes," she says, and stares hard at me for a moment before she casts her gaze over the rest of the group. "Come, back to the encampment. I will explain to those who have been assigned to relocation."

"No," I say quickly. "No. We're not going back to the camp."

Her eyes snap back to me, her forehead spots clustering near the center.

"What?"

"I'm not going to let the Faloii deal with this while I go hide in the mountains," I say. I wonder if my voice shakes or if it just feels that way.

"Octavia . . . ," Alma starts.

"Stop it, Alma," I snap. "You can go back if you want. I know you don't understand. None of you do. You don't hear what I hear. You don't—" I pause, a lifetime of my father's teachings like a dam in my mouth keeping me from speaking the words. "You don't . . . *feel* what I feel. We were all born here, but I don't know if you have chosen Faloiv as your home. N'Terra isn't home. It's just . . . a place."

They all regard me silently. I don't dare look into the Artery: I'm afraid of what silent judgment Kimbullettican and Hamankush exchange.

"If not the encampment," Hamankush says slowly, "then where?"

"To the archives."

CHAPTER 24

"There are more of the N'Terran beasts," Hamankush tells me as we make our way through the thickest part of the jungle I've yet seen. Jaquot had said there were mountains to the north, but we pressed west and have met mountains here too. Rondo and Alma walk ahead with Kimbullettican, the path getting steeper and steeper. They look back occasionally as Hamankush and I talk, Alma frowning.

"I figured," I say. "I didn't think he would stop with just the vasana that killed my mother."

"How many?" she says.

"I don't know. I have no idea how difficult a procedure it is. But now that he has successful trials, he will probably just keep going."

"For what purpose?"

I think back to the last day I had seen Dr. Espada alive, when my mother had dragged me to the Greenhouse to consult with him. "Weaponization," my mother had said, and Dr. Espada had known exactly what she meant.

"I think the animals whose brains he's tampering with are just part of his bigger plan. They're tools to get what he wants."

"Bigger plan," she repeats.

"To . . . you know. Take over. He wants to strip Faloiv of its resources to take back to the Origin Planet after he gets what he needs to leave."

"We will not give him what he needs."

"I—I know," I stammer. "I wasn't saying you should."

Hamankush walks on in silence.

"Is this a part of being human?" she asks eventually. "I do not think the Faloii remembered your people as having been this way."

"Remembered? What do you mean?"

"From the Faloii's first encounter with humans. I do not believe we would have let you stay if we had known."

"You, as in, me?" I ask. "Or . . . us?"

"All of you," Hamankush says, her forehead spots clustering with impatience. "If we had known this was your way, I do not think the invitation would have been extended."

"No, probably not." I sigh. "But it's not what we remember either. I mean, I don't know much about where we came from. It's not something we talk about."

"Why is this?"

"That's the question Alma is obsessed with," I say, gazing ahead at her. "And I guess me too, now. Our past has a lot of mystery. But I'm trying to put the pieces together. I think if I do, things will make sense."

"Your people are people of science," Hamankush says. "Your grandmother, your mother . . . they spent many years finding answers to questions. If there are no answers to questions about yourselves, then this is a willful ignorance."

I want to argue, but she's right. For so many years our only goal was uncovering the mysteries of this planet and, in the process, to forget about the one we came from. My ignorance about our own history feels like an unforgivable void in my mind.

"I can't explain it," I say. "There were questions it didn't occur to me to ask. Alma asked, but never got anywhere. It . . . never occurred to me that they would be lying. Covering it up on purpose."

Hamankush regards me sideways, her forehead spots rising, peaking above one eye. "When a people are cut off from their history, this can only damage their future."

Something about the way she says this makes the words grow larger in my ears. A question burns on the tip of my tongue, and it's as if she can see it glowing there, for her eyes remain fixed on me, even as we climb the steepening face of the mountain.

"I know Rasimbukar and Adombukar knew about the beasts made in N'Terra," I say quickly, before I can change my mind. "He was in there with them. He knows what they did to the vasana."

"Yes," Hamankush allows. She's not looking at me anymore.

"Why?" I say. "Why did they let your Elders think that the igua was something new? If they knew what N'Terrans were doing in the labs, they would have understood why you did what you did. That you had to."

"I did not have to," Hamankush says. I'm out of breath from the mountain's incline, but she doesn't seem to be fazed. "It was a choice, like many choices."

"You know what I mean." I try to catch my breath so that my next question is coherent. "Is this related to why Rasimbukar was mad you showed me the memory? The one about war?"

At this I think I catch a glimpse of her smiling. Perhaps it was an expression of exertion, but I can't mistake the subtle rise of her facial spots.

"You are clever" is all she says.

"Not clever enough," I push, frustrated. "Otherwise I would understand. Why does Rasimbukar keep so many secrets?"

"The same reason your people do," she says. "Because sometimes the past requires protection."

"From?"

"From everything."

Ahead, Kimbullettican pauses on the path. In this moment,

the entirety of the planet is one endless tangle in my mind: a knot of vines that I can only imagine making sense of with the slice of a blade. A lazy way of solving a problem, I think as Kimbullettican and Hamankush converse silently; slicing it in half rather than disentangling all the parts that make it a problem. But when I think of all that Albatur has knotted up in the creation of N'Terra, a blade seems, momentarily, like the only feasible solution.

"We are close," announces Kimbullettican, assumedly after confirming this with Hamankush. Kimbullettican sounds cheerful, as if their eagerness rises at the same rate as the mountain. I wish I was carrying the map my grandfather had sent rather than its being tucked away inside my suit. I can't remember now if he had sketched the archives on an illustration of a mountain. How had he mapped the whole planet? *Had* he mapped the whole planet?

Hamankush pushes ahead to surpass Kimbullettican. Kimbullettican follows eagerly, leaving me and Rondo and Alma to gather behind them, struggling up the path. Alma's entire face is shining with sweat.

"How . . . much . . . farther," she pants.

"Very near," Kimbullettican says over their shoulder, their facial spots high and jovial.

"Thank . . . stars . . . for . . . this suit," Alma says. "I would die."

"We all would," I say.

● ● ●

With the elevation, I expect the trees to thin the higher we climb, but they remain dense, even if less spongy somehow than the jungle below. My eye craves something that leaps out of the green like a fang, and I realize I'm looking for another capsule. The pod I'd already found, far behind us now in the clearing, *must* have mates. Its naming of "3" demands it, and the certainty of another's existence is like a splinter lodged just under my flesh, aching to be drawn out and examined. But the only discernible change is that many of the roots of the trees jut above the ground before diving back below the soil: they resemble the brown knuckles of human hands, clinging to the mountain with clenched desperation. Rondo sees me looking and nods at the roots.

"Kind of creepy," he says, his breath stretched with the effort of climbing. "I wonder how the Faloii picked Hamankush to live all the way up here? Alone? I wouldn't want the job."

"Ahead," Hamankush calls. "You can hear it, if you listen."

I'm so accustomed to "listen" being used as an instruction for the Artery that at first I think what I hear is there, and not my actual ears. But the noise carries down the mountainside the higher we climb, a chorus of rising and falling sounds echoing between the trees, both raucous and musical. Its presence is in the Artery too, of course, the consciousness of many animals, all the same species but still unique from one another somehow, in a way my mind isn't sophisticated enough to perceive.

"Are those birds?" Alma asks.

"Yes," Kimbullettican says, but does not elaborate.

"I see a building," Rondo says, pausing on the path to point at something farther ahead.

"These must be the archives," Kimbullettican says with a tone of affirmation, but I sense a sparkle of excitement in the Artery. This is new for them too. I wonder if they've ever left Mbekenkanush before Rasimbukar had sent them through the jungle to my side.

"I will let the archivist know you have arrived," Hamankush says.

"What?" I say. "I thought you were the archivist."

But she is gone, disappearing around the next curve of the path, delving into the jungle that clutches the trail like mist clings to early morning grass. A moment later the boisterous sound of the unnamed birds stops abruptly, midnote, as if there had been a signal for silence that every beak obeyed.

"Yeah, definitely creepy," Rondo murmurs. Something about the sudden silence raises goose bumps on my arms under the suit, every skin cell prickling as if to sense the danger the birds might have scented. Then I realize that *we* are probably the danger they sense—the truth of it slows my feet. Every step deeper into the planet feels like an invasion.

We have just rounded what I think must be the final corner between us and the archives when Rondo grabs my arms and jerks me backward with a gasp.

"Look out!" he shouts, and I'm immediately prepared to run, my body already turning, hunting for an escape route. But I catch sight of what Rondo thinks he's protecting me from, and it's as if all my fear transforms into something familiar, like a diagram in a text I've studied once before, my memory twanging as it tries to remember.

A figure in a dark cloak. They stand just before us on the path, the cloak's hood obscuring their face, its folds hiding their body the way my memory hides the place where this figure originated in my mind. The things that make it familiar feel fuzzy the way details from dreams do, the edges lacking clarity, the way I had dreamed of my grandmother after I thought she had died. . . .

My mind latches on to the memory just as the cloaked figure's hands rise to the material obscuring their face. I have seen this figure before, in one way many years ago, but not with my own eyes. Through the memory of the tree; the scene I watched unfold long, long ago, when N'Terran war touched Mbekenkanush for the first time. This person is the ageless presence, respected even by the trees.

The fingers that lift the edge of the cloak are deeply brown and lined, age giving them the appearance of wood, polished smooth by years. Behind the figure stands Hamankush, and I wonder how old they must be to have shrunk so in size: they only reach Hamankush's chest, the cloak hiding the ancient body that I know must be curled by a century's hands.

When the cloak falls away, I first take in the eyes. Not galactic and glowing like Rasimbukar's, not even black with the beginnings of a universe within like Kimbullettican's. The eyes are the shape of raindrops laid sideways, the color clear and brown, the whites only slightly yellowed with age. They peer out from a face that looks no older than my mother's but which I am sure somehow has known more years than I can fathom. Their clarity is unmistakable. And unmistakably human.

"Who are you?" I hear myself saying, logic failing me. The person before me, the person I had seen in the memory of the tree, is human. My eyes rush over her face, looking for something that makes sense. She wears a headwrap under the cloak, dyed bright red and tied in a decorative knot. Her lips droop at the corners but she is somehow still smiling, her eyes lacking the galactic sparkle of the Faloii but still managing to dance.

"Here she is, here she is," the woman says. She lets her hands drop to her sides again, the folds of the black-green cloak falling over them, hiding all existence of any part of her but this ancient face. It makes her look even tinier, with Hamankush towering behind. "A child of my home. A pebble of my rock. Hello!"

"H-hello," I stammer. "But . . . who are you? I saw you . . . I saw you when the drones came to Mbekenkanush. . . ."

The lips that had somehow been smiling are not anymore, a light frown turning her mouth serious. "The drones? A little young, aren't you? Confusing, confusing."

"No, I mean, I wasn't there . . . ," I start, but Alma steps forward to interrupt.

"Hello," she says, and her voice carries an ache inside it, an ache which silences me. "I'm Alma. This is Octavia, and he's Rondo. We're from N'Terra."

The young-old woman's eyes shift to Alma, a bit of the dance returning to them.

"Oh, seekers. That's what you are, aren't you? A herd of seekers. A seeker sees an old woman and sees answers. That's all right. You're not wrong."

"An *old* woman?" Alma says, raising her eyebrow. She doesn't see it? The fact that this woman is more than she appears to be? Does she not see her frailty? The years layered across her shoulders?

"But your questions will have to wait until I've fed the eyenu," the woman continues. "Come now."

"The eyenu?" I say. "My grandmother . . ."

"Soon," she says.

And with that, she turns back on the path she had come down, her hands drawing the cloak up over her head again. With her back to us, she could be anyone, anything. A flowing mirage, the color of the jungle, traveling autonomously through the trees.

Who is she? I ask Kimbullettican as we follow.

"I am June," the woman calls over her shoulder in a strong voice. At the sound of her name, its throaty single syllable, the raucous cries of the unseen birds rise again like so many handfuls of dust thrown into the air. Their sounds shower us, growing louder as we follow June up the mountain path, which is leveling out now. We're nowhere near the summit, but we seem to have reached a landing of some kind, a place on the mountainside where the ground goes flat before rising again somewhere ahead, through the band of trees too thick for my eyes to break.

"There's something strange about her," Rondo whispers, pulling up between me and Alma. "I can't put my finger on it."

"She's old," I say. "Very old. She has to be." I tell them what I had seen in the memory Hamankush showed me. "She was old then. And she felt . . . ancient? Part of Faloiv. Somehow I think she was here . . . before the *Vagantur*."

"Impossible," Alma says.

"I know," I say. "But . . . the trees knew who she was."

"Kimbullettican," Alma says. "Who is she?"

"This is not a story I have been told," Kimbullettican says, and by the look of their forehead spots, they're as confused about the presence of this woman at the archives as we are.

"What's that smell?" Rondo says, and I flinch, thinking of the stench of the violet flowers by the river and how it had meant the approach of the dirixi. Every smell, every sound on this planet seems to mean something, a meaning that often goes right over my head.

"The eyenu," Kimbullettican says. They are quiet for a

moment and then add, "But I have never seen one before."

"Really?" Rondo says. "I would have thought you'd seen . . . you know, everything."

"Faloiv is a small planet, but it carries many life-forms. I am aware of the eyenu's existence but have never come into contact with one."

"So this is exciting for you too," Rondo says.

"Yes," Kimbullettican admits. "It is. When I reach maturity, I will be permitted to travel the planet as Adombukar does, logging the species I have been assigned. Until now my experience outside Mbekenkanush has been limited."

"Like us," Alma says.

"Yes, I suppose that is true," Kimbullettican says. I don't think they like the idea that there are suddenly many things they don't know.

"Here they are!" June's voice rises again, louder still to be heard over the chorus of eyenu. "My little ones. My little, little ones."

Ahead is another meadow of sorts, June standing on a rocky outcrop that looks out over the clearing. Since we left the meadow with the *Vagantur* capsule, we'd walked for nearly five hours to reach the mountain we've been scaling. Now the sun is almost at its highest point in the sky, and the meadow blazes near white with the heat of the day. The plants have changed with the altitude, I note: their green paler and their stems thinner. More thorns. Fewer bright swatches of color common in the lower jungle. But the eyenu are bright enough on their own.

They roam the meadow in small groups, not the birds I had expected. They are ground dwellers, probably flightless by the look of their massive legs and small wings, and are grouped into two colors: an intense aquamarine and a shade of fuchsia that almost hurts the eyes. Their necks are long like vasanas', with shaggy feathers that hang in a curtain from their throats. Their beaks are long and spiked, and as they bend to the meadow ground, I find that they are using their beaks to root in the tough mountain soil. Though occupied with whatever they are searching for in the ground, there is a near-constant din rising from their numbers: melodic in a way, but off-key somehow, the notes ragged and disorderly.

"Beautiful," Kimbullettican says, and I feel their consciousness doing something I can't explain in the Artery: to describe it as taking notes doesn't do it justice. They are recording, in a similar way, I think, that the ogwe had recorded the event of the *Vagantur*'s crash onto Faloiv and the following landing discussions. Kimbullettican's mind is a sponge, soaking up the sight of the grazing eyenu in the meadow, sensing and recording biological details my mind isn't even aware of. They are a living text.

"They are," June says proudly. "They are!"

Her cloak flutters around her, a breeze from the mountain-top winding its way down and working its fingers through my hair. She reaches inside the flapping material of her shroud, fishes around, and then withdraws a black case.

"An izinusa," Rondo says quickly. "You have one."

"Why yes," June says. "Necessary in my line of work."

With that, she clicks open the shining black case, revealing the delicate instrument within. It's smaller than the one I've seen Rondo play, but everything else is the same: the warm-hued wood, the ten waiting strings. The bow is nestled in the case alongside it, curving over the instrument itself like the path of a shooting star.

June withdraws it from the case with care, and I can feel the hunger for it rolling off Rondo like a scent. The woman brings the instrument to her chin inside the lip of the cloak and then gently lays the bow against the strings. She pauses, waiting for something. From here I can only see a sliver of her face not obscured by the hood, and just as I'm beginning to think about the purpose of the cloak, and if she wears it for similar reasons to Albatur, she begins to play.

The notes are soft at first and seem to circle in on themselves. They circle and circle, an almost hypnotizing pattern that grows in strength the longer she plays. I can't help but sway to the sound, and so do the eyenu.

They only sway at first, their brilliantly colored bodies rocking almost imperceptibly out among the flat green-yellow grass, as if moved by a gentle wind. But then it's as if that gentle wind moves them toward us, the notes from the izinusa gathering them, petals on a still lake suddenly drifting on a course charted by breeze. They circle like the notes, the small groups of the animals coming together in larger knots, dispersing and regrouping, always flowing toward the outcrop where June stands playing her melody. She rocks from foot to foot under the mass of the dark cloak, her eyes closed, her unsmiling lips somehow smiling. Around us, the music seems to multiply.

When the eyenu are close enough to stand before us, a small sea of vibrant feathers, I realize that the song has swelled because the eyenu have joined it. The disjointed music of their cries has smoothed, finding the melody of the izinusa and clinging to it like tributaries joining a rushing river. Their beaks are barely open, but their throats convulse to emit the music, a haunting melody that fills the meadow with a sound as vivid as vision.

Their throats are swelling. With music, yes, but with something else as well. The curtain of feathers that hang down from their necks becomes tighter, and the music becomes more resonant. The izinusa plays on as before, but the sound the eyenu offer thickens, amplifies. Their throats convulse, as if the music is too much to bear, as if there is something greater than music that they wish to speak but are unable.

The eggs drop one by one. Not the way I have seen other birds lay eggs, and I know immediately that these eggs are not meant for nests. These luminous balls carry another meaning, and they slide from the mouths of the eyenu like stars emerging from black holes. The eyenu bend their long graceful necks one at a time, allowing the kawa to drop gently from their beaks to the ground around the outcrop. June plays on. She plays until the birds have all offered their gifts, and the music from their throats fades to a hum. Only then does she stop, and when she turns to us, all I can see beneath the cloak is her broad smile.

"They were hungry," she says. "But now they are fed."

CHAPTER 25

When night has fallen and we have helped June guide the eyenu into the natural stone quarry where she says they like to sleep, all of us but Hamankush sit around a warming oven inside a qalm that June calls a cabin. Hamankush is outside somewhere. I'd asked where she was going and all she said was "To watch."

Kimbullettican sits closest to June, and if a week ago I'd been told that there was someone pushier with their curiosity than Alma, I wouldn't have believed it. But here we are, Kimbullettican asking endless questions, while I try to get a word in wherever I can.

"Have you never been to Mbekenkanush?" Kimbullettican says. They are eating from a smooth wooden bowl, one of four or five that June passes around, all with a different food that we each eat a bit of before passing it along and accepting the next bowl. Kimbullettican barely eats; they're too busy asking questions and soaking up the answers.

"Once. A long time ago," June says, and I know she's talking about the memory I had seen. She eats with a shiny, slender instrument I've never seen, a rounded hollow at one end with tiny spines extending from the hollow at the bottom. She alternately uses the tines to skewer the food or the hollow to scoop it when applicable. I've never seen anyone not eat with their hands or with bread as the vehicle for getting food from bowl to mouth. I almost laugh when I see her use the tool the first time.

"Why only once?" Alma breaks in, taking advantage of Kimbullettican's stopping to chew.

"Those I need to see come to me," June says. She doesn't bother to wait until she's finished chewing to speak.

"You don't get lonely?" Rondo asks.

"When you've lived a life like mine, child, loneliness is a waste of resources."

All these are things I want to know, but I'm impatient as my friends pluck the answers from June like berries. In my mind, there is only one question that matters in this moment.

"Your flock," I say. "The eyenu. They make kawa?"

"*Make* is an interesting choice of word," June says. She looks at the ceiling as she chews now. "*Make.* A machine makes."

"Not necessarily," Alma butts in. "A person makes a child, for example."

"Creates," June says, her eye swooping down from the ceiling as if on wings, alighting on Alma with a fierce but cheerful shine. "A person *creates* a child."

Alma's lips crack as if to offer argument, but they close again, opening only to mutter, "Pedantic."

I shoot a look at her to hush. "So the eyenu *create* kawa?" I say, turning back to June, who never seems to stop chewing. "How?"

"You could say that," she says. "They do many things."

"You feel strange in the Artery," Kimbullettican says. "Different."

If they had said anything else, I'd be annoyed at their interruption of my line of questioning. But at this I pause, waiting for June's explanation. I had felt it too—the way her presence in the Artery feels stiff and oddly shaped, like a tree that grew around a boulder, taking the stone into part of its trunk: warped but still very much a tree.

"That's because I was the first alteration." June chuckles. A chewed shard or two of zarum is ejected from her mouth but she doesn't seem to notice or care. The qalm is illuminated by piles of kawa, not all of which glow, but those that do are like globular lanterns, and June's square teeth reflect some of this light at Kimbullettican when she smiles at them. "When I met your family for the first time, it was a long way from here and we had to try to communicate the old-fashioned way. Oh, I was a young thing then. Twenty years old! I'd never seen anything like your family but we took a liking to each other right away, and they invited me to come back here with them."

"You mean from another planet," Alma says, her voice soft. Between us all, the oven, glowing with warmth as it bakes the flatbread June had arranged inside, makes a hissing sound.

"Yes, baby. The same one your people are from, unless there is another place in this universe that creates children who look like us."

"How?" I say. "How is this possible? You're telling us the Faloiv came to the Origin Planet before we ever landed here? Before the *Vagantur* ever crashed here?"

"The Origin Planet," she repeats with a laugh. She reaches up to scratch her head and her fingers seem surprised to find that she still wears the red headwrap. She unwinds it carefully, layer by layer, and when the cloth has fallen away I'm staring at coiled white hair, thick locs like the ones that once hung from my mother's scalp. She laughs again. "Is that what they call it?"

"The Origin Planet, yes," Alma says. "Why? What do you call it?"

"I call it by its name, child!" She laughs, and uses the red headwrap to whisk away the crumbs from her lap. "I call it Earth."

"Earth," I echo, and I think Alma and Rondo say it too, the

round heavy word like a single stone dropped among us in the small cool qalm. Like earthquake. Like soil. A basic thing, a thing from which things and ideas grow. It's so simple, but it makes sense in my mouth and in my mind.

"Why did they bring you here?" Kimbullettican says, their confusion apparent. "An extraterrestrial with no knowledge of Faloiv?"

"I can't say," June says. She accepts the bowl Rondo is passing to her and uses her small shining tool to scoop up some waji. "I suppose because I wanted to come. There was nothing for me there, or so I thought. No family, at least. I left behind much more than I thought, of course. You think you have everything you need except that which you want when you're twenty."

"How old are you now?" I blurt.

June's shiny eating tool pauses halfway to her mouth and her eyes pause on me. "I'm one hundred and eighty-two," she says, and then grins as an afterthought. "Give or take a few. It didn't occur to me to keep track right away."

"How?" Alma breathes.

"I have my flock to thank for that," she says. "I give something to them, they give something to me."

"Symbiosis," I say.

"That's right, baby."

"My nana calls me baby," I say softly, mostly to myself.

"How old is your nana?" she says, putting her eating tool down.

"I'm not sure," I say. "I think she was in her thirties when the ship crashed. They say we've been here forty years."

"Yes, forty years." June nods. "I remember when you came. I'd been here many years by then. It was a shock to see those people come off that ship. At first they wore their yellow suits, their high-tech masks. Then they learned the air was good. I saw the masks come off and it was like my heart leaped through space."

"You must have been happy," Alma says, "to see someone like you. Your own kind."

"To tell the truth, I was terrified," June says, chuckling, a low sound that has less humor in it than another laugh might. "I didn't know what kind of people these would be. I'd seen all types on Earth. A lot of bad ones."

"They say that's why we left," Alma says. "To escape the ruin that they made of the planet."

"Say again?" June says, her eyes refocusing. Her gaze had wandered, blurring as she stared at the stove, her thoughts elsewhere.

"That's why the *Vagantur* left . . . Earth?" Alma says, trying the true name out again. "To escape what had been done to the planet?"

June's harsh laugh startles me and I almost drop the bowl

I'd been cradling. I snap my eyes up to her face, alarmed. "So that's what they've been telling you all this time!" June says. "Well, honey, I don't know much, but I know a scam when I hear one."

"A what?" Rondo says. He's put down the bowl in his hands, listening intently. I follow suit. Kimbullettican sits motionless, listening.

"A scam! A con. They might have ruined the planet, but that's not why they came. Not to escape. No, no. They came for something to take back. At least, some of them did. From what I've heard told."

"What do you mean?" I say. We're getting close to something important.

"This was my understanding as well," Kimbullettican says, their spots clustered in a knot at the center of their forehead. "I understood the humans' plight to be that their planet died, and that Faloiv was a haven of coincidence."

"Staying here was the coincidence," June says. She toys with her eating tool, its hard, shiny material catching the light of the many kawa. "Staying. For some of them. I might even take the risk of saying *most*. But every ship has a rat, I guess you could say."

I blink, this reference lost on me. "Hamankush said she didn't think the Faloiv remembered humans as having been this way," I say. "I didn't think this is what she meant."

"Hamankush doesn't often say what she means," June says,

chuckling again. "She's a puzzle, that one."

The food around us is forgotten: the past has filtered in through the skin of the qalm and casts a dizzying spell on us all, even Kimbullettican.

"One thing I've learned about this place," she goes on, "is that symbiosis is survival. To exist here—truly exist—you must have something to give. I worked in a library on Earth. A silly thing to love. They stopped caring about such things long before I was born. But I liked putting things in order."

June's eyes have taken on the preoccupied quality I recognize from the sole time I'd stood in my father's office in the Zoo. Blurred with the past, memories and places far away swirling in to take the place of the here and now. I have no idea what a library is, but I say nothing, waiting. I'm afraid Alma or Kimbullettican will jump in with one of their questions, but they sense it too: the feeling of standing at the edge of something important, rocking in an invisible wind.

"Your family," she says, gesturing vaguely at Kimbullettican. "They are scientists of a respectful nature. Exchange, always exchange. I have been the keeper of their exchanges these last two hundred years. What they take, I look after. All here with me."

"What do they take?" I say, barely louder than a whisper.

"Oh, so many things. I've never been a scientist, not really. What catches a scientist's eye is a mystery to me. I love the eyenu because they're beautiful, and I know what makes them tick. Perhaps we only truly love that which we understand."

Her gaze wanders from where it's been fixed on a space beyond the oven, eventually landing on my face. We lock eyes and I take in the wrinkles of her skin, the even hairline, the wide arch of her nose. The ache I'd heard in Alma's voice, the ache that has been slowly sprouting in my stomach, surges into a full flower. One hundred and eighty-two years old. And here she is.

"Can we see the archives?" I say without fully meaning to.

She purses her lips, still studying me. "I was going to show you tomorrow . . . ," she says, and some flash of disappointment must flicker across my face, because she trails off. "But none of you look all that tired just now. So we might as well go on down."

"Please," I hear myself say.

"Let me just take this bread out before I burn down the cabin."

"Please," Kimbullettican says, sounding alarmed.

"Don't worry," June says, misunderstanding. "We'll eat it on the way."

A moment later, June wraps each of her hands in thickly woven cloths and grasps either side of the oven she had used to bake the bread. Rondo and I both move forward to help her, but she waves us off, scooting the clay oven to the left a little at a time. Beneath is a colorful mat that she kicks aside.

A hole. Almost perfectly round, and completely dark from

where I sit, as if below the qalm we all rest inside is not the ground, but an endless nothing that we're floating above. I crane my neck, looking for a hint of light, but June is already blocking the way, lowering herself into the maw, gripping what must be a ladder by the sound of her echoing feet. When none of us move to follow, she pauses, only her head visible above floor level now, and casts a quick glance around.

"We could wait until tomorrow if you're too tired," she says, but she sounds like my mother when she says it; there's an order in that statement that makes me rise quickly from where I'd been watching her. A moment later I'm descending into darkness, the light from the qalm above blotted out after me by Rondo and the others as they follow us.

The ground under my feet is soft, not squishy like mud but loose, as if the soil had been recently dug up and hasn't yet resettled. I can't see anything, just the halo of light from the qalm glowing down on us but not strong enough to reach the ground. I pause, motionless, noting how my suit seems to enjoy the cool air that smells of minerals. June disappears into the dark to my left, the sound of her footsteps muted in the sinking soil.

There's a sudden glow in the shadowy space we all stand within, a floating orb of light that appears like the abrupt birth of a moon. As it floats toward us, I realize June holds it between her palms, and it's not until she gets closer that I see it's not a power generated by her hands but light emitted from a nearly round kawa.

"Do you want me to carry it?" I say, and my words sound loud in what I can now vaguely make out as a cavern. "It looks heavy."

"It is," she says, her smile ghostly above the glow of the egg. "But I can bear it. Besides, it needs me in order to stay lit. This little one was shaped by my cells. And we're not going far."

"You are altering the kawa that the eyenu produce?" Kimbullettican says. I can feel their brain doing the complicated things it does that I can sense but not understand. They read the biology of the kawa like a line of text.

"Altering isn't quite accurate," June says, turning away from us, the kawa held in front of her like a torch. "Influencing is more precise."

"How?" Kimbullettican says, the first to follow as the woman moves slowly down what I realize now is a tunnel. Only in certain movement does she feel ancient. "This is not something I have learned in Mbekenkanush."

"No? That's why they have Hamankush on the job, I'd expect. We've spent a lot of time learning this process together."

"What process, exactly?" Alma pipes up. We cluster close on June's heels in the low-ceilinged passageway, our voices echoing tightly around us.

"The kawa, I've learned, are incredible conduits for power," June says.

"Yes, I know," Kimbullettican and I say at the same time.

"But," June continues, with a tone of patient impatience,

"they can be convinced to absorb other kinds of things too. Light. Memory. Heat."

"Convinced?" I say.

"Yes."

The sound of our footsteps in the passageway spreads in my ears, a signal that the tunnel is widening.

"Wait," June says, and moves forward without us. The halo of light from the kawa shrouds her but only her: straining my eyes at what awaits beyond in the dark is useless. The globe of the kawa seems to float down toward the ground as she bends, lowering it into what I can just make out as some kind of crater.

"Just a little wiggling," she says to herself, her voice drifting back over her shoulder to where we wait eagerly. The darkness of this place is complete: it's hard to believe that somewhere above ground is the sky and its stars, a moon that lights the jungle. This kind of dark is a mouth; it swallows us all.

And suddenly the dark fades. From where the dim figure of June crouches, there comes a thunk, and the halo of light from the kawa spreads onto the floor like a puddle. But then it seems to leak forward, on and on, as if in a vein that fills with light like blood. It gains momentum, the light snaking in a straight path ahead in the passageway for at least two hundred yards before veering abruptly to the right for a short distance and then snaking back toward us. The light creates a glowing rectangle, giving off illumination a similar shade to dawn. The light streaks back toward the kawa in its vein and then seems to feed into the egg on its other side, a complete circuit.

"Stars . . . ," Alma whispers, motionless, but I'm already moving past her, down the three carved steps beside the kawa, toward the rectangle of light and what it contains.

It's like my father's office, but far more vast and strange. Skeletons, some massive and some small; the enormous ones rooted on the floor with wooden supports, the small ones elevated on white clay podiums. Square transparent cases with the intricate bodies of leaves and roots crystallized inside. Clear cylinders as tall and thick as Kimbullettican filled entirely, from what I can tell, with soil: some of it richly black, some reddish. One cylinder farther down the row seems to contain a fine blue powder that gives off a slight glow. Many long trellises, transparent like the cylinders, with rows and rows of seeds, arranged by size, suspended within.

"These are the archives?" I breathe.

"On Earth we would just call it a museum," June says. She's moved down the steps as well and stands with one steady, wrinkled hand on a cylinder bearing mottled green soil. "Here, it is a record of all the places the Faloii have been and what they brought back."

"I do not understand," Kimbullettican says. They have not moved from the steps. In the Artery, their confusion is a shifting cloud of deep blue.

"This may come as a surprise," June says gently, "but your people used to travel."

"We are a stationary people," Kimbullettican says, seeming stubborn for the first time.

"It's been a long time." June pauses, taking in Kimbullettican's clustered facial spots. "Humans aren't the only ones who keep secrets."

"Why did they take all this stuff?" Alma says, wandering slowly down one row of artifacts.

"To learn from," June says. "To observe what other planets and their species do well. The Faloii are mostly stewards on Faloiv, but occasionally they step in to help species . . . improve."

"It is rare," Kimbullettican says, finally coming down closer to the rows of archived materials. "We do not like to do it. But it is the purpose of voyages like Adombukar's. To monitor ecosystems and ensure they are functioning effectively."

"What kind of changes do you make?" Rondo says. He stands near a glass case as tall as he is, studying what appears to be the fossilized form of a massive insect.

"Small ones," Kimbullettican says, their eyes sweeping over the many objects the archives contain. "What the humans call 'tweaks.' Mostly to encourage symbiosis. If one species develops a new adaptation, it may affect other creatures in its ecosystem. Sometimes these changes mean extinction of another species, which may be the best possible outcome. Other times we need to tweak other species in the ecosystem to ensure their continued survival."

"Wouldn't that happen on its own? Eventually?" Alma says.

"Sometimes." They turn to June. "Why did my people enter the stars? Leave Faloiv? It is not something I have ever been told of."

"Those tweaks," June says. "Some of the material they needed to make those tweaks wasn't on Faloiv. They went far to get it. As far as Earth."

"Where are the artifacts from Earth?" Alma says, turning to June, who has moved farther down the row. It's hard to focus on one thing here: there is so much to take in. Soil. Bones. Plants. In some cases, vials of what looks like air, or fumes of some kind, swirling endlessly, trapped within the transparent containers.

"Just here," June says, gesturing. Alma is at her side in a flash, but I move toward her more slowly. My heart has begun to pound, sending blood thrumming through my veins in a war dance of . . . what, I can't decide. Anxiety. Anticipation. Part of me would rather walk back toward the steps carved into the ground and disappear down the black tunnel toward June's qalm. But the greater part of me is magnetized. I am drawn toward June's cloaked back, and when I stand at her shoulder, I'm surprised by how little there is to see.

"This is all?" Alma says, her voice dropping.

"Our people had already been on a path of destruction for some time," June says, her eyes hovering just above the artifacts, as if she doesn't want to look right at them. "By the time the Faloii came, there wasn't much left of our natural world."

I stare at the two objects, one suspended inside a transparent cube on the surface of a smooth white-gray clay pedestal. The second is a smaller cylinder of soil, about half my height, rising from the floor beside the pedestal.

"What kind of animal is that?" Alma says, indicating the form of the creature suspended in the cube. Poised as it is in air, it's difficult to tell whether it was made for land or water or both, but the animal itself appears unremarkable. Pentaradial, its five legs splayed symmetrically, its skin bearing a thick and rubbery appearance. Two tentacles extend from its back, which I have to move to one side of the cube to fully gauge the length and function of. It appears to have many little pouches, circular and close to what appears to be a flexible body. The specimen appears to have been perfectly preserved, but its anatomy is a puzzle I can't decipher.

Then it moves.

Rondo and I both jump back, but Alma edges closer.

"It's *alive?*" she says.

"Yes. I don't know how, so don't ask," June says. "The kawa keep me young, but I don't know about our little starfish."

"But it's not a fish," Alma frowns, peering at its rippling appendages. "What is it?"

"They called it manducavirosa on Earth," June says. "It doesn't have a name here. It just is."

"Why did the Faloii bring it here?" Rondo asks.

"It was known for pulling the toxins out of water and turning them into food," June says, watching the creature with an almost loving expression. "It ate electricity, bacteria. Converted viruses into healthy cells—never a shortage of meals on Earth, in that case. They brought it because it's a survivor. The same reason they brought me."

"And the soil?" Kimbullettican says.

"Soil was something your family took from every one of their stops. Every planet has many different kinds, but they always take whatever they find most interesting."

Alma crouches down next to the canister of soil, her eyes simultaneously focused and dreamy. Her palm pressed against the container, just that bit of glass between her and the planet she has longed for; her yearning seems to expand like a bubble, filling the air around us with a substance that, though unseen, holds us suspended as if we too are a handful of other artifacts, crystallized and waiting to be remembered.

"This has come a long way" is all Alma says.

She stands abruptly and turns to June, nostalgia on her face disintegrating into a sudden anger. "Why don't we remember anything? Why is this all there is?"

June's eyes remain on the soil. Her hands don't touch the canister, but I can almost see her caressing it in her mind's eye. "I left almost two hundred years ago," the young-old woman says. Sadness has leaked into her voice. "And even then the world was being flattened."

"What does that mean?" Alma demands. "What do you remember?"

"Oh, I've put those things away," June says softly. "I've had too many other things to carry to carry that too."

"And what does *that* mean?" Alma says again. "You don't remember anything? Nothing?"

"A gray world," June says. The unsmiling smile fades completely. "A world with no sky. Metal and metal. Storm after storm. The rest I've put away. Those memories haven't hatched in some time."

"But what about us?" Alma says. "The people? Who *were* we?"

"We were trapped," June says. She has allowed her eyes to fall on the soil and the manducavirosa, flexing almost imperceptibly. Her eyes seem to focus, harden for a moment. "I remember their factories. My mother died in one."

"What did they make?" Alma says, latching on like a blood-sucking insect. "In their factories?"

June fixes her with a short, sharp gaze. "Stuff."

"So all the Faloii took was soil and the . . . creature?" I say, looking back at the pair of Origin Planet objects. "The Faloii went all that way and they only found two things worth taking?"

I thought we were getting to something that would make sense of what I have unearthed about Albatur: the reasons that brought him here, the coincidence that June calls the humans' decision to stay.

"Three," June says, her sliver of a smile more genuine now. "If you count me."

"And what did they leave behind?" Rondo says. He's leaning with his hands on his knees, peering intently at the soil, as if he'll find something sparkling in the grains of it. "You said the Faloii always exchanged, right? What did they exchange for the soil and the animal? And you?"

"They tried to give what was needed," June says, rubbing her hands together as if cold. "They weren't always right."

"What does this mean?" Kimbullettican says quickly. I glance at them but can't tell from the arrangement of their facial spots whether they are defensive or not. I think back to what they said that night in the qalm—*this all must be very strange—discovering a side of your people that you never knew existed.*

June sighs, a long deep breath that seems to leave her hollow. "Well," she says, turning away from the pedestal and the cylinder of soil. "I might as well show you."

She moves farther into the archives and I follow, enchanted, gazing at the rows of artifacts on either side of us like quiet sentinels. They seem to stare back as I trail her down the long wide aisle, the light from the kawa surrounding us in its glowing rectangular cage. Dozens of cylinders of soil, uniform white clay pedestals bearing various objects, crystallized specimens, the bones of creatures from planets even farther than my own people's. June approaches the last pedestal within the light the kawa provides—beyond is a narrow bit of dark empty ground before it runs into the flat cavern wall—and I know before June speaks that I recognize the object on the platform's surface.

"This," June says, reaching out and taking the narrow black cylinder in her hand, "is what your family left behind on Earth."

"A kawa," I say.

"A piece of one," she replies.

She opens the cylinder, letting the object slide out onto her palm. It shines deep purple, its edges jagged. I'm not sure how I even recognized it in its broken state: it's a feeling that emanates from the object in June's hand. A warmth, vibrating with power.

"This bit came back home," June says, "in one of those capsules from the ship."

"One of the capsules?" I say. "You've seen one of the capsules?"

She ignores me. "This is what was given in exchange for these few objects. Not an even trade, I would say. But the Faloii were generous. Too generous."

"What do you mean?" Alma says. "What do the kawa *do*?"

"What do the kawa not do?" she counters. "For Faloiv, they carry the promise of new species. They are coded with the past and the future. Energy. Humans call them eggs, but they are more akin to seeds. Faloiv cannot go on without them."

"But what about for Earth?" Rondo says. "The humans

wouldn't have been interested in creating species for a new planet."

"Power," June says. "Energy. That's what was needed, and the Faloii try to give what's needed, don't they? Leave it to our people to ruin this gift, and then dare come looking for more."

"What are you saying?" I interrupt. "The Faloii gave Earth a kawa, and then the humans came to N'Terra to get another? To get more?"

"I'll give them some credit," June says, as if she hadn't heard me. "They figured out how to use the kawa they did have as a map. Somehow they accessed its memories and it led them back here."

"Because Earth was dead?" Alma says. "They decided to come here?"

"Mostly dead," June corrects. She stares lovingly at the piece of kawa. "Most of them boarded the ship to make a home here. But every ship has its rat, as I said. *Every ship has its rat.*"

Beneath my feet, the ground seems to give a long shuddering sigh.

"What was that?" Rondo says, looking around. I do the same, expecting, perhaps, the thick bones of one of the larger fossils to be coming to life, thundering toward us. But the archives are still, the cylinders of soil and other artifacts as dead and motionless as before. The only response at first is another shudder through the ground.

"Is it going to cave in?" Alma says, jerking her chin up, her eyes searching.

"No," June says, but she frowns, tipping the purplish piece of kawa back into its cylindrical nest, placing both back on the platform. Her eyes look slightly unfocused. Listening, I think.

"It is a storm," Kimbullettican says, and their forehead spots frown too, concerned. "So sudden. I did not smell this coming."

"That's thunder?" Rondo says when the ground shakes again. I'm suddenly glad we're underground, away from any trees that might be felled by lightning. But now that Alma has said that about the ceiling caving in, I don't feel safe here either. The qalm seems so flimsy compared to the thick walls of the N'Terran compounds; I've never been beyond their boundaries for one of the gales that blow in from the jungle. I always assumed the storms weakened by the time they reached our settlement—now we're here in the thick of it, where the thunder and lightning begin.

I wouldn't be so nervous if Kimbullettican didn't also seem unsettled. They take several steps away from the pedestal, back toward the entrance that leads into June's qalm, but before they can get much farther, Hamankush appears at the end of the archives' long aisle, at the top of the three stone steps.

"Quickly," she says, her voice echoing toward us. "The eyenu."

• • •

Above ground, the rain has not yet come, but the smell of it ripples through the air, heavy and thick as the breath of a beast. The jungle is hushed, even the night dwellers, the Artery full of murmurs. Hamankush and June lead us back along the worn path toward the quarry where we had left the eyenu, and every time the thunder rumbles in the near distance I leap in my skin, expecting both sky and ground to open and for us all to vanish into one or the other.

What do you plan to do? Kimbullettican says to Hamankush, allowing me into the conversation as well.

We need to move the eyenu into their cave, she replies. The anxiety I sense emanating from them does nothing to settle my nerves. I trip on a stone and find Rondo's hand on my shoulder, steadying me. *This storm's suddenness is very strange. Ordinarily we would have more time to prepare.*

"What's going on?" he says when the next roll of thunder has died. "Do you know something we don't know? Feel something we don't know?"

"Not exactly," I say. "It's just something is weird. From what I can tell from Hamankush and Kimbullettican, this storm wasn't expected."

"Storm after storm," Alma says to herself, and it takes me a moment to realize she's echoing June's words about the Origin Planet in the archives. It puts shivers down my spine in spite of the hot veil the thunder seems to lay across the land.

"Don't animals usually protect themselves during a storm?"

Rondo asks. We round what I remember to be the last corner on the way to the eyenu's sleeping grounds, June hurrying ahead now with surprising agility.

"I think the eyenu are different," I say.

As soon as the animals are in sight, I know I'm right. Where the other creatures in the jungle are surely hidden away in strong trees or below ground, the eyenu cluster together in the open of the circle of rocks June had called their nest. When the lightning cracks the sky, it illuminates their wide eyes, all fixed on June where she comes hastening down the slight hill. In the electric light, the colors of their bodies, which had seemed so glorious in the daylight, look pale and washed out, the storm and their fear draining their brilliance.

Why are they still? Kimbullettican says. As June hurries down toward her flock, the rest of us pause, awaiting instruction. Above, the thunder rumbles on. It feels nearer, its breath hotter and stronger.

They rely on the archivist for much, Hamankush says.

"Why did they take her?" I call to Hamankush over the rising din. "Why is June here?"

This is what they do not want you to see, she tells me, and I'm jolted back to the jungle near Mbekenkanush, where she had shown me the memory. *The Faloii are as hypocritical as your own people.*

June turns and I sense that she and Hamankush are communicating, their eye contact and the blur of Hamankush's thoughts extending out to the woman like an arrow.

"What?" I shout. "I need to know! Why does June keep the kawa? Why June?"

"When my people traveled the stars, they were searching for perfect cells. They found them in June. Part of her lives within the eyenu. She has made them perfect."

Two planets, June says as she tends to her flock. *Two that need my blood.*

If your people knew, Hamankush says silently, *they would take her home. And they would believe they have a claim to the kawa.*

This *is home,* June says.

"What is going on?" Alma shouts, looking back and forth between us.

A roar of thunder silences any response.

"Come," Hamankush says to all of us. "We must help the eyenu to the cave!"

June moves through the crowd of the eyenu slowly, touching each of them, delivering them from their fear, at least momentarily.

"Where is the cave?" Alma yells. The wind has picked up. The animals of the jungle are silent but the trees are not: the whipping leaves and the groaning trunks fill the air with a violent noise, dense and green. Alma's voice barely cuts through.

"Just here," Hamankush says, but we can barely hear her. I get the feeling she is not accustomed to raising her voice.

Instead, when the wind shrieks, she shows me the way in the Artery.

Just there, she says, laying out the route. Up the mountain a little way, toward higher ground, the cave a mouth in the rock that extends deep. *Form a line, give the eyenu something to follow.*

"Come on!" I shout to Rondo and Alma, and Kimbulletti-can follows too, the four of us fighting the strengthening wind as Hamankush and June work on gathering the animals.

Wait here, I tell Kimbullettican when we've gone a little way. *When the eyenu reach you, keep moving toward us.*

"What are we doing?" Alma shouts. The just-risen moon is obscured by clouds, dimming by the moment. The storm is sweeping in, ready to swallow the light.

"The cave is just up here," I shout back. "We need to guide the eyenu to it. When we get to this outcrop, wait there until June brings them up!"

Between the whistles of the wind I can hear the eyenu chorus beginning to rise, still as scattered as it had been when I'd first laid eyes on them, but shrill, fear turning their song desperate. From this distance I can barely sense June in the Artery, but she's there, reassuring them, coaxing them to higher ground. Now that I know, their connection makes sense: they are part of her, and she of them. She had come from a rock across the galaxy and found what is, in a way, her true self. Her birth on

Earth was a coincidence, somehow: the green language shows me the way her biology aligns with the eyenu's, a miracle of genes and chance. June, like me, is between two worlds. Except she doesn't feel stuck. She feels like she's where she belongs.

The first drops of rain land on my forehead.

"Hurry," I call to Rondo, who is a few paces behind me. The ground has gotten steeper and we struggle upward. I don't want to imagine what the soft soil under our feet will become once the rain comes down.

"I think I see it," Rondo shouts, and when I look ahead there's a yawning hole where the dark is even darker. In the Artery I hear Hamankush encouraging the eyenu upward with gentleness that feels foreign coming from her.

"Keep going," I yell when Rondo reaches me. "I'll wait here for the eyenu."

"No, you keep going," he argues, pausing.

"Rondo, *go*," I say, pushing him upward. "I need to be after Alma in case the animals get confused! I need to hear them!"

He starts to say something but is stunned into silence by lightning so intensely bright that when I blink afterward, there's a glowing seam across the dark of my closed eyes. A clap of thunder leaves my ears ringing. Every hair on my body seems to rise, drawn up by the storm. Another few drops of water spatter my head and shoulders.

"Hurry up!" I shout, pushing him again. Only when he turns

reluctantly do I cast my eyes back down the mountain, peering through the thickening dark for a sign of the coming flock. At first I see nothing, but the next crack of lightning illuminates them: the dozens of wide and rolling eyes, making their way higher, led by June, tailed by Hamankush.

Come now, babies, June is telling them in her way. *A little more, a little more.*

I catch sight of Kimbullettican, waving an arm for June. Their confusion has not abated, and they reach out in concern to Hamankush.

Why did we not know? they say, about June and the eyenu. *The source of the kawa?*

The Faloii cannot very well demand much of humans, Hamankush says, *when we rely on one of them so much.*

The kawa, I say. *We used it for power. What do you use it for?*

Everything, Hamankush says. *Power. Memory. We pass the kawa to the Isii to balance the planet's lifeblood. Before June, we searched the universe for cells like hers, cells that would join with Faloiv's and create what could not be created by Faloiv alone, flexible cells with change embedded within. Her biology was wasted on Earth, but Earth did create her. In that way the kawa belong to humans as well—so they should be allowed them. They should be allowed to use the power to destroy themselves.*

Only the one they were given, June says. *They must only be allowed what they were given.*

This storm, Kimbullettican says. Their energy feels elastic, as if they are stretching toward Hamankush, needing something. *It is strange. Why?*

At this Hamankush communicates in Anooiire, and my own concern is left dangling before being knocked sideways by thunder so mighty that the very mountain seems to tremble. I crouch, pressing my hands against the ground. My fingers find grass in the near dark and grip it, as if clinging to these frail roots will tether me to the ground. When the rumble dies, the cries of the eyenu rise again, bridging the distance between us.

Here, I try to tell them. *Come up. You're almost safe!*

Their fear is purple in the Artery, but I feel them recognize my reassurance and continue upward, June still at the head of the flock. They've reached where Alma stands waiting and she now turns to make her way up toward my post on the trail.

That's when the sky splits open.

It's as if the spattering of raindrops that had fallen on my forehead were part of an exploratory mission, the first travelers out of a ship, scenting the air. What comes now is the invasion. The rain is not rain. It is an endless army, all its ferocity unleashed at once, turning the ground to mud and the air to water, transforming everything on the planet to a limp version of itself.

Quickly, Hamankush says to anyone listening.

The eyenu have almost reached me but they stall, Alma between their numbers and me, her hair plastered down by the rain's viciousness, her mouth open and shouting but inde-cipherable. She won't be able to hear me, so I just point, point hard, my finger a spear aimed at the cave one hundred yards beyond, its mouth almost invisible in the downpour. Alma scurries upward, slipping and sliding.

Hurry, babies, June says, her presence as calm as ever. The eyenu slip and slide after Alma, whose suit glows white in what's left of the moon. I look down at my own suit and find it glowing as well. I don't know if it's a result of saturation or because it knows I need light.

Almost, almost! I tell the eyenu. Their feet, clawed talons as thick as my own legs, struggle through churning mud. There is nothing I can do, no help I can offer. June says they'll be safe in the cave, and the only thing I can do is get them there.

The thunder cracks above like two meteors colliding in space, the reverberation shaking the ground, causing the mud to shift under my feet. I fall, my back slamming against what had been the ground but is now more like a slow-moving water-fall. It slides down toward the eyenu, and the animals balk at the sight of me, struggling in the mire.

Something is wrong, Kimbullettican says.

I'm fine, I answer, trying to right myself, trying to get my feet under me as the rain drowns out the moon. The only thing I can see clearly is myself, the white of the qalm-grown suit like the inner flesh of a shell, exposed to the light.

But they mean something else. The realization hits me and

the eyenu at the same time. Up until this moment, June has been keeping them calm, her silent murmuring in the Artery like a spell that keeps the flock moving up the mountain, even under the assault of the rain. But something stirs them from their near hush. Their throats open and the raucousness slices through the roar of the storm. I try to shout something at June, but my mouth fills with water.

They're here, someone says, maybe two someones, maybe everyone, maybe the whole planet, the words echoing in from the trees, already screaming from the fury of the storm. But by the time I realize who "they" is, they are upon us.

They come from lower on the mountain, their shadows emerging from the trees the way the qararac had come from the underwater gloom: they appear like haunted beings, the rain giving shape to their bodies but the thunder and water masking all sound of their attack. They are barely present until the moment that they're not. Three gwabi, their eyes white and empty, so empty they are like hollow bone, so empty that the only thing about them that remains familiar is the smell of the Zoo steaming off them like heat rolling before a wildfire.

"No," I whisper, too late, and by then there's already blood on the ground, mixing with the mud, everything stirred by the lashing of the storm, a cyclone of screams and violence toppling in waves down the mountainside.

And then the buzzguns. Lightning to my ears, at first, until the spark of one catches a fleeing eyenu in its graceful neck, the smell of smoke filling my nose, the explosion of fuchsia feathers, the screech that erupts from its beak to join with the clamor of thunder, shaking the world.

"Not the birds!" shouts a voice from the dark. "Shoot the others if you have to, but not the birds!"

I watch the eyenu fall and without choosing to, I'm running toward it, my hands outstretched, as if I reach it before it falls, everything will be okay. If I can keep its blood from joining the soil, I can stop this blur of horror and set everything right.

I reach the animal's body at the same moment as another person: a person wearing a gray suit, their face obscured by a mask that looks like glass, glowing crimson with some infrared vision, something that makes them a friend of the storm. The lightning flares like a volcano in the sky, and maybe behind the mask they smile. I try to run downhill: if Alma, Rondo, and the other eyenu could reach the cave, they can stay concealed. The graysuit drags me backward and flings me down, mud filling my mouth and eyes. Somewhere in the dark I hear June's scream splitting the air like a century of mothers before even she is lost in the rain.

CHAPTER 26

They march us all night, through rain that renders every tree uniform. The deluge conceals the scents I'm accustomed to, the darkness disguising everything familiar. But the graysuits seem to know where they're going, or perhaps it's the Albaturean gwabi that lead our tense procession. It is only June, the eyenu, and me. When they had eventually paused our march near daybreak, they lit a fire and lounged around it, their captives bound and set to the side like rubbish.

"If it's not cooked, I don't want it," a man's voice says says.

"Why would I offer you food if it wasn't cooked?" says another.

"I don't know why you do the things you do."

"Oh, shut up. At least we're finally drying out."

"Barely. The humidity is murder."

I can't see them, only hear them. My face is pressed into the damp soil. Inside my suit, the sharp edge that I know to be Captain Williams's pin stabs me, undiscovered with my grandfather's map.

"Watch the sparks," one voice says, a woman. I recognize it: Manx. "You're going to char my meat."

"A little char makes it taste better."

Meat. I force myself not to inhale—I know I will be sick if I do. Meat. After everything that has happened—that's still happening—N'Terrans are eating dead animals. Anger and revulsion flood through me, and I breathe out hard through my nostrils.

"It's too hot for a fire, honestly," one of the male voices says.

"Almost," says the other. "But as long as it keeps the beasts away, I don't mind a fire."

"You mean besides our beasts," Manx says, chuckling.

"Is that what he likes to call them? His beasts?"

"No, that's just what Dr. Jain calls them. Albatur probably calls them something more sophisticated than that."

I struggle against my bonds, but June's voice is immediately in my head.

Be still, June tells me, and I almost jerk at her nearness. She doesn't feel like Kimbullettican and the other Faloii in the Artery. Her Arterian feels softer, weaker. Like my mother's. Like Dr. Espada's. Human.

Where are you? I ask, trying to keep from wriggling.

Behind you.

Do you know if my friends . . . ?

I don't know if they survived, she says.

I squeeze my eyes shut. Alma had carried on past me up the mountain, toward the cave, where Rondo had been waiting. Had they made it? Had they managed to hide themselves? What about Kimbullettican and Hamankush? I remember the gwabi's jaws flashing in the swirl of dark and storm, fangs that had seemed to float. Had those fangs found flesh? This all feels so much like the night my mother died: the blur of noise, the uncertainty about what had befallen whom. Separated from my loved ones. Again.

Three of my children dead, June says, her grief thrumming in the Artery thick and blue. I remember now, her wail breaking through the storm like its own shrill thunder. The comfort I offer her is weak: my mother's death is too near for me to comfort her now; all the condolences I give seem aimed, at least in part, at myself. I focus instead on the stretching ache of my arms' tendons, bound uncomfortably behind my back.

Why are they doing this? I think, not to June but to the entire Artery, as if the world might answer, as if the stars themselves might offer something solid.

Someone told them it's right, June says.

Nearby I hear a scuffle of movement, a faint whine reaching my ears. I stiffen, my eyes cracking open.

"They're moving again," one of the people by the fire says.

I wonder if they're still wearing masks, the reflective shields that had rendered them inhuman there on the mountain. Are we still on the mountain? The sun has risen now, but I can't tell where we are.

"Let them move," Manx says. "They're not going anywhere."

This time I roll slightly sideways, an inch at a time, my cheek still pressed into the soil, but my eyes taking in the people sitting around the fire. They wear the predictable gray suits, darkened by the crush of rain. They turn from where they sit on stones and wood, looking over their shoulders at the eyenu, almost in a pile, their legs and beaks bound with what I can only guess is the same fibrous material that binds my wrists against my lower back. Some sort of chariot is parked nearby, a wide flat bed at its rear. I can only assume this is how the eyenu were transported. The three Albaturean gwabi crouch nearby, on guard.

"I don't know what he's going to do with them," Manx says, turning back to the fire.

"I heard it's like the bones," one of them says. "Something that will give energy."

"I thought they got the bone machine to work?"

"They did, but you need the bones to do it, don't you?" Manx snaps.

"We were so close to getting the Faloii on the mountain. That would have been something."

They're silent for a moment and I merely watch them

through the slits of my eyelids, a feeling like hate roiling within me.

"*Something* would be finding our egg," Manx says. She pokes at the fire with a stick, sending sparks up into the canopy. "*That* would be something. He won't be happy when he hears we found one of the pods but nothing inside."

They found one of the pods. Was it the same one I found with Kimbullettican?

"It has to be in the aliens' city," one of the men says. "The humans who turned sides had to have taken it with them. He'll find it when we finally go in."

Aliens, I repeat mentally, trying to make sense of it.

They mean the Faloii, June says.

That doesn't make sense. How can they be aliens on land that's theirs?

This . . . this is something I remember.

Her energy in the Artery seems to swell with something, something that swims as it looks for its name.

What are you talking about?

The rats in the ship. The man who now leads your people and makes these monsters—he was a rat, a young man at one time. This has begun to feel like Earth. He brought it from there.

What do you remember?

There is nothing to remember. They killed my mother for loving who she was. She was from a place called Trinidad. She wanted to remember and they hated her for it. When the Faloii came, I couldn't wait to leave.

And they took you with them, I say. *They wanted you.*

I was special, she says. *Somehow. My genes were made for the stars. But now Earth has followed me through them, and I wonder what it was all for.*

"The lady doesn't look so good," a voice says.

I dart my gaze back to them. The three people around the dwindling fire are all standing, moving toward us.

Manx and one of the men clutch strips of meat, tearing at them with their teeth. The image of knocking those teeth out of their mouths flashes across my mind unbidden. The other man carries a buzzgun.

"They're tied up, Rand," his compatriot sneers. "It's a tiny woman and a kid."

"The lady bit me when I grabbed her before," the one called Rand says. "Look, I have a mark."

"Yeah, yeah."

Manx reaches us first. "Hey, kid," she says. "We know who you are."

I stare back at her from my twisted position on the ground, glaring at the meat in her hand. She takes a bite, chews hard, looking me in the eye.

"Do you know where your friends went?" she says.

I can't help it—my chin quivers. If the graysuits don't know where Alma and Rondo are, then that at least means they aren't dead. These three people didn't find Kimbullettican or Hamankush, and they didn't personally shoot my friends. If they're not here tied up, they're free. For now.

"Brave, huh?" Manx says. She looks almost sorry. Maybe just disappointed. "Well, it would be better if we had you all. Their parents are worried, Octavia. Doesn't that bother you?"

I grit my teeth. It does bother me. But that's not what's important here. My voice finds itself at the back of my throat, and when I open my mouth I sound like I'm croaking.

"You're making things worse," I say.

Her eyebrows lower for an instant, maybe because she can't understand me, or maybe because she doesn't like what I have to say.

"For who?" she says. "Not for us. Haven't you learned anything from your daddy?"

It's like a slap. June cringes in the Artery. The graysuits turn their attention to her.

"So who are you, exactly?" Rand says, using his gun like a finger, pointing. "And why do you have so many of the egg things?"

"More importantly," Manx interrupts, "do you have ours? Albatur has had us looking for the *Vagantur*'s forever. You'd save us a lot of trouble if you gave it up now."

"If I kept track of everything that fell from the sky," June says, "I would have a lot of rain."

"You know that the storm last night wasn't normal, right?" I break in. "You know that the planet is starting to change? Because of you. Because of us."

Manx's eyebrows lower again, but they spring back quickly, arched with annoyance. "All the more reason we need to get the hell out of here," she snaps. "Now, what did you do with our egg, lady?"

I've twisted away from her, but behind me, June hums to herself. I imagine her eyes closed, hiding the century that shines out from them. The heat is rising. Dawn is passing into day.

"What about your birds?" Rand says. "We were watching. We saw them give the eggs. How does it work? He's going to want to know."

"It's not work at all," June says, then resumes her humming.

"You know you're human, don't you?" Rand insists, using the gun to point again. I keep my eyes trained on the empty black mouth of it, hoping it doesn't speak. "Who do you really think you're helping?"

Behind him, the eyenu make stifled sounds beneath their gags. They're watching the human proceedings with fear-filled eyes. I wonder if they think June is their mother, if they feel as helpless as June had on Earth, watching her mother be dragged away. The thought fills my heart with grief, but I'm too cowardly to look into the Artery and feel what they feel. It might overwhelm me, sodden my reflexes with sadness, and I need to be sharp.

"There are other ways to do this," I say. "Don't you know there are a hundred or more people living in the city with the Faloii? Perfectly happy? Everything was fine until Albatur started messing everything up."

"Don't you know anything?" Manx snaps now, crouching down before me. "He's right: you are just like your mother. Think you have it all figured out, don't you?"

Rand laughs, an ugly sound, small under the eye of the jungle. Manx rocks back on her heels, still eyeing me. "You think it's about working things out here. It's about working things out here so that we can *leave*," she says. "If Albatur has his way, we can keep Faloiv for its resources but finally go *home*. Why don't you understand that?"

"But this *is* our home," I whisper.

She rolls her eyes skyward, as if my ignorance is a bird that she follows to the treetops. "It doesn't have to be. You're a kid: you don't know. Before Williams died, they got what they needed from her: the ship will only run on the kawa it was built with. We need *that* egg."

Only one will make it run, I think, the words etched on the captain's cell wall glowing behind my eyes.

They must only be allowed what they were given, June says.

"Don't do that," the one called Rand says. "You're doing the talking thing, aren't you? Albatur said you probably could.

Don't. Whatever you want to say, say it out loud."

"You found all those kawa," I say, almost laughing. "But he still can't get what he wants."

Manx looks like she wants to hit me. "N'Terrans have been searching for years," she says. "We know the aliens have the *Vagantur*'s power cell. If they just give it up, we can go."

My heart begins to pound. June somehow has a piece of the *Vagantur*'s kawa in the archives. They must not know it's there, or this conversation would be moot. I have to keep it that way.

"Go back *where*?" I say, diverting the conversation. "To Earth? It's probably a shell by now."

"That's why we need the eggs," she says, smiling as if she finally found a way to get through to me. "The *eggs* will not only fix the ship, they will fix the planet. All the power we need."

"That's what he says," I say.

"Yes, that's what he says," she snaps back, angry again.

"And what if he's wrong?" I say. "What if he's wrong?"

"Don't bother," Rand says to her. He lets the buzzgun fall now, its mouth shouting silently at the ground. He turns back to what's left of the fire. "Waste of time. Let her die in a cell like Williams."

"At least we have her," Manx says, shrugging carelessly in my direction. She too goes back to the embers, to the smoking bodies of dead animals. "She's wearing the suit he was talking about. It will be good to make a few of those before we leave this shit planet."

Are you all right? I say to June.

I'm tired, she says. *I thought I was finished being tired.*

I don't know what to do, I say, and my eyes fill with tears, because it feels like I'm talking to my mother and at the same time it feels like I never had one.

She doesn't answer, and this makes the tears burn even hotter. To keep them at bay, I focus on the gwabi and the eyenu, the vast space between what each of them is feeling. I wonder if, under all the modifications Albatur and the others have made, the animals still retain anything of their own, or if they've been changed beyond recognition, all that they used to be weeded out by the force of violence. I think of the metal world I'd seen in June's memory and wonder the same about myself and my fellow humans. Have we retained anything that isn't destructive?

Was it ever good? I ask June in the silent tunnel. *Was there anything worth saving?*

She doesn't answer right away. I can feel her attention focused on the remaining eyenu of her flock, her heart aching for them, her anger stronger than her body. When she finally turns her energy toward me, it's purple and heavy with grief and memory.

Of course, she says. *There is always something to save. But what was good, we made ourselves. My mother's pin. Such a small thing. She wanted to remember the place she came from, before she started working for the River's factories. I remember now. I remember there were no jobs, except with them: two companies owned everything. She had to feed me. She worked for them. They cut off her locs. They erased her tattoos. What is there to pass on from a world that has been flattened?*

They started doing the same thing in N'Terra, I tell her. I have to work hard not to let her grief sink into me from the Artery. It's as strong as last night's storm, threatening to saturate me. *People had banners from the Origin Planet. From Earth. Flags. They started replacing them with N'Terran banners.*

This man, this Albatur, she says. *He wants a metal world. If there is good, it's made ourselves.*

The three graysuits are sitting and eating. It might be meat. I can almost hear them chewing, can hear their low laughter, keeping their conversation quiet enough to remain secret from me and June. I stare blankly, trying to envision the world they imagine going back to. A flat world. Is that where my father longs to return? A colorless world. What besides blood makes us family? The vivid colors of Faloiv surround the graysuits, and I decide to stare at those instead. Crimson. Aquamarine. Violet.

Violet.

My eye passed over the tall purple flower the first time, just one more bright thing in the jungle. But as it seems to rise, I lock my gaze onto it. It does rise, inch by inch, its stalk emerging from the brush. A vusabo.

There is no breeze, but it sways. So friendly. So harmless.

One more flower of Faloiv . . . at least that's what it would like passersby to think. But I know better.

The first time I noticed the green language of Faloiv, far away in Mbekenkanush—or was it earlier? In N'Terra? The ogwe and their messages of first calm and then warning?—it wasn't a language I could fully understand. But something has shifted—maybe inside me or maybe inside the planet. I hear it more clearly now. The vusabo almost makes sense to me, and I can feel it hunting.

Rand and the other graysuits continue their conversation, oblivious to the threat. The almost threat. The vusabo hasn't yet decided what it will do: the slight shift I sense in Faloiv isn't complete; it's a process, a message that spreads slowly through the planet's veins. Maybe it flows from the Isii. I can't tell. But the plant that normally hunts birds is making up its mind, sizing up the humans, weighing whether they are predators, and therefore prey.

I know immediately what I must do. If there is good, it's made ourselves.

The green language doesn't come naturally to me the way Arterian does. I know I will never speak it as the Faloii do. But I can feel some cave of my brain grinding open as I force what feels like a forest of vines apart to make room for the words.

Humans, I say. *Danger.*

It's as if the vusabo was waiting for permission. Two quills fly like wasps from the stalk, burying themselves in Rand's neck. The vines spring from the bush a moment later.

"Holy hell," he cries, leaping up. I stare, unmoved, knowing the venom is spreading through his veins. I know there is no voice in the Artery telling him where he will find the antidote. I have just helped the vusabo kill this man, but the only thing I feel is the green language thrumming through me.

Manx screams, leaping up, using the stick she'd used on the fire as a weapon against the vines, which are wrapping around Rand's legs like two snakes.

Hurry, we need to move now, I tell June. She stares at me in bafflement, and I can't tell if she's impressed or horrified by what I've done, what I have decided to be. *Now!*

I remember a graysuit cuffing Rondo's wrists, and Rondo wriggling out of them. I begin to do the same, urging June to follow my lead. The graysuits ignore us, their cries rising as they battle the vusabo, which shoots another set of quills but misses. My bonds have begun to loosen, but not quickly enough. One of the graysuits has freed Rand, ripping one of the vines clean off the vusabo's stalk. I yank at my wrists, my pulse climbing. Captain Williams's pin jabs me through my suit, spurring me on.

Manx raises her buzzgun, aims at the flower of the vusabo, and fires. The sound echoes through the jungle and bright violet petals and plant matter scatter to the ground. The stalk will likely survive, but it is too damaged to attack further, dashing my hopes.

Rand, however, remains panting, dizzy. He will be gone soon, I think, fighting a flood of remorse. Instead I feel sorry for the vusabo. It had been too small a predator against too dangerous an adversary. The small fangs of the stalk were not enough to do what I needed them to do. I needed a bigger beast.

A bigger beast.

Do not, June says in the Artery, seeing my plan before it has fully hatched in my mind, but I know already that I'm going to.

My wrists are not free, but my fingers can reach the place on my hip where Captain Williams's pin is concealed within the flesh of my suit. The suit opens for me, revealing the hard edge, the point of the wings which, long ago, the woman who flew our ship had used to carve her words into the wall. I grip it hard. I will not let it fall.

I take a deep breath, the wings in my hand, the wings that had come so far across the universe. I press the edge against my left palm, wincing already. I press. I press until my mouth opens, releasing a small breath. I press until I feel the blood release from my skin, a small river, a signal. I imagine it as the reddest thing on the planet as it drips down my wrist into the soil. I imagine it as a siren, a beacon shining into the sky, demanding the jungle to part like water.

Nothing happens.

Rand is still clutching his buzzgun, but it hangs limply to his side. His mouth moves, rambling an endless stream of nonsense as his fellow graysuits cluster around him, trying to figure out how to help.

"Poison?" one says. "Check the packs on the gwabi. There has to be some kind of antidote that the whitecoats sent out!"

"Rand, what's happening? Where does it hurt?"

Please, I think. *Please. Come on. We're right here.*

Manx aims her buzzgun at me and June.

"Don't even think about moving," she says. "As soon as we deal with this, I'm retightening those bindings!"

Please, I pray to the sky. *Albatur can't have June. He can't have the eyenu. Please. Please.*

And then I notice the quiet.

It spreads across the jungle like wind, everything becoming still, the very trees listening. The graysuits barely notice. They are accustomed to not noticing, and their attention is elsewhere.

The first time the ground shakes, it's a mere tremor.

Oh, child, June says, her fear growing large.

Get ready to move, I tell her.

The ground shakes again, this time enough to make the grass around me tremble just slightly, as if shuddering in a mysterious breeze.

"Did you feel that?" the third graysuit says, looking away

from Rand for the first time. Rand is still on his feet. I think it must take longer for the venom to travel through someone his size.

"Feel what?" Manx says.

The rumble in the ground answers. My heart matches it, thundering in my ears. I begin scrambling at my bonds again, not caring if they notice.

"I felt it that time," Manx says. She's standing now, her eyes fixed on the jungle. "Leftover from the storm maybe?"

How can they not know?

"It's so quiet," the third graysuit says, and these three words float out into the air between them, a seed. I can almost see it being planted, the way it grows roots in their minds.

"Oh god," Manx says, and suddenly the buzzgun is a metric of her fear: alert, erect. She aims it at the jungle, at nothing, at everything. She clings to it like it might offer something besides noise when the time comes.

"Be quiet," she says, her voice as soft as the soil against my cheek. "Be quiet *now*. Don't move. Don't speak."

They obey. Silence consumes the small clearing. The fire has long faded, its embers cracking only occasionally and so softly I don't think even a dirixi would notice. I work blindly, madly at the material that ties my wrists, imagining that I feel the fibers stretching, that freedom is only a few twists away. June is motionless behind me, as still as the jungle and as silent. I wonder if her wrists move, if she is struggling to free herself,

AN ANATOMY OF BEASTS

or if she has resigned herself to whatever happens next.

"Did it stop?" Rand whispers. Only the shape of his words reaches me.

"Quiet," Manx hisses.

My wrists burn. The jungle is still silent.

"I don't hear it," Rand whispers again, fear and poison making him stupid.

"Quiet!"

The ground does not shake. Perhaps the beast is listening. Perhaps it has chosen other prey. Perhaps it raises its monstrous tongue to the air, scenting other beasts that might earn its wrath. I remember its scales. The way it had approached the *Vagantur* without fear, despite the ship's size, confident in its fangs. The way its only concern was blood, leveling the jungle in pursuit of its needs, and the way the jungle had gone silent before it, within and without.

I am alone in the Artery when I open it wide inside my head.

Come, I say into the void. *We're here.*

A long moment of stillness, of silence.

Then the ground begins to tremble.

CHAPTER 27

June is already free. I don't know how she did it, but as the graysuits get lost in their panic, their fear rising to replace the flames of their dead fire, I catch sight of her slipping across the small campsite, dodging between the streams of light the breaking sun provides. She is fast and agile, the weight of her many years lifted by urgency. Even with the Artery closed, her purpose eclipses all else: she is going to save her babies.

"The walls are yellow and blue," Rand cries, as if behind the delirium of the venom he still understands the fear. "The doors are falling!"

The third graysuit scrambles for a buzzgun. It's the only thing they know to do. The Albaturean gwabi have risen from where they lay resting. Their blank eyes show no fear, but I wonder if threads of it are still sewn into their muscles, if inside they are twitching to run but are held in place by the Zoo's bonds.

I struggle at my own. I'd risen to my knees at some point, shoving Captain Williams's pin back into the fold of my suit with my grandfather's map, the soil still clinging to my face and finding its way into my mouth. My hand throbs, wet with blood. What I've done seems to spiral down from the sky like a wide-winged oscree, down and down until it lands on my shoulder and whispers in my ear: *It's coming for you. You called it with your blood; now the dirixi will answer.*

The graysuits are shouting and they shouldn't be, but they've realized June is trying to free the eyenu and they can't decide whether killing her is more important than saving their own skins. The dirixi could be a mile away, it could be five miles away. All we know is that it will be here soon.

One of my wrists feels loose. I stumble to my feet, unbalanced without my arms to help, and use all my strength to pull my hands in opposite directions. The bonds, whatever they're made of, cut into my skin, and perhaps more blood emerges into the thick jungle air, but it doesn't matter. One drop. A hundred. It's enough.

The bonds snap just as June frees another eyenu. I start to move toward her across the clearing, but Rand whirls on me, his buzzgun aimed at my chest.

"The comet is too big!" he shrieks, delirious. His eyes are wild but as empty as the gwabi's. The beasts don't move. The third graysuit appears to be searching frantically for their remotes, hoping the gwabi will defend against the coming threat. He has no idea that what he's hoping for is smoke. That the gwabi, if they had their own minds, would already be fleeing. Only humans think this is something that can be fought.

Frozen, my eyes move toward my hand, the blood wandering down from my palm to my wrist. Bloodshot with venom, Rand's eyes follow mine, and when they settle on the red ribbon running from my skin, he stares blankly for a moment.

"You . . . ," he starts, but can't finish. He doesn't need to. Despite the effect of the vusabo, he knows I did this.

Manx has attacked June. They wrestle on the ground, all but one eyenu free. The birds squall with terror, the nearness of the dirixi competing with fear for their mother. One rushes to where the two women fight, bringing its long beak down on the graysuit's shoulder with ferocious speed. Manx screams, and the beak comes away red. Two more eyenu rush to help, and Manx falls away from June, who lies shaking on the ground. Without her cloak she looks small and frail, every bit of her almost two hundred years. Rand watches this scene over his shoulder, his mouth opening and closing soundlessly, the buzzgun still trained on my chest.

I leap forward, grabbing the long muzzle and shoving it skyward. I expect it to fire, but it doesn't; Rand merely grunts in surprise and stumbles backward toward where the third graysuit fumbles with one of their packs. Rand and I are still struggling when the other man withdraws a square black remote.

One of the gwabi immediately becomes alert as a button on the remote glows red. Its eyes, still blank, narrow into slits. It moves forward, its gait as jerky and unnatural as it had been when it had tracked me to the *Vagantur*'s escape pod. If it's even the same one. With their selves stripped away, there is no differentiating between the creatures Albatur has stolen.

The roar from the dirixi rends the jungle, turning everything static; the air ripples like water. My fist connects with Rand's face in the moment he allows fear to make him still, and the impact makes me cry out, one of the knuckles of my already injured hand cracking, the blood still moving in a slow line from my palm. When the gwabi leaps, I find myself holding the buzzgun, and when it fires, the bolt of light leaving my hands and snapping through the air into the massive airborne body is as if all my worst dreams have flowed from inside my head and gathered in a swarm before my eyes. The gwabi falls, twitching, the eyes still blank but now somehow blanker, life leaving the grand muscles and traveling elsewhere, somewhere far. I drop the gun, my hands shaking like the ground. Everything is shaking.

June is gone. Manx hauls herself from the ground, bleeding, screaming obscenities at her two comrades. Rand crawls away from me, afraid of the gun when he should be afraid of everything else. I scream too, but it doesn't sound real: I don't hear myself. All I hear is the echoing silence of the jungle, watching us and knowing that the noise I have brought is what will put us in the soil.

When the dirixi breaks through the tree line, it pauses. It's smaller than the last one I had seen. I stare at it, empty. My fear is a planet—I live on it. The flaming eyes pass over the scene before it, blazing with gleeful hunger. Manx, streaming blood from the wound inflicted by the eyenu, is closest. She stumbles sideways, then backward, her escape slowed by her desperate need to keep her eyes on the thing that means her harm. Maybe she's still screaming, maybe instinct has silenced her. It doesn't matter because it doesn't save her. I watch her disappear into that jagged mouth, shreds of her visible for only a moment before they are lost in the black hole of the dirixi. It rises onto its back legs, screeching victory.

Buzzguns fire and I am running. The jungle swallows me and I make my way down its green throat, even when something hot and sharp strikes my shoulder, sending me down into the dirt, the pain erupting like a scream. My suit screams too: I feel its pain, a thousand tiny fibers recoiling from the burn, trying to repair themselves against this unknown assailant. I stumble to my feet again, my breath coughing in and out, my legs wobbling as if I am not a creature made for land. Beneath me, that land shakes. There's no way of knowing how far or how near I am to death, or how near death is to me. It is near enough. It is near enough for every roar to turn my skin into water.

Water.

The gentle sound of its movement had reached me when I'd awoken in the camp and now it reaches me again between roars. Soft. A whisper of a trickle, or the lap of a wave. In my mind, I imagine the river and its bowing plants, the noxious bubbles rising to save me from the death that hounds my heels. I can make it. I can make it there. I don't hear the rush of other animals to this source of safety, but I tell myself they are already there, collapsing into nausea like a cool, safe bed. I force my legs onward. The river. I will make it to the river.

I think behind me I hear screams. One person. Two? I tell myself the screams don't belong to June. Every time my foot strikes the ground I tell myself it is her foot, carrying her and her flock far up the mountain, back to the archives, underground where death can't reach them. Every breath I take blows her toward safety. I smell the water now. It fills my nose with hope.

The pain in my shoulder screams louder and louder. The place where I cut my palm throbs. I think I can smell my own blood, mixing with the hope that drives me onward. I can still feel my suit trying to repair itself, but it's struggling, and it can't heal me, the hole in my body left open to the air.

Air. I almost run out into it. The ground ends. Something

pulls me back, some last shred of sense that sends me scrambling backward, my butt landing hard on the rocky ground, pain lancing upward. Stones slide under my feet, pitching out into the nothing. There is no river.

I might whisper a curse, or perhaps something sadder, a groan that comes from my bones. The water I smelled was not the river. There are no clusters of bending plants here, no shaggy predators leaping from the trees to save me with their symbiosis. The air is devoid of bubbles. It's devoid of everything except the smell of my blood, joined a moment later with the sky-shattering shriek of the dirixi. The heat rises on Faloiv, the sun's crimson eye like a balm on my skin, but the fear clings to me like ice. I can't move. I stare far down—far, far down, impossibly far. Water there at the bottom of the nothing. A vast blue lagoon laid like a disk across the land. Behind me there is only jungle, the smell of death creeping out like fingers over the soil, seeping through to reach my feet. The death smells familiar. It could be my own.

The dirixi hulks out of the trees on all fours, its nostrils flexing, taking in the fumes of the trail I left behind. The blood dripping from my hand is a breadcrumb compared to the soaking feeling of pain that is a red sponge on my shoulder. I wonder if the beast sees me, or if it sees only my blood, my body a mere vessel that contains what it requires. I breathe shallowly, not to be silent but because I know no other way. My breath is gone, leaking away like my blood.

"Thank you," I say, the words falling clumsy and strange from my lips. The Artery is a wide hallway in my head: I lack the control to close it. Inside, the dirixi's hunger and joy are unbearably bright. It's almost beautiful, the perfection of its savagery.

Each step toward me shakes the ground, sending more stones flying out into space, where maybe they eventually fall. Or maybe they float. I'm too weak to care. When I find myself floating, my surprise is more real than the breath in my lungs. I don't know if I jumped, if I fell. I float down. All I smell is blood. All I hear is the roar that rips the air and not my skin, and in the Artery, all the joy growing spines of rage.

CHAPTER 28

I'm some version of asleep when I hit the water, dreaming of the gwabi I shot, a nightmare in which all the animals of Faloiv have had their souls cut out by Albatur's scalpel. The crash and slap of the surface wakes me, but barely. I'm tired. So tired that when I begin to sink, I don't struggle. The water's so cold it's sharp, needles that prickle every patch of exposed skin. The cold of it presses on my injured shoulder and palm, tighter the deeper I go. As I sink, I notice the tickle of algae brushing my face, my chest: I descend through their gardens, an astronaut through the strangest reaches of space. But I'm not afraid of this blackness, of the soft density that crushes in around me. I'm not even afraid when I feel the creep of slime across my face, the slow crawl of something I can't see, its grip like a gentle veil.

I'm breathing. Shallow breaths that leave me slightly dizzy, but breaths nonetheless. Not algae on my face, then, but my suit—even in its weakened state it is trying to help me survive, and the guilt of that realization seems to pull me down farther still in the depthless water.

I don't know how much time has passed when I realize that I'm not merely sinking. A current carries me, down through the tunnels that I sense were dug by the multukwu. A current of water and . . . something else. I realize, in my numb acceptance of whatever fate awaited me, I have not been listening. I look into the Artery.

The green language perceives me keenly from above and below. I'm surrounded by it. It feels like only yesterday that it had been too obscure for me to comprehend. Even now its words are beyond me, but I grasp its meaning the way I grasp communication from any species on Faloiv. Only this feels . . . larger. In constant motion. As bright and endless as the stars.

And it beckons me.

There is a trail in the Artery, and it hails me, signaling the organism of my suit as well. I have a choice, I feel. I can choose to be borne along in the current that is carrying me, following something like a scent that the green language has decided I should see. I can also choose to die.

Curiosity guides me. The suit feels my decision and allows me to be pulled along in the current, the water getting warmer and warmer as we go. I sense we are rising from a great depth, and I know I'm right when light looms larger and brighter ahead, the plants thinning into what looks like fine moss. I'm in a tunnel. It slopes upward.

Soon I lie in the shallows, staring at my fingertips, almost unrecognizable in their wrinkled state, feeling the mask my suit provided receding off my face. My shoulder, which the pressure of the water had seemed to soothe, now aches anew, as if the sunlight had reminded it that we are indeed a body and that we have lost blood. I wonder how much. I wonder what my shoulder looks like, if there's a hole in me for the light to pass through. I glance at my palm, and the wound stares back.

I raise my head, looking first over my shoulder at the water. If I'm at the edge of a lagoon, it's bigger than any I've seen so far. I can't see the other side, its surface endless and an otherworldly green. A sea. I look ahead again, at my arms resting in black sand. Beyond is the welcome sight of jungle. It's different, somehow, from the rest of Faloiv: the trees are tall, as tall as ever, but I don't recognize their smell—sharper than the ogwe and the syca, almost acrid. It makes me thirsty. But greater than my thirst is the call of the green language. I force myself to stand.

The ground beyond the sand is green and springy, paler than the jungle ahead. It seems like a good place to lie down— to rest, or maybe to give up—but something pulls me onward. The trees will have answers, I tell myself. At the very least, hydration. I drag myself in their direction, imagining the smell of water.

I push through the jungle. At one point, I might have tried to classify the plant species, all new to my eyes. That person feels far away. N'Terra feels like a vestigial organ that I've slowly evolved out of my body. Whatever part of me it had occupied has shrunken into a memory. Something else has taken its place, the green language rushing in and planting seeds. It grows inside me. It had heard me whisper *Danger. Humans.* It thinks I have chosen a side. Maybe it's right; maybe this is why the vine that had once encircled me and Rondo has seemed to wither. What pulls me toward Faloiv pulls me away from his heart.

I haven't gone far when the smell of water trickles out of my imagination and into reality. It grows stronger as I press on, my feet finding the edge of a ravine, bordered with crags. A stream runs along its bottom, a small rush of water whose gurgle barely reaches my ears as I stand gazing down. There looks to have been a trail once, used by animals, perhaps, to reach the water when it still flowed more strongly. Now vines cross what had once been worn, stones where they shouldn't be. My dry tongue drives me down to the ravine's floor, slipping and sliding, showers of rocks preceding every step. Twice I catch myself with my bleeding palm, the pain shooting up my arm, reminding me that after water, I need to find medicinal flora.

But more than healing and more than water, something else

calls me. The thing the green language wants me to see. When I reach the tiny stream's edge, I let my eyes wander, searching the shallow water. I direct my eyes to the wall of the ravine, which bears traces of having once been under water: wavy lines that pattern the stone in gentle sweeps. I follow their trail with my eye, wondering what caused a river to dwindle to a stream.

And then I see it.

A boulder. Almost round, almost white. One end tapering off to prevent it from being a true sphere. Moss grows along its surface, a fine coating like green lace. Along one side grows an orange-blossomed tree, its trunk bonded with the pale surface as if the two were born intertwined. The tree may think the boulder is organic. I know better.

Yes, this, the green language seems to say.

If I could, I would run to it. The object is a glowing planet: I'm helpless, drawn in by its gravity, and I splash through the stream to reach it. When I press my palms against its surface, peeling away the moss, swiping away the layers of dirt, forty years' worth, my heart freezes in my chest until my eyes land on the faded red letters. I need to see them, I need to know that I'm right, even though wrong is impossible.

Vagantur Capsule 2.

"Here you are," I whisper. "Here you are."

Just as with the capsule's sibling, the indentation in the shape of wings is just below the red letters. Ignoring my aching shoulder, I reach for the hidden pocket within my suit and with shaking fingers withdraw Captain Williams's pin, waiting there for me like a prophecy. It slides into the indentation with the same satisfying sound, and after what seems like an eternity, the door slowly, slowly opens, a few ragged inches at a time. The closed smell, a smell of strangeness, drifts out and over my face, a mask that shrouds me in the past. I don't hesitate. I step inside and achingly sink down onto the single white seat, encircled by the transparent walls of the capsule.

I sit, numbed by all that has transpired. I can picture the jaws of the dirixi snatching up Manx, one gnash of its teeth turning her into nothing—but I feel empty. It is one death of many deaths. I had thought my mother's was the first, but June's memories tell me that the blood has been flowing for much longer than that. Not a planet swallowed by natural disaster but a place destroyed by its people. This is our legacy after all. The heritage Albatur wants to re-create is this: he wants to destroy the place we'd come for refuge and then go back to the Origin Planet and continue his path of desolation. This world, the last world . . . they both feel so heavy that I can only lean forward onto the dashboard, my fingers spread wide, and slowly lower my forehead to rest on its long-dead surface. I hear nothing but my own breath, not even the far-off sound of birds. The silence is complete.

Until it's not.

The sound starts low, like a whisper. I don't even sit up at first, mistaking it for the wind, for the brushing of leaves against other leaves, or maybe even the water, trickling around the base of the pod as it has been forced to do these past forty years. But the sound grows, increasing to a crackle: an unnatural sputtering that latches a microscopic hook inside my ear and tugs gently. I raise my head, looking beyond the window first to see what is making the noise outside. But it's not outside: it's a staticky hiss emerging from a small rectangular screen, no larger than the length of my hand. It's trying to unscramble an image, pieces in the wrong order sparkling across the screen, breaking up and then rejoining, over and over, the rustle of audio snapping in and out, trying different formations until they make sense.

And suddenly they do. A face appears on the screen, all its pieces and parts in the correct order: the face of a woman with the same deep brown skin as me, high-arching eyebrows, her lips slightly parted as she peers out of the screen, squinting as if unsure. Above her head floats the tightly coiled shape of her Afro. Her voice drifts out of the screen slightly delayed after the movement of her lips, and I can only stare at the image of her with my mouth hanging open.

"This is Captain Yolanda Williams, pilot of Ship *OVD* 92, otherwise known as the *Vagantur*. If you are receiving this message, I am likely dead." She pauses and seems to think, her eyebrows low and rigid. "But . . . that also probably means I was successful in what I am attempting to do, so I can live with that."

Behind her on the small screen, another person appears, a woman whose face I can't see, only her body up to her neck. Captain Williams turns to look at her.

"Ready?" the woman says in a low voice. "Now or never."

"Just about," the captain says, and turns back to the camera. The faceless woman remains in the frame. "My crew and I— the ones that I trust—are sabotaging the *Vagantur*. The crash will not be an accident. If there are casualties, we are responsible and we are so, so sorry. I will do my best to land the ship safely."

She pauses again, bowing her head. When she raises her chin, her eyes are resolute.

"We determined this was the best option for saving lives— both human and otherwise. This ship was meant to carry families hoping to start fresh on the Planet X, where we determined we might find sympathy—the mission was infiltrated by River Corp. I repeat, we were infiltrated: Eric Albatur is a River Corp agent."

"We need to hurry," the woman behind her says.

"Just a minute, LaQuinta," Captain Williams snaps, but her eyes shine with tears. She addresses the camera again: "I don't know what's going to happen next. If anyone gets hurt . . . I'm . . . so sorry. Please understand that we did what we thought was best."

"LaQuinta Farrow," I whisper.

LaQuinta Farrow is moving toward the exit and I catch a

glimpse of her face as she cracks the door and peers out into a hall. Short in stature, her hair in thick plaits hanging from either side of her face. She was involved from the beginning.

Captain Williams leans in toward the camera.

"Our ship was built using energy from an egg from the Planet X," she says, whispering fiercely. She's standing now, about to shut down. "I have dismantled the ship's power cell. And concealed it, split in three. One piece in each of three pods—I'm hoping they make it outside the atmosphere of Planet X: if they are reunited, they will bond again, giving the River Corp agents the power they need to exploit this new world. With what I have done, we will be trapped here, but that's better than the alternative: two planets destroyed. We come with nothing. We have been robbed for so long by the people of River Corp. Now I'm hoping to steal us another chance."

She pushes away from the desk, reaching beyond the lens she'd been staring into. Whatever she fiddles with makes echoey scratching sounds in the audio. Behind her, LaQuinta Farrow whispers something I can't catch, and I'm leaning into the screen, straining my ears, when its surface goes black. The hissing carries on for another minute or so, and I crouch there frozen, poised for more, until it finally fades to nothing, returning the interior of the pod into a capsule of silence. I continue staring out through the grimy transparent walls of the pod, at the jungle beyond, at the bit of the sky I can see beyond that. Time bends along with the truth, past and future reshaping themselves before my eyes. But at the center of my mind, I only think of Captain Williams, her lonely skull in the gloomy cell of the *Vagantur*: how the woman who made an impossible choice ended up dying alone in the dark.

I push back from the dashboard and let my eyes wander over the few buttons and levers. She had sat on the *Vagantur*, her sweat gathering on her scalp and at the center of her palms, right before she released this very pod into the stars, hoping it would stay there. She had done the best she could, but the capsule had made its way here to Faloiv, the planet she then knew only as X. My gaze falls on the compartment beneath the dashboard, just a slim bit of a handle visible from where I sit. I don't know what it was built to contain, but I know even before I open it what it contains now.

A violet eggshell. One of three. What Albatur wants so badly, I hold easily in my hand. The captain had thought that by removing the power cell, she would remove Albatur's ability to harm Faloiv. She was wrong, and I wonder if she died know-ing it, if when her eyes closed for the last time, she knew that some of us had come here looking for peace and still caused only pain.

I step back out into the ravine, clutching the piece of kawa, my palm stinging and my knuckle aching. But I barely notice the pain; the kawa feels warm and pleasant in my hand, and it draws my mind back to the first one I had ever held: Adombukar's, far away in the main dome of the Mammalian

Compound. I thought it was as simple as giving him energy, like the vitamin compound Alma had injected me with when we escaped the Zoo.

It's so much more, and even the thought of Alma—of Rondo—isn't enough to distract me from the thing that is growing larger in the Artery, a feeling of certainty that sprouts first roots and then branches.

The Isii has made a decision. And that means it's time to choose.

I turn back toward the open shell of *Vagantur* Capsule 2, the ghost of Captain Williams invisible but present.

"I'm sorry," I say. "I know what you tried to do. But I have to undo it."

The kawa in my palm seems to sense my intention, or perhaps I only imagine it vibrating at the prospect of being united with its other pieces. At my feet, the stream trickles on, and, kneeling, I slowly lower my aching palm to the water.

At first nothing. I don't know how long I remain crouched there, waiting. Maybe it was a matter of the message finding me, or maybe it had taken the green language that long to decipher what I was searching for. But eventually I hear it. A message. Something my grandmother left for me.

Look to the sky.

I hesitate only a moment before I turn and race to the ravine's edge, scrabbling up its bank to level ground before tearing through the jungle. This time it feels as if the trees give way, the branches that had torn at my hair and suit parting to allow me passage. Or maybe I am numb to their thorns. I break out of the jungle, cross the springy green ground, and arrive back at the clear green sea I had dragged myself out of less than an hour before. I see nothing but the wide expanse of water. I'm looking the wrong way, I sense. I need to be higher.

I return to the jungle, pocketing the piece of kawa, which thrums hot and alert against my skin. I stare at the trees, all too large to climb. But I don't need to climb.

The springy ground beneath me comes to life.

I sway, then lurch sideways as what reveals itself to be a massive leaf rises into the air—what I had been walking on was not ground at all but a carpet of these mobile plants. All around me the leaves seem to seek the sun, their towering stalks shooting toward the sky, and I am carried up as well. I scream in spite of myself, the air rushing past my face. I fall to my knees, clinging to the plant that bears me up, and it's not until my palms connect with its surface that I understand this is no coincidence.

I said I needed to be higher, and the green language heard.

I gaze around, my fear melding with my wonder in a hand-shake of emotions. The setting sun turns the ground—now far below—orange and gold, the colors of ripe fruit. There's a disk of water ahead, maybe a mile, if this height allows any sense of distance: a lake. Its waters glisten pink and gentle in the dimming light, and for a moment my fear falls away like a shed skin.

And then I see the smoke.

Red. Redder than the sun. It crawls up into the air from its origin, obscured by the trees, but I don't need to see to know where it came from. My nana's message. The Faloii have chosen war.

Under me, around me, inside me, I feel the shift of the leaves that hold me. As always, their language is complex and multilayered, a thousand voices, woven together in dense green speech.

Rage.

Unlike the smoke, it is unseen, but I inhale it like oxygen: it fills me up, and with every bit of space it fills, it clears away the feeling of desolation, the pale helplessness that has bewitched my bones. I pull myself to stand, swaying a little on the platform the plant provides, staring intently at the smoke. It's a sign of what has happened and what is to come.

I feel the plant understand that I've seen what it wants me to see. There are no animals here, but this is Faloiv in all its angry green vibrancy.

Do you know? it seems to say. *Do you know what it is you must do?*

I shield my eyes from the sun, spreading its darkening blood across the jungle far below. There will be war: the Isii has named humans as parasites. It is time to choose a side, but my choice has always been made. I don't need to speak the green language to communicate what it is I wish to tell it.

Yes, I say. *I choose Faloiv.*

ACKNOWLEDGMENTS

My deepest thanks to every reader of this series: every page you turn makes the world in my head feel more real. In that vein, eternal gratitude to Zoé Samudzi, who has believed in this world from the beginning—I continue to learn so much from you, and one day I hope to do for you what you have done for me just by existing.

Librarians everywhere, you are magical.

Eric Smith, you have allowed yourself to become a punchline in your support of this series. I will never, ever forget it.

Ashley Woodfolk, at the time of my writing this, we haven't even met in person, and yet you get all my jokes and answer 11 p.m. texts. You are honest and vulnerable and your *Parable of the Sower* sh*t is real.

My editor, Ben Rosenthal . . . you believe in these books and I appreciate you for always trying to be a good partner, even when I'm the bull in your shop of breakable objects. Thank you for seeing Faloiv and understanding why it's important.

My agent, Regina Brooks, thank you for your patience and for at least not sighing audibly when I ask the same thing for the millionth time. There are so many things happening in my head at once and I appreciate you trying to parse through them.

Minda Honey, Lucie Witt, and Kaitlyn Soligan Owens . . . the makings of Monday night mischief. Thank you for your tacos and your trash talk. Minda, thank you especially for your plants and your laugh. You gather people together in a unique way, and my life and my writing (and my writing life) have so vastly improved since I allowed myself to open up to you.

The Kentucky Governor's School for the Arts, thank you for making a home for me and my vision, and the vision of so many young artists. And to my students . . . every summer you remind me of why I do what I do.

Amani and Monae, you always wear your promo shirts even when you haven't read the book yet. I see you and appreciate you.

Caralanay Cameron and Dana Lynch, my best best besties: thank you for planning all my events and for knowing everything I'm not even aware of not knowing. You are in my blood the way not even family can be.

And finally, thank you to my daughter and my husband, my greatest inspiration. Earth is only worth it if you are here beside me.